weaves folklore through a story of self-discovery that touches on what it means to be a daughter, the ramifications of the past and daring to follow your heart'

Kate Sawyer

'I've been lost in *The Lost Storyteller*'s marvellous pages . . . brilliantly written and high concept with a moving story and vivid characters. But it also has that special indefinable SOMETHING. One of my books of the year'

Tracy Rees

'Captivating, moving and profound. I loved it! A spellbinding novel about the power of the stories we tell both to ourselves and to others'

Tracey Emerson

'Absolutely beautiful . . . A cleverly wrought tale of fathers and daughters, and a bond buried so deep that it is lost to folklore'

Polly Crosby

'*The Lost Storyteller* is a deeply evocative book about family and the redemptive power of stories, all wrapped up in some of the most beautifully affecting fairy tales I've ever read. If you like stories that tug at your heart and show you a different way of looking at love, loss, betrayal and redemption, you will enjoy this heartwarming tale . . . I loved this book'
Buki Papillon

'Completely engaging . . . A lovely reflection on the power and magic of stories'
Marianne Cronin

'Beautifully revealed, with a lovingly drawn conclusion'
Zoe West, *Woman & Home*

'Beautifully, sensitively told. Block reminds us that people don't always behave as we want them to, and maybe because of that, there are few things so powerful as the ability to be kind'
The Wee Review

'A captivating and richly mesmerizing read'
Buzz Magazine

'A beguiling, gorgeous book about fathers and daughters and the stories that bind and redeem us'
YOU magazine

About the Author

Originally from Devon, Amanda moved to Edinburgh in 2007, where she attained a master's degree in creative writing. Since then, she's divided her time between ghostwriting, editing and tutoring.

Amanda's writing is often inspired by myths and fairy tales, which she uses as starting points to tell new stories. Her work has been shortlisted in contests such as the Bridport Prize and the Mslexia Short Story Competition.

The Lost Storyteller is her first novel.

THE LOST STORYTELLER

AMANDA BLOCK

HODDER studio

First published in Great Britain in 2021 by Hodder Studio
An Imprint of Hodder & Stoughton
An Hachette UK company

This paperback edition published in 2022

1

A CIP catalogue record for this title is available from the British Library

Paperback ISBN 9781529360806
Hardback ISBN 9781529360783
eBook ISBN 9781529360813

Typeset in Adobe Caslon Pro by Palimpsest Book Production Limited,
Falkirk, Stirlingshire

Printed and bound in Great Britain by Clays Ltd, Elcograf S.p.A.

Hodder & Stoughton policy is to use papers that are natural, renewable
and recyclable products and made from wood grown in sustainable forests.
The logging and manufacturing processes are expected to conform to the
environmental regulations of the country of origin.

Hodder & Stoughton Ltd
Carmelite House
50 Victoria Embankment
London EC4Y 0DZ

www.hodder-studio.com

For Mum and Dad, without whom I'd be lost;
And for Joely, my favourite storyteller.

'No, you are all wrong,' said the little man meekly. 'I have been making believe.'
'Making believe!' cried Dorothy. 'Are you not a Great Wizard?'
. . . 'Not a bit of it, my dear; I'm just a common man.'

L. Frank Baum
The Wonderful Wizard of Oz

PART ONE

1

The Journalist

The sign was askew. Rebecca noticed this as soon as she arrived in the new office: the company's name was drooping downhill. Who had hung it up? More importantly, why hadn't they done it properly? She prodded the transparent plastic, trying to nudge it straight, but it was screwed in too tight.

It was all very well for everyone else, she thought, edging past the boxes stacked around her reception desk; they wouldn't have to stare at it all day. From here, though, there was little else to look at, aside from a weeping fig tree, a line of grey tub chairs and the water cooler that had been delivered the previous afternoon. Even the glass front door only offered a view of a gravel courtyard, where, every once in a while, a besuited employee of a neighbouring office strolled in and out of sight, like an actor crossing the stage in the world's most tedious play.

After checking the company's emails, Rebecca resolved to ignore the crooked sign and instead began to restock her desk drawers from a box marked *RECEPTION*. Mostly, it contained stationery, but there were a few personal knickknacks too: her spare running sunglasses, two lip balms, a metal Eye of Horus that had lost its keychain. She was tracing a finger along the lines of this pendant, trying to remember where she'd bought it, when the phone rang.

'Sudworth and Rowe Surveyors.'

'Yeah, hi – morning.' The male voice on the other end of the line sounded scratchy from sleep. 'I was wondering if I could speak to Rebecca Chase?'

She considered the mobile number on the display screen. 'Who's calling?'

'It's Ellis Bailey, I'm a journalist from SideScoop. I'm following up on an email I sent her last week . . .'

Rebecca's stomach gave a little lurch, though she kept her voice steady: 'Just a moment, please.'

With the exactitude of someone setting down a brimming cup of tea, she hung up the phone. As it bleeped, the display screen cleared, but her insides still felt knotted. She needed to find out how to retrieve and block that number.

When she looked up, Gerry Rowe was letting himself into the building. He was a portly man with a short white beard and a seemingly endless collection of novelty ties – today's was stamped with sailing boats. Tucking his access card back into his shirt pocket, he bade Rebecca good morning, noting, 'You're in early.'

'Lots to do,' she said, indicating the boxes behind her.

'Indeed, indeed – sign looks good, at least.'

'Mm-hmm.'

'Knew that drill would come in handy . . . I don't suppose we have internet yet?'

'We do. New password's *SudworthRowe2016*. All one word, capital S, capital R,' she said, her mind still on the journalist. Would he call again? What if he spoke to someone else? The email had been bad enough, but phoning her at *work* . . .

'Doesn't seem to be connecting,' Gerry murmured, frowning down at his phone.

'Capital S, capital R,' Rebecca repeated, glancing down at her lengthy to-do list, then adding *block journalist* right at the top.

'Ah, yes.' Satisfied, Gerry started towards the main office, but was distracted by the new water cooler. 'Here we are . . .' He patted its plastic bulk, as though greeting a dog. 'Didn't get a chance to look at it last night – very nice. Now, how do you get a cup out?'

'There's a lever on the—'

But Gerry had already stuffed his arm into the top of the adjoining tube and, after a few seconds of straining, he withdrew a paper cup.

'Not the most practical of contraptions, is it?' he muttered.

He helped himself to water, then, seemingly unsure what to do with it, raised his cup in a sheepish toast. 'Well, to the new office – and a new era.'

Rebecca's attention had returned to the phone – she was half-expecting the journalist to ring back at any moment – but she waved her empty mug in Gerry's direction.

'Speaking of new eras . . .' he continued, inching towards her desk. 'Have you had a chance to sign that contract yet?'

'Um – no, not yet,' she said. The document had been lying on her coffee table for over a fortnight. 'I will, though.'

'No rush, of course,' Gerry assured her. 'It's just—' he chuckled, smoothing down the little boats lining his paunch, '—we want to keep you, that's all.'

She managed a smile. 'Thanks, Gerry.'

When he eventually departed, Rebecca succeeded in recovering and blocking Ellis Bailey's number, but banishing him from her mind was proving more difficult. No matter how hard she tried to concentrate on the morning's tasks – fielding further requests for the Wi-Fi password, restocking the printers with paper, claiming shelves for files and a cupboard for stationery – the journalist kept returning to her thoughts. What if he called again from a different number? Should she respond to his email, make it clear she couldn't help, or would that just encourage him?

By midday, Rebecca was unpacking a box of ancient ring binders when Chris Fenton, the only member of the surveying team remotely close to her in age, sauntered over to reception, reeking of aftershave.

'All right, Chaser? Oi oi, this looks fancy.' He pushed at the water cooler, like he was trying to provoke it, before groping the cylinder of cups. 'How does it work, then?'

'On the side, there's a—Never mind,' she sighed, as he wrenched at least four cups from the bottom of the tube.

'Not great, is it?' Chris said, examining the crush of cardboard in his fist.

He balled it up and threw it towards the door, missing all three recycling bins, then leaned against the edge of the reception desk, watching her. They had friends in common outside the office, so Rebecca tried to tolerate him, though he tested this resolve on an almost daily basis.

'Coming to The Crown tonight?' he asked.

'Can't,' she murmured, trying to decipher a binder's faded label.

'Go on, everyone'll be there. And there's a pool tournament – you can be on my team.'

'I'd rather be on the *winning* team . . .'

Chris snorted and gave her a smile that was probably meant to be appealing, only it exposed his protruding front teeth, which – along with his dedication to hair gel – gave him the look of a damp rodent. The previous year, after a similar Friday evening at the pub, Rebecca had made the mistake of going home with him, and now always had the impression he was angling for a repeat performance. Dispirited by the thought that nothing remotely romantic had happened to her since, she returned to her binders.

'You won't even come out for a bit?' Chris wheedled.

'It's my grandmother's birthday.'

'Ooh, wild night for you!'

Rebecca, however, felt slightly cheered by the prospect of seeing Lillian; even if she'd wanted to join Chris at the pub, she never would've missed her grandmother's dinner.

Chris began to kick at a leg of the desk, making the entire tabletop shudder. Rebecca readied herself to send him away, but was distracted by the bleat of the intercom.

'Oi oi – first visitor!'

As far as Rebecca knew, no external meetings were booked in today – which was just as well, because the office was in no fit state to receive anyone. She turned to the monitor to get a better look at the unexpected guest, but Chris reached over her head.

'*Don't*,' she snapped, too late: he'd already jabbed the button to unlock the door.

The man who wandered into reception a few seconds later had a mop of sandy-coloured hair and horn-rimmed glasses, and was wearing jeans and a wrinkled green T-shirt. A cycle helmet was clipped to the strap of his canvas messenger bag, the underside of which bore a dark blue stain, presumably from a leaky pen. Clearly, he wasn't a client, and Rebecca might've assumed he was a student at the university, only something about his unhurried manner – his self-assurance, maybe – suggested he was closer to 30 than 20.

Chris straightened up, eyeing this newcomer with suspicion. 'All right, mate?'

The man, who'd paused to study the wonky sign and crumpled cups on the floor, said, 'Yeah, thanks . . . I'm looking for Rebecca Chase?'

His gaze slid over the desk, and Rebecca tensed as they both realised – perhaps in the same instant – who the other was.

'Ah – Ellis Bailey,' he said, offering his hand.

She ignored it and stood up, demanding, 'What are you doing here?'

He flipped his palm, turning his rejected handshake into a gesture towards her phone. 'I did try and call to tell you I was passing, but,' he shrugged, 'I must've got cut off.' There were faint dimples in his cheeks, as though he were repressing a smile. Rebecca gripped the edge of her desk.

'Anyway, I'm here now, so maybe I could buy you a coffee?' the journalist suggested, while Chris made a spluttering noise. 'I just have a couple of questions about your—'

'I don't have anything to tell you,' Rebecca blurted out. 'I haven't . . .' She checked herself in front of Chris, who was watching them both intently, his arms folded. She wished he'd go away. 'Look, this isn't a good time.'

Ellis nodded like he'd expected this and backed towards the tub chairs lining the wall. 'I can wait until you're on your lunch,' he offered. 'Or we could talk here?'

He flicked at the lever on the side of the water cooler, looking pleasantly surprised when it dispensed him a paper cup. Rebecca glared as he fiddled with the taps, sending plump bubbles swarming through the bottle like jellyfish.

'All right,' she snapped, 'there's a meeting room – we can go there now.'

'But—' began Chris.

'You can mind things here for five minutes, can't you?' she told him, before adding in a chilly undertone, 'You already know how to work the intercom . . .'

The meeting room only made her more irritable. It was gloomy, but when Rebecca adjusted the metal blinds by their knotty cords, the space looked even worse: daylight illuminated the dust suspended in the air, the rectangular shadows on the walls where posters had once hung and the stains on the carpet, which was grey and speckled like ash. Eyeing the table, chairs and floor, which were cluttered with a miscellany of objects that hadn't yet found a home – a stack of measuring wheels, a tangle of extension cords and old phone chargers – Rebecca couldn't imagine a less welcoming space. Although perhaps, in this instance, that was no bad thing.

The journalist seemed unfazed by the mess and pushed aside a plastic clock and a pile of rolled-up site plans to make space at the table. Rebecca resented this, just as she'd resented him playing with the water cooler; she was still finding everything its place in the new office, yet this thoroughly unwelcome visitor had already made himself at home.

'Do you mind if I record us?' asked Ellis, when they'd sat down.

'Actually, yes.'

'Fair enough.'

Unperturbed by her sharp tone, Ellis tugged his grubby bag onto his lap and searched its depths until he'd located a spiral-bound notebook and biro. Rebecca eyed these objects with scorn: what did he think he was going to write about?

'Well,' he said, flicking through several pages of notes, 'as I said in my email, I'm a staff writer at SideScoop – you know SideScoop?'

She nodded. 'So you write those online lists and quizzes?' she asked, hoping to embarrass him. '*Twelve Cats That Look Like Household Appliances*? *Can We Guess Your Age Based on Your Favourite Pizza Toppings?*'

'I have done,' he said, with a smile.

'That's some pretty highbrow journalism.'

'You know, most people are quite excited by the name SideScoop,' he remarked, although her derision seemed to interest him. 'And to be fair, we've been branching out into serious news stories lately: investigative stuff, big think-pieces . . . You know, to complement the quizzes and pictures of baby animals.'

Rebecca said nothing. She was already familiar with SideScoop's content, given she often scrolled its pages at her desk, but wasn't about to admit that to one of its so-called journalists.

'Anyway, we also like nostalgia,' he continued, 'and that's why I've been working on this feature about children's TV stars from the 90s, which I'm hoping will turn into a bit more than just a fluff piece. I've already interviewed Arnie Hooper from *Can you Capture the Castle?*, a couple of the guys who were in *The After School Club* and most of the cast of *The Wishing Well*. But the person I want to talk to most of all – the person I can't imagine this article without – is the Stowaway himself, Leo Sampson. Only, I'm having trouble tracking him down . . .'

Having read and deleted Ellis's email the previous week, Rebecca was prepared for this and able to keep her expression blank. But it was harder than she'd anticipated, especially as that name had prompted a tingling between her shoulder blades; it'd been so long since she'd heard it, *Leo Sampson* sounded unreal, even mythical. The journalist might've been searching for Robin Hood or Merlin.

'I'm guessing *you* might know where he is, though?' asked Ellis.

'I'm afraid you guessed wrong.'

He scanned her impassive face for a few seconds, his eyes narrowed behind his glasses: he didn't believe her. 'You don't ever see him or speak to him?' he persisted.

'No.'

'You've no idea where your dad is?'

'None at all.'

Her spine still felt shivery, but she was using her work voice, which was light and brisk.

'Huh.' Ellis rolled his pen over the blank page of his notebook, re-evaluating.

'I said I didn't have anything to tell you,' she reminded him, pleased he now seemed stumped. 'Unfortunately, you've had a wasted journey.'

'What do you mean?'

'I assume you came from London?'

'Oh – yeah. But I'm heading to Cornwall anyway, to see a cousin.' The dimples reappeared in his cheeks. 'I didn't come all this way for you, you know.'

To her annoyance, Rebecca felt herself blush. Of course he hadn't journeyed all the way to Exeter on the off-chance she would answer his questions.

'Well, good,' she decided, 'because I can't help you.'

Growing serious again, Ellis asked, 'When was the last time you saw him?'

'I don't know.'

'Ten years ago?'

'More like twenty,' she admitted, with an unexpected sting of humiliation. 'He left when I was little.'

If this surprised the journalist, he didn't let on, but scribbled a note down on his pad. 'Was that before or after *The Stowaway*?'

'I've no idea.'

Ellis started to ask another question, but Rebecca cut across him.

'Really, that's it: he left when I was little, end of story.' She made a show of checking the clock beside them – which had stopped – and, trying to conclude the conversation, added, 'But I'm sure that if you can track *me* down, you'll have no problem finding him.'

'Tracking you down was easy,' Ellis said. 'Two minutes online threw up all sorts of stuff: your old school, your profile on the Sudworth and Rowe website, your social media – which you should make more private, by the way. It's not difficult to find people these days. That's what makes this so strange . . .' He stared at his largely blank page, murmuring, '*Where is Leo Sampson?*'

This almost sounded like a headline, and though Rebecca's body tensed, like a runner poised on starting blocks, she remained in her seat.

'If you search for him online, there's tons of stuff about *The Stowaway*, as you'd expect,' Ellis continued, 'and a few bits and pieces about some of his other acting jobs. But after '97 there's nothing. It's like he vanished.'

'Maybe he's dead?'

The journalist looked taken aback and Rebecca, too, felt a prickle of unease at the flippancy and finality of her own suggestion. Then she shrugged: what difference would it make to her now, whether or not Leo Sampson was alive?

'But then you'd have heard about it, surely? And there'd be a record of his death, and an obituary – he was the Stowaway!' Ellis frowned at the windows, apparently seeing something far beyond their grimy blinds. 'It's almost like the show itself, isn't it? When he used to disappear?'

Something about this comment caused Rebecca's heart to twitch. Trying to ignore the feeling, she reached out to neaten the rubber band securing the nearest roll of site plans. The snapping noise returned Ellis to the room.

'You don't agree?' he said.

'I don't know what you're talking about, I never watched it.'

'You never—*Really*?' He seemed more thrown by this than anything she'd said so far. 'Leo Sampson's daughter never watched *The Stowaway*?'

'Like I said, he left when I was little.'

Ellis either missed or ignored the edge in her voice. 'They're all online now, if you're interested. I've been watching a few episodes here and there – purely for research, of course. It stands the test of time, when not many of those old shows do. And Leo Sampson, he was something else . . . You don't look like him, by the way.'

Good, thought Rebecca.

'You're more . . .' Ellis straightened his shoulders and clasped his hands together, mimicking her rigid posture. 'I never would've known you were related. Although, I suppose there's *something* . . . Maybe it's your eyes.'

He leaned back, tilting his head as he studied her. Rebecca felt her insides writhe with discomfort, although whether this was because she was being scrutinised by this stranger or compared to her father she didn't know.

'Do you remember him?'

She shook her head, not in answer to the question, but because he'd fired it at her so suddenly, as though to catch her unawares. When Ellis's expression turned sceptical again, she wanted to clarify this – but then, there was no need to explain herself; not to him, not to anyone.

'I should be getting back to work,' she said, standing up.

'Yeah,' said Ellis, unsurprised. 'Sure.'

They walked back to reception in silence, and it felt to Rebecca like they'd been away much longer than a few minutes. Not that anything had changed in the interim: the sign was still squint, the paper cups were still lying on the floor, the boxes were still towering around her desk. Among them, Chris was slumped in her swivel chair, so engrossed in a noisy game on his phone he didn't notice them return.

Rebecca accompanied Ellis all the way to the entrance, pressing the door's release button on his behalf. Sunlight flared against the glass as it swung open, and a slight breeze plucked at the wisps of hair around her face. She glanced up at the sky; it was endlessly blue.

'If you remember anything that might help me find him, perhaps you could drop me an email?' said the journalist. 'Or maybe someone in your family has an idea where he is . . . ?'

He still doesn't believe me, thought Rebecca, frustrated; she'd been almost completely honest with him.

Ellis threw his empty cup into the recycling bin and offered her his hand again. This time – because it was goodbye – Rebecca shook it, but as soon as he'd stepped out into the courtyard something compelled her to call him back. 'Hey?'

As Ellis turned, the automated door began to close between them, so she jabbed at the button again. What was she doing? He was finally leaving, and she didn't care about any of this, not really. But maybe, after all his questions, she wanted to ask one of her own.

'What did you mean before, that he used to disappear?'

'On the show?' The journalist had unfastened his cycle helmet from his bag; he bounced it from hand to hand a few times, like a basketball. 'At the end of each episode, after the Stowaway had finished the week's adventure, he'd crawl into a rabbit hole or a serving hatch and then the credits would roll. But the next episode he'd spring out from somewhere completely different, like a tree house or – I don't know – a ship's cabin.' Smiling, Ellis began to back away across the gravel. 'As a child I always used to wonder where he went, how he got from one to the other . . .' He shrugged. 'I guess I'm still wondering.'

Again, something tugged in Rebecca's chest, even stronger than before. But when the door started to shut for a second time, she pushed at the edge of the glass, striving to close it quicker than it wanted to go.

2

Lower Morvale

Halfway to the village, Rebecca abandoned the motorway for the more meandering countryside route, where sun-drenched lanes were striped with the shadows of surrounding trees. She had learned to drive on these back roads, and usually it was satisfying to anticipate their every bump and bend. This evening, though, the journey's familiarity meant her unchecked thoughts kept straying back to her conversation with Ellis Bailey – the conversation she'd been trying to ignore all afternoon – until her musings snagged on one question in particular: *Do you remember him?*

Of course she did. Leo Sampson might've been exiled to the back of her mind long ago, but it was still so easy to conjure him: his wide blue eyes and dark tangled hair; his tuneless singing and booming laughter. She could even recall the smell of him – fresh and green, like grass clippings. Yet there was no point in all this remembering. He had left. He was gone.

The church bells were tolling seven when she finally dipped down a steep track and emerged into Lower Morvale. Her foot hovered over the brake pedal as she continued to slide through the village, winding past dozens of thatched cottages until she splashed through the copper-coloured water at the ford. There were children playing by the war memorial, and every one of the picnic tables outside The Three Tors was occupied by locals or ramblers done with Dartmoor for the day. After waving to her grandmother's yoga teacher outside the village hall, Rebecca steered down the track that led to Primrose Cottage, her body tensing as she caught sight of her childhood home.

Her mother was upon her the moment she parked the car.

'*There* you are! I was about to arrange a search party!'

This evening, Rosalyn Chase was wearing a sleeveless peach-coloured dress with a lacy collar. It complemented her slender figure and long auburn hair, yet Rebecca thought she looked pale and oddly old-fashioned, like a figure on a cameo brooch.

'I took the back route,' Rebecca explained, ignoring her mother's accusatory tone and submitting to her embrace.

'Whatever for?'

'I don't know, it's a nice evening?'

Rosalyn tutted, motioning Rebecca towards the vanilla-hued cottage. 'I was going to ask you to help me finish the cake, but I've had to do it all myself now . . .'

In the porch, Rebecca was struck by the inimitable aroma of home, which was woody and sweet, save for a lingering suggestion of bleach. To her mother's cries of, '*Shoes, shoes, shoes!*', she kicked her ballet flats towards the rack beside the front door and trailed after Rosalyn into the kitchen. Most of the ground floor of Primrose Cottage had been made open-plan, although the sparkling marble worktops and state-of-the-art cooking appliances were offset by dark beams overhead and a wall of original stonework that included a fireplace.

'Now, something to drink?' said Rosalyn. 'We'll be plied with wine at Daffy's, so let's be virtuous for now. I've some rather nice elderflower fizz in here somewhere . . .'

She disappeared behind the fridge door and Rebecca, disappointed alcohol was not yet an option, pulled herself up onto a stool at the breakfast bar. There was a hiss from Brontë, her mother's monstrous tortoiseshell cat, who was glaring at her from the window, her flanks drooping over the side of the sill.

'Aren't you going to compliment me on my cake?' Rosalyn called.

Rebecca glanced over at the towering confection on the counter. She hadn't realised it was a cake, because whatever sponge it contained was almost entirely obscured by a mound of summer berries.

'I thought Nana asked for chocolate?'

'What?' Rosalyn popped back into view clutching a narrow green bottle. 'Oh – *you*!' she huffed, catching sight of Rebecca's smile. 'Silly!'

She poured out two glasses of the fizz, and Rebecca was just beginning to relax when her mother cast a disapproving glance at her blouse and cropped trousers. 'Are you wearing that tonight? Obviously, you look *lovely*, but do you think a dress might be better . . . ?'

'I'll change in a minute,' muttered Rebecca, once again wishing her drink was stronger. 'Give me a chance, I came straight from work.'

'Of course you did.' Rosalyn beamed. 'Oh, I'm just *so* pleased to see you, Becca-Bell! It's been weeks and weeks!'

She wound her arms around her daughter's shoulders and Rebecca, who was used to these sudden surges of affection, patted her on the bony elbow. This evening, after the upheaval of the office move – and especially after that unexpected encounter with the journalist – the predictability of Primrose Cottage was almost comforting.

'I ran into Debbie Jarvis in the tearoom the other day,' continued Rosalyn, her chin digging into Rebecca's collarbone. 'Do you know, she's hardly seen Amy since she moved to London.'

'No?' At the mention of her oldest friend, Rebecca experienced a pang of sadness. Amy felt so far away now.

'Debbie's quite distraught, Amy being the last to leave the nest and so on,' continued Rosalyn. 'It made me feel very lucky to have *my* girl so close. *Very – lucky – indeed.*' She emphasised her final sentence by squeezing Rebecca's shoulders on every word.

Rebecca, deciding enough was enough, unpeeled her mother's arms, and Rosalyn returned to the other side of the breakfast bar, where she picked up her navy leather-bound address book, which was stuffed with Post-it notes.

'You've remembered Nana and I are away from Sunday? For her little birthday trip?'

'Yes.'

As her mother flipped through the address book, the rustle of the pages returned Rebecca to that messy meeting room and Ellis's spiral-bound notepad. What else had he written about her father in there?

'I've asked Carol to pop in every day to feed Brontë and keep an eye on the plants, but I'm not entirely sure I trust her.'

'Carol?' repeated Rebecca, trying to focus on the subject of Rosalyn's innocuous old neighbour. 'Why not?'

'She's been quite forgetful lately, and twice given me the wrong change at the shop. I think she might be going a bit, you know – ' Rosalyn lowered her voice, —'*gaga*. So I've told her if she can't get hold of me, she can call you.'

'Right,' said Rebecca, now wishing she'd got a proper look at the journalist's notes.

'I'm sure she'll be fine. I've marked out all the numbers she could possibly need; the plumber and so on. We've decided on North Devon, did I tell you that?'

'Um, yes.'

'Ilfracombe. Nana's not been for years. We'll go to Clovelly too, I expect – well, it's more picturesque, isn't it? – and then there are those gardens on the way . . .'

While Rosalyn chattered, Rebecca continued to mull over her meeting with Ellis – who would also be on holiday this weekend, she remembered. He hadn't come all the way to Exeter for her, but he'd stopped off there because, long ago, Leo Sampson had disappeared.

If anything, it was strange she didn't think of her father more, in this place he'd once lived. But Leo had been scrubbed from Primrose Cottage years ago, and so thoroughly that Rebecca couldn't recall ever finding any trace of him: no scuffed shoes hiding at the bottom of a wardrobe, no dregs of aftershave lurking in the bathroom cabinet.

Of course, this must've been her mother's doing. Had they talked about it at the time, this erasure of Leo? Rebecca couldn't remember – she'd been young, and the circumstances of her father's departure were foggy – but she doubted it. On the few occasions she'd mentioned him since, her mother had clammed up, until, as a teenager, Rebecca had finally summoned the nerve to ask about her father outright. Even now, it was excruciating to recall Rosalyn's tearful accusations of insensitivity, her wails of: *Aren't I enough?* The conversation had left Rebecca feeling cross, confused and guilty – which was why, she supposed, in the intervening years, it had been easier to emulate Rosalyn and pretend he'd never existed.

But he *had* existed, and if Rebecca put her mind to it she could see him, seeping back into this house like smoke. Here in the kitchen, they'd attempted to bake cupcakes together; behind her, between shabbier sofas, they'd built a den out of sheets and clothes horses; and in the doorway, they'd created a puppet theatre with little cardboard cut-outs sellotaped onto sticks from the garden. Rebecca had forgotten the plays, but could still see those hastily painted figures bobbing across the space: birds and fairies, pirates and sea monsters, woodsmen and witches . . .

Do you remember him?

Recalling how the journalist had flung out that question, like something hot she might catch before she realised it would burn, Rebecca eyed her mother, who was unloading the dishwasher. Perhaps it would be easier to ask about Leo now she was an adult, now even more time had passed. She twisted the stem of her glass, daring herself to speak.

'Mum?'

'Hm?'

Rebecca took a steadying breath. 'Do you know where my dad is?'

Knives, forks and spoons clanked as Rosalyn dropped them into the compartments of the cutlery drawer, one by one. Had she heard? After a moment, Rebecca began to doubt she had even asked the question out loud; perhaps she'd simply tested it out in her head. But after shutting both the drawer and dishwasher with a little more force than necessary, Rosalyn spun around, her expression hard.

'You've been contacted by that journalist, haven't you?'

Rebecca hadn't expected this, but, of course, Ellis would've tried to talk to her mother too.

'I told him — I *warned* him to stay away!' continued Rosalyn, her voice rising, her pale face now oddly flushed.

'When was this?'

But her mother wasn't listening: 'It's harassment, that's what it is – a gross invasion of privacy! Although I don't know why I'm surprised, when you hear about all the phone hacking and goodness knows what else these people get up to . . . You didn't email him back, did you, Rebecca? You didn't speak to him?'

It was easier to lie: 'No.'

'Well, you mustn't, it's none of his business – it's nobody's business! I've a good mind to make some sort of complaint—'

'Mum, it doesn't matter,' Rebecca cut in, anxious to curb this tirade. 'I just ignored him.'

Rosalyn returned to the breakfast bar, twisting her dainty watch around and around her wrist. When Rebecca held her gaze, she seemed to relax.

'Of course you did. I knew you would.' She attempted a smile, then pinched the face of her watch between finger and thumb. 'Petal, it's almost twenty-past – I really think you should go and change, don't you? Daffy will harp on if we're late, and carrying that cake along the road will slow us down. In fact, I need some sort of tin . . .'

While she started opening cupboards and clattering through their contents, Rebecca slid from her stool and headed back to the car for her overnight bag. It was only after she'd returned inside, and was trudging up the stairs towards her old room, that she realised how neatly Rosalyn had sidestepped her question.

As she leaned closer to the cake, Lillian Chase tucked her short silvery hair behind her ears, a galaxy of beads and buttons glittering on her indigo cardigan. She directed a few weak breaths towards the candles, before gesturing to the twins – who were still shouting the final '*ooo*' of the *Happy Birthday* song – and they generated a lot of noise and spit as they blasted lungfuls of air at the tiny flames.

Rebecca's Aunt Daphne led the applause from the other end of the table. She was a younger, softer version of Rosalyn, radiant tonight in a floral tea dress and pearls. Ignoring her young sons, who were now poking at the heap of berries, Daphne cried, 'Oh, Rozzy, that looks *magnificent*! What a treat!'

Rosalyn didn't respond. She was glaring at the twins, her lips thin.

Suppressing a smile, Rebecca switched on the main light, illuminating her grandmother's dining room once again. The solid oak table had been extended to seat seven, but there was barely enough room for the crockery and crystal glassware among all the frothy flower arrangements – which, Daphne had informed them, were fresh from the garden.

'Is there any ice cream?' asked Uncle Morton, eyeing the cake with distrust.

'If you want to spoil it,' huffed Rosalyn.

'Ice cream!' gasped Daphne, as though he'd asked for ketchup. 'Morty, it's covered in *real* cream!'

Morton made a grab for the decanter of claret. Unlike his sisters, he was thickset and dark-haired, with prominent eyebrows lodged in a near-permanent scowl.

'Shall I dish up?' suggested Lillian, before her children could start sniping in earnest.

In the end, though, it was Rebecca who cut up most of the cake, keenly observed by her mother, who then rejected her slice in favour of one half the size.

Once everyone had been served, and Rosalyn's baking abilities roundly praised, Daphne cast around for another conversation topic. So far, Rebecca – whose mind was still turning over that meeting with the journalist – had managed to zone out while her aunt had updated them on her husband's unfathomable work in finance and spoken at length about Thomas and Daniel's adventures at summer school. Now, though, Daphne's attention landed upon her.

'So, Becca, how's it all going?'

'Um – fine, thanks.'

Rebecca braced herself, conscious she hadn't been subjected to: *Are you seeing anyone?* in a while. Really, it had almost been worth enduring Adam and his arthouse film obsession for a year and a half, just to swerve moments like this.

Daphne, however, had a different query in mind: 'How's your job? Are you still working for those surveyors?'

'Yes,' said Rebecca, after wincing at the word *still*. 'It's fine – I mean, it's good.'

She began to nudge a blueberry around her plate, hoping the discussion would move on. To her right, Morton refilled her wine glass.

'Becca's office manager now,' announced Rosalyn, who had probably been waiting to say this all evening.

'Oh, *fab*!' cried Daphne.

'Well, not yet,' said Rebecca, grimacing as she pictured the contract she'd discarded on her coffee table, unread and unsigned.

But Rosalyn wasn't about to pass up an opportunity to engage in some competitive bragging with her sister. 'All right, maybe you're still waiting for the job title, but you've been managing that office for years – I expect the place would fall apart without you.'

Rebecca tried to feel flattered but couldn't quite manage it. She wished her job was as important as her mother was implying, and that her colleagues were as admiring of her efforts. After everything she'd done to facilitate the office move, all anyone had talked about since was that wretched water cooler . . . Did Rosalyn, who adored her own job at the library, realise how dull it could be at Sudworth and Rowe? Did she remember that Rebecca had once had bigger ambitions? Perhaps none of that mattered to her, not when her daughter had a decent job – a soon-to-be stable job – and remained close by.

To Rosalyn's obvious irritation, the conversation soon degenerated from Rebecca's promotion to local gossip. Rebecca, though, was pleased she was no longer the focus of attention. After finishing her cake, she yawned into her palms and turned her watery gaze on her eight-year-old cousins, who were sitting opposite. Clearly, they didn't care that the landlord of The Three Tors was having another affair – this time with the girl from the stables – so were taking it in turns to swipe at the flame of the nearest tealight.

Their grandmother tapped at the tabletop to gain their attention. 'Watch this,' she said, licking her thumb and index finger and then pinching out the flame. Thomas and Daniel looked briefly disappointed, until Lillian pulled one of the taller candles from its bracket and held it several centimetres above the smoking wick, causing it to blaze back to life.

'Woah!'

'Nana, how d'you do that?'

She smiled as she replaced the candlestick in its holder. 'Magic.'

Rebecca, who'd seen her grandmother perform this trick before, asked, 'Isn't it something to do with the vaporised wax in the air?'

'If you say so, dear.'

'So it's science.'

'Only once you know,' said Lillian, nodding towards the twins, who were now inspecting the tealight as though it were somehow different from the others on the table. 'And until then, there's nothing wrong with a little magic, is there?'

Perhaps this was the sort of thing Leo used to say, because at that moment he popped back into Rebecca's mind, as vividly as the tiny flame.

It was more difficult to picture him here than at Primrose

Cottage, yet he would have come to this house; he would have sat down to countless birthday and Christmas dinners at this very table. When had she last seen him? She had no recollection of their parting. Perhaps he hadn't even bothered to say goodbye.

At this thought, Rebecca tried to dismiss him again – this evening was about Lillian, not Leo – but looking between her grandmother, Morton and Daphne made her wonder: did they know where he was? He'd once been part of their lives too, so they were all complicit in erasing him from their shared history. *And so am I,* realised Rebecca, who, somehow, had always known she wasn't to mention him.

Finally, she contemplated her mother, who was spearing a strawberry with her cake fork. It seemed unlikely Rosalyn was ignorant of the whereabouts of her ex-husband, the father of her only child, yet what reason could she have for keeping it secret? And what right? Rosalyn had said it was nobody's business, but surely Rebecca was entitled to the truth.

'Penny for them?'

Rebecca blinked, realising her unfocused gaze had been boring into a stout vase of yellow roses.

'It's not like you to be off in a daydream,' continued Lillian.

'Oh – no.' Carefully, so as not to smudge her make-up, Rebecca rubbed below her eyelids. 'It's been a bit of a busy day, that's all.'

'Is everything all right?'

Rebecca turned, studying her shimmering grandmother, who was small but straight-backed. Lillian had a round, girlish face and dark eyes that curved into crescents when she smiled, although now she looked serious. If anyone else had asked, Rebecca would have insisted she was fine, simply tired, but her grandmother was difficult to deceive.

'Nana, can I ask you something?'

'Of course.'

After checking Rosalyn and Daphne were still happily gossiping, Rebecca bent closer to her grandmother and, in an undertone, asked, 'Do you know where my dad is?'

It took Lillian a few seconds to react, but when her face slackened it wasn't from shock, as Rebecca had expected, but something closer to sorrow.

'Leo?' she whispered.

She was probably just stalling, but, like earlier, when Ellis had explained who he was looking for, Rebecca felt as though something momentous had been uttered; she couldn't remember Lillian even alluding to her father before, let alone saying his name.

The table creaked as Morton leaned forward on his elbows. 'What about him?' he grunted.

Rebecca and Lillian froze like a pair of schoolgirls caught passing notes in class.

'What about *who*?' called Daphne.

'*Le-o* . . .' said Morton, grimacing as he dragged out the name's first syllable.

'Oh!'

With a nervous giggle, Daphne looked at her sister. Rosalyn was sat very still, her gaze darting between her mother, brother and daughter, as though they were an opponent's chess pieces and she was trying to work out which posed the greater threat.

'What about Leo?' Morton insisted.

Rebecca forced herself to meet his glare. She couldn't help feeling a little betrayed; she and her uncle were usually on the same side, whether they were scoffing over the village newsletter together or exchanging weary looks when the twins started scrapping. But it always irritated her when Morton became overbearing – as though, just because he was a man, he considered himself head of the family.

'I've been wondering where he is,' she said, remaining defiant.

'Why?' Morton demanded.

Rebecca wasn't sure. Because she'd been goaded by some journalist? Because Rosalyn had refused to tell her? Or, deep down, had a part of her always wondered what had happened to Leo, and why he had left her?

'Because he's my dad,' she decided.

'Not much of a dad,' her uncle muttered. 'Not much of a man, really.'

'Morty . . .' Rosalyn's voice held a warning.

'Well he wasn't, was he?' Morton glowered around the table, daring any of them to contradict him. 'What sort of man behaves like that? What sort of man just gives up on his wife and little girl? He was a coward. I told him so the last time he was here, and wherever he is now, I'll bet he's still a selfish, spineless—'

'Morton, that's enough.'

Perhaps it was the effect of her sparkly cardigan, but authority seemed to crackle off Lillian like electricity. Morton shrugged and reached once more for the decanter of wine. Rosalyn inhaled, as though to speak, but Lillian shook her head.

'Enough.'

There was a long silence, save for the guttural ticking of the grandfather clock, which seemed unusually loud and slow. Then the twins began to snigger. Daphne shushed them and declared she wanted more cake, though there was still half a slice on her plate.

Rebecca felt slightly stunned. Morton was usually monosyllabic and Lillian always stayed out of squabbles, while she herself was rarely the cause of any upset – yet one mention of Leo had been enough to transform the family's whole dynamic. Then she caught sight of Rosalyn, who was blinking rapidly, as though repressing tears, and a lump of regret began to thicken at the back of Rebecca's throat. Lillian patted her hand, which made her feel worse. She was no better than that journalist, trying to ambush her family into answers they could or would not give. To avoid her mother's distress, Rebecca glanced down and realised she'd been dragging the end of her fork around her plate, for there were three parallels lines running through a smear of cream, like tracks in fresh snow.

3

Seven Tales

'Nana? We're heading off soon.'

Rebecca nudged open the door to discover Lillian propped up against two pillows on the right side of the bed. She was wearing a polka dot nightdress and purple reading glasses, and frowning down at the tablet Daphne had bought her for Christmas, tipping it from side to side like a steering wheel.

'Becca, what's an e-card?' she asked.

Grateful to delay the moment she'd be alone with Rosalyn again – her mother had been subjecting her to dark looks since dinner – Rebecca perched on the edge of the bed and helped Lillian navigate a link in an email from her godson. They both gave a start as music blared from a bunch of cartoon balloons.

'Well,' said Lillian, once Rebecca had switched off the device, having established there was no other message but *HAPPY BIRTHDAY GODMOTHER!!* 'I suppose it's the thought that counts.'

She wriggled into the centre of the bed, towards the side once occupied by Grandpa Archie, and patted the space she'd just created. Rebecca moved up until they were sitting next to one another and she was breathing in her grandmother's scent, which was warm and lightly floral, like an expensive candle.

'How's everything downstairs?' asked Lillian.

She'd slipped away shortly after the cake, so had missed an uncomfortable hour of Rosalyn aggressively tidying, Morton rattling about in the drinks cabinet and Daphne and the twins growing increasingly bored and shrill.

'Yes, fine,' Rebecca lied, aware that her mentioning Leo at dinner was at least partly to blame for the evening's tension. 'I think Mum wants us to go in a bit, though.' Again, she winced at the thought of the long and likely silent walk back to Primrose Cottage.

'Before you do, may I ask you something?' Lillian removed and folded up her glasses.

Rebecca, anticipating gentle chastisement, said, 'I didn't mean to ruin your dinner.'

'I happen to think you're perfectly entitled to ask about your father. I'm just curious about what made you do so tonight.'

After Rosalyn's reaction, Rebecca was reluctant to mention the journalist, even to her grandmother. 'I guess I just think about him sometimes, that's all.'

This was true, though she'd never admitted it before. No matter how hard she tried to forget him, Leo had a habit of bounding back into her head around her birthday, at Christmas, every Father's Day. And, occasionally, something smaller and more unexpected would bring him back: certain nursery rhymes, the taste of lime cordial, the lengthening of her shadow on a summer evening . . . She couldn't remember the details of these associations, exactly, but the surprise cameos they prompted felt raw, until, regardless of how long it'd been and, in spite of her feelings of abandonment, she even wondered whether she *missed* him.

Like before, the thought of Leo seemed to trouble Lillian, and Rebecca was tempted to change the subject. But, as she fiddled with the edge of the quilt, she wondered whether she was being presented with a second chance.

'You don't know where he is, then?' she asked.

Lillian shook her head. 'I'm sorry.'

She seemed sincere, but Rebecca began to consider what else her grandmother might be able to tell her. Before she'd thought of a question, however, Lillian asked, 'Would you fetch me something, dear?'

Almost relieved, Rebecca rose from the bed.

'In the wardrobe, on the shelf at the top, there's a box . . .'

Rebecca, who'd been anticipating a request for a novel from the bookshelf or perhaps a hot chocolate from downstairs, turned the ornamental key in the wardrobe door. Inside, Lillian's perfume was stifled by a musty, cupboardy smell, and all her brightly coloured blouses, dresses and jackets looked curiously dull when dangling, disembodied, from a row of hangers. Feeling slightly awkward, Rebecca stood on her toes and began to search along the top shelf, her fingers brushing past the brims of hats and heels of shoes.

'Are you sure it's here?' she asked, worried Lillian was getting muddled.

'Yes – it's wooden, with a little latch on the front.'

Rebecca's hand made contact with something solid, half-hidden behind a stack of scarves. It was about the size of a shoebox, but far heavier and, as she slid it from the wardrobe, she saw it was made of a dark, mottled wood, possibly walnut. When she brought it over to the bed, Lillian threw open the lid and began to rummage through a random assortment of objects: handwritten letters, a man's wedding ring, an envelope marked *M's first tooth*.

As she sat down again, Rebecca picked up a photograph depicting a surly dark-haired boy of around ten, next to two red-headed girls in matching dresses, the taller thin and pensive, the smaller gap-toothed and sunny.

'They haven't changed much,' she remarked.

Lillian didn't respond. She was now tossing aside keepsakes

– a christening bracelet, a square of embroidery – as though they meant nothing.

'Nana, are you all right?'

'Of course, dear – ah, here we are!'

From the very base of the box, she withdrew a book. It was small and narrow, with a faded olive-green cover, and would've been unremarkable – the kind of volume lost to the shelves of a second-hand bookstore or junk shop – had it not been for the gold lettering of its title, which was glinting in the lamplight:

Seven Tales.

A little bewildered by this choice of reading material, which was not in keeping with the cheesy romance novels her grandmother usually favoured, Rebecca started tidying the other mementoes back into the box, asking, 'Do you want me to put this back now?'

'I want you to stop fussing and look at this.'

'Hm?'

'It's yours.'

Rebecca turned to find Lillian offering her the book, which she assumed was a volume of fairy tales or fables, and her puzzlement turned to concern: her grandmother wasn't often mysterious, nor prone to strange bequests. Hopefully this wasn't anything more serious than post-birthday exhaustion.

'Nana, I'm almost twenty-six,' she said, trying to laugh it off.

'Meaning?'

'Meaning . . .' Rebecca reached for the book and skimmed through its pages, catching sight of a few titles: *The Voyage to the Edge of the World*; *The Enchanted Lute.* 'Meaning I'm a little too old for children's stories.'

'Actually, I think you might be exactly the right age,' her grandmother said. 'It's long overdue, anyway – I should've passed it on years ago.'

Rebecca, who was growing impatient with these cryptic comments, decided to be more direct: 'Nana, you're not getting confused, are you?'

Lillian shot her an arch look. 'I assure you all my marbles are accounted for, thank you.'

'Then why are you giving me this?'

'Because it's yours,' Lillian said again, now sounding a little impatient herself. 'Because he left it for you.'

'Who did?'

'Leo.'

Rebecca looked down at *Seven Tales,* suddenly acutely aware of how it felt; its scant weight, its downy clothbound cover. Balanced on the tips of her fingers, the book seemed to hum, like something sentient. She wished she'd known it was from him; now, she felt tricked into taking it.

'I shouldn't have kept it this long,' Lillian was saying. 'But I didn't realise you still thought about him, you never mention him, and Rozzy said—'

Rebecca wrenched her attention from *Seven Tales*. 'What?' she asked, more sharply than she intended. 'What did Mum say?'

Lillian squirmed, as though the pillowcase at her back was filled with needles. 'After he left, she told me you didn't want anything to do with him.'

Rebecca's impulse was to deny this but, again, she couldn't remember his departure, let alone any conversation she and Rosalyn might've had about it at the time.

'Back then, holding onto it seemed the right thing to do . . .' Lillian continued, her eyes growing filmy.

'It's fine,' Rebecca said, relenting in the face of her grandmother's distress. 'It doesn't matter. It's only an old book.'

'But you'll keep it?'

'If you want.'

'And you'll read it?'

'Um, maybe . . .'

Rosalyn's voice floated in from the hallway: '*Becca*?'

'I'm with Nana!'

Lillian gripped at Rebecca's sleeve. 'He wanted you to have it. If you read the stories, you'll understand, and then we can—'

'What are we all doing in here?'

As Rosalyn swept into the room, her cheeks pink, Rebecca slipped *Seven Tales* under her cardigan. She doubted her mother would acknowledge what had happened at dinner, especially in front of Lillian, yet it seemed unwise to flaunt this book of Leo's in her presence.

'I thought we were going, Petal? Morty's out for the count in his old chair – *as usual* – and Daffy's threatening to wake him, which will only end in tears.' Rosalyn spotted the wooden box on the bed. 'What's that?'

'I was just showing Becca some old photographs.'

'Oh.' Rosalyn wrinkled her nose as Lillian held up the picture of her, Morton and Daphne as children. 'Well, are you all right, Mum? Do you want me to make you a cocoa before we go?'

'I'm fine, my love, thank you.'

While Rosalyn went to plump pillows and smooth down the quilt, Rebecca slid from the bed and retrieved the memory box. She poked down its contents so everything would fit inside again, and only then did she see what was neatly stitched into the square of embroidery she'd noticed earlier: *Rebecca Adeline Sampson 03.09.90.* This unnerved her a little – she had no recollection of ever having his surname, the keepsake could've been meant for a stranger – so she quickly shut the box's lid and slid it back into the wardrobe, out of sight.

'Night night, then.' Rosalyn kissed Lillian on the cheek. 'And happy birthday, Mum.'

'Night, Nana,' Rebecca added, turning the key in the wardrobe door.

Lillian blew her a kiss. 'Keep your eyes peeled for badgers on the way home,' she advised. 'I saw two by the Websters' farm the other night.'

'Will do, will do,' said Rosalyn.

As Rebecca followed her mother to the door, she felt a dig to her side, like someone had nudged her in the ribs. Automatically, she glanced back at her grandmother, but Lillian was still nestled in the bed, her dark eyes on Rebecca, her expression imploring. It was Leo's book, Rebecca realised, remembering she'd bundled it under her cardigan. She wished she'd given it back. In spite of her curiosity, she didn't want anything of his. She should've returned it to that box when Lillian wasn't looking. But it was too late now – Rosalyn would see – so Rebecca fastened her arm more tightly to her side, securing the hidden book in place.

Rebecca's old room in Primrose Cottage was a perfectly preserved shrine to her teenage tastes. Along with magazine clippings featuring once beloved celebrities, the walls were still dotted with postcards of ancient ruins: Pompeii, Ephesus, Angkor Wat. A map of the world as imagined by a 16th century cartographer remained pinned above the chest of drawers and black-and-white photographs of Mary Leakey and Gertrude Bell on their respective dig sites still hung on either side of the door.

Now, Rebecca lived in a neat new build in Exeter, whose interiors were sleek and largely unadorned, and perhaps this was why she felt like an imposter whenever she came back here, as though the room belonged to someone else. She needed to clear it out: take down the pictures and donate all the old clothes, trinkets and school textbooks to charity shops or Higher Morvale's monthly jumble sale. It was childish, holding onto this rubbish, retaining these reminders of the unworldly little person she'd been before university. Yet at the same time, Rebecca envied the girl who'd grown up here, dreaming of discoveries; at least *she'd* known what she wanted.

Sitting cross-legged on the single bed, her eyes sticky with fatigue, Rebecca contemplated *Seven Tales*. She was still tempted to sneak it back to her grandmother somehow, or even throw it away – she wanted answers, not a load of children's stories – but now, studying it more closely, she saw it was an unusual-looking book. There was no barcode and nothing to indicate a publisher or even an author, other than a symbol at the bottom of the cover, embossed in gold like the title; a circle and a squiggle, which looked to Rebecca like the outline of a bulb that had briefly sprouted before wilting.

She found this motif repeated on the second page, under a dedication of just two words:

For Birdie

Rebecca stared. The little black letters were dwarfed by the expanse of blankness around them, and the longer she looked the more they seemed to be retreating from her, dissolving into cloud. She traced them with the tip of her index finger, pinning them in place.

She had forgotten the nickname. Now, though, as she whispered it to herself, she could hear him calling it, calling her: *Birdie!* Like the room and its clutter, the name seemed to belong to a different person.

He hadn't just left her this book, Rebecca realised, her pulse ticking in her throat as she turned over the page; he'd written it. These stories were for her.

The First Tale: The Collector and the Nixie

Once upon a time there was a boy with no family. He lived in a gloomy orphanage, where he was forced to wash in icy water, dress in sacking cloth, and eat cold and lumpy porridge for every meal. Until, one day, a man known only as the collector visited the orphanage, on the hunt for a young cleaner. The boy was frightened of the collector, who wore a long dark cloak and a hat that was pulled low over his eyes, but he was more afraid of staying in the orphanage for the rest of his days, so agreed to work for the sinister-looking man.

The collector lived on the outskirts of town, in a house so grand it was almost a castle. When the boy was shown around, he soon learned the reason for his employer's mysterious name, for the house's huge study was crammed with jars, cases and cabinets of magical specimens. The boy, who had never seen such creatures, gazed in wonder at the shimmering wings of fairies, the nimble limbs of pixies, and even the glittering scales of a baby dragon. The collector had trapped them all behind glass, and the boy didn't know which unnerved him more, the ones that were dead, their bodies floating in chemicals, or the specimens still alive.

The house had a vast garden which was full of fragrant flowers and tangled thickets. The collector declared this garden out of bounds, but because he was often away, hunting for new specimens, the curious boy began to sneak out to this forbidden place. One day, he wandered so far into the tall trees he found a clearing surrounding a great green pond, and next to it the biggest fishing net he had ever seen. In the hope of finding some frogspawn or a newt, the boy dipped the rod between the lily pads and began to drag it through the water, until he felt something heavy catch in the net.

He assumed he had trapped a big fish, and with great excitement began to pull at the rod. But when the net emerged from the water, the boy realised it was not a fish he had captured, but a woman. She thrashed against her bindings, wailing with fear, and he was afraid, too, for he knew this was no ordinary woman. With trembling hands, he tugged at the net, and together they succeeded in untangling her.

The boy expected the strange woman to dart away at once, but instead she stood there, watching him. She was dressed in a gown of waterweeds, and her long hair was threaded with green, but she was very beautiful and her skin shone like light on the water.

'I thought you were the collector,' she said, in a voice that rippled through the clearing. 'I see I am fortunate.'

The boy explained who he was, and that he had been looking for frogspawn.

'Well, you have caught a nixie instead,' she told him, 'which means you are fortunate too. For if a nixie is caught, she must grant her captor a wish.'

Delighted, the boy began to pace around the pond, wondering what to wish for. But before he could decide, a shriek of fright tore through the air, and he turned to see the collector throwing the net back over the nixie. She screamed and struggled, but the collector was too strong and stomped back to the house with her bundled over his shoulder.

The boy, who had witnessed this from the opposite bank, ran after them, his heart drumming. He couldn't bear the thought of the nixie becoming another specimen, but was afraid that if he confronted his master, he might end up in a glass case himself. So he paused at the door of the study, his ear to the keyhole.

'Grant me my wish, nixie!' the collector was snarling. 'Grant me my wish!'

But no matter how much he raged, the nixie gave no answer.

The next morning, after the collector had set out for his day's hunting, the boy snuck into the study. The nixie was imprisoned in a large tank of water, its lid fastened with many bolts and padlocks.

'If you grant him a wish, perhaps he will free you?' said the boy.

'The wish is yours,' she replied. 'Tell me, what do you desire?'

Still, the boy didn't know. What did he want most in the world? A hot meal every night? A home to call his own? He considered asking for piles of gold, for that would buy him both.

'I need more time to think about it,' he told her, 'and while I am thinking, I will find a way to free you.'

Yet over the next few days, although he searched the whole house, he could not find a single key that would fit any of the locks on the nixie's tank. Meanwhile, the collector gave up his hunting trips in favour of remaining in his study, where his demands for a wish mingled with the nixie's eerie cries.

Before long, she grew thin, and her skin started to lose its shine, as though she were permanently cast in shadow. Every night, the boy crept downstairs to the study, and although there was little he could do to help her, she was comforted by his presence. He told her tales of the orphanage, she sang him songs about the enchanted world beneath the water, and sometimes he would raise his small hands to the tank while she pressed her long, webbed fingers against the other side of the glass.

Once, he grew frustrated with her: 'If you can do magic, why don't you free yourself?' he asked.

In response, the nixie simply shook her head, now almost too weak to speak. The boy's heart ached for her, this curious creature he had come to love, and at last he understood what had been lacking from his life.

'You have decided,' she whispered through the water. 'Before it is too late, tell me what you desire, and I will make it so.'

The boy put his hands to the glass, and in his mind's eye he could see them: his mother, his father, perhaps a brother or sister too; the family he should have had. Then he looked into the nixie's sad green eyes and said, 'I wish for your freedom.'

For just a moment, she matched her fingers to his, and then she was gone. She had vanished from the tank, and the only sign she had been there at all was a trail of watery footprints leading from the study to the garden.

When the collector learned of her escape, he took a hammer to the empty tank until the floor was flooded with water and broken glass. He never guessed she'd had help, but this did not ease the great loneliness that seized the boy's soul after the nixie left. As the years went by, and he dreamed of a day when he had saved enough of his scant wages to leave the collector's service, he would often return to the pond at the bottom of the garden. But no matter how many times he trailed his net through the water, he never caught the nixie again.

Rebecca didn't read much fiction. On the rare occasions she deviated from biographies or history books, she would usually pick up a detective story, although secretly she enjoyed trashy Tudor-set novels now and again, despite their inaccuracies. It had been a long time since she'd read a fairy tale, and she was a little embarrassed even to have skimmed this infantile story of wishes and water spirits.

Embarrassed and disappointed, too, because she'd hoped *Seven Tales* would contain more than this. While everything about its appearance suggested it was a book of children's stories, there had to be a reason Lillian had chosen to pass it on tonight, right after Rebecca had asked about Leo for the first time in years. It had to contain more of *him*.

She flipped back to the beginning, certain she must have missed something – an introduction, perhaps, or an author's note – but all she could find were a few small words on the inside cover:

Fletcher & Sons, 1999

What had Ellis Bailey said? *After '97 there's nothing. It's like he vanished.* Was this book the only proof of her father's existence beyond that date, or had the journalist not been thorough in his research?

Again, she tried to remember when she'd last seen Leo. She was fairly sure he'd bolted from the village in the mid-90s, when she'd been about five, so assuming he really was the author of *Seven Tales,* he'd tried to get these stories to her long after he had left.

Did anyone else know about this book? Rosalyn definitely didn't, otherwise Rebecca was sure it would have been destroyed. She wished she'd asked her grandmother more questions: when, how and why had Leo passed this on? But if Lillian had held onto it for so long, what else might she be keeping back?

Rebecca flicked through 30 or so pages to the end of *Seven Tales*; perhaps there was some kind of afterword. But aside from a small black-and-white illustration inside the back cover – a collection of trees with keyholes in their trunks, a detail Rebecca assumed would feature in a later tale – the volume contained nothing but stories. She even turned it upside down and gave its spine a shake, but no note or letter tumbled out. It was just a book of fairy tales.

'Stupid.'

She clapped its covers shut and dropped it onto her bedside table, where it knocked against a plastic statuette of Anubis. Maybe Lillian had just wanted to get rid of it. Most likely, she'd passed on *Seven Tales* as a distraction, just as Rosalyn had diverted the conversation from Leo earlier, and now Rebecca felt annoyed at herself for even contemplating – for even *caring* – that the book might have some greater significance.

After reaching out to steady the wobbling jackal-headed god, she switched off her lamp and flopped back against her pillow. When she closed her eyes, the pages of *Seven Tales* remained imprinted on her vision, their words now muddled, meaningless. Impatiently, she waited for them to disappear, to melt into the darkness like the statuette, the posters and all the other junk that belonged in her past.

On the screen, the cursor blinked in anticipation. It reminded Rebecca of a clock radio she'd once had. She started to count its flickers while her fingertips traced the edges of her laptop keys, resisting the urge to check over her shoulder. Her spine felt taut. Though she lived alone and knew her flat was empty, she couldn't shake the suspicion that she was being watched. Or maybe she just felt guilty.

I don't have any other choice, she told herself for the fifth or sixth time that afternoon. She'd rather have questioned her grandmother further but she hadn't managed to speak to Lillian since the night of her birthday – and by now she and Rosalyn would be halfway to Ilfracombe. Rebecca might've tried her mother again, but it hadn't seemed worth upsetting her; the morning after the family dinner, Rosalyn had been back to her usual bustling self, as though Leo had never been mentioned. So Rebecca supposed she was forgiven, especially as, by the time she'd left Primrose Cottage, her mother had used all her normal ploys to delay her departure: making a fresh pot of coffee; exhibiting her latest watercolours; pretending she couldn't find the bits of Rebecca's post that still came to Primrose Cottage.

Upon returning to her flat, Rebecca had thrown these envelopes onto the coffee table, along with *Seven Tales,* which she wasn't sure what to do with. The post, however, was now much more appealing than staring at the now-blank screen of her laptop, so she began to open bank statements for an account she no longer used, coupons for shops she rarely visited and the latest alumni magazine from the University of Exeter, whose previous editions had never made it out of their shrink-wrap.

Under this debris, she discovered the contract for the office manager position at Sudworth and Rowe. Rebecca considered signing it now – it would only take a few minutes to read through the document, check her details and scribble her name – but halfway through the first paragraph her attention began to wander. It was too dull; she was too preoccupied.

Her mind kept circling back to *Seven Tales.* Leaving it in Primrose Cottage for Rosalyn to find had seemed unwise, but neither did Rebecca want it here in her flat. Against the magnolia walls and pale laminate flooring, the dusky green book looked too bright; it didn't belong. There wasn't much point reading the other stories – she wasn't a child anymore – she should probably just throw it away. Only, when she pictured tossing the small volume in the kitchen bin, on top of potato peelings, oily packaging and balls of used kitchen roll, something – *For Birdie,* perhaps – caused her fingers to tighten around its spine.

In the end, Rebecca bundled the book under the coffee table along with her unsigned contract. Then she returned her attention to the laptop screen, and – with mounting trepidation about what she might find – finally typed her father's name into the search bar.

Predictably, most of the relevant results concerned *The Stowaway.* Ellis hadn't exaggerated about the programme being a cult classic: it already featured in a number of existing SideScoop articles, including *How Many of These 90s TV Shows Do You Remember?* and *21 Reasons TV Was Better When You Were a Kid.* Rebecca found links to a DVD, *The Stowaway Series One and Two: 10th Anniversary Special Edition*, released in 2005, and most of the episodes had been uploaded to YouTube, just as the journalist had said. The programme also had a Wikipedia page, and even a few fan sites, many of which hadn't been updated in several years.

When Rebecca clicked on Images, her heart gave a disobedient judder at all the stills and publicity shots of Leo in character as the Stowaway. She was surprised by how familiar he was. There were no photos of him in Primrose Cottage, yet this was almost exactly how she remembered him: wide smile, bright blue eyes, dark hair – its messiness exaggerated for these pictures, backcombed around his head so he resembled a sunflower. There were only a few details she'd forgotten, or perhaps not noticed as a child: the crooked front tooth, the off-centre nose. Again, she was thankful she looked nothing like him.

Promptly clicking back, Rebecca typed in *leo sampson*

daughter. Once again, all the results related to *The Stowaway: . . . In episode four, the Stowaway (***Leo Sampson***) encounters a miller's* ***daughter****, whose father has boasted she can spin straw into gold . . .*

Searching for *leo sampson family* produced much the same outcome, although one fan site seemed to have a little more biographical insight than the others: *. . . In the early 90s,* ***Sampson*** *took a break from acting to spend more time with his* ***family*** *. . .*

After flexing her fingers over the keyboard, Rebecca typed *leo sampson 2016* and, a few minutes later, was forced to conclude Ellis had been right: there was no trace of him after 1997, which was apparently when he'd left *The Stowaway*. Rebecca wasn't sure what to make of this – especially as the fairy tale book was dated two years later – although when *leo sampson death* and *leo sampson obituary* produced only a memorial to an old Texan, she felt a tiny flutter of relief.

Mostly, however, she was annoyed: it was absurd, to be researching her own father online. If only Lillian hadn't gone away, because even if her grandmother didn't know where Leo was, Rebecca needed someone to confide in. Not for the first time, a bothersome little part of her brain then reminded her there *was* someone else; someone who might know more than Lillian, someone who had his own reasons for wanting to find out what had happened to Leo Sampson . . . But, again, Rebecca dismissed the idea, closing her laptop with a definitive snap.

For the rest of the afternoon, she tried to reclaim what was left of her weekend: she went for a run around the river; tidied her flat and watered her plants; chose an outfit, prepared a lunch and packed her bag for the next day. Until, satisfied there was nothing else to do – the contract could wait another day or so – Rebecca settled on the sofa with a cup of tea, trying to recall what had happened in the Swedish crime drama she'd started last Thursday.

Yet she soon found her concentration wavering. She kept forgetting to read the subtitles, because her gaze was drifting under the coffee table, towards *Seven Tales*. *Should* she read the other stories? When the lead detective's shocked expression and a crescendo in the soundtrack implied she'd missed a pivotal revelation, Rebecca sighed, paused the TV and went to retrieve her laptop.

Dear Ellis,

Rebecca scowled at the screen: this was painful. If she was going to pursue this, she wanted to do it alone, and certainly not with someone like him.

Following our meeting on Friday, I was wondering whether you could keep me updated on your search for Leo Sampson? I would be interested to hear if you find him.

Best regards,
Rebecca

She read the message several times, hoping it sounded offhand. She didn't want him calling the office again, so after some deliberation added her mobile number. When she finally pressed *send*, the tension in her back began to drain towards her toes and she reached for the remote to rewind her programme.

Two episodes later, the ringing of her mobile coincided with the lead detective finding a blood-spattered dossier. Rebecca, now so engrossed that the sudden noise off-screen made her jump, fumbled for her phone.

'Hello?'

'So you really don't know where he is?' Ellis said, without preamble.

Rebecca checked her watch and noted it was now almost 7.00 pm; a ridiculous time to call, especially on a Sunday. 'I thought we'd been over this?'

'Yeah,' the journalist agreed. 'And you want to be kept updated, do you?'

'If you wouldn't mind,' she said, forcing herself to be polite, though she thought she'd been more than clear.

'I wouldn't mind,' Ellis confirmed, sounding cheerful enough, though Rebecca sensed an impending *but* . . . 'I'm just wondering what's in it for me?'

'I'm sorry?'

'What do I get out of this arrangement?'

For one wild moment, she thought he was propositioning her. She pictured the unkempt but amiable figure who'd sauntered into the office on Friday; he'd been pushy, not sleazy. Did he want payment? Again, Ellis Bailey didn't seem the type to be motivated by money – if he were, surely he'd be better dressed?

What would a journalist want from this situation? Information, she supposed – but what did she know that he didn't? The existence of *Seven Tales* was the obvious answer, but what use was an old book?

'I think my grandmother knows more than she's letting on,' Rebecca said eventually, hoping this sounded promising but vague. 'She's away at the moment, but I can talk to her when she gets back? Let you know what she says?'

'Yeah? Sounds good.' Ellis's tone was so nonchalant Rebecca suddenly wondered whether he'd been teasing her. Maybe he would've helped regardless. The suspicion made her feel half-embarrassed, half-furious – until she reminded herself she had no intention of actually passing on anything Lillian shared.

'Hey, you know Richard Lowrie?' Ellis continued.

'What?'

'Richard Lowrie, the actor – I'm interviewing him this week in London.'

'Okay . . .' She pictured the snowy-haired stalwart of British film and TV, then wondered why on earth the journalist was talking about him.

'Richard Lowrie was in *The Stowaway*,' he explained. 'I forgot you haven't seen it. He was always the king or father character. I thought, in case I can't find your dad, I'd line him up for my article – I've got to have *someone* from *The Stowaway* – and it'll be good to hear about his time on the show, see if anything interesting comes up.'

'Right,' said Rebecca, wondering exactly what he meant by *interesting*.

'Why don't you come along?'

'What, to London?'

'Yeah, then you can hear what he has to say for yourself. It's this Tuesday at 2.00 pm. I'll get you a press pass – we can pretend you work for SideScoop.'

Rebecca could think of plenty of reasons why this was a bad idea. Going to London for the day would be expensive and, although she had plenty of annual leave left, it was extremely short notice for work, especially so soon after the office move. Then there was Ellis himself, this stranger sniffing around her family. Asking to be kept informed was one thing, but meeting up with him was definitely disloyal, especially after she'd assured Rosalyn she'd had nothing to do with *that journalist*.

Above all, where was the sense in pursuing this? Why should she go to all this bother for a man who hadn't been bothered about her in years? Leo Sampson had contributed nothing to the last two decades of her life. Nothing but a book of fairy tales . . .

'Rebecca? Are you still there?'

'Oh – yes.'

'It was just a suggestion,' said Ellis. 'If it's too much hassle, I can let you know afterwards if he—'

'No, I'll go,' she decided as, beneath the coffee table, the gold lettering of *Seven Tales* glinted up at her like coins in a wishing well. 'Why not?'

PART TWO

The Second Tale: The Golden Door

Long ago, deep in the woods, a gentle old woman was collecting kindling for her fire when she discovered a baby. He had been laid in a cradle of twigs and moss, and was fast asleep under a blanket of petals. The old woman searched and called through the trees, but there was nobody around and she concluded the child had been abandoned. The woman had no family of her own, and as she peered into the cradle her heart quickened with love.

When she returned home, she realised the little foundling was not like the other children in the village. His fingers and toes were too long, his ears too pointy and his eyes were as green as holly leaves. Though she loved him very much, she knew the villagers would be troubled by his strange appearance, so she made him extra-large gloves and shoes, and a little cap to hide his ears. There was nothing she could do to cover his eyes, but she didn't mind that, for she thought them very handsome.

As the boy began to walk and talk, it became more obvious still that he was different. His gait was quick and light, his laughter sounded like distant bells and those who looked directly into his large green eyes often forgot where they were. While the other children teased him, the adults whispered behind their hands and the priest grew grave. But the old woman, who was a healer, was well-regarded in the village, so for a time the people let her little foundling be.

The foundling himself didn't mind being unusual. As he grew up, he began to realise he had powers the other children did not possess.

His skin was tough, not easily grazed or bruised. He could breathe underwater as though he had gills. Best of all, he could talk to the animals in the woods.

These animals spoke to the foundling of his homeland. They told him he was a prince of a great kingdom and had been smuggled into the human realm when war had endangered his family. The boy didn't know whether he believed this, but sometimes, when he was deep within the trees, he caught glimpses of a doorway shimmering gold in the half-light of the woods, always just out of reach.

When the foundling was almost a man, the old woman caught a chill and died. The youth was overcome with grief, it felt like his heart was cast in shadow and he mourned her for many months. The village too was saddened, but the priest, who had always been jealous of the healer's standing within the community, saw her death as an opportunity to assert his authority.

'Out of respect for our wise woman, I have held my tongue,' he told his congregation, 'but now she is with God, let me speak plainly: I believe that creature is a changeling brought here by the Devil, and an innocent human child is trapped in Hell in its place.'

When the people heard this, they were very afraid and begged the priest to tell them what to do.

He replied, 'Tie the beast to the church gate and beat the wickedness from its skin.'

The villagers did as they were told and struck the youth with sticks and stones. He wasn't hurt, because his skin was as hard as bark, but he was greatly distressed, and when the villagers finally freed him, he dashed into the sanctuary of the woods. There, the animals gathered around him, trying to offer comfort by telling him once more of the realm to which he belonged.

The youth asked, 'But how do I return there?'

The answer, no matter which of the animals he asked, was always the same:

When oak meets ash,
And ash meets thorn,
There you will find
Where you were born.

The foundling searched the woods far and wide, and although he found oak and ash and thorn trees, they never seemed to grow together, nor offer him any way home. Eventually, he returned to the healer's house, wishing his dear old mother was still alive. As soon as he was spotted in the village, however, the people grew afraid once again.

'If the wickedness cannot be beaten out of the changeling, it must be washed out,' the priest advised.

So, a band of villagers seized the youth, dragged him to the river-bank and held his head under the water. Any other man or beast would certainly have drowned, yet the foundling breathed as easily as if he had been taking in great lungfuls of air, and when the villagers finally let him go, they were more afraid than ever.

'Changeling!' they cried. 'Devil's child! Creature from Hell!'

The youth sped back into the woods, anguished yet uninjured, and repeated to himself the words of the animals:

When oak meets ash,
And ash meets thorn,
There you will find
Where you were born.

But no matter how hard he searched, he could not find a place where oak and ash and thorn grew together.

'I must look further afield,' he decided. 'I will explore beyond these woods.'

Yet as he was packing supplies for his journey, he was set upon by a mob from the village, who dragged him back to the church and tied him to the gate again. This time, they did not pelt him with sticks or stones, and nor did they hold his head underwater.

'Fire is the only punishment the Devil understands,' said the priest. 'We shall burn the changeling, and then the Devil will be forced to return its human brother from Hell.'

The villagers began to push logs and branches against the gate, and the foundling grew very afraid, because he knew he could not withstand flames.

'Help me!' he cried, as the first kindling was lit. 'Please, help me!'

The animals heard his cries, and the mice, who were the bravest, darted through the logs to nibble at the youth's bindings. But even when they had chewed him free, he was still trapped in the middle of the smoke and flames.

'Burn him!' screamed the priest, his voice shrill with triumph. 'Feed the fire so he burns!'

The terrified villagers did as they were told and hurled great branches onto the pyre. One man threw a bough of oak, another one of ash and a third one of thorn, and as these branches met at the feet of the weakening youth, a shimmering golden door appeared.

The villagers cried out in alarm, backing away from the blaze and seeking instruction from the astonished priest. But the foundling knew this glimmering portal was for him, so with the very last of his strength he pushed open the door and leaped through.

Afterwards, many of the villagers claimed they had caught a glimpse over the threshold of that mystical door before it was devoured by the flames. Some said they had spotted lush green land, while others swore they had seen a majestic man and woman holding out their arms in welcome. Nobody was sure, though, and upon the advice of their priest they strove to put the whole incident, and the foundling, from their minds.

4

The Actor

'Found it okay?'

Ellis gestured at the bar. It was a bustling two-storey building with a bluish glass façade, which gave it the look of an aquarium. It seemed too busy and exposed, too *modern* a venue for Richard Lowrie, who must've been approaching his eighties. But, according to Ellis, the actor had specifically requested it for the interview, as he was in final rehearsals nearby for a production of *The Tempest*.

'Yes, fine,' Rebecca replied, though she'd compulsively checked her phone and every map she'd passed since arriving at Paddington. London made her nervous – its size felt impenetrable – and though she was still questioning why she'd agreed to this meeting, now she'd come all this way she was anxious not to miss it.

Ellis was sat at a sunlit table next to one of the vast windows, sipping at a swamp-coloured smoothie. He looked much the same as he had the previous week, only his crumpled shirt – didn't he own an iron? – was patterned with red and purple plaid, its sleeves rolled up to below his elbows. As Rebecca joined him, he handed her a menu printed on dog-eared recycled paper and pinned to a plywood clipboard. When they'd agreed to meet for lunch to discuss the interview before Richard Lowrie arrived, she'd imagined something slightly more professional than this. Even the purple lanyard hanging around Ellis's neck did little to convince her he was there in a work capacity – although at least its colour matched his shirt.

'They do great veggie food here, by the way,' he remarked, as she flicked an old lentil off the edge of her clipboard. 'You should try the falafel, it's amazing.'

Presumably this meant he wasn't a meat eater himself and, irritated by his unsolicited recommendation, Rebecca scanned the menu for the least vegetarian dish she could find. This was difficult, firstly because it was mostly *cauliflower steaks* and *quinoa bowls*, and secondly because Ellis kept besieging her with questions about the journey from Exeter. She told him she'd spent most of it reading a whodunit, neglecting to mention that she'd intended to use the time to finish *Seven Tales.* Only, she hadn't managed to get past the second story, as she'd found the misadventures of the changeling, or whatever he was, just as inane as its predecessor, and had felt a little too self-conscious reading fairy tales on the train.

After a waitress took their order, Rebecca supposed it was only polite to ask about the journalist's weekend in Cornwall, although she barely listened to his responses. Normally, she might've been interested to hear how he'd cycled to the castle, caves and coast of Tintagel – places she knew from her own summer holidays – but today she was too consumed by what had brought her to London.

'So, I don't suppose you've had much of a chance to work on your article since we last spoke?' she ventured.

'Nah, not really – and I doubt Richard Lowrie will know where your dad is. But I'm curious to hear what he has to say about their time on *The Stowaway*, considering it was right before Leo disappeared. Oh yeah . . .'

He retrieved a plastic folder from his shabby bag. It looked like it was stuffed with paper, but after a few seconds of rummaging Ellis fished out a purple lanyard that matched his own.

'Welcome to SideScoop,' he said, sliding it across the table.

The lanyard was emblazoned with the familiar outline of a scoop and a curl of ice cream, while its card read *PRESS*, her name and the words *SideScoop: an extra dollop of news and entertainment*.

'You *are* a Rebecca, aren't you?' Ellis asked, nodding at the pass.

'What?'

'Not a Becky?'

'Oh – no, definitely not.'

'Becca?'

Not to you, she thought.

'Becs?'

'Rebecca is just fine,' she told him firmly, looping the lanyard around her neck and instantly feeling more purposeful; ugly though it was, the pass allowed her to pretend she had no personal stake in this. 'What do you want me to do at this interview, anyway?'

'Oh, just look interested, maybe take a few notes. I'll try to keep him on *The Stowaway* as much as possible, but he can be difficult . . .' Ellis lowered his voice. 'My friend interviewed him a few years back, said he was a bit of a nob.'

Rebecca knew little about Richard Lowrie and had only seen a few of his films and TV shows; most recently, he'd starred in a sprawling adaptation of a Dickens novel. He usually played the villain, so it was easy enough to imagine him being less than friendly in real life. But she found Ellis's conspiratorial manner grating, so resolved to give the actor the benefit of the doubt.

When the waitress returned with their food, Ellis moved his folder from the table to the empty chair between them, where Rebecca read her father's name through the clear plastic.

'What's all that?'

'Huh?' Ellis was getting to grips with the sizeable falafel wrap he'd just been delivered. 'Oh, that's my Leo Sampson file – all the research I've done so far for this article. Man, this looks good,' he added, ducking towards his lunch.

Rebecca frowned: the folder was so full its popper wouldn't fasten.

'I'm trying to compile it into a kind of timeline,' Ellis continued, through a mouthful. 'Mostly for the biographical part of the article, but I also thought it might give me some clue as to where Leo's gone.'

While he bent to slurp at the dregs of his smoothie through a cardboard straw, Rebecca began to pick at the Caesar salad – with extra bacon – she'd ordered, which was drenched in dressing. But her attention was soon drawn back to the folder.

'Can I have a look?' she asked, pointing with her fork in an attempt to look casual.

'Yeah, sure.' Ellis sounded mildly surprised, perhaps because she'd been a lot less interested on Friday. He relinquished a hold of his half-eaten wrap, wiped his fingers on a napkin and slid a handwritten sheet of paper from the top of the folder.

'This is what I've got so far for the biography . . .' he began, but seemed to hesitate before handing it over. 'Actually, as we've a bit of time, maybe we could go through it together? You might be able to fill in some of the gaps?'

Rebecca doubted she'd be any help, but was too curious to admit this. 'Good idea.'

Ellis held up the paper, as though trying to see it in a better light. 'All right, what have we got . . . ? According to public records, Leo Sampson was born in Ashford, Kent, on the 1st of June 1965.'

He looked at Rebecca for confirmation, who nodded, though she'd never given her father's birth a moment's consideration. Whenever he sidled into her thoughts, he existed only in the context of her own life: he'd bounded into being during her earliest memories and ceased to endure beyond their last parting, whenever that had been. The idea that there was a before – and possibly an after – was unfamiliar.

'He must've grown up in Kent, or at least returned there,' continued Ellis, 'because in 1980 he starred in the Ashford Youth Theatre's Christmas play – as Aladdin, in case you're wondering.'

'How do you know that?'

'The archives of *The Ashford Examiner* are online. So he was there when he was fifteen, but then there's a bit of a gap before he crops up again five years later, in 1985.'

Once more, Ellis paused, offering Rebecca the opportunity to contribute. Partly to disguise her ignorance, she asked, 'And what happened then?'

'His acting career started to take off: a show at the Edinburgh Fringe; a job touring with a children's theatre company in Scotland. Then he found himself an agent in London and did some bigger stuff down here . . . This is all on his Wikipedia page, by the way, and *The Stowaway* fan sites have more or less the same biography.'

Inwardly, Rebecca admonished herself for not being more meticulous in her own research. She felt unusually unprepared, not to mention uninformed: shouldn't she know all of this? He was her *father.*

'He did *Peter Pan* at the Circle in the summer of '89,' Ellis went on. 'It was a big production, that one – a big deal – but then he went quiet for a while. Oh, yeah . . .' Without looking up from the page, the journalist nodded at Rebecca. 'That's because he moved to Devon, married Rosalyn Chase and had a baby, born on the 5th of September 1990.'

Rebecca stiffened: she might've grudgingly accepted that this journalist was probing into her father's past but wasn't prepared to feature in his investigation herself. Despite defining Leo by his contribution – or lack of – to her own life, she disliked the idea of being so much as a footnote in his.

'I've no idea what he got up to in Devon,' Ellis continued, oblivious to her discomfort, 'whether he had a job or what, but he next appears in '95, in *The Stowaway*, which he did for two years, and then—' He clicked the fingers of his left hand. 'That's it. There's nothing else.'

Rebecca thought of *Seven Tales* in her bag, and the date on the book's inside cover: 1999. Still, she wouldn't mention it. She barely knew what to make of it herself and, in comparison to the journalist's research, a collection of children's stories would sound trivial.

Unwilling to persevere with her soggy salad, she laid down her fork and returned her gaze to the folder, where a photocopy of a newspaper article was now visible.

Wednesday 6 December, 1995

The Stowaway *commissioned for second series*

The Stowaway, *the children's storytelling show that debuted this autumn, is to return for a second series.*

Starring Leo Sampson as a boyish hero who unwittingly becomes entangled in famous fairy tales, the programme has been a huge hit with audiences, averaging around nine million viewers each week.

'We've been overwhelmed by its popularity,' said creator and executive producer Larry Wilkinson. 'We couldn't have predicted how much the public would embrace our little show.'

Speaking about the newly commissioned second series, Wilkinson hinted the programme's focus will widen to include myths and stories with a more international flavour. 'But Leo and the rest of the cast will be back,' he said, referring to the seven-strong troupe who perform a variety of roles each week, 'so the faces will be as familiar as the format.'

The second series of The Stowaway *will begin filming in Bristol in the new year. The final episode of the current series will air this Sunday at 5 p.m. on BBC One.*

The article was accompanied by a picture blanched by the photocopier.

'Hold on,' said Ellis, when he saw Rebecca squinting at the image, 'I've a colour version of that somewhere.'

He withdrew a print from his folder and offered it to her. It was a publicity shot depicting a band of attractive people in doublets and puffy dresses, accessorised with crowns, swords and magic wands. Six of them were tussling over a glass slipper, while a seventh messy-haired figure was sat cross-legged in the foreground, beaming at the camera over the giant pumpkin resting in his lap.

Rebecca could sense Ellis studying her reaction and was relieved to have recently encountered similar images of Leo online: this photo, her father's face, it didn't faze her – not much, anyway.

She let the picture fall to the table and reached for the folder instead. 'What else have you got in here?'

She pulled out another photograph, a paparazzi shot of Leo, his arms around two other people. On his right was a pretty blonde woman wearing dark lipstick and a tight dress. To his left was a handsome square-jawed man clad entirely in denim. Their clothes and the quality of the picture put them firmly in the nineties, when they wouldn't have been much older than Rebecca was now.

The photograph had been taken at night, presumably outside a bar or club, and the three figures looked very bright against the darkness. Yet Leo stood out in comparison to his companions, despite their more conventional good looks; while they were looking coyly at the cameras, his expression was distant, almost wistful.

'Those two were in *The Stowaway* as well,' said Ellis. 'They always played the prince and princess characters – you know, Cinderella and Charming, Sleeping Beauty and whatever her man was called. The Stowaway always ended up helping them get together.'

Rebecca examined the publicity shot again, spotting Cinderella, Charming and Richard Lowrie among those fighting for the glass slipper. But her attention swiftly returned to her father. 'You said he was the Stowaway for two years – did they just do the two series, then?'

'They did three. The last one was with a different guy, a different Stowaway.'

'And that was in '97?'

'Yeah.'

In the paparazzi shot, Leo's T-shirt was a little stained, his dark hair looked lank and there was a sheen of moisture above his brow. He was leaning forward, urging his companions on.

'Was he fired?' Rebecca asked.

Ellis hesitated before answering. 'Not officially, no. All the press from the time suggests he quit to pursue other roles – and there are a lot of articles about his departure; it was big news.'

'But *un*officially?'

'I don't know, it's a bit weird. First, because *The Stowaway* was at the height of its popularity, so he would've struggled to find a better TV role, let alone one that suited him so well. And second . . . Well, he didn't do anything else, did he? As far as we can tell, he never acted again.'

'Maybe he was fired but they got rid of him quietly, to avoid a scandal,' speculated Rebecca.

Ellis nudged the bridge of his glasses further up his nose, watching her intently, and Rebecca felt she'd finally contributed something to the discussion – although it wasn't much of a stretch to imagine the dishevelled man in the paparazzi shot losing his job as the face of a wholesome children's TV programme.

'Yeah,' said Ellis, 'I think you might be right – and it's certainly something to ask Richard Lowrie.'

The actor arrived 40 minutes late, trailed by a petite dark-haired woman, and announcing, 'At last – I've escaped! We're in the middle of tech rehearsals, and it's the biggest bloody bore.'

He was shorter than Rebecca had anticipated, although his height was exaggerated by a long dark coat and trilby, both of which seemed unsuited to the warm weather. His pale eyes were as icy as they were onscreen, but out of make-up and away from studio lights his narrow face was speckled with age spots and thread veins. This made him look ordinary, and Rebecca, who'd never met anyone famous before, wondered whether all celebrities were slightly disappointing in person.

After Ellis had introduced himself and Rebecca, the actor shook their hands, but did not divulge the identity of his own female companion, who was presumably a publicist or assistant. Instead, he attempted to dispatch her to the bar for wine, and when she tried to object, he snapped, 'No, please – just do it. Tech days are an exception. In fact, get a bottle, I'm sure this young man will reimburse you.'

As she departed, Lowrie peered down at Rebecca and Ellis's table, which was now clear of papers.

'I'm desperate for a smoke, let's go to the balcony upstairs,' he said. 'Oh, don't worry about Jenny, she'll find us,' he added, when Rebecca and Ellis both glanced towards the bar. 'She never lets me out of her sight . . .'

He led them on a slow slog up the wooden stairs and, when

they eventually arrived at a table, Lowrie clamped a cigarette between his downturned lips and began to fumble with a lighter. 'Not a great view,' he muttered, 'but needs must.'

Rebecca thought he had a point about the scenery: the balcony faced a row of boxy red-brick buildings, and the only greenery in sight was a lone tree.

'She wanted you to come to the theatre or my hotel,' he continued, perhaps referring to Jenny, 'but I've told her time and again, we won't be bothered in public. Who's going to look twice at an old codger like me?' Lowrie smiled, either at his own self-deprecation or because he'd finally lit his cigarette.

By the time both Jenny and a waiter had found them with the wine, Ellis had produced his spiral-bound notebook and asked the actor's permission to record their conversation. Lowrie responded with a magnanimous nod, so the journalist tapped at a button on the screen of his phone, which made a chirruping noise, and enquired about the progress of *The Tempest.*

Unfortunately, this pleasantry inspired Lowrie to launch into a lengthy monologue about his latest role – and an uninterested Jenny to begin scrolling through her phone. Though it was his first time playing Prospero, Lowrie declared he'd been after the part for many years, 'eager to tackle a character with such a complex sense of morality: . . . *the rarer action is / In virtue than in vengeance,*' he intoned, so loudly that people at the neighbouring table turned to stare. He praised the play's director – 'a true visionary' – and discussed the adaptation's immersive staging, explaining that the audience would take their seats to the sights, sounds and smells of the ocean.

Rebecca, who'd been writing random words on her own notepad to look busy – *character, visionary, ocean* – was suddenly plunged into her past as a recollection crashed over her like a breaking wave. Leo, on a beach, digging a hole with a red plastic spade. Gulls were griping overhead and the briny scent of seaweed was circulating on a warm breeze. Leo's bare shoulders were striped with undissolved sun cream and his dripping hair and the spray of sand at his back made him seem more dog than man . . .

Rebecca frowned, dislodging this gleaming memory from her mind and forcing her attention back on the interview. Ellis didn't appear frustrated by Lowrie's endless opinions and long-winded anecdotes, but his eyes were a little unfocused. When was he going to ask about *The Stowaway*?

Jenny, meanwhile, was now contemplating Ellis over the top of her phone, her expression appraising. Amused, Rebecca tried to ignore the journalist's creased shirt and thatch of hair and concentrate instead on his broad shoulders and the strong contours of his face . . . She supposed he was *almost* attractive – or would be, if he tidied himself up a bit.

After about 15 minutes, Lowrie paused to refill his wine glass and Ellis seized his opportunity. 'Mr Lowrie, obviously you've become known for these big, complex roles like Prospero, but many of SideScoop's readers will have first encountered you in *The Stowaway.* So maybe I could ask you a couple of questions about your time on that show? For the article I mentioned in my email?'

Ellis glanced at Jenny, perhaps hoping for back up, but she'd returned to her phone. Lowrie, however, seemed happy to indulge him. 'I'm often asked about *The Stowaway*,' he said. 'It was one of my first forays into television, and probably my most successful. I had young grandchildren at the time, you see, so I wanted to be in something we could watch together – and I must admit I was charmed by the idea of it, how each episode was a different fairy tale.'

His gaunt features seemed to soften. Ellis, clearly keen to

press his advantage, said, 'It's difficult to believe it only ran for three series—'

'Two and a half, actually,' Lowrie corrected. 'We were cancelled halfway through our third year.' His voice was curt, his dreamy expression gone.

'Do you have any idea why?' Ellis asked, undaunted by this change in the actor's demeanour.

'I know exactly why: because of *Leo Sampson*.' His enunciation made it sound like a vocal warm-up, not a name.

Rebecca's pen quivered a few centimetres above her page, but she didn't dare look up. Beside her, Ellis made a show of flicking through his own notebook.

'You mean, the actor who played the Stowaway?' he asked, giving a convincing impression of someone only just keeping up.

'Yes – that man was a nightmare, but after he left it didn't work. Nobody liked the new Stowaway. Do you know, I can't even remember his name . . . *Craig* someone? Whoever he was, he was awful.'

After a cautious glance towards Rebecca, Ellis voiced the question at the forefront of her mind: 'In what way was Leo a nightmare?'

'In *every* way: he was always late, he never learned his lines, he was constantly losing his script, or his props or bits of his costume. The man was a complete mess.'

Jenny, Rebecca noticed, had looked up from her phone again; evidently, this topic didn't come up in every interview.

'And why was that, do you think?' asked Ellis.

He sounded wary: Lowrie seemed to be enjoying himself for the moment – perhaps he'd grown bored with *The Tempest* or being asked the same old questions – but Rebecca suspected his willingness to gossip was only temporary.

'Why was he a mess?' the actor pondered. 'Oh, a number of

reasons, I suppose – the first being he was a colossal egotist. Look, I'm not denying Leo was the star of *The Stowaway*. He was born for that part. But the success of the show went to his head. He became completely obsessed with that character; it drove Larry and the writers to distraction.'

'Obsessed? How?'

'Oh, he wanted to know who the Stowaway was, where he'd come from before he'd ended up in all those stories. He even wanted to know the Stowaway's *name*, for God's sake – as though it were real!'

'Was he trying to better understand the role?' Ellis suggested.

This sounded reasonable, especially as Lowrie had just spent several long minutes dissecting his Shakespeare character, and Rebecca felt grateful that Ellis was remaining impartial. The actor, however, looked sour.

'I believe it was a little more devious than that. The Stowaway might have been the main part, but mostly he was an observer. He never had a storyline of his own and that bothered Leo, which was where all the claptrap about his character came from. He wanted more screen time, more attention.'

Lowrie's untidy white eyebrows met above his nose, and he reached for his lighter.

'You said there were other reasons?' Ellis reminded him. 'Other explanations for Leo's behaviour?'

'Yes, well, his personal life was all over the place. He'd married young, if I remember rightly, and his wife had thrown him out shortly before he'd started on the programme . . .'

With slightly shaking fingers, Rebecca made a genuine note of this. On Friday, Morton had denounced Leo for giving up on them, not the other way around. So what was the truth?

Her father's departure was a blank in her mind, but she had a vague recollection of lying awake in Primrose Cottage, trying to shut out the stifled sobs coming from her mother's bedroom. Had she snuck through and crawled under the covers of the vast double bed to offer comfort? Rebecca couldn't remember – just as she couldn't be sure the memory had anything to do with Leo – but somehow, she doubted she'd have been welcome; Rosalyn was too proud.

'Good for her, I say,' continued Lowrie, 'although I can't understand why she agreed to take him on in the first place – anyone with half a brain could see he was wild. So he was cut up about that when we were filming the first series, and he was upset about his daughter . . .' Rebecca looked up, giving a small start as Lowrie's lighter flared. 'It wasn't the best of beginnings.'

Keeping his tone neutral, Ellis asked, 'Why was he upset about his daughter?'

'His ex-wife was making it difficult for him to see her, something like that. I suppose he felt he was missing out on being a father. But that was his own fault, wasn't it? He shouldn't have messed up his marriage.'

As Lowrie took a drag on his freshly lit cigarette, Rebecca suppressed the urge to knock it from his lips; she hated the careless way he was talking about her parents, though Leo hardly deserved defending.

The actor exhaled, his pale-eyed gaze fixed on one of the red-brick buildings across the road. 'Looking back on it, how he pined for her, I think that little girl was the only person in the world Leo cared about – aside from himself, of course. He certainly didn't care about any of us or he wouldn't have behaved the way he did. He was an exceptionally selfish man.'

He tapped at his cigarette, scattering ash all over the table. A few specks landed upon Rebecca's page, and her latest scribblings: *filming, own fault, daughter* . . . Her heart clenched as she wondered how reliable Lowrie's testimony was. Did she dare believe what she'd just heard?

'Leo decided to leave after the second series,' Ellis began, and for the first time Rebecca was annoyed by his line of questioning. Unlike earlier, she wanted to stay on the subject of herself; if her family remained tight-lipped, this might be her only chance to actually learn something.

Lowrie snorted. 'He didn't *decide* to leave, he was fired.'

While Ellis feigned surprise, Jenny sat up a little straighter, whispering, 'Um, Mr Lowrie—'

'Oh, this was years ago,' he told her, 'and it was an open secret at the time. They couldn't keep him, not with the way he was carrying on. Not with his little problem.'

'What little problem?'

The words had left Rebecca's mouth before she could stop them. Ellis and Jenny both glanced at her in surprise, but Lowrie seemed to be enjoying his story too much to register she'd spoken for the first time.

'*Drugs*,' he said, with relish. 'Don't ask me what he was taking, but he was bouncing off the walls. It's not uncommon in the industry, of course, but considering he was the *Stowaway* . . .'

Rebecca presumed that Lowrie had kept back this revelation until the last moment, for maximum dramatic impact. It had certainly worked on Jenny, who had lurched forward in her seat, anxious he should stop this potentially slanderous story. Yet when Rebecca thought back to the paparazzi shot, in which Leo had looked clammy and unfocused, it was difficult to feel too shocked – and easier to understand why her mother, who valued rules and appearances so highly, refused to talk about him.

'So, he was fired for substance abuse?' asked Ellis, who appeared almost irritated by the turn the conversation had taken.

'Yes,' Lowrie replied, ignoring the sound of Jenny clearing her throat. 'Well, they had to, didn't they? He could hardly hold himself together.'

'Were you there when he was dismissed?'

Lowrie hesitated. 'As it happens, no. I had a morning off when it all blew up, which I was quite pleased about at the time, because a school group was visiting, and—'

'But you know for certain he was fired, and why?' Ellis persisted.

'Of course I know! The producers told us, didn't they? All right, not in so many words – they had to protect the show – but we all *knew*. And the stupid thing was everyone was so shocked! Not me, though. I've been in this business for over 50 years and I've seen dozens like Leo Sampson: young, reasonably talented and utterly self-destructive. I realised at once that *The Stowaway* was finished. It couldn't go on with him and it couldn't go on without him. I just wonder whether he ever considered our careers when he was busy throwing away his own.'

Lowrie snatched up the wine bottle, discovered it was empty, and dropped it back into the cooler with a clunk. 'Why are we talking about this, anyway?' he demanded. 'Are you going to put it in your article? No one will care, it happened so long ago . . .' Too late, he seemed to realise, he'd said too much.

'I won't put it in my article,' Ellis assured him. 'But — did you ever see Leo after he was fired?'

'Why are you asking these questions? I thought this was about *my* career?' He rounded on Jenny. 'Isn't it time we were getting back?'

Rebecca shot Ellis a sharp look, willing him to do something: Lowrie mustn't leave without answering the question that had brought them here.

'You're right, I've got distracted,' said the journalist smoothly, holding up his hands. 'Obviously, the article will focus on you. After all, you're by far the most famous member of that cast . . .'

Lowrie, who was tucking his cigarettes and lighter back into his coat pocket, paused. 'Yes, I suppose I am.'

'Why do you think I was so keen to speak to you? It's not like you hear anything about the rest of them anymore. I mean – ' Ellis laughed ' – where the hell's Leo Sampson these days?'

'I dread to think,' said the actor. Then, in the same nonchalant tone, he added, 'You know, he's probably dead.'

Rebecca remained determinedly seated as Ellis accompanied Lowrie and his assistant back inside. She watched as they shook hands and followed the actor's progress as he began to shuffle down the stairs, until his black trilby had bobbed out of sight. Her whole body was pulsing with anger, but she wasn't sure why. Lowrie's callous assumption was the same theory she had offered Ellis the previous week, but for some reason hearing it from another person felt more painful – more plausible.

When Ellis returned, he stopped the voice recorder on his phone and flopped into his chair. They both stared at the side of the table recently vacated by Lowrie, which was still dusty with ash.

'What a tosser,' said Rebecca.

After a flicker of surprise, Ellis grinned. 'Don't hold back, Rebecca, say how you *really* feel . . .' The end of his sentence was muffled as he rubbed his eyes beneath his glasses.

'You're not going to include that stuff he said about my dad in your write-up, are you?' she asked.

She was thinking less of Leo's reputation and more of her family. Could they be dragged into this? Even being publicly associated with her ex-husband would embarrass Rosalyn, so Rebecca could only imagine how she'd react to being linked – however tenuously – to a scandalous story of drug abuse. Which was to say nothing of Morton's inevitable anger, nor that strange sadness that seemed to envelop Lillian every time Leo was mentioned . . .

Ellis emerged from his fingers. 'Nah, I'd need more than an old man's rant to prove it. And I'm not really interested in spoiling anyone's memories of *The Stowaway*. To be honest, it's unlikely I'll be able to include Leo at all.'

'Seriously?' Rebecca was unable to keep the scepticism from her voice. Had all his work been for nothing? She'd been quite impressed by Ellis's research, and especially by how much he'd managed to extract from the actor.

'I've nothing to say about him,' said the journalist, shrugging. 'It's supposed to be a kind of *Where are they now*? And he could be anywhere, have a new identity even . . .'

A little troubled by this idea, Rebecca asked, 'Could we contact some of the others from *The Stowaway*?'

'I've already tried his mates from that paparazzi shot, but she knew less than Richard Lowrie, and I couldn't get hold of him – he's moved to Canada, I think. I've left a few messages for Larry Wilkinson, *The Stowaway*'s executive producer, but he's retired now, and I doubt he'll want to talk to me, considering what we've just heard . . . No, I think we've reached a dead end.'

'Really?'

How could he say that after everything they'd just discovered? Although, when she thought about it, much of what Rebecca had learned that afternoon had come from Ellis himself, before the interview.

'I don't know what else to do,' said Ellis, still slumped in his chair. 'I've tried everyone I can think of: you, your mum, *The Stowaway* lot . . . I've even been emailing the agent he was with before he moved to Devon. Ah – ' he tapped the end of his pen against his notepad ' – what about your grandmother?'

'Um, she doesn't know anything,' lied Rebecca, who'd forgotten this was part of the deal they'd made over the phone. Then, feeling this sounded insufficient, she added, 'I mean, she was talking about him the other day, but I think she was getting confused, you know?'

She thought this might elicit sympathy, but Ellis's expression was shrewd. 'There you go, then,' he said, with another shrug. 'That's it. Either nobody knows where Leo is, or nobody's telling.'

Rebecca wondered whether this was a dig – but then she *didn't* intend to share anything her grandmother might reveal. To ease her conscience, she told herself it probably didn't matter anyway, not now Ellis seemed to have given up.

Still, it felt strange to say goodbye to him. Over the past few days, the journalist had been the one constant; while her own feelings had started to shift, his ambition to locate Leo had remained unchanged. Yet after they'd parted at the bar – he to pay for the wine, she to hurry for her train – Rebecca realised that if she wanted to find out more about her father, it looked likely she'd have to do so by herself.

She was almost at the station when she realised that she should've asked Ellis to send her the recording. If she were never subjected to Richard Lowrie's voice again it would be too soon, but there had been that one shining moment she now longed to revisit: *I think that little girl was the only person in the world Leo cared about . . .*

5

The Stowaway

The next morning, Rebecca was confronted with 26 unread emails, a stack of unopened post and an elderly surveyor panicking about his expired antivirus software, but otherwise Sudworth and Rowe seemed to be running as normal. Unfortunately, the same couldn't be said for Rebecca herself. She felt distracted, dissatisfied; no matter how much of her to-do list she crossed off, she couldn't help but feel bothered that Leo Sampson's whereabouts remained a mystery.

Then there were the memories. Until a few days ago, Rebecca's recollections of her father had been shut away in a near-forgotten place at the back of her mind, like a cupboard stuffed with toys she'd outgrown long ago. But now she'd peeked inside, it was hard to close the door again, so the contents of that cupboard kept threatening to tumble out. Still, she continued to push against it all. What good were memories to her now?

During her lunch break, she shunned the sunshine to remain at her desk, where she pulled up a new window on her computer and, after checking her colleagues were all occupied, typed into the search bar *leo sampson fired* and *leo sampson drugs.*

Neither query returned anything relevant. If Richard Lowrie had been correct and Leo's dismissal had been an open secret, the producers had done a good job at keeping everyone quiet. Rebecca discovered one article announcing the casting of the new Stowaway for the third series, but nothing in it suggested the circumstances of Leo's leaving were in any way scandalous. Instead, the writer parroted the line that Leo had quit to pursue other projects, and then speculated whether the programme would be the same, commenting, *It's almost impossible to imagine anyone else being able to inhabit this now iconic role.*

'Oi oi!'

The yell, along with a pungent waft of aftershave, warned Rebecca that Chris Fenton was approaching. She quickly minimised her search window.

When he reached her desk, Chris began to prod at her salad, which was still in its Tupperware, untouched. 'You on your lunch?'

'Yes, just catching up on some emails.'

She hoped he'd take the hint, but he pulled over a chair, spun it around and sat down, his arms and legs dangling around the backrest. 'Did Stretch text you?'

'Who?' asked Rebecca, before registering he was referring to their mutual friend, Steph. She disliked the nickname: Steph wasn't *that* tall – just taller than Chris.

'*Stephanie,*' said Chris, rolling his eyes. 'She's asking about the quiz tonight – you coming?'

Who played the title role in the BBC children's TV series, The Stowaway?

Once, that question had come up during a quiz at university, catching her completely off-guard – so much so she'd almost dropped the round of drinks she'd been carrying back from the bar. None of her teammates had known Leo Sampson's name, but they'd all sworn they could picture him. Flustered, Rebecca had assured herself her friends would never make the connection between her and a half-remembered figure from their childhoods, but she hadn't been able to write down the answer, not even for the points, so had told them she'd never watched it – which was true.

Was that the last time she'd heard Leo mentioned, before Ellis's visit to Sudworth and Rowe?

'Chaser? Hello?'

Chris was clicking his fingers in front of her face.

'*What*? I mean—' She sighed. 'Yes, I'll be there.'

While Chris began to boast about how many answers he'd get – an optimistic outlook, Rebecca felt, given he was usually only good for questions about football – she made a decision: if she wanted to find out more about Leo, she had to be patient and wait for Lillian to return from her holiday.

Until then, Rebecca would have to let the matter drop, just like Ellis. After leaving the bar yesterday, she'd thought it only polite to text and thank him for letting her sit in on the interview.

No problem, shame it wasn't more useful, he'd replied. *Good luck if you keep at it.*

This had sounded final, but she couldn't help refreshing her messages every so often, quietly hopeful that, in spite of his apparent withdrawal, he might've stumbled across something since.

After work, her head was still buzzing, so she went running without music and instead tried to focus on the sound of her snatched inhalations and the soles of her trainers smacking against the stony track. It was still warm outside, and the air was weighted with the tang of the river and the sweet scent of the nearby meadows, where rabbits were skittering around the hedgerows. Rebecca didn't stop to watch them: she sprinted until her legs were searing, her lungs straining, because usually – if she went fast enough – her mind would quieten. Only this evening it wasn't working; it wasn't possible to outrun her hounding thoughts.

Why couldn't she let this go? Her father's absence hadn't troubled her for years, not really. At some point long ago, presumably when she'd realised that he wasn't coming back, she'd resolved not to think of him anymore. To forget him. And though that hadn't been quite possible – she still remembered, she still *wondered* – it had seemed less painful to at least try.

So what had changed? Why should she care about him now, this man who had walked out on her as a child? But she knew why. It was because of that dedication in the fairy tale book, and what Richard Lowrie had said: the only person . . . It was the knowledge that – for a time, at least – Leo had cared about her.

Swiping through a cloud of insects flickering in the low sunlight, Rebecca considered the other revelation from Lowrie's interview. She had scant experience with drugs, outside of the few occasions she'd smoked weed and a misguided attempt to take magic mushrooms with Amy, which had resulted in them both throwing up outside the village hall. The closest she'd ever come to hard drugs was during her first and only term at Oxford. A group of girls in spangled dresses had staggered into the accommodation's communal bathroom and started cutting lines of coke and Rebecca – already in her pyjamas, toothbrush in hand – had felt so young and lonely, she'd wanted to cry.

So she could only guess at what Leo had been taking. She tried to picture him with track marks up his arms, like the addicts she'd seen in crime dramas, and felt a little sickened. Whatever he'd been using, it had cost him his job as the Stowaway. *He could hardly hold himself together*, Lowrie had said, and, all things considered, perhaps his and Rebecca's initial theory concerning Leo's fate had been correct, in spite of the lack of obituary or death notice – yet Leo couldn't have died before 1999, Rebecca reminded herself, recalling that date in *Seven Tales*.

She leapt over a clump of nettles spilling onto the path, wishing she had more to go on than the grumblings of an embittered actor and a book of children's stories. She needed more than old fan sites, the research of a prying journalist and the scraps thrown to her by otherwise tight-lipped family members.

Do you remember him?

She slowed her pace, considering Ellis's question anew, finally allowing herself to throw open the door of that toy cupboard in the back of her mind.

Despite the years she and her family had spent pretending he'd never been there, the Leo inside Rebecca's head existed almost entirely in Lower Morvale. She could see him there now: sitting on the wall of The Three Tors, daring her to bite off the bottom of her ice cream cone; bent over her bare foot in the garden, inspecting her first and only bee sting; jigging through the lanes after Midnight Mass, competing with her as to who could do the loudest rendition of *Hark! The Herald Angels Sing*.

Then there had been his stories, which felt like memories, because at the time she'd believed they were true. She'd tiptoed past a knobbly boulder on the moor because he'd whispered it was a sleeping troll; left a tuft of sheep's fleece caught in barbed wire because he'd insisted it was the beard of a gnome who'd want it back; scattered a trail of biscuit crumbs through the woods at Midsummer, because he'd convinced her the trees liked to move around on the longest day, and otherwise they might forget the way back.

Rebecca pressed her knuckles against her sternum, as though the ache now clogging her chest could be dislodged like a morsel of partially swallowed food. These weren't useful memories. Had he been unhappy, troubled? He must've been, his marriage was falling apart. But she could only picture him full of joy, like a crinkly foil balloon tugging against its string for the sky.

She felt hot now – a little too hot – and her strides shortened again as she continued to exert her memory. Somewhere, there had been a purple door. It flickered in the mists of her mind, distant and detached. They had been eating sweets from paper bags and Leo had held up a blackcurrant gummy, pretending it was no longer visible against the door's paintwork. His feigned indignation at misplacing that little sweet had made her laugh until she'd hiccupped.

Where had that been? According to Richard Lowrie, Rosalyn had made it difficult for Leo to see Rebecca during his *Stowaway* days – *difficult*, but not impossible. The show, she recalled, had been filmed in Bristol. Was that where he'd gone after leaving the village? Rebecca dragged an arm across her sweaty brow, striving to ignore an increasing sense of wooziness, and wondered whether she'd ever seen Leo as that character in real life, whether she'd visited the set, seen him in costume, and . . .

. . . And there's a couple wearing masquerade masks, the lace of their sleeves fluttering as they wave to a crowd. Nearby, a man is juggling with black and white clubs, and girls are dancing in a row, their toes tap-tapping against cobbles slick with rain. She needs to stop, ask one of these people if they've seen him, but she's being swept under a canopy of umbrellas, buffeted along by elbows and shopping bags, towards that dark passage where the ground slips away into nothing. She mustn't go near that place – she *mustn't* – but the current of the crowd is too strong, and she is too small, and there's so much noise. All the cheering, clapping and laughter is smothering her own voice, so nobody hears the one word she's wailing, over and over:

Daddy!

Disorientated, Rebecca blinked. It took her a few seconds to work out she was just along the road from her flat: her feet had brought her home.

Her heart was drumming, but not from exercise; that scene had startled her into stillness. Had it been real? She couldn't think where she'd been. Certainly not a TV set or anywhere in Exeter. The jumble of sights and sounds had seemed more like a dream than a memory, as did the way it'd all enveloped her so swiftly, so completely. Yet that feeling of being lost, that fear . . . It was too acute to be imaginary.

Shaken, Rebecca let herself back into her flat and began to gulp down a pint of water. She felt drained. What was going on? She wished she had a flatmate, someone she could talk to – or someone who could talk some sense into her. On any other matter she would've confided in her grandmother, or maybe Rosalyn, who was especially good for practical advice, even if it was sometimes unsolicited: which A levels to take; what bank account to open; the best outfit to wear for a job interview. Suddenly, it seemed pitiful that the only person who had any inkling of what was currently consuming her was a stranger from SideScoop.

She laid down her glass and, in an attempt to forget that obscure memory or vision – whatever it'd been – stared around her living room, trying to root herself in the present. She'd chosen her flat for its proximity to town and, at the time, had been drawn to its square sensible interiors, which had felt far removed from both Primrose Cottage and the shabby house she'd shared with friends during university. Now, though, the space felt anonymous, unfriendly. Without all her pot plants, it would've been as spartan as a show home. Rebecca knew she should string up some fairy lights, scatter about a few candles and cushions, but living here – living alone – was supposed to have been temporary; a short but necessary pause while she figured out where she wanted to be instead.

Her reverie was broken by the buzzing of her phone, and she soon found several messages from the various members of We Mean Quizzness, asking where she was. Rebecca rubbed at her eyes. How could she have forgotten the quiz when Chris had pestered her about it earlier? What was the matter with her today?

After showering and changing into her pyjamas, Rebecca stirred a handful of cherry tomatoes and the dregs of a jar of pesto into some spaghetti. She then opened her laptop, and – deciding it unlikely she'd be able to concentrate on anything else that evening – typed *the stowaway* into YouTube.

Series One, Episode One: Cinderella was the third result, boasting tens of thousands of views and an unusual number of positive comments:

Anyone still watching this in 2013??

The stowaway >>> prince charming

my childhood!!!!

Had Rosalyn ever forbidden her from watching *The Stowaway*? Rebecca could remember her mother once snatching the TV remote from her fingers and scolding her for not playing outside – which had felt unfair, because Rebecca had been blackberry-picking with Lillian all afternoon. Possibly, that overreaction by Rosalyn had been *Stowaway*-related, but Rebecca wasn't sure she'd been banned from the programme, exactly. But then, her mother had never needed to veto anything, not when, somehow, Rebecca had always known what would and wouldn't meet with her approval.

Besides, Rebecca had never been that curious about *The Stowaway*. By the time she'd fully appreciated what it was, and the significance of Leo's role, the show was off-air. She'd outgrown it. Even if she hadn't been trying to ignore her father's existence, *The Stowaway's* subject matter was about as appealing to her as that of *Seven Tales*. Now, though, she wanted to experience it first-hand; to understand what Ellis and Richard Lowrie had been talking about. If nothing else, familiarising herself with the programme felt more productive than dwelling on disjointed, indecipherable recollections. And, if she saw her father moving and talking – if she saw him *living* – maybe she'd remember more?

Taking a deep breath, Rebecca pressed play.

The fuzzy picture quality immediately dated the programme, as did the graphics of the opening credits, which featured an unseen hand flicking through the pages of a storybook. As the folky theme tune petered away, the episode opened with a view of a tree house balanced between branches of overlarge and oversaturated flowers. When its round yellow door was thrown open, a brightly coloured figure appeared on the threshold, tripped over his own feet and almost tumbled from the tree. He caught hold of a branch just in time, clinging to it with his arms and legs, like a koala.

'Oh – hello there!' He beamed at the camera, unfazed by his near fall. 'I'm the Stowaway!'

Rebecca jerked back in her seat. She'd been prepared to see him, of course, but not for this; he was looking right at her.

'Now, I'm afraid I have an unfortunate habit of finding myself in other people's stories,' continued the Stowaway, still hanging from the branch, 'but I'm always searching for my way home, so maybe this time . . . ?' He took an exaggerated look at his surroundings, disturbing the nest of a bird puppet, who glared down its beak at him. 'Nope, I don't think I'm home – hold on!'

He untangled himself from the branch and returned to the tree house covered in twigs and leaves. As he dusted himself down, the camera lingered on his costume: a baggy white shirt; green and yellow striped trousers; shoes that curled up at the toes. He looked like a slapdash jester, although instead of a hat his dark hair had been tousled into peaks.

He's so young, Rebecca thought. When she was a child, he'd always seemed grown up, but here he must've been around thirty – only a few years older than she was now.

Onscreen, the Stowaway had spotted someone on the ground: a blonde girl dressed in rags, sobbing into her apron. He clambered down the tree trunk, accidentally upending the bird's nest as he went, and landed next to the girl with a soft thump.

'What's the matter?' he asked, extracting a long string of green and yellow handkerchiefs from his pocket. 'Why are you crying?'

'Oh!' wailed the girl, who seemed to think nothing of strange-looking men leaping out of trees around her. She took one end of the handkerchiefs and, as she dabbed at her eyes, Rebecca recognised the actress from the publicity and paparazzi shots. 'I'm crying because my stepmother and stepsisters are so cruel to me! I work from dawn 'til dusk scrubbing and sweeping the house, and by the end of the day I am covered in dirt and ash!'

There followed a montage of the Stowaway attempting to help Cinderella mop the floor, bake the bread and feed the animals, only he unintentionally sabotaged each task through clumsiness, greed or making an enemy of a puppet goat. It was a little like a pantomime, only it never descended into total farce, nor were there any tongue-in-cheek jokes or references for the benefit of adult viewers. There was a sincerity to its silliness, a freshness to its familiarity and, though she was far from its target audience, Rebecca could understand why it'd been so popular.

As the episode continued, she concentrated on the Stowaway himself. It was difficult not to, for it was his energy and enthusiasm driving the story and, as he veered between pratfalls and quieter moments of contemplation, he seemed to embody the very spirit of the show. So much so that it was difficult for Rebecca to pick out her father from the character; when the fairy godmother informed Cinderella the spell would end at midnight, the Stowaway listened intently, his head tilted to one side, and Rebecca was sure this was how Leo had looked when she herself had told him something important.

Though she hadn't intended to, she watched right to the end of the 20-minute episode. In the final moments, the Stowaway dashed after the prince – played, Rebecca noted, by the other man in the paparazzi shot – to inform him there was a girl locked in the cellar of the house he'd just visited, and to suggest that perhaps she might try on the glass slipper, too. Once Cinderella and the prince were married, and the stepmother and stepsisters thrown from the wedding reception, the Stowaway sneaked away from the party and into the palace gardens, tossing aside the yellow bow tie he'd donned for the occasion.

'Well, that was a bit of fun!' he told the camera, before growing more forlorn. 'But I really would like to find my way home . . .'

As he glanced around, he saw the hedge beside him was part of a great maze. Excited again, he skidded towards a gap in the greenery, peering into the leafy passage beyond.

'I wonder . . .' he grinned over his shoulder. 'Let's see!'

After he disappeared, the picture lingered on the mouth of the maze for a few seconds, until Rebecca half-expected the bright impish figure to double back for one final stunt or joke. But he didn't, and as the screen faded to black, she was unable to suppress a pang of disappointment.

'Petal, are you listening?'

Rebecca replied in the affirmative, but midway through her mother's call the following morning her gaze had drifted from her muesli towards *Seven Tales*. The book had been sitting on her table since her trip to London, its fuzzy green cover putting her in mind of something turning to mould. Yet in spite of her apathy towards the tales themselves, every so often she found herself flipping to the dedication page, checking *For Birdie* was still there.

'I said, I'm worried about Brontë!' cried Rosalyn. 'According to Carol, she's hardly eating – not even her treats!'

'Well, she could do with losing a bit of weight.'

'Oh, it's not funny! What if she's ill and I'm not there?'

Rebecca rolled her eyes, torn between amusement and exasperation that her mother had worked herself into a such a state over that ridiculous animal: why was she always *fretting*?

'Mum, I'm not sure what you want me to do about this . . .' she began, trying to sound sympathetic.

'I think you should go round and check on her after work.'

'*What*? You want me to drive all the way to the village? Why can't Morton or Daphne do it?'

'Morty hates Brontë—'

'So do I!'

'—And you know Daffy's *allergic*,' continued Rosalyn. 'Please, Becca-Bell – for me?'

Rebecca considered inventing plans for that evening, before she glanced back at *Seven Tales*, realising Rosalyn's absence would provide a rare opportunity to check whether all evidence of Leo truly had been erased from Primrose Cottage. If she were to search through the drawers of Rosalyn's desk, for instance, what might she find?

Did she dare? Rebecca rarely caused trouble for her mother and, in return, Rosalyn had turned a blind eye to her minor transgressions over the years: laughing at the Morris dancers on May Day; pilfering Aunt Daphne's make-up to experiment with at a sleepover; returning from a school disco reeking of alcopops and sporting a very obvious love bite . . . But rifling through Rosalyn's private papers was hardly a minor transgression, and would be far worse than talking to Ellis or watching *The Stowaway*. Yet the temptation of the unoccupied house was difficult to resist.

'Fine, I'll check on her,' said Rebecca, hoping to keep any eagerness from her voice.

When she walked into the open-plan kitchen later that evening, the absence of all her mother's bustle and chatter made the space feel too still, too quiet. The smallest of noises seemed amplified: the clink of her keys; the hum of the fridge; the hissing of Brontë.

'Charming,' Rebecca told the cat, who was lolling in her usual spot on the windowsill. 'And hello to you, too.'

Lillian had bought the cat for Rosalyn after Rebecca had left for university, so they'd had little to do with one another over the years. Nevertheless, it seemed obvious to Rebecca that the animal was absolutely fine; as glossy and grumpy-looking as always, plus no longer on a self-imposed diet, going by the empty food bowl on the floor. She searched the cupboards until she found a bag of treats and held out a foul, fish-shaped morsel. The cat hesitated, torn between greed and disdain, then heaved herself to her stumpy legs, waddled across the work surface, and gobbled the food from Rebecca's fingers.

Brontë fine – has eaten all her food and a treat x

Rebecca took a photo to accompany the message, stepping back in order to fit Brontë's significant bulk into the frame. When the flash went off, the cat yowled.

'Oh, *shush* . . .' Rebecca murmured, heading back towards the hallway.

Rosalyn's study was a cramped room at the back of the house. Its furniture – an antique desk and a bookshelf that stretched to the ceiling – felt too big for its modest dimensions, and the only free wall was covered by a print depicting the entire text of *Wuthering Heights.* It was also extremely tidy and, as Rebecca edged over the threshold, she began to feel a lot less optimistic that her mother might have left something important lying around for her to find.

Regardless, she approached the desk. Its red leather top was bare, save for a Tiffany-style lamp, a framed photograph of Rebecca at her graduation and a *Keep Calm and Ask a Librarian* mug doubling as a pen pot. Trying to ignore the twinge of guilt inspired by the photo, Rebecca began to search the desk drawers, discovering art supplies, old greetings cards and gift tokens, and an excessive amount of stationery.

The desk's middle drawer was locked. Rebecca tugged at its handle to check it wasn't just stuck, then put her eye to the tiny keyhole. What was in there? She rummaged through the other drawers and the librarian mug for several minutes, trying to find a key, until she was startled by a sudden rattle from the other side of the house. Convinced Brontë must be keeling over out of spite, Rebecca dashed back to the kitchen, only to realise the sound had been her phone vibrating against the marble worktop.

Thanks for checking – so relieved!! Love you xxxx

'How do you do that?' Rebecca murmured, guilt gnawing at her once again.

She had to stop this. It was so irrational, risking her relationship with the parent who'd raised her for the one who hadn't. In any case, Rosalyn would have guarded against such an event; if there existed any papers concerning Leo, they'd be boxed away somewhere or with a solicitor.

Her phone clattered again, and this time Rosalyn had sent a photo of herself and Lillian looking windswept on a beach, posing in front of an anchor-shaped monument. Rebecca smiled, but as she looked at the picture her mind returned to that day on another beach, when Leo had been burrowing into the sand with his red spade. He'd lined that hole with shells, pebbles and driftwood, she now remembered, then he'd lain down and buried himself from his toes to his neck. He was the remains of a legendary lost king, he'd told her; if she dug him up, she'd discover riches beyond measure . . .

Rebecca felt a prickle of self-contempt. Was that how it had started, her fascination with ancient treasures? If so, she'd forgotten, but perhaps it was fitting: here was yet another disappointment associated with her father.

Returning her focus to the blustery beach on her phone screen, she saw Lillian was hugging her daughter with both arms, while Rosalyn's cheek was resting against the top of her mother's head. All at once, Rebecca's plan of waiting to talk to her grandmother about Leo seemed naïve. Would Lillian really tell her anything Rosalyn didn't want her to know? Was she even a reliable source of information? Lillian had kept back the fairy tale book because she'd believed Rosalyn, who'd told her Rebecca didn't want anything to do with Leo – something Rebecca was finding increasingly difficult to imagine her younger self saying.

Defeated, she picked up her keys and threw Brontë a resentful look. The cat had leapt up onto the breakfast bar – which even Rosalyn didn't allow – and was now heaped over the marble like a fluffy pudding.

'Get down,' Rebecca said, giving her a prod. 'Go on, shoo!'

The animal merely rolled over, revealing Rosalyn's address book underneath her tawny belly. Tutting, Rebecca began to brush cat hairs from the Post-its poking from the pages, before she paused, her brow furrowed. It felt too simple a solution, but it would be foolish not to check – it was right here. But when she flicked towards the S section and searched through the names of family friends, she could find no *Sampson.*

Rebecca's frown deepened: her mother had had this address book for as long she could remember – had she never had any contact details for her ex-husband? Perhaps they were recorded somewhere more private, like that locked drawer. Or was her mother just as oblivious as she was?

She was about to close the book when her fingertips snagged against an unexpected edge. Rebecca angled the page towards the light: it looked as though a white label had been cut to fit the exact dimensions of one of the contact boxes. *Sadler, Cathy* – one of Rosalyn's Exeter friends – had been written on the new surface, but who was underneath?

Excited, Rebecca turned to the beginning of the address book and ran her fingers over every page, checking for other labels. After a few minutes, she found another in S, and marked both places with her mother's post-its, wondering what to do. She'd seen enough detective shows to know sealed envelopes could be opened with steam, and after consulting the internet, she discovered ironing the label under a tea towel was the recommended method of melting the glue in real life. So, watched by a suspicious Brontë, Rebecca dragged the ironing board from the hall cupboard and set to work.

She started with the label towards the beginning of S, only leaving a little residue as she peeled it away. Anticipation jolted through her as she saw the name *Sampson,* but it was accompanied by *Patricia,* and an address in Kent. Impatiently, Rebecca moved onto the second label, and managed to prise *Sadler, Cathy* away from the page, her breath hitching as she caught sight of the name beneath:

Sampson, Leo

Was this it? Had she found him? It felt disconcertingly easy, but it was right there, in her mother's neat handwriting: his name, an address in Bristol and a telephone number.

Before she could lose her nerve, Rebecca snatched up her mobile. Her hand trembled as she tapped in the number, which took longer than usual, because her mind was churning with questions. What if he answered? What would she say? Why was she even calling? She had absolutely no idea how she felt about her father anymore . . . But no sooner had she put the phone to her ear did an automated female voice start to drone: *The number you have called is not recognised. Please check the—*

Rebecca hung up. Of course, he wasn't there. He couldn't be, not after all these years. It was too close, too convenient. A quick online search confirmed the address – the whole block of flats, in fact, no longer existed. She wondered whether that had been the location of the purple door where he'd lost his purple sweet, and didn't know whether to feel disappointed or relieved.

She turned back through the pages of the address book until she reached *Patricia Sampson*, who lived in Huxley House in Kent. Hadn't Ellis said Leo was born in Kent? The article in the local paper about his youth theatre production suggested he'd grown up around there too. Could Patricia Sampson be Leo's mother, or sister? What if she was a *second wife*?

Rebecca picked up her mobile once more. Oddly, the prospect of phoning a total stranger was almost as daunting as the possibility of talking to her father again. She thought of Ellis, and how brazenly he'd pursued a meeting with her; he wouldn't think twice about making this call.

'Patricia Sampson speaking?'

The voice on the other end of the line was deep and plummy. Rebecca froze: she hadn't expected so swift a response.

'Um – hi. I was wondering if you could help me? I'm looking for some information about Leo Sampson . . . ?'

She hesitated, deliberating over how best to explain herself, but before she could continue the other woman said, 'I think you must have the wrong number.' Her tone was frosty – too frosty for a simple misunderstanding. Besides, it was unlikely Rosalyn had made a mistake.

'You don't know anyone called Leo Sampson?' Rebecca persisted. 'Because I'd be really grateful if—'

'Who is this?' Patricia interrupted. 'How did you get this number? Actually, never mind . . .' Her voice grew faint, as though she'd lowered the phone.

'Please!' cried Rebecca, before blurting out the only thing she could think of to keep the call going: 'He's my dad.'

'Your—*What*?' Patricia sounded stunned, and Rebecca wondered whether she'd been expecting a journalist, like Ellis, or someone connected to *The Stowaway*.

'My name's Rebecca Chase. I came across your name in my mum's address book and I thought you might be related to him, to Leo.'

There was a long silence, during which Rebecca feared she'd be cut off. Then, unexpectedly, Patricia asked, '*Chase,* did you say? What's your mother's name?'

'Rosalyn.'

'Yes, that was it . . .' Her tone grew pensive. 'She wrote to me once – I'm afraid I never replied.'

'Wrote to you about what?' asked Rebecca, eager to seize upon this new information.

'About Leo.' Patricia let out a long, resigned sigh, then admitted, 'He was my nephew.'

'*Was*?' Rebecca turned suddenly cold, Richard Lowrie's words returning to her: *he's probably dead.*

'Is, was, I don't know. I haven't seen him in over 30 years.'

Before me, then, thought Rebecca, after a ripple of relief. Before even Rosalyn and his move to the village. 'I don't suppose you know where he is, do you?' she asked.

'No. Don't you?'

'No.'

'Hm.'

Patricia's tone wasn't encouraging. Once again, Rebecca wished she had Ellis's knack for getting people to talk.

'You don't have any old contact details for him, anything like that?' she ventured. Then, feeling she should explain herself, added, 'I guess I'm looking for him – or news of him, at least. I haven't seen him for a long time either, since I was a child.'

'Hm,' Patricia repeated, but Rebecca sensed she was softening. 'Well, I'm afraid I can't help you. Like I said, it's been decades since I saw that boy.'

'You knew him when he was growing up, then?' Rebecca asked, as much to keep her on the line as anything else.

'I did.'

'What was he like?'

Rebecca heard a sharp sniff, but Patricia said nothing. Her lack of response seemed telling, and when several seconds had passed, Rebecca felt obliged to fill the silence: 'I've never thought about his childhood,' she confessed. 'I don't know anything about his family – *my* family,' she added, realising this only as she said it.

'Yes,' agreed Patricia, quietly, 'I suppose we are, aren't we?' She sighed again. 'Look, I'd rather not discuss all this over the phone. Let's meet in person. Are you free for lunch this Saturday?'

'Um—' Rebecca was thrown, both by the abrupt change of subject and the invitation itself: she wanted information, certainly, but did she really need to meet with this officious-sounding woman? 'It's a bit of a long drive . . .' she began, hoping they could just continue their conversation now.

Patricia, however, seemed encouraged by her reticence: 'Where do you live?'

'Exeter.'

'Oh, that's miles away. Well, you can stay the night if you like, to make the journey worthwhile. It'd be good for you to spend a bit of time in the family home.'

Suddenly, this was moving very fast, and out of Rebecca's control. She was determined not to waste the opportunity – not to spurn the only family member willing to talk to her – but was it wise to stay with a person she'd never met, even if they were a relation? She wondered what to do. What would Ellis do?

'Do you have my address in that book of your mother's?' continued Patricia.

'Huxley House?'

'That's the one.'

Ellis would go, Rebecca thought. He'd work out how to get Patricia onside to find out what he wanted, just as he had with Richard Lowrie. Just as he had with *her*.

'Well then, I'll see you on Saturday, shall I?' continued Patricia, though Rebecca hadn't agreed to anything – this was just like dealing with Rosalyn. 'Why don't you phone again in the morning, so I know what time to expect you. I'll also need to give you directions, because it's a nightmare to find the driveway . . .'

While she talked, Rebecca was struck by an idea, one she didn't have long to ponder because she sensed Patricia was trying to wrap up the call.

'Um . . . Mrs Sampson?' she began, because *Aunt*, or even *Great-Aunt*, seemed a little presumptuous.

'It's Miss, dear, I never married. But you can call me Patricia.'

'Patricia, then. This Saturday – can I bring a friend?'

6

The Aunt

'I like your car,' said Ellis, opening the passenger door.

'Yeah, yeah . . .' Rebecca was too used to people – men, in particular – making disparaging comments about her bright green Nissan Micra to feel offended. 'Come on, get in. I'm not supposed to stop here.'

'I'm serious,' insisted Ellis, clambering in beside her and throwing his rucksack into the back. 'It's a great colour, very . . .' he deliberated over the right word . . . '*vibrant*.'

Was he teasing her? 'It used to belong to my grandmother,' she said, deciding to give him the benefit of the doubt. 'She gave it to me when I passed my driving test.'

'First time?' he asked, as she pulled away from the curb.

'Second,' she admitted, reluctantly.

'Took me three attempts,' said Ellis. 'It was always the roundabouts that got me . . . I'm a good driver now, though, if you want to swap?'

'I'm fine, thanks – I stopped for a coffee.'

In truth, Rebecca would've appreciated a break – she'd been on the road for almost three and a half hours already – but she didn't trust him with her car.

Ellis peered at her phone, which was perched on the dashboard, directing her back to the M25. 'So where are we actually going?' he asked.

'Huxley House, which is near Ashford, apparently.'

'And you've never been?'

'Like I said on the phone, I didn't even know Patricia Sampson existed until a few days ago.'

'That's mad, isn't it?' said Ellis, cheerfully. 'To suddenly discover a long-lost relative.'

'Just a little,' said Rebecca, who was still adjusting to the idea of having a great-aunt – or any kind of family beyond the Chases.

'I started looking into the Sampson side myself,' continued Ellis, 'but gave up when I discovered his parents were dead.' This was news to Rebecca, but before she could ask about it, Ellis said, 'How did you find this Patricia, anyway?'

In more detail than was strictly necessary, Rebecca described her visit to Primrose Cottage. It felt good to have discovered something for herself, by her own initiative. But when she'd finished, the journalist's only comment was, 'You stuck the labels back on, right? In the address book?'

Rebecca confirmed she had, and then stared at the stretch of A-road ahead, trying not to feel disappointed: she supposed Ellis dug up contact details all the time.

'How's the article going?' she asked.

'Huh?' he sounded surprised by the question.

'The *Where Are They Now* piece?' she clarified.

'Oh – yeah, fine. Just missing a Stowaway.'

'Well, maybe this weekend will help with that.'

'Yeah, hopefully . . . I assume Aunt Patricia doesn't know I'm a journalist?'

'No,' said Rebecca quickly, thinking of her own initial reaction to him, and Rosalyn's. She doubted Patricia's would be any different. 'No, let's not mention that.'

Ellis made a noise of assent, before opening and closing the glove compartment. 'Hey, Becs?'

'*Becs*?'

'I thought you didn't mind Becs?'

'I never said that.'

'All right, *Rebecca* – can I put some music on?'

'If you want.'

Crunching on a sweet he'd evidently just found, Ellis began to fiddle with the radio, listening to a snippet of each station before moving onto the next. As this continued, Rebecca's hold on the steering wheel tightened.

'Are you going to do that the whole way?' she enquired. 'Because if you are, I might have to drop you back in Clapham.'

'If you want,' he said, changing the station one more time. 'My flatmate's opening a bar next week, and I was supposed to be helping with some last-minute painting this afternoon.'

Deciding to ignore that he was calling her bluff, Rebecca asked, 'Then why are you here?'

'Aside from the article, you mean? I guess this sounded more interesting, more *intriguing* . . .' he turned to look at her. 'You know, I'm still waiting to hear why you invited me.'

Rebecca kept her gaze on the road, considering why – as soon as she'd finished speaking to Patricia on Thursday – it had been Ellis she'd called. Going alone had felt too daunting, but she could've asked someone else. Probably no one in Exeter, but she could've picked up Amy on her way past London; she was already feeling guilty for not telling her best friend she'd been there earlier this week. But Amy knew nothing about Leo – none of her friends did – whereas Ellis was already involved.

'We had a deal, didn't we?' she reminded him. 'You said you'd keep me updated, and I said I'd—'

'—Speak to your grandmother,' Ellis interjected. 'Which you did, and she didn't know anything.'

Tensing at the memory of this lie, Rebecca said, 'Well, now

I've found you another relative, haven't I? A blood relation – someone who knew Leo as a child.'

'Right,' said Ellis, sounding amused. 'So you're just keeping up your end of the bargain, are you?'

Rebecca sighed. Was he always this exhausting? She was well aware he was toying with her, trying to make her admit she needed him – and the worst thing was, it was true.

'Obviously, you're also more experienced in this than me,' she said, resenting every word, 'so I'm sure you'll be able to persuade Patricia to talk. I mean—' she dropped her voice to a mutter '—Richard Lowrie was a handful and you got a lot out of him.'

Ellis didn't respond immediately, but opened the glove compartment again and helped himself to another sweet. He chewed on it for a few seconds, then remarked, 'That sounded like a compliment.'

'It was an observation,' she assured him.

A few miles past Ashford, when the satnav on Rebecca's phone told her to drive into a river, Ellis tried to make sense of Patricia's directions and, two wrong turns later, they located the overgrown track that led to Huxley House. It was a hotchpotch of a building: its ivy-strewn bulk was undoubtedly grand – as was its position at the heart of a large garden – but Rebecca, whose architectural instincts had been honed working at Sudworth and Rowe, thought there was something incongruous about the russet-coloured roof and Tudor-style bow windows. To her, the house was too muddled; it looked as though it had been built over several centuries, and no one had had the sense to keep the design true to one era.

By the time she'd parked in the gravel driveway, she was feeling a little sick, and not just from the heat. But escape was impossible, for as soon as she switched off the car's engine, two black Labradors come bounding across the driveway. Feeling that knocking out one or both of her great-aunt's dogs would make a less than favourable first impression, Rebecca opened the driver's door with care and tried to avoid the bright pink tongues and rancid breath of the two animals leaping up at her.

'Down, girls, *down*! Just give them a shove, they know they're not supposed to jump up!'

Rebecca turned in the direction of the commanding voice, whose owner was emerging from the house. Patricia Sampson was a large woman. Not overweight, exactly, just tall and broad, with boxy shoulders. She was wearing a linen shirt, and taupe trousers tucked into sturdy leather walking boots. In her right hand, she clutched a knobbly wooden walking stick that curled at the top like a shepherd's crook.

'My, what a bright little car you have!' she cried, advancing across the driveway. She held out a hand and crushed Rebecca's fingers with her own. 'Hello, dear, I am glad you came. Now, let me look at you . . .'

Rebecca took the opportunity to survey her great-aunt in turn: she had a square face, a ruddy complexion and her dark grey hair was pulled into a short, straggly ponytail.

'I didn't expect a redhead,' Patricia remarked. 'You don't look like him, do you? I see practically nothing of the Sampson side.'

'Oh, I look like my mum,' Rebecca said automatically, for she'd been told this all her life.

'But there *is* a little of Adeline about you,' Patricia continued, still scrutinising her. 'Yes, you've her big blue eyes . . .'

'Adeline?'

'Your late grandmother, dear – goodness, we've a lot to talk about! Who's this, then?'

Ellis was emerging from the back of the car with their bags, but Rebecca was too distracted to respond to Patricia's question.

The notion of having a grandmother other than Lillian was peculiar enough, but a grandmother called *Adeline* . . .

Perhaps realising he'd have to introduce himself, Ellis hoisted his own backpack onto one shoulder in order to offer his hand to Patricia. As she gripped it, she regarded him with a look that suggested she was temporarily reserving judgement. Today, the journalist was wearing a T-shirt and a pair of cargo shorts, which, Rebecca now noticed, revealed a graze on his left shin that had scabbed over. She wished she'd told him to look a bit smarter.

Patricia, meanwhile, was puzzling over his name: 'Did you say *Ellis*?'

'Yeah, like the island.'

'What island?'

He grinned. 'Never mind, I like your dogs – what are they called?'

'That's Bonny behind you,' Patricia said, visibly brightening, 'and this is Poppy, who needs to lose some weight, don't you, girl?' She gave the animal a sharp poke with her stick.

Ellis crouched to pet Bonny, and the freshly chastened Poppy soon skidded over to compete for his affection. Patricia regarded this interaction with a more approving expression, though Rebecca hung back. She wasn't fond of dogs. The previous landlord of The Three Tors in Lower Morvale had had a gigantic Irish wolfhound called Baskerville, that had scared her senseless as a child.

'Come on, then,' said Patricia, perhaps feeling her dogs had had enough attention. 'Let's give you the grand tour.'

The house's interior was a gloomy contrast to the sunshine outside. The rooms of the ground floor, which all ran off a narrow corridor, were full of tatty furniture and faded arts and crafts-style wallpaper. There was a permeating smell of both damp and dog, and the doors and floorboards creaked like old bones.

'The original building dates back to the 1400s,' said Patricia, as she led them down a few steps into a kitchen that, for some reason, had been built half a metre below ground level. 'It fell into a bit of a state over time but was restored in the middle of the 19th century, given new windows and whatnot.'

'Is it just you here?' enquired Ellis, who was inspecting an old-fashioned range.

'Me and the dogs, yes – it's far too big, of course, but I can't bring myself to sell it, not when it's been in the family for generations. Although . . .' she considered Rebecca for a moment '. . . until the other day, I believed *I* was the last Sampson.'

Rebecca, uncomfortable with the implications of this remark, tried to move the discussion along. 'So you've lived here all your life?'

'Oh no, I grew up here, but moved out when Victor and Adeline were married. I lived on the outskirts of Ashford for nearly 20 years. But I came back eventually, and Victor left me the house in his will – another reason I can't quite bear to part with it.'

'So Leo grew up here too?'

Rebecca and Ellis had spoken simultaneously. She frowned at him over Patricia's shoulder and he raised his hands in surrender.

'He did. In fact, Leo was born here.'

Rebecca's gaze drifted towards the ceiling, where it lingered on a long crack that had fractured into smaller lines on either side, like the veins of a leaf. She'd given her father's childhood little thought over the years, but never would've guessed he'd spent it in a crumbling old house in the Kentish countryside. She would've imagined him somewhere far more colourful, more transient; a circus tent, perhaps, or a canal boat. Although that might've been the result of having recently watched *The Stowaway*.

After they climbed back out of the kitchen, Ellis ducked into a small bathroom and Patricia signalled Rebecca to follow her further down the dingy corridor.

'I thought you said *Alice* on the phone,' she whispered, her forehead creased with concern.

'Sorry?'

'I didn't realise your friend would be a man.'

Rebecca wasn't sure why this was relevant. 'Um – yes, he is.'

'I should tell you now, I've put you in separate bedrooms . . .'

'Oh!' Rebecca felt herself redden. 'Yes, that's completely—'

'But I consider myself a *modern woman*, Rebecca,' Patricia ploughed on, 'so if you do want to share, it's absolutely none of my—'

'No!' cried Rebecca, a little too forcefully. 'I mean, we're not, you know, together.'

Patricia seemed first relieved, then looked slightly as though she wanted to pursue the point, but at that moment Ellis reappeared, trailed by Bonny and Poppy. Rebecca watched as he scratched the ears of the dog to his right, his smile cleaving deep lines into his cheeks, but when he looked up, she couldn't meet his eye.

'Now, there's just one more room to see down here,' Patricia said, 'my favourite, as it happens. Then I'll show you where you're sleeping. You have excellent views of the woods from your bedroom*s*,' she added, leaning heavily on the sentence's last letter.

Patricia's favourite room turned out to be the study, which was located at the opposite end of the corridor from the kitchen. Unlike the rest of the house, it possessed an air of orderliness – the bookshelves, cabinets and large low table in the centre of the room were all made of the same dark wood – but it felt empty too. For a study, it contained very few books, and instead an odd assortment of curios were dotted across the many surfaces: an antique microscope; a sheep's skull; an empty bell jar. It reminded

Rebecca of an old-fashioned museum, and her eye was drawn to the only splash of colour in the room; an overgrown spider plant sprouting miniature versions of itself all the way to the floor.

'This is where Victor spent all his time, bent over his petri dishes and notebooks,' explained Patricia.

'Was he a scientist?' Rebecca asked, peering at the sheep's skull, similar versions of which she'd stumbled across on Dartmoor.

'He was a doctor – a GP – but biology was his true passion. He spent hours on all his investigations and experiments. If our father hadn't encouraged him to pursue medicine, I feel sure he would have become a botanist or entomologist.'

'A what?'

'Someone who studies insects, dear. He used to have these tanks of beetles and stick insects and goodness knows what else, and he liked butterflies best of all. Here—'

She handed Rebecca a flat wooden case with a glass cover. Inside, nine butterflies had been mounted on a white board, and underneath each one both their common and Latin names had been recorded in small neat handwriting: Painted Lady, *Vanessa cardui*; Holly Blue, *Celastrina argiolus*; Speckled Wood, *Pararge aegeria*.

'There used to be dozens of those cases,' Patricia said, 'but I donated most of them to local schools, and the books went to libraries and universities. It's a shame,' she added, looking over Rebecca's shoulder, 'because they're very pretty, aren't they? But I'm sure the children will get more pleasure out of them than me.'

Rebecca wasn't so sure. The butterflies' powdery wings looked garish against the sterile backdrop, and a silver pin pierced each furry body. She offered the case to Ellis, who seemed reluctant to take it, and then spotted something much more appealing on a bookshelf to her right: a framed photograph of three figures standing in a garden.

'This is them, isn't it?' she said, picking it up so as to better study the image, which had the syrupy quality of a scene from the 60s or 70s.

The child at the front, who looked about five years old, was unmistakably Leo. The lopsided smirk on his pink-cheeked face was so familiar Rebecca thought she would've recognised him even without context. He was wearing a striped T-shirt and blue shorts, clutching a wooden toy truck and peering up at the camera from beneath a tangle of hair.

Victor Sampson, positioned behind and slightly to the right of his son, was tall and heavy-jawed like his sister. His dark hair had been sliced by an immaculate side parting and plastered to his head. He looked hot and uncomfortable in his tweed jacket, one arm hovering around his wife, the other clamped rigidly at his side.

While Leo and his father were peering directly at the camera, Adeline Sampson's gaze was lowered. She was small and slender, with long blonde hair and a washed-out complexion. Her yellow summer dress seemed several sizes too big. There was something insubstantial about her; a gust of wind might've carried her away had she not been clinging so tightly to the shoulders of her son.

As with the house, these were not the parents Rebecca would've imagined for her father. She might've pictured nomadic performers or hippies before these two, and wasn't sure who was more surprising, the stern-looking Victor or the waif-like Adeline.

Ellis, who had moved to stand beside her to see the photograph, asked, 'How old was Adeline here?'

It was a good question. Adeline looked far younger than Victor, almost child-like – although that might've been the effect of her overlarge dress.

Patricia took the frame, opened up the back, and read, 'August,

1970. So she must have been twenty-four. She was a year younger than me – although sometimes it felt like more.'

Clearly, this was a pointed comment, but Rebecca was too intent on having another look at the picture to query it, especially as Patricia now seemed unwilling to hand it back.

'Most of the photographs are in the attic now, but I always keep this one out. It was Victor's favourite.' She studied it herself, her smile sad. 'I suppose it was the last picture of them all together.'

'The last?' said Rebecca.

'Didn't you know? Adeline died young – the summer after this was taken, in fact.'

A chill seeped through Rebecca's body. Patricia still had the picture, but the image of Adeline – of her other grandmother, eternally young – seemed to shimmer at the forefront of Rebecca's vision.

'How?' she asked.

'There was an accident,' said Patricia, 'a terrible thing.' She let out a short sigh, replaced the picture on the shelf, and brushed the dust from her stubby fingers. 'Now, did either of you bring sensible outdoor shoes? There's no point being inside in this weather, so after you've seen your rooms, I think—'

'What kind of accident?' Rebecca asked.

Patricia drew in her chin, and Rebecca had the impression she wasn't used to being interrupted. She wondered whether she was about to be scolded.

'I'm not sure now is the time to be discussing that sort of thing,' said Patricia, sounding more flustered than stern. There was an awkward pause. 'Now, what was I saying?'

Rebecca was tempted to ask when the right time was, but Ellis cut across her. 'You were suggesting going outside?' he reminded Patricia, quietly.

'Ah – yes,' she said, clearly trying to recover. 'Yes, we should go for a walk. I'll show you around the woods. I'm sure the dogs will be keen . . .'

She continued to talk as she strode from the study. Rebecca, still stunned by the idea of Adeline's early death, opened her mouth to speak, but Ellis shook his head. This annoyed her – just as it annoyed her that Patricia was already halfway down the corridor – but she managed to swallow her questions.

The woods around Huxley offered further respite from the heat, yet, unlike the house, the speckled shade between the trees blazed with life: bees crawled over clutches of honeysuckle and burrowed into late-blooming foxgloves; birds warbled to one another from distant branches; living, unshackled butterflies jittered in and out of view, their wings aglow as they passed through strands of sunlight.

Leo must've played here as a child, Rebecca thought, as she and Ellis followed Patricia and the dogs along a dry, cracked path. They had this in common, she and her father; Lower Morvale was surrounded by similar woodland, which they had once explored together. Rebecca found herself scanning these new surroundings for evidence of a child's presence; initials carved into a tree trunk, perhaps, or an abandoned rope swing. Now she was here, she longed to know more about her father's past, to understand what his childhood had been like in this isolated place.

'You have to be more patient,' murmured Ellis, as, up ahead, Patricia stopped to talk to someone she knew.

'What do you mean?'

Ellis slowed his pace, directing his reply to the dusty earth. 'You need to let her share stuff in her own time, as though it's her own idea. Don't push her.'

He was probably right, but Rebecca was too hot to be lectured: sweat was pricking under her arms, and loose strands of hair were sticking to the back of her neck. 'I don't remember asking for your advice,' she told him.

'Right,' said Ellis, with a small smile, 'then why am I here?'

Fortunately, Rebecca was spared from answering, as Patricia chose that moment to chivvy them along. But for the rest of the walk she decided to heed Ellis's advice, and instead concentrated on gaining a better understanding of Leo's aunt. Patricia, it emerged, had worked for many years in the visitors' centre of a local National Trust property, though she was now retired. She was a keen walker, horse rider and bridge player, although most of her enthusiasm seemed to be reserved for dogs, and Bonny and Poppy were only the latest in a long line of canine companions. She reminded Rebecca of an old country bachelor: robust, headstrong, impossible to imagine with a partner.

Back at the house, Rebecca slipped away for a much-needed shower, fiddling with the crosshead taps until the water dribbled out, almost cold. It took a while to rinse the conditioner from her hair, but she didn't mind lingering under the lukewarm trickle, mulling over the day so far.

Why had Patricia really invited her here? Eyeing the mould-stippled ceiling and remembering her great-aunt's comment about being *the last Sampson*, Rebecca hoped she wasn't set to inherit this dilapidated old house. If Sudworth and Rowe had taught her anything, it was that old buildings were far more hassle than they were worth.

When she returned downstairs, Rebecca found her great-aunt in the kitchen, which smelled of roasting meat.

'It's all organic,' said Patricia, waving a peeler over mounds of potatoes, carrots, runner beans and broccoli – far more food than was necessary for three people. 'I get a box from one of the local farms. The chicken's from there as well . . . You're not a vegetarian too, are you?' she demanded, suddenly stern.

After Rebecca shook her head, Patricia glanced towards the corridor and pulled in her chin again, a show of disapproval presumably intended for the absent Ellis.

Rebecca was soon set to work washing and chopping the vegetables and, although she made a few attempts to engage her great-aunt in conversation, it was clear from Patricia's monosyllabic responses she considered cooking a largely silent activity. Most likely, this was simply the result of living alone for so long, but Rebecca feared her own pushiness in the study was also affecting her great-aunt's willingness to talk. Whatever the reason, it was worrying. So far, she'd learned very little about Leo's childhood and nothing that might help her understand why or where he had gone.

In spite of their tense exchange in the woods, she was buoyed by the reappearance of Ellis, who offered to lay the table and made enthusiastic and probably disingenuous remarks about the smell of the cooking. He smelled of soap and his fair hair was still damp from the shower; a tuft was sticking out at the back and, as Rebecca helped him arrange the cutlery, she had the strongest urge to reach out and smooth it down.

Huxley's dining room looked out onto the back garden, its French windows fringed by moss-coloured velvet curtains. An old Ordnance Survey map of Kent was framed on one of the walls and a drinks trolley had been parked by the door – not too recently, if the sticky necks of the bottles and decanters were anything to go by. Otherwise, the space was dominated by a long dark table and eight high-backed chairs. Rebecca, Ellis and Patricia arranged themselves around one end, but the presence of so many empty seats suggested they were still waiting for others to arrive.

Patricia studied Ellis intently as she handed him an empty plate and told him to help himself to vegetables, which looked dry and dull without gravy. It seemed she was trying to work him out, because after a cursory '*do start*' she asked, 'So are you from Devon as well, Ellis?'

'Brighton, actually – although my mum's American.'

Rebecca, reflecting on his laidback and slightly offbeat demeanour, found these facts as unsurprising as his vegetarianism. Still, as she took her first bite of rubbery chicken, it occurred to her she knew very little about this person she'd allied herself with.

'I live in London now, though,' Ellis continued. 'Clapham.'

Patricia gestured between them with the pepper mill. 'So how do you two know each other?'

'University,' said Rebecca quickly. 'We both went to Exeter, although we were on different courses. I did History and he did . . .' she faltered, conscious she was overdoing it, '. . . English. But we were in the same halls.'

'And we shared a house in our final year,' Ellis decided. 'You wouldn't think it, but Rebecca's really messy.'

Rebecca raised her eyebrows at him, but he merely mimicked the action back at her.

'I think I would have studied History too,' Patricia mused. 'But I didn't go to university – well, it wasn't so common for women back then. Victor did, of course. UCL. Father was so proud.'

'Is that where he met Adeline?' asked Rebecca, aware the age gap between them made this unlikely, but keen to keep the conversation on Leo's parents.

'Oh no, she was a local girl – in fact, we went to the same primary school. Victor didn't meet her until after he'd graduated, when he started working at the surgery down the road. She was one of his patients.'

There was a note of disapproval in her voice, which Rebecca decided to emulate. 'Is that allowed?'

'It shouldn't be,' Patricia said at once. 'Adeline was completely wrong for him: far too young and fragile. She was only seventeen when they married.'

'Seventeen?'

'Yes, and she acted like it. All the Lockwoods were a bit *unusual,* but she was the worst. *Adeline should be locked up,* we used to say at school. But Victor liked looking after her. He never seemed to mind how delicate she was, how weak.'

Patricia's disdain was obvious now, to the extent that Rebecca already knew the answer to her next question. 'So you didn't really get on, you and Adeline?'

Patricia pursed her lips. 'She frustrated me, I don't mind admitting that. But I think I could have come to care for her as a sister if she'd just—When it came to affection, she really wasn't—' Patricia let out another of her curt exhalations. 'Put it this way, I don't think she loved Victor as much as she should have. My brother would have walked over hot coals for that girl, but with him she was always . . . *distant.* And it wasn't as though she didn't have the capacity for love. Oh no, we saw that quite clearly when the *boy* came along.'

As casually as she could, Rebecca asked, 'They were close then, Adeline and Leo?'

'Too close, probably,' said Patricia, with a flash of spite. Then, relenting, she continued, 'Oh, I don't mean there was anything *unnatural* about it, only that Adeline seemed to consider the boy hers, and hers alone. It was like that from the start, when she made such a fuss about calling him *Leo* – which isn't a family name, by the way. The two of them were always out there—' She nodded towards the garden '—Playing their secret games, telling their secret stories. Victor said he didn't mind, that it gave him the opportunity to continue with his studies, but I'm not so sure . . .'

Rebecca turned her gaze towards the garden, which was veiled in the mauve evening light, thinking about the games and stories Leo had shared with her as a child. She could only remember snippets – knocking on tree trunks to see if anyone was home, sticking feathers in their hair and clothes so they could fly – but wondered whether this was how he and his mother had played together. Was it from her he'd inherited his boundless imagination?

'Victor didn't spend much time with Leo himself?' Ellis asked.

Patricia pondered this for a moment. 'I don't think so. It's difficult to remember now, considering everything that happened later. But no, they didn't have much of a chance when Adeline was alive, and – who knows – perhaps if she hadn't smothered that boy so much he might have had more respect for his father. You know, *afterwards*.'

Patricia started to saw at her chicken, while Rebecca took a sip of wine, unsure how to proceed. Once again, they'd landed upon the subject of Adeline's death, and though morbidly curious to learn more, Rebecca feared Patricia might shut down the conversation as abruptly as she had in the study.

Ellis, perhaps sensing her indecision, said, 'It must've been very hard for Victor, when Adeline died.'

'Yes, it was.' Patricia's knife scraped against the plate. 'In fact, I don't think he ever recovered, not fully. As I said, he'd devoted himself to caring for her and suddenly she was gone.'

Ellis nodded, but Rebecca experienced a ripple of annoyance on behalf of the third figure in the photograph; the little boy in the striped T-shirt clasping his toy truck.

'How old was Leo?' she asked.

'Six.' Then, as though reading Rebecca's mind, Patricia added,

'And of course it was very hard for him too. I'm no psychologist, but I'm sure losing his mother like that was the root cause of all his bad behaviour.'

Losing his mother like how? Rebecca wondered. But, again, she remembered Ellis's advice in the woods and urged herself to be patient, to not push Patricia – particularly with regard to Adeline. 'He was badly behaved?' she asked instead.

'Very. He'd been quiet as a child – rather odd, now I think back on it – but when he turned twelve or thirteen, he started coming out of his shell, and not in a good way. The number of letters and phone calls we received from his school . . . It was ridiculous.'

'What did he do?'

'Not his work, that's for sure. He didn't show up to half of his lessons, or if he did he was disruptive, and sometimes he just left the school grounds in the middle of the day . . . He claimed the other children were picking on him – calling him names, ducking him in the pool, that sort of nonsense – but it's hardly an excuse, is it? It put such a strain on poor Victor. The headmaster kept pressuring him to intervene, but what could he do? He couldn't *make* Leo behave, could he?'

Rebecca knew she should agree, possibly even sympathise with *poor Victor*, like Ellis. Instead, she pretended to be intent on cutting up a piece of broccoli, perplexed by her own reluctance to take sides against father.

Patricia, however, needed no encouragement to continue: 'The boy was suspended a few times, naturally, but eventually that school washed its hands of him, which was hardly surprising . . .'

'You mean, he was expelled?' said Rebecca, who did find this surprising – though only because she'd rarely been in trouble at school herself.

'Oh yes.' Patricia stabbed at a potato with her fork. 'It was such a bother, because of course Victor had to find somewhere new to take him on and in the end he had to go to an expensive private school. Although he did board during the week, so it was probably worth the money.'

Rebecca's gaze lingered on a piece of peeling botanical wallpaper behind Ellis's head. Huxley's faded grandeur made it difficult to ascertain how wealthy the Sampsons had been – how wealthy Patricia was now.

'And did he do any better at the new school?' asked Ellis.

'Not really,' said Patricia. 'If anything, he got worse. I remember him once being in huge trouble for climbing all over the school roof – it was an old building and he damaged part of a historic turret, something like that. He also kept wandering off. He went missing on a school trip to the coast, which sent everyone into a total panic for an afternoon. Then there was the lying, the stealing—'

'*Stealing*?'

Clearly, he'd had many failings, but Rebecca wouldn't have thought her father dishonest or deliberately deceitful.

'Yes, he became rather light-fingered as a teenager,' said Patricia, 'although if you ask me, he wanted to get caught – everything Leo did was purely for effect.'

'Maybe that's why he got into acting?' suggested Ellis.

'Because he was an attention-seeker, you mean?' Patricia snorted. 'Undoubtedly.'

Rebecca felt irritated with Ellis for siding with their host, or at least pretending to, though she herself had employed this same tactic only minutes ago.

'What happened after Leo finished school?' asked Ellis, before pondering, '*Did* he finish school?'

'He did, believe it or not. We were quite surprised by that. Although his last year coincided with his time in a local theatre group, which straightened him out for a bit – he was slightly less trouble when he was doing those plays in Ashford. And it wasn't as though he was top of the class, far from it. I think he managed to scrape a few O levels, but they weren't exactly As and Bs. Nothing like Victor had achieved at the same age, so the boy must have inherited his mother's brains – or lack of.'

A stray morsel of potato or chicken was wobbling on Patricia's cheek as she spoke. Rebecca, gripping her cutlery tighter than usual, decided not to let her know.

'Still, Victor was pleased Leo had at least a couple of O levels,' continued Patricia. 'He thought if the boy stayed in school, perhaps he'd be able to get a few A levels too, and then maybe he could go to university – not to study medicine, of course, but I think Victor hoped he could salvage something from his school years. As always, though, Leo had other ideas.'

'You mean, he wanted to act?'

'Indeed,' said Patricia, scathingly. 'He was desperate to move to London and do . . . Well, whatever one does to become an actor. Auditions and suchlike, I suppose?'

She looked at Ellis, as though he might be able to confirm this. Instead, he made a show of wiping at his face with his napkin, although Patricia didn't pick up on the hint.

'And Victor didn't approve?' guessed Rebecca.

'No, but he didn't try and stop him either. He even gave the boy some money to start him off – well, I knew that was a bad idea. It would have been less wasteful to flush the money down the lavatory.'

'What happened?'

'The same thing that always happened: Leo messed up. Oh, I'm not sure *how*, exactly,' she added, intuiting their next question. 'We didn't hear anything from him for about six months after he left, because the ungrateful little so-and-so took the money and bolted. But then, as usual, when he got into trouble it was Victor they called.'

'Who called?' asked Rebecca.

'The *police*,' said Patricia, with as much triumph as Richard Lowrie had said *drugs*.

Reluctantly – for she was picturing her father being dragged from some hovel, a needle protruding from his arm – Rebecca asked, 'What had he done?'

'They'd arrested him for trying to break into a private park in the middle of the night. Apparently, they found him clutching at a locked gate, blind drunk, singing at the top of his voice and . . .' Patricia's chin was now pulled in so tight she looked like tortoise glowering from its shell ' . . . And *stark naked*.'

Relieved, Rebecca let out an involuntary snort of laughter. Her aunt seemed so incensed, whereas she'd heard of worse drunken antics during her time at university – nothing involving herself, exactly, but people she'd known.

'Hay fever playing up again?' Ellis said, mildly.

'What?' Rebecca noticed her great-aunt's flinty expression was now directed at her, and hurriedly sniffed a few times. 'Yeah, maybe.'

'What happened after the arrest?' Ellis asked.

'Victor had to go up to London and sort it out, didn't he?' Patricia sighed. 'He was away for days.'

'How come?'

Their host gave a jerk of her wide shoulders. 'Search me. Victor didn't want to talk about it – not even to his own sister! I think he was ashamed. That boy had disappointed him too many times.'

Rebecca inhaled to speak, but Ellis got there first: 'What do *you* think happened?'

'They had a big argument, I know that much. And Victor

and Leo never argued. They tended to avoid each other as much as possible – neither of them liked confrontation.'

'You mean, they argued about the arrest?' pressed Ellis, before Patricia could head off on another digression.

'I assume so – and probably about Leo's lifestyle in general. He was obviously drinking too much, and I'm fairly sure he didn't have any work. Whatever was said, though, that argument did it for them. They never spoke to one another again.'

'Never?' said Rebecca, startled.

'Never. And to add insult to injury, a few days after he returned to Huxley, Victor discovered one of his credit cards was missing. The bank cancelled it, naturally, but not before Leo was halfway across Europe. Although, in retrospect, that was probably a blessing: with the boy gone, my brother finally had some peace and quiet.'

As Patricia nudged the last of her gravy-soaked peas onto her fork, Rebecca frowned, wondering why – in spite of everything she'd just heard – she didn't feel as appalled by these stories as perhaps her great-aunt had intended.

'What about when Leo returned to the UK?' asked Ellis. 'When he started acting professionally?'

'What about it? I saw his name in the paper once or twice, but I never showed Victor, and if he read it himself, he never mentioned it. As I said, we had no contact with Leo after that incident in London.'

Now it was Ellis's turn to frown. 'But you knew about his wife – or she knew about you, at least.' He looked to Rebecca. 'Wasn't this house in your mum's address book?'

She nodded, grateful at least one of them had remembered this. Looking uncomfortable, Patricia tugged her napkin from her collar, as though worried it might choke her, and scrunched it into a ball.

'Yes, she wrote to me once, years ago: *Rosalyn Sampson.*'

Patricia considered the name, which, to Rebecca, might've belonged to someone else's mother. What had she been like, Rosalyn Sampson? More easy-going? Less bothered about what other people thought of her? Content?

'She told me she and Leo had recently married,' Patricia continued, 'and were expecting a baby – goodness, that must have been you! You don't have any siblings?'

Rebecca shook her head.

'It was a nice letter. She seemed to understand there had been problems. I think she was trying to bring about some sort of reconciliation. She said she wanted us to be part of their lives – of your life, when you arrived – but by then it was too late.'

'Too late?'

'Victor was gone. He passed away in '88, and your mother's letter must have come a year or two later, so Leo couldn't have made amends. I doubt he wanted to – I suspect it was all her idea – but I'm afraid I didn't bother to find out. Victor's death was still very raw. He'd had a heart attack, completely out of the blue. He was only fifty-three.'

Patricia seized her crumpled napkin and wiped roughly at her face, finally dislodging the blob of food clinging to her cheek. Her hazel eyes were shiny, like two clean pennies.

'It was a mistake, not writing back – I see that now,' she continued, her voice unsteady. 'I was too focused on the idea of seeing Leo again. Frankly, I didn't think I had the energy for him. It never occurred to me I'd miss out on seeing Victor's granddaughter grow up . . . *Anyway.*' She sniffed loudly. 'You're here now, aren't you? You made it to Huxley in the end.'

Rebecca, unwilling to hold her gaze, thought she now understood why Patricia had invited her here, yet couldn't fully accept the notion of being Victor Sampson's granddaughter. She'd never been close with Rosalyn's father, Archie – not like she was with Lillian – but at least she'd known him.

'And, of course, none of this is a reflection on *you*,' Patricia added, as though it'd only just occurred to her Rebecca might be offended by her scorn for Leo. 'You can't help who your father is. As I said, he was too much like Adeline, too much of a *Lockwood*. You, though . . . You might not look like one, but I can tell you're a Sampson through and through.'

Clearly, this was intended as a compliment, but Rebecca didn't feel particularly flattered. She was spared from responding, however, because Patricia then asked, 'Now, have you both had enough?'

This was in reference to the food, but Rebecca thought she'd had her fill of family history too, at least for now. Though she still had plenty of questions, she longed to retreat and let everything she'd just learned crystallise in her mind.

But for the moment, she forced herself to contribute to the tidying up effort, collecting the debris now scattered across the table – the used napkins, the cork of the wine bottle, a few stray peas – while Ellis amalgamated leftover vegetables into one pot.

'Yes, good,' said Patricia, pausing to watch their progress. 'There's a trifle in the fridge, then I thought we'd see what's on the box . . . No, leave the scraps, Rebecca – the dogs will have them.'

7

Huxley

Tucked into the cushioned window seat of the guest room, Rebecca gazed down onto Huxley's shadowy back garden. She had pulled the floral curtains shut around her and opened the latticed window as far as it would go. The night felt close. It was the sort of atmosphere that gave her mother headaches, and could only be shattered by a storm.

Rebecca had been sitting in this spot for over an hour, one hand wrapped around her bare knees, the other picking at a loose thread of the seat cushion. She'd given up on sleep long ago. It was too warm and she couldn't relax when everything she'd learned over the past few hours was still rattling around in her mind.

Why wasn't she more shocked by Patricia's account of Leo's many transgressions? Generally, Rebecca had been well-behaved as a child, and never undergone an especially rebellious phase – although it occurred to her she might be on the brink of one now. Even to her, though, Leo's misdemeanours didn't sound so bad. Admittedly, the credit card theft was pretty deplorable, but skipping classes and wandering off? It was no worse than anything Amy – who'd once released all of an old farmer's sheep because he'd called her a tart – had tried over the years. And when Leo's actions were considered in the context of his mother's early death they became, if not justified, at least understandable.

How *had* Adeline died? Both Patricia and the photograph had inferred Leo's mother had been delicate, and Rebecca's thoughts kept circling some kind of illness, perhaps one Adeline had endured for many years – that would explain the close relationship she'd formed with her doctor, Victor. But Patricia had said an accident had killed her; an accident she was reluctant to discuss, all these years later. She might've been lying, but what would be the point? Even if the idea of a shocking accident was easier to bear than that of a drawn-out illness, it wasn't as though anything needed to be censored for Rebecca's benefit. Before today, she hadn't known Adeline Sampson had existed.

A slight breeze fluttered the curtains behind her and, as the inside of her makeshift den billowed with cool air, Rebecca wondered whether Leo had ever sat where she was now. She was still struggling to picture him at Huxley at all, but this might have been his room – although its flowery furnishings seemed to date back several decades. Perhaps Ellis had Leo's old room. She would ask him tomorrow.

The journalist had snuck upstairs during the tedious railway documentary Patricia had subjected them to after dinner and Rebecca hadn't seen him since. What did he make of it all? It was too late now, but she almost wished she'd knocked on his door after Patricia had gone to bed and suggested they find a drink somewhere, just to talk over everything they'd learned – although where the nearest pub was, she had no idea.

Besides, Ellis could hardly help her fathom her own attitude towards her father, which was puzzling Rebecca most of all. Nobody seemed to have a good word to say about him – Patricia, Richard Lowrie, even her own uncle recalled Leo with nothing but contempt. So why was she beginning to feel stirrings of sympathy? It wasn't as though she owed him anything; a few years of parenting wasn't enough to earn him much loyalty. Was it simply some primal predisposition, her increasing bias towards her own blood? Or did she sense another person beneath the stories she was being told, a figure more in keeping with her own hazy memories?

Glancing down, Rebecca discovered one end of the window seat's cushion cover was unravelling. Quickly, she dropped the thread she'd been pulling and smoothed it into the seam, hoping Patricia wouldn't notice. She was still wide awake but couldn't sit anymore – her legs were cramping – so padded back towards the bed and withdrew *Seven Tales* from her overnight bag.

She wasn't sure why she'd brought it to Huxley. Before now, she hadn't planned on reading any more of the stories, but as she climbed on top of the bedcovers, book in hand, it occurred to her she owned nothing else from or even of her father. He must have given her presents for her first few birthdays and Christmases, but Rebecca couldn't recall a single one of them. The thought of all those lost toys made her grip the olive-green book more tightly. Maybe that was why she'd packed it: as well as evidence of his affection, it was a talisman, a tangible connection to him.

After pausing, once more, at *For Birdie,* she turned to where she'd left off.

The Third Tale: The Voyage to the Edge of the World

There was once a young sailor who had been wrongfully imprisoned. For several miserable weeks, he huddled in a dark, dank cell, trembling as he listened to the guards discussing the terrible tortures that would soon be visited upon him. They called him a cheat, a thief, a criminal, and did not seem to know or care that none of this was true.

One night, the guards decided to move the sailor to a darker, danker cell, and tied his hands with thick rope for the trudge through the prison. But the sailor was an expert in knots, so, seizing his opportunity, he managed to wriggle out of his bindings, overpower his captors and escape.

He fled straight to the docks and, knowing the authorities would be following close behind, accepted work on the first ship that would take him, which was heading east. For the next few months, he kept sailing in that direction, eager to put as much distance as possible between himself and his homeland, for he was still haunted by the guards' terrible threats and false accusations. He worked hard on dozens of vessels, and once he had accrued both gold and experience, was able to afford a ship of his very own.

Now a captain, the sailor and his new crew continued east, further than any of them had gone before, until they had long since passed the ports they knew, and the water hummed and sparked with a strange magic. The crew felt uneasy, but, reluctant to appear cowardly in front of their captain, they said nothing and journeyed on.

Eventually, they reached a dark patch of sea, where creatures were carousing, frolicking in the water. At first, the men took them to be large fish or dolphins, but up-close the silvery, sinewy figures resembled beautiful women, and when the crew heard their eerie song they grew afraid:

What sailors are you,
Who dare to sail through
The sirens' forbidden domain?
We'll sing you to sleep,
Then drag you down deep,
Forever with us, you'll remain.

Soon, the sinister lullaby caused the men's eyelids to grow heavy, and the sirens began clambering up the side of the boat, baring their pointed, shark-like teeth. But the captain, who had clamped his hands over his ears, called down, 'We meant no offence, crossing through your waters! We only wish to keep sailing until we can sail no more! Please, let us pass!'

The sirens paused, smiled, and then continued their singing as they slipped back towards the water.

You truly must be
The fools of the sea
If the edge of the world is your fate.
But just for our fun,
We'll let you go on,
In case you return, we will wait.

Safe, for the moment, the men sailed on, yet the captain's mind lingered on the sirens' warning about the edge of the world. No sailor had made that dangerous journey in living memory, and legend told that men were changed forever when they peered beyond the end of the earth. But the captain was more afraid of being dragged back to his homeland to face those false charges and, realising nobody would dare pursue him so far, convinced his crew of the fame and glory a voyage to the edge of the world would bring.

A few days after they set their new course, another ship appeared on the horizon. It was flying a black flag, and before long pirates had jumped aboard the captain's vessel, demanding gold and jewels. Once more, the crew were frightened, but the captain kept his head.

'We have nothing of worth to give you,' he told the pirates. 'We are not merchants, but explorers travelling to the edge of the world. Please, let us pass!'

The pirates, who had never ventured so far themselves, were impressed, and after finding no treasure on the ship, invited the captain and his crew to dine and drink with them. After that, both vessels sailed side by side, for it felt safer to travel those unfamiliar waters together.

They didn't see land for many weeks, but just as their supplies of food and fresh water were running low, they spotted a rocky green island in the distance. The pirates steered straight towards it, but the captain was more cautious, and advanced upon the island slowly.

No sooner had the pirates alighted on the green rocks did the ground beneath them begin to quake. Crying out in fear, they tried to head back to their ship, but a gigantic tentacle rose from the water, smashing the vessel clean in half. Too late, the pirates realised they had not landed on an island, but on the back of an enormous sea monster.

The captain ordered his own ship closer to the beast, in spite of the objections of his trembling crew. Taking the wheel, he steered around the creature's lashing tentacles to pull aboard the few pirates brave enough to swim out to his ship. Those who remained cowering on the creature's back he was forced to leave behind.

The monster had spooked the survivors, who had never encountered anything so large or ferocious in all their time at sea. So, when the captain insisted they sail on, his crew and the remaining pirates staged a mutiny, and threw him into a rowing boat with nothing but a compass, some rope, a tin of stale biscuits and a bottle of rum.

'Good luck at the edge of the world!' they sneered, before sailing away.

The abandoned sailor, now the captain of just one soul, realised he had little choice but to take up the oars and row. After a few agonising days in the baking sun, he began to notice a rushing in the water, as though a strong current was pulling him towards the horizon. He rowed towards a jagged rock, around which he knotted one end of the rope, and then guided his little boat forward.

The captain had always pictured the edge of the world as a tabletop, from which he would look out onto endless sky. But as he approached, he saw his destination lay beyond a vast curtain of sea and foam, stretching up into the clouds like a giant waterfall. He refused to be daunted by this curious sight, and when he arrived at the cascade, he shut his eyes to protect them from the crashing water. Though he could not see, he felt his boat tumble through the tempest, before bobbing out into smoother seas.

When the captain opened his eyes, he was surprised to find it was still dark. Not completely black, like the view behind his eyelids, but dull and gloomy, as though the sun had gone in. The sea beneath him was the colour of pitch and, ahead, a jagged rock rose from the water, the murky twin of the one he had tied his boat to. The captain's little vessel, his oars, even his own hands, were now dark and insubstantial, as though made of nothing but shadow.

Cold, sick and more afraid than ever before, he realised this world was a dark reflection of the one he knew. He had to leave, but the current was pulling him on, deeper into that sinister place, and he felt horribly weary, as though his body had been robbed of strength as well as substance. Worst of all, he could hear someone or something whispering – cheat, thief, criminal – and for the first time, the captain felt these accusations might be true.

'I must escape this place,' he said to himself, 'or I will be lost forever.'

He summoned all his remaining courage and began to pull himself back by the rope. It was hard work against the current, but he heaved and heaved until he was back at the waterfall. When he opened his eyes on the other side, he was dazzled by colour and sunlight, but only paused long enough to detach his rope from the jagged rock and take up his oars again.

Eventually, when the flow of the sea had returned to normal, the captain collapsed. Lost, and weak from hunger and thirst, he was certain he would die, but his boat had strayed into the path of a merchant ship, and the kindly crew took him aboard and nursed him back to health. Nobody believed his stories about sirens and pirates and sea monsters, nor his babbling about a land of shadow beyond the edge of the world. Yet they humoured his request to avoid both a rocky green island and dark patch of sea, where, through a telescope, the abandoned sailor glimpsed the sirens sunning themselves upon the wreckage of his former ship.

No longer a captain, the man was eventually delivered to his homeland, although he felt no satisfaction at being back, nor fear that he might be recognised and recaptured. Venturing beyond the edge of the world had filled his heart with shadow, and sometimes he imagined he caught sight of that dark realm when he looked out of a window or into a mirror or heard those menacing whispers again. Usually, it was nothing, but he feared that place for the rest of his life, and never set sail upon the sea again.

Rebecca stared at the page until the words began to blur, and when she finally looked up, she was startled to find herself in the unfamiliar guestroom of Huxley House, which was dark beyond the glow of the bedside lamp. For a moment, she felt she too had been transported to the shadowy land beyond the edge of the world, and in spite of the warmth of the night, she shivered.

Why had her father left her this book? She wanted a letter or a journal; something about *him,* not these fanciful stories. How had he even come up with them? She supposed the captain's false imprisonment might've been influenced by the arrest Patricia had described at dinner, but where had Leo got the inspiration for a youth trying to return to a magical realm or a mermaid – no, a *nixie* – being captured by a man who imprisoned fairies in cases and tanks?

Unbidden, an image from earlier that day flashed into Rebecca's mind: the glass-fronted case of butterflies in the study. Victor had collected specimens too. Not fairies, of course, but insects. He'd been an amateur – what was it? – *entomologist.* According to Patricia, the entire room had been full of cases and tanks.

That can't be right, Rebecca told herself, trying to ignore a creeping comprehension, plus the tingling of her skin, which had turned to gooseflesh. Because if the collector in that story was meant to be Victor, it wasn't too difficult to figure out who the little boy and the captured nixie represented . . .

She closed the book, dropping it onto the bed as though it might scald her, but this didn't stop the questions now zipping through her head. Was Leo trying to tell her something about his childhood? If the first and maybe third tale were autobiographical, were they all? Or was it all just make-believe, and the lateness of the hour and peculiarity of the house were tricking Rebecca into searching for connections that didn't exist?

Swinging her legs off the bed, she picked up her phone – noting it was 2.07 am – and slipped out into the upstairs corridor, grateful for the honking snores reverberating from behind Patricia's door. Using the dim light of the phone screen to illuminate her path, Rebecca crept along the passageway and began to descend the staircase, mindful of where she placed each foot. For some reason, she'd always been unduly paranoid about tumbling down stairs, and it didn't help that each of these steps creaked in protest to her presence.

By the time she'd reached the ground floor, her eyes were adjusting to the darkness, and a little moonlight was filtering through the diamond-shaped panes of the downstairs windows. Rebecca didn't believe in ghosts or the supernatural, but as she lowered her phone the shadows pooling in Huxley's corners seemed to yawn towards her, and she quickened her pace towards Victor's study.

There, she risked turning on a dusty banker's lamp, and pointed her phone's camera around the room, briefly wondering why the last picture she'd taken was of a crabby-looking Brontë. Patricia had said most of Victor's possessions had been given away, but Rebecca wanted a record of the few objects still contained within this room: the butterfly case, the microscope, the empty bell jar, even the sheep's skull and spider plant. She wasn't wholly convinced she was looking at the basis of the sinister character of the collector, but she wasn't about to dismiss her new theory either.

Edging further into the room, Rebecca took a close-up of the framed photograph of Leo, Adeline and Victor, pondering the three figures in the garden long after the flash had faded. It wasn't as though she'd expected the image to have changed – Victor hadn't acquired a hat and cloak, Adeline hadn't grown gills – but it still seemed odd her father and these grandparents she'd never known looked exactly the same as earlier, when now she knew so much more about them.

Rebecca was almost back at the stairs when she heard clinking at the other end of the corridor. She froze, fleetingly afraid Huxley had been invaded by a burglar, or a spirit – or perhaps by the collector himself. But these wild imaginings were soon stifled by logic: there were only two other people in the house, and she was certain one of them was still snoring in her room.

Sure enough, when she peered into the kitchen, she discovered Ellis sat at the table, fully dressed and eating a sandwich.

'Oh, hey,' he said, almost as though he'd expected her. 'Couldn't sleep either?'

'No.' She noticed he'd also poured himself a glass of milk and felt slightly affronted on Patricia's behalf. 'What are you doing?'

He frowned at his sandwich. 'Is that a trick question?' Then, poking at a chunk of cheese that was threatening to escape the bread, he said, 'I fancied a little protein.'

'Ah,' said Rebecca, remembering the dry vegetables he'd been served at dinner, and regretting her tone. In an attempt at levity, she remarked, 'You'll have funny dreams.'

'In this creepy old house? Surely not.'

She smiled, which seemed to distract Ellis from his sandwich, for he leaned back in his seat, studying her as he had in the office, the first time they'd met. Though his attention was on her face, Rebecca was suddenly aware that she was wearing tiny pyjama shorts and an old T-shirt with no bra underneath. She folded her arms over her chest in what she hoped resembled a casual gesture, and asked, 'What?'

Ellis shook his head. 'Nothing – what are you up to?'

'Um, water,' she decided.

She descended the trio of steps into the kitchen, flinching as the soles of her bare feet touched the stone floor. After searching a few overhead cupboards for a glass, she ran the tap and, as she waited for the water to cool, glanced over her shoulder. Ellis was now focused on his sandwich again – but why had he given her that look?

On her way back out, Rebecca nudged a chair under the table as she passed and when its legs scraped loudly against the floor, two shadows leapt from the corner of the room.

'*Shit*!' she gasped, water slopping over the edge of her glass. 'I didn't realise they were here!'

Ellis bent down to restrain an excitable Bonny and Poppy, who promptly began snuffling at his legs.

'They're terrible guard dogs,' he said. 'They slobbered all over me when I came down, then just fell asleep again.'

Her heart still thudding, Rebecca watched him divide one of his crusts between the two black Labradors and then turned back towards the door.

'What's the Great West Run?' Ellis asked.

'What?'

'On the back of your T-shirt.'

'Oh, it's a half marathon. You run twice around Exeter, I did it in—'

'—2013, I see that.' Ellis took another bite of bread. 'I can't run, it hurts my knees. I don't really do any sport.'

'None?'

Rebecca neither admired nor believed this statement: he didn't have the physique of someone who didn't exercise, though she resented him for drawing her attention to this.

'Well, I cycle to work most days, I guess that counts.'

Rebecca pictured Ellis on a spindly, impractical bike, weaving in and out of London traffic. 'Is it safe?'

He grinned. 'Are you worried about me?'

'No,' she said at once, embarrassed. 'Just— Don't get squashed by a bus until we've found out what's happened to my dad, all right?'

'All right.' He nodded solemnly. 'But after that, I'm not promising anything: I'll ignore red lights, I'll hover in drivers' blind spots, I'll throw out all my reflective gear . . .'

'Oh, shut up.'

The two dogs had retreated back to their cushions in the corner, and Rebecca – feeling it was foolish to continue a conversation from a doorway – returned to the table and sat opposite Ellis. He made no comment about her decision to stay, but continued to eat the last of his sandwich.

'Your room upstairs . . . ?' she began.

'I don't think it was your dad's. I had a poke about. Or if it was, she's got rid of all his stuff. By the sound of it, he was probably kept in the cellar.'

Obviously this was a joke, but Rebecca couldn't help but think of the little boy in the first of the *Seven Tales*, tiptoeing fearfully around the collector's residence. Huxley was the second house she'd been in where all evidence of Leo had been removed. What was it about him that inspired people to clean up so thoroughly in his wake?

'You feel sorry for him,' Ellis said, keeping his gaze on his plate as he pressed his index finger against the last of the breadcrumbs.

'A bit,' she admitted. 'Imagine growing up here, and losing your mother so young . . .' Then, because it had been bothering her since their arrival, she said, 'My middle name's Adeline.'

Now, Ellis looked up. 'Really?'

'I never knew why. My mum's into all those classic novels, I assumed it was from one of those.'

She wondered why Rosalyn hadn't changed it, as she'd changed their surname. Maybe she'd forgotten where *Adeline* had come from.

'Did you tell Patricia?' asked Ellis.

'No – do you think I should?'

'Probably not. If your middle name had been *Victoria* . . .'

Guiltily, Rebecca thought of everything else they'd kept from Patricia. It had been a lot easier to deceive Richard Lowrie. 'We shouldn't have made up all that stuff at dinner, about meeting at university,' she said.

'You started it. Anyway, maybe I *did* go to Exeter.'

'You did not.'

'Yeah, I went to Durham. Why did you stay in Devon?'

He shot the question at her, just as when he'd asked *Do you remember him?* and Rebecca's instinct was to wrong-foot him. 'I didn't, actually, not at first. I went to Oxford, but—Well, it didn't work out.'

She hadn't thought this through. In trying to throw him, she'd accidentally revealed something too personal. Uneasily, she waited for his inevitable interrogation.

'Now, *that* you should've told Patricia,' said Ellis, getting up and heading towards the sink to wash his plate. 'If she knew you'd got into Oxford, she could've attributed it to Victor's brains.'

Relieved, Rebecca looked from his now empty glass of milk to her own untouched water, and said, 'You know, I could do with a proper drink.'

Ellis turned off the tap. 'Now you're talking. Wasn't there some kind of bar cart in the dining room?'

He threw the tea towel he'd been holding back onto its hook and departed the kitchen, presumably to investigate, while Rebecca was left pondering her sudden desire to stay up and drink. Perhaps she wanted a distraction: from Leo; from her own jumbled feelings; from the melancholy that seemed to permeate this house. Or maybe, she thought, as the window squeaked on its hinge, she was a little spooked after all.

Quietly, so as not to wake the dogs again, she crossed the kitchen and pushed open the window until it wouldn't go any further, just as she had upstairs. She stared out into the back garden. Beyond the edge of a well-trimmed lawn was a dense copse, presently just a dark outline against the night sky. They'd not ventured between those trees during their afternoon walk and, at the time, Rebecca hadn't given them a second thought. Now, though, she wondered whether, if she were to venture through that thicket, she might find a great green pond and, in the depths of its water . . . What, a nixie? She was being ridiculous.

'Everything all right?'

She turned to see Ellis in the doorway, clutching a crystal decanter.

'Yeah, fine – it's just cooler over here, that's all.'

'Good plan,' he said, passing her the drink and fetching two chairs.

Rebecca poured some of the honey-coloured spirit into a couple more glasses and handed him one, asking, 'What is this, anyway?'

'No idea – cheers.'

It was brandy. Sweet and warming, it felt completely wrong for a humid summer night, although she welcomed its sharp aftertaste. It reminded her of Christmas, of staying up with Morton after the rest of the family had burned themselves out, the pair of them grumbling about whatever was on TV as they picked at the last of the pudding. What would her uncle think if he knew where she was now?

Resisting the urge to down the drink in one, Rebecca lowered herself into the chair on the right, tugging at the hem of her pyjama shorts before tucking her mostly bare legs out of sight. Ellis, meanwhile, was stretching out in the neighbouring seat, propping up his ankles on the sill of the open window, so his feet hung out into the darkness. Rebecca wasn't sure she approved of this disregard for both Huxley's architecture and Patricia's hospitality, especially as it gave her a close-up of the graze on his shin, which she now saw was an archipelago of smaller scabs.

'Was that from cycling?' She nodded at the injury.

'Huh? Oh – yeah, but in Cornwall, not London. Got up too close and personal with a drystone wall.'

'See, cycling's dangerous,' Rebecca said, before explaining, 'When I was little, I broke my arm falling off my bike. I still have a scar somewhere . . .' She twisted her right arm one way then the other, trying to glimpse the thick silvery line beneath her elbow.

'I see it,' said Ellis.

He pointed at the same time as she moved and his fingertip inadvertently brushed her bare forearm. It was the lightest of touches yet it sent a jolt of electricity through Rebecca's skin.

Unsettled, she cupped her elbow with her other hand, and gabbled, 'It's weird, but I can't remember falling off. I have this really clear picture of the bike itself – light blue and covered in stickers and ribbons – but I've no memory of the actual accident . . .'

She thought of her mother, who brought up that tumble over the handlebars all the time – so much so that Rebecca thought the incident must've contributed to Rosalyn's overprotectiveness. 'Anyway,' she said, with a shrug, 'where were you in Cornwall again?'

Unlike the last time this had come up, Rebecca was keen for details as to how and where he'd spent the previous weekend. In comparison to Huxley, her neighbouring county – the destination of so many summer holidays – felt friendly, and they soon discovered a mutual appreciation of Tintagel.

'They've dug up some amazing stuff there,' said Rebecca.

'Obviously, everyone's always trying to link it to the King Arthur myth, but the artefacts themselves are fascinating.' She was about to elaborate but stopped herself; Ellis had twisted in his seat to look at her and she suddenly felt awkward. 'I was really into archaeology when I was younger,' she admitted, a little embarrassed by how childish this sounded.

'Yeah? Is that why you took History?'

She nodded, recalling she'd revealed this at dinner: how much of what she said had he filed away?

'Archaeology always looks so cool . . .' said Ellis, crossing one ankle over the other on the windowsill.

'It's hard work,' Rebecca told him. 'After my A levels, I volunteered on this excavation in Tuscany, and it was exhausting.'

She took another slug of brandy, wondering why she'd brought this up; she never talked about archaeology anymore. Perhaps it was because Ellis seemed genuinely interested. Maybe it was because, after tomorrow, she'd probably never see him again. Most likely, it was just the drink.

'What did you find?' he asked.

'Ceramics, coins, animal bones – someone dug up a human skull while I was there. Apparently, we were at an old dumping site, which is why there were so many random artefacts . . .'

She trailed off, still able to feel the bumpy arid soil beneath her knees, her hands sweating in the gardening gloves she'd borrowed from Lillian, the sting of the sun on the back of her neck as it crept under the brim of her hat. Many of the other volunteers had grown frustrated over the course of the week. It was disheartening spending hours, even days, painstakingly removing layers of dirt from something that turned out to be a piece of old rubbish. But Rebecca had enjoyed it all: the meticulous methodology; the time outdoors; the prospect of easing from the earth a genuine piece of the past.

'So, shouldn't you be crawling through an ancient tomb right now?' asked Ellis. 'Uncovering some legendary lost artefact?'

'I think Hollywood might've misled you about how exciting archaeology actually is.'

'Come on, human skulls? That's exciting.'

Rebecca didn't know how to explain it, though she'd already let slip about Oxford. Sometimes, though she knew it was twisted, she wished something truly terrible had happened during her first and only term there: a bad boyfriend; a bad drug trip; a bad *something*. It would be easier to explain than *it was too difficult*. She wasn't sure exactly when she'd abandoned her ambitions of archaeology, but it hadn't been long after her return to Devon that Christmas, and certainly before she'd started at Exeter the following September. Archaeology had been for the Rebecca who'd been top of the class at a small rural school, not the drop-out still reeling from the discovery she was ordinary.

'It didn't work out,' she said again. Then, in attempt to divert the conversation, she added, 'You know, you ask a lot of questions.'

'Maybe I should do it for a living?'

'*Funny*. Did you always want to be a journalist?'

'Nah, I wanted to be a vet. I kind of just fell into journalism.'

'What do you mean, you *fell* into it?'

After a fair amount of prompting – Ellis seemed less used to being on the receiving end of a questioning – she learned he'd started writing when travelling around Central and South America after school. By the time he'd returned to the UK, he'd had a few articles published online and in magazines, and one had even found its way into the Sunday supplement of a national newspaper. He'd taken up his deferred place at Durham, but moved to London as soon as he'd graduated, where he'd worked freelance until being offered a full-time position at SideScoop.

As she listened, Rebecca couldn't help but feel impressed, even a little envious; it all sounded so spontaneous, so *easy*. She was about to ask him about SideScoop when she caught him glancing away, too quickly. Only then did she register that, at some point during his story, she'd eased her cramping legs from under the chair and hooked them over the windowsill, next to his. They seemed very pale and smooth in comparison, although the dark red polish of her toenails matched his scab. When had she stretched out? And how long had he been looking? All of a sudden, Rebecca felt even warmer than before, though pleasantly so, like she'd sunk into a freshly drawn bath.

'How do you become an archaeologist, anyway?' asked Ellis, directing his question to the hinge on the other side of the window.

Instantly, the bath drained. 'You have to do a Masters, and lots of work experience. It's really competitive.' Rebecca's breath fogged the edge of her now-empty glass as she sighed. 'I don't want to do it anymore.'

'No?'

'No.'

'Huh.'

Rebecca turned on him, frowning. 'What's that noise for?'

'Nothing,' he said, with a shrug. 'It's just I can see you as an archaeologist now, that's all.'

At first, she thought he was mocking her again, but as he held her gaze, she realised he was being earnest. She was grateful – and grateful he was here, that she hadn't come to Huxley on her own. She wanted to tell him so, to thank him, but couldn't think how to say it, especially when they were sitting so close.

Instead, she reached towards the floor for the crystal decanter. 'Another one?'

The next morning was cooler, though there had been no storm. It helped to dispel a little of Rebecca's post-alcohol fuzziness, as did the brisk walk across the back lawn. She hadn't met anyone on her way downstairs, and there had been no noise to suggest Ellis, Patricia or either of the dogs were even awake. Yet she maintained a swift pace all the way to the thicket, unwilling to be spotted from one of Huxley's windows. She wanted to undertake this expedition alone.

Once she reached the trees, Rebecca slowed down, partly because she was now concealed from view and partly because the vegetation impeded her progress. Wiry branches plucked at her clothes and the exposed parts of her skin, lumpy roots tried to trip her and at one point she had to pull something sticky from her hair, which turned out to be a spider's web.

Soon, she found the pond, just as she'd expected. Its water was so clogged with lily pads and duck weeds, its surface seemed solid and she felt she could've walked right across it without wetting her feet. On the opposite bank was a bridge that might once have been picturesque, only now its stone was smothered with lichen and moss, as though it were being reclaimed by the land. The whole clearing looked and smelled too green, too potent; it felt fetid, like an impressionist scene gone to seed.

Rebecca advanced a few steps, first testing the ground with her toes, as it was difficult to tell where the bank ended and the water began. Now what? She had found a pond at Huxley, just as there had been a pond at the bottom of the garden in the first of the *Seven Tales*. Presumably, this meant her theory that Leo had based the character of the collector on his own father was now a little less far-fetched, but otherwise what was the point of this mission? There was nothing else she could learn here, nothing else she could do; she wasn't about to dip a net into the water and attempt to fish out a nixie.

Besides, though there was a great green pond here, how could there exist a doorway that led to another realm or a threshold where the world turned to shadow?

A sudden swishing and rustling made her turn: Patricia was swiping her way through the thicket with her walking stick, Bonny and Poppy at her heels.

'I thought I saw you up ahead! How did you sleep?'

'Good, thanks!' Rebecca raised her hand in greeting, deciding not to explain her presence among these trees.

'Do excuse the mess,' Patricia continued, gesturing at the weeds as the dogs went from sniffing Rebecca's legs to nosing experimentally at the surface of the water. 'I keep meaning to pay one of the local boys to have a go at it.'

She seemed breezy today; maybe she was a morning person. It made Rebecca even more reluctant to voice the question she knew she couldn't depart Huxley without asking:

'Is this where Adeline died?'

Patricia paused in the act of jabbing at some nettles with her stick. 'How did you know that?'

'I think my dad must've mentioned it, years ago,' said Rebecca, the lie popping into her head as readily as the realisation of her grandmother's fate. 'I only just remembered.'

'What a thing to tell you! I never saw any point in dwelling on it myself – it's not going to bring her back, is it?'

'No,' agreed Rebecca, but then asked, 'Did she drown?'

She thought Patricia might clam up again, as she had in Victor's study. But after fixing her with an evaluating sort of look, her great-aunt said, 'Yes – although goodness knows how, that water's only waist-deep. I expect she got herself tangled in the weeds.'

Rebecca stared at the flecks of murky water visible beneath the greenery. 'Was she swimming?'

'I don't think so, I'm not sure she knew how to swim. Victor never really talked about it – he was too heartbroken – but she was fully dressed when they found her, so she must have fallen in. That poor, silly girl.' Patricia sighed. 'She'd wandered off first thing in the morning, so nobody even knew she'd gone.'

Perversely, Rebecca's mind overlaid the scene in front of her with another image: small, delicate Adeline lying face forward in the water, her long blonde hair glistening around her head.

'Who found her?' she asked, although she suspected she knew.

'The boy. He was the first to go looking for her, and almost drowned himself trying to pull her out. But he was too small and it was too late.'

Rebecca clutched at her collarbone: shock and sorrow were squeezing so hard at her windpipe it was difficult to breathe.

'I'm sorry, dear,' Patricia said, still prodding at the ground with her stick. 'This is why I didn't want to say anything, it's all too morbid – and it practically destroyed Victor.' She glanced over her shoulder, towards the house. 'Look, why don't we head back? I was going to make a cooked breakfast before you set off, although goodness knows what our vegetarian friend will have. Does he eat *eggs*, do you think?'

As Rebecca was beckoned away, she chanced a last look at the overgrown pond. Was Adeline truly the nixie? Had she been trapped somehow by Victor's collector? And did Patricia even know how or why her sister-in-law had died? Because in the first of the *Seven Tales,* the nixie had wanted – no, *needed* – to return to the water . . .

'Actually, I'm glad I caught you on your own this morning,' said Patricia, as they emerged from the thicket. 'I was wanting a quick word before you left.'

Pushing aside thoughts of fairy tales, Rebecca braced herself for some kind of cross-examination, possibly about Ellis – or maybe Patricia had noticed her decanter of brandy was a little emptier than it had been yesterday evening.

'You said you hadn't seen your father since you were young, is that right?'

'Um – yes.'

With the air of someone advancing with caution, her great-aunt continued, 'You said you wanted to find out about his childhood and so on, but you also asked if I knew where he was, whether I had any contact details – I assume, then, you also want to find *him*?'

As they continued across the lawn, Rebecca realised she'd not yet confronted this question herself: it had been hanging ahead of her for the past few days, like something visible but blurred in the distance, and Patricia had just nudged her towards it.

'Yes,' she said. 'I think I do.'

She half-expected her great-aunt to reproach her, or perhaps launch into another lament about her late brother. But, to her surprise, Patricia reached for her hand.

'I'm glad you came to see me, dear.' She clasped Rebecca's palm between her calloused fingers. 'It's made my heart glad to see Victor's grandchild, to know we Sampsons march on. You're a good girl, and I hope we'll stay in touch – your mother too, if she'll pardon my past rudeness. Perhaps you'll even come back and see me again sometime?'

'I'd like that,' lied Rebecca, wincing at both her great-aunt's grip and the thought of Rosalyn's horrified reaction if she ever received a letter from a relative of Leo.

'I can't tell you what to do about your father,' said Patricia, her expression suggesting she wished this weren't the case. 'It's up to you, of course – but if you do find him, I'd rather not hear about it. The way he behaved, the strain he put on Victor . . . It would be too painful for me.'

'Of course.'

'That goes for Huxley too. As I said, its doors are always open to you, but I'm afraid Leo isn't welcome here anymore.'

Rebecca nodded. 'I understand.'

'Well, then – that's good. Very good.'

Patricia exhaled loudly, perhaps relieved she'd made herself clear. After releasing Rebecca's hand, she thrust her stick in the direction of Bonny and Poppy. 'Come on, girls – inside! Then breakfast all round!'

Rebecca thought it likely this command was intended for her as well as the dogs, but hung back as Patricia disappeared through the front door. Trying to flex some feeling back into her fingers, she stared up at the ivy grasping at Huxley's façade, now consumed with another question: why would Leo ever want to come back here?

8

SideScoop

'I think we might have a new lead . . .'

In the passenger seat, his head bowed over his phone, Ellis waited for Rebecca to respond. But she hardly registered what he'd said – it was all she could do to keep her concentration on the road. In her mind, she was still in that tangled thicket, but years earlier, watching a little boy try to pull his mother from the murky water.

'Becs?'

'Hm? I mean—' She shook her head. 'Don't call me that.'

'You okay?'

'Yes.' She gripped at the steering wheel. 'Just thinking about Huxley.'

'Do you reckon it was worth going?' asked Ellis.

'Of course. Why, don't you?'

'I guess. Don't get me wrong, I enjoy staying in weird old houses for the fun of it – and it definitely gave us some insight into Leo's childhood – but I'm not sure we're any closer to finding out what's happened to him.'

'No . . .'

Was this the moment to tell Ellis about *Seven Tales*? She could explain her theory that the stories were semi-autobiographical, and even set him on interpreting them. But something stopped her: the book was private, from Leo just for her, like the shadow animals he'd taught her to make with her hands or the badger trails he'd found for them in the woods. And she liked having this secret. When Ellis had strolled into her life with all his questions and that folder of research, he'd exposed how ignorant she'd been about her own father; now, she knew something he didn't.

'*Anyway*,' said Ellis, raising his phone again, 'I might have something else here: do you remember I told you I'd emailed Leo's agent?'

'Did you?'

'Yeah, her name's Priya George. She represented him in the late 80s, before he moved to Devon. I messaged her a couple of weeks ago.'

'Right,' said Rebecca, whose thoughts were still occupied with the fairy tales. 'Did she reply?'

'She did, actually – yesterday, although Huxley's signal was so bad it's only just come in. I thought she'd been ignoring me, especially as I mentioned Leo by name, but she's offered to see me.'

'Really?' Now he had Rebecca's full attention. 'When?'

'This Thursday. She's based in Soho, so it's kind of bad timing for you – I'm guessing you won't want to make the journey to London again so soon. But I could report back afterwards?'

'No, I'll come and meet her,' said Rebecca, glossing over the fact she hadn't been invited. 'I'll drive back that morning, or—Or maybe I'll just stay in London.'

'Yeah?' Ellis seemed surprised.

'Why not?'

A week ago, she wouldn't have considered this for a moment, as it meant taking four more days off work with no notice. Today, though, Sudworth and Rowe wasn't important. What if this agent knew where Leo was?

'We have a comfy sofa if you need a place to crash?' offered Ellis.

'I'm fine, thanks,' said Rebecca, unenthused by the idea of spending multiple nights on a sofa, then curious as to who he meant by *we*. Housemates? Parents? A girlfriend? 'My best friend moved to London last year and she's always saying I should come and stay.'

Later, when Ellis was subjecting them to another questionable radio station – this one featuring endless tracks of discordant jazz – Rebecca said, 'You know that folder? The one you showed me before we met Richard Lowrie?'

'Yeah?'

'Can I take another look at it?'

'Sure. I don't have it on me, but I can photocopy it and bring it on Thursday. Or you could swing by the SideScoop office before then if you're passing?'

'Thanks.'

He opened the glove compartment. Guessing what he was up to, Rebecca held out her left hand.

'Pass me one,' she said.

There was a lot of rustling as Ellis rootled around in the sweet packet. 'Strawberry or – what's this green one – lime?'

'Lime.'

'Seriously? Who prefers lime to strawberry?'

'I do,' said Rebecca, making a hurrying gesture with her fingers.

He unwrapped the sweet and placed it in her palm. Rebecca supposed Lillian had smuggled them into the car the last time she'd given her a lift into Exeter. Enjoying the nip of slightly sour sugar on her tongue, she chanced a look at Ellis, now examining the packet again, presumably anticipating his next helping. She'd be saying goodbye to him shortly, but the meeting with the agent now meant she'd see him again in a matter of days – twice, if she went to pick up that folder. For reasons she wasn't quite ready to acknowledge, even to herself, it was the most comforting thought she'd had all morning.

'Come on up, it's the fifth floor,' a husky voice crackled through the intercom. 'And don't be a nob and take the stairs, I know what you're like.'

Rebecca grinned as she was buzzed in without being given an opportunity to speak and, deciding to heed her friend's advice, she stepped into a lift so sleek she hardly felt it move.

Amy Jarvis was waiting for her, slouched in the doorway of an otherwise anonymous corridor, dressed in a bright pink vest top and spotty harem pants, her blonde hair wet and scrunched into a topknot. 'What's this, eh? A country mouse in the big smoke?'

She all but collapsed onto the soft, bare shoulders of her oldest friend; it felt like days had passed since she'd seen anyone or anything familiar.

'This is very affectionate,' Amy noted, patting her on the back. 'Who are you and what've you done with Becca Chase?'

'Funny,' said Rebecca, before noticing a chemical odour was competing with Amy's sugary perfume. 'Why do you smell like the Chemistry lab? Did you clean for me?'

'*Please*. I was dyeing my hair when you called – don't worry, it's rinsed out now,' she added, as Rebecca swerved out of the way. 'I get greys now, can you believe it? Anyway, come in . . . Is that all you've packed for the week?'

'It was a last-minute trip,' Rebecca admitted, picking at the strap of her overnight bag as she followed Amy inside. 'Hey, this is great.'

The flat, which was in a modern complex in Greenwich, was probably of a similar size to Rebecca's, only it looked far more lived in. The sofa was strewn with magazines and crumpled clothes, while the coffee table was straining under game controllers, used crockery and several candles that had burned down to the wick. Rebecca could never have stood so much untidiness in her own living room, but here it felt welcoming.

'We've Tim's family to thank,' said Amy, referring to her boyfriend. 'We never could've afforded the rent for a place like this.'

'Where is Tim?'

'Football,' replied Amy, and whether this meant watching or playing Rebecca didn't know – or care, if it meant she had her friend to herself for a while. 'Here, come and look at this . . .'

Amy beckoned her towards a casement door, which led to a small balcony that could've benefitted from a few plants. There, they spent a couple of minutes contemplating the gap between the identical flats opposite, where it was just possible to see Canary Wharf and a sliver of the Thames.

Privately, Rebecca felt this view paled in comparison to Dartmoor, but as a latecomer to Lower Morvale, Amy had never been particularly attached to the village and its surroundings. She'd always felt the lure of London and hadn't seemed fazed that moving here might be difficult, or even a mistake. By contrast, Rebecca felt unadventurous, unsophisticated; aside from that brief, miserable term at Oxford, she'd lived in Devon all her life.

Back inside, her request for a cup of tea was ignored and Amy instead produced a bottle of white wine from the fridge, which she sloshed into two mismatching glasses.

'So,' she said, after they'd settled into the squashy blue sofa, 'what's going on, then?'

'It's quite a long story,' warned Rebecca.

'That's all right – my plan this afternoon was to do a face mask and read all this crap.' She gestured at the magazines Rebecca had just tidied into a neat pile at one end of the coffee table. 'I'd much rather hear a long story.'

'Okay . . .' Rebecca took a sip of wine as she considered how to begin. 'I don't suppose you remember *The Stowaway*?'

Amy gave a start, which struck Rebecca as a slightly odd response, even to such a random question.

'It was this children's TV show from when we were younger, I think it aired—'

Amy held up a hand. 'Yeah, yeah, I remember. We always used to watch it with our tea.'

'The Stowaway – the character, I mean, not the show – he was played by an actor called Leo Sampson, who . . .' Rebecca stopped, finally understanding Amy's reaction. 'You already know what I'm about to tell you, don't you?'

'No,' said Amy at once. Then, 'Okay, maybe. I don't know, there was a rumour going round the village for a while that your mum's mysterious ex-husband was the Stowaway, but I never really believed it. It seemed so random, especially as your mum's so . . . you know, *proper*.'

Rebecca processed this in silence. Naturally, anyone who'd lived in or around Lower Morvale for a significant amount of time would have known who her father was, but the Jarvises had moved there long after Leo had left. Rebecca supposed it was a testament to their friendship that Amy had never mentioned this rumour. In fact, Amy had only asked her about her father once – in the playground during their last year at primary school, over a shared bag of salt and vinegar crisps – and after Rebecca had changed the subject she'd never brought it up again.

'Well, it's true,' said Rebecca, 'the Stowaway's my dad.'

Amy extracted a bejewelled purple phone from the clutter on the coffee table, tapped at it for a few seconds, then held it next to Rebecca's face. 'Pull that expression, will you?'

Rebecca looked sideways to find a photo of Leo in character, wide-eyed and open-mouthed with mirth.

'Piss off,' she said, swatting the screen away.

'I can *sort* of see it . . .' Amy's eyes flicked between Rebecca and the picture. 'But mostly you look like your mum. Why's this coming up now, anyway? You've never talked about him before.'

As Rebecca began to explain, Amy reached towards the coffee table for a bottle of gold nail varnish. Wordlessly, she then lifted one of Rebecca's hands onto a cushion and set to work. Somehow, this made talking easier; Rebecca had always enjoying watching Amy sweep neat lines of polish over her nails. For a moment, she might've been back in her friend's childhood bedroom, perched on the creaky camp bed, nursing a hot chocolate loaded with whipped cream and marshmallows – an indulgence Rosalyn would never have allowed. They might've been talking endlessly of their friends, boys and their hopes for the future; in those days, Amy always had a glamorous new aspiration each week – fashion designer, film director, wedding planner – while Rebecca had been set on archaeology, even then.

These thoughts were so soothing she found it hard to focus on her account of the past week. Of course, it was just nostalgia; her mind must've edited out any bleaker moments, as it had with her returning memories of Leo. Nevertheless, Rebecca couldn't help but feel that life had been a lot simpler when it had revolved around sleepovers, school and mucking about in the village – and that she'd been a lot happier.

'I'd forgotten Richard Lowrie was in *The Stowaway*,' Amy remarked. 'He looks like a dick and all. Do you want another drink? No, I'll get it – those aren't dry.' She nodded at Rebecca's shimmering nails.

When she returned with the bottle and poured the remainder of the wine into their glasses, Rebecca started to describe her visit to Huxley.

'Wait, let me get this straight,' interrupted Amy, sinking back into the sofa. 'You went to stay at some random house in the middle of nowhere with a strange man . . . ?'

'I'd met him twice before – and it was my great-aunt's house.'

'Your aunt you'd *never* met – Becca, you might've been murdered in your bed!'

'Don't be silly.'

'Who is this journo, anyway? What's he up to?'

'What do you mean?'

'Well, it sounds to me like you're doing half his work for him.'

'Actually, I think it might be the other way around.'

'Good,' said Amy, picking up her phone once more. 'What's his name again? Ellis—?'

'Bailey.'

'And he works for SideScoop, as in—?'

'All those lists and quizzes, yeah.'

'I love SideScoop,' murmured Amy, scrolling through her phone. 'The other day, they had this thing about British food, and how it's always—Um, *hello*.'

Gleefully, she turned her phone around to reveal Ellis's profile on the SideScoop website. As Rebecca peered at the colour photo heading the page, something twitched in her chest like a lost hiccup. His hair was a little shorter, though still untidy, and he had different glasses, which made his eyes look very green. Were they that green in real life?

'Is this your journalist?' demanded Amy.

'He's not *my* journalist . . .'

'Becca, he's cute!'

Rebecca didn't think she could convincingly refute this anymore, so took another sip of wine.

'Is he single?'

'Amy, stop it – he's not exactly my type.'

'Why, too attractive? Too interesting?'

'*Ouch*,' said Rebecca, recognising this as a dig at her only serious boyfriend, Adam – although a dig not totally undeserved.

'Don't tell me you don't think he's cute,' continued Amy, cradling the phone and shooting Rebecca a mischievous glance. 'I see now why you wanted an overnight stay . . .'

'Oh, shut up – a minute ago you thought he was going to murder me!'

Amy shook her head. 'I must've meant your aunt.'

Rebecca snatched the phone from Amy's hand and placed it on the coffee table, keen to end this discussion as quickly as possible. Because what did it matter if, yes, she found Ellis *slightly* attractive? She doubted he felt the same way about her. He probably had a girlfriend, plus they lived miles apart and were completely different from one another. Nothing was going to happen.

'Do you want to hear the rest of this story or not?' she asked.

Perhaps it was the wine or that Amy was now applying a second coat to her nails, but it didn't occur to Rebecca to leave out *Seven Tales* from her account, nor her tentative theory that Leo had based the stories on his own life. Somehow, she felt Leo would've approved of Amy and her being let in on their secret. Rebecca couldn't think of anyone she trusted more than her oldest friend. A few days ago, she might've said her grandmother – but Lillian had withheld *Seven Tales* all this time, so now she wasn't so sure.

'Can I see this book?' asked Amy.

'It's in my bag . . .' Rebecca waggled her newly polished fingers.

Amy prised herself from the sofa again and when she returned Rebecca was pleased to see she was handling *Seven Tales* so carefully she might've had sticky nails herself.

'I like this,' she said, tapping at the embossed gold squiggle on the cover.

'I don't know what that is,' Rebecca admitted, studying the symbol. 'I thought it might be the logo of a publisher, but it's not a proper book or anything.'

Amy blinked at her, then laughed. 'Becca, it's the author! Look . . .'

She grabbed one of the magazines from the floor, flipping through it until she reached the horoscope page. The symbol on the front of *Seven Tales* was right at the top: apparently, it was Leo's month. Rebecca, who thought astrology was nonsense, felt slightly disappointed that the squiggle didn't represent anything more profound – and irritated she hadn't worked out its meaning herself.

'I always think the Leo one looks like the head of a girl with a high ponytail,' remarked Amy, before examining the fairy tale book far more gently than she had the magazine. 'Are these the stories? *The Collector and the Nixie*—'

'That's the one about Adeline.'

'—*The Golden Door*, *The Voyage to the Edge of the World* . . . This sounds great.'

'Really? You don't think it's a bit childish?'

'What's wrong with that? I miss stories like this. All I read these days are reports on water pollutants or shite like this.' She pushed the horoscopes back onto the floor with her toe. 'Ooh, what happens in *The Witch and the Sphinx*?'

'I don't know, I've only read the first three.'

Amy stared at her. '*Becca*!'

'I didn't think they were important until last night!'

Amy mimed hitting her over the head with the book. 'Read the rest, you div! Hey, maybe there's one about you!'

Rebecca wasn't sure this made her any keener to read on. 'I'll finish it, I will. But for now, I think it makes more sense to concentrate on real life: to have a look through Ellis's research, to see this agent . . . Those fairy tales aren't going to help me find him, are they?'

Amy didn't reply, and was evidently following her own train of thought, for she looked unusually solemn as she closed *Seven Tales*. 'Becca, have you considered there might be a reason you haven't heard from your dad in all these years?'

'You mean, have I considered he might be dead?'

Even Amy, who was used to her candour, looked a little taken aback. 'Erm, yeah.'

'Well, there's no record of his death,' said Rebecca, parroting what Ellis had told her in the office. 'There's no obituary – and surely there would be, for someone like him. For the Stowaway.'

'Yeah, I guess . . .' said Amy, fiddling with a strand of her hair, which was now dry and bright blonde.

She sounded doubtful, but didn't press the point, and for this Rebecca was grateful. It was becoming increasingly difficult to feign indifference, especially in front of someone like Amy. Leo might've been absent for most of her life, but the more Rebecca learned about him – the more she considered him as a person in his own right, not just a disappointing bit player from her past – the more she dreaded discovering that their separation was permanent; that at some point he'd departed for a place where he couldn't be found.

The Fourth Tale: The Enchanted Lute

Many years ago, there lived a young man who was down on his luck, for he had no work, gold or companions. One day, while walking in the woods, he slumped down on a fallen tree trunk, closed his eyes and said, 'Oh, how I wish I had an occupation! One that could take me all over this land, make my fortune and bring people great joy!'

He did not expect anyone to hear him, as his surroundings seemed deserted, but then there came a voice: 'You must take the wood of this tree to a luthier and ask him to craft you an instrument.'

The man opened his eyes and to his great surprise saw a strange but striking woman standing before him. The leaves of her robe were sewn together with cobwebs and her dark skin was dappled with lichen, so at first, he mistook her for a weathered bronze statue. But she told him she was a dryad and had lived in the old tree before it had fallen in a storm.

'Its wood is still imbued with my magic,' she explained, 'so if you do as I say, your wish will come true.'

Eager to change his luck, the man hurried to a luthier, who was amazed how easily the old wood bent to his hands and tools. In just a few days, the craftsman finished the most magnificent lute he had ever made, and, when the young man took it, he felt as though he were slipping his hands into a pair of perfectly fitting gloves. He had never played a note in his life, but his fingers seemed to know what to do and, as he plucked at the lute's strings, the workshop was filled with the most beautiful music he and the luthier had ever heard. It was a sound so sweet that, when he finally stopped, the room felt wintry and full of shadows.

'Keep playing,' commanded the luthier.

But the delighted young man was now impatient to see his wish come true, so he ignored the craftsman's request and set out on the road with his new instrument.

Over the next few years, he journeyed across the land, playing his lute in taverns, town halls and village squares. He earned great riches and saw many wonderful places, and everywhere he went his joyful music made people smile and laugh and sing. But the lute's song was so enchanting that nobody, including the musician himself, ever wanted it to stop. When his fingers grew tired, and he was forced to set down his instrument, it always felt as though night had come early or an icy draught had seeped under the door.

Over time, the lute's music grew even sweeter and its hold over both the young man and his listeners more powerful. He began to ask for payment at the beginning of his performances, so when he was finished he could flee while his audiences called for more. But he was as unhappy as they were when the music ceased, so he would often play and play until he was almost at the point of collapse.

His mind felt clearer if he left the lute for a while, and during these quiet periods he would consider destroying it and ending the power it wielded over him and anyone else who heard its song. He thought about throwing the instrument off a cliff or into a lake or tearing it apart with his bare hands, but could never bring himself to act upon these intentions.

Once, his travels took him back through the woods in which he had encountered the dryad. He walked between the trees calling for her, and when she eventually appeared, he told her of the lute's terrible power.

'You wished for an occupation,' she said, unmoved. 'One that would

take you all over this land, make your fortune and bring all around you great joy.'

'But the lute has made me its slave!' cried the musician. 'I fear it will destroy me!'

'Then you should destroy the lute,' advised the dryad. 'Before you do, though, consider this: what will you be without it?'

Miserably, the young man thought back to how his life had been before he had first entered these woods, when he'd had no gold, work or company. He could not bear the thought of returning to that existence now.

Several years passed and the musician played on, until one day the King heard of his skill and invited him to perform at the palace. The young man had little choice but to obey this royal command, but did so with dread in his heart, for he knew he would never be able to run away when the King demanded more music.

At court, and like always, the song of the lute was so beautiful it seemed to cast a spell over everyone in the room. As the young man had known, the King commanded he play through the night, through the next day and on into the second evening. Food and wine were brought in to sustain the listeners and many people fell asleep in their chairs, but the musician was compelled to play on and on.

During the third night, the King's middle daughter arrived. She had been born deaf and had not been invited to the performance, but curiosity had drawn her from her quarters. In the throne room, she was met by an extraordinary sight: her parents, brother, sister and all the lords and ladies of the land were completely spellbound by something, only the princess couldn't work out what.

The sole explanation was the lone figure swaying and stumbling in front of the throne. He was hunched over like an old man, and though his eyes were drooping shut, his blistered, bleeding fingers continued to pluck at the strings of a lute. As the princess watched him, her heart full of pity, the musician met her gaze.

'Please!' he cried. 'Help me!'

Of course, the princess could not hear him, but by now she had guessed what was wrong. She strode across the throne room, seized the lute from the musician's hands and smashed it against the floor three times. The wood splintered and broke, and a puff of green smoke burst from the hollow of the instrument and disappeared.

At once, the royal family and all the courtiers began to blink and stretch, as though waking from a deep and dream-filled sleep. The young man, who now felt lighter and happier than he had in years, dropped to his knees and kissed the feet of his rescuer, full of gratitude and devotion. Unused to such admiration, the princess laid a hand upon his head and silently promised she would always look after him.

Perceiving this affection between them, the King then granted them permission to marry. After a grand wedding, the young man became a prince, and, with his beloved wife at his side, lived out the rest of his days in comfort and company.

The SideScoop UK office was a large open-plan space divided by purple partitions, each of them stamped with the company's logo. This motif was everywhere – on purple mugs, umbrellas, and badges – and even the furniture was on-brand, as the office's silver stools had rounded seats, which gave them the appearance of giant ice cream scoops.

A pink-haired woman directed Rebecca to wait next to a low table scattered with flyers and bowls of foamy ice cream-shaped sweets. Rebecca couldn't see Ellis, but had a good view of some of SideScoop's other employees in their clunky noise-cancelling headphones. A few purple hoodies were slung over the backs of stools, but otherwise there didn't seem to be much of a dress code, and in just one glance Rebecca noted a waxed moustache, a sprawling shoulder tattoo and a panama hat. She was wearing a spotty summer dress and ballet pumps, an outfit she'd been pleased with this morning; now, she suspected she looked a little prim.

Perhaps this was why Rebecca felt tense, and when she caught sight of Ellis strolling across the office she leapt from her scoop-shaped stool as though it really had been chilled. Ellis's headphones were canary yellow and currently dangling around his neck. As Rebecca's eyes traced the bright curve round his throat, she experienced a small spasm in her chest and silently cursed Amy for making her feel so muddled.

'You made it,' said Ellis, stooping to help himself to a handful of the sweets on the table, and then gesturing around the office. 'What do you think of the place?'

'I think it looks like a sixth form common room.'

He grinned. 'That's probably the idea.'

As he began to rummage through his bag, Rebecca studied the sandy hair spiralling from his crown, before remembering they were far from alone.

'Well, here you go . . .'

He handed her a transparent folder, neater than the version she'd seen the previous week.

'Thanks, I—'

'Hey, Bailey?' The man in the panama hat was standing up behind his desk. 'I've got that video you've been chasing.'

'Yeah?' After a quick glance at Rebecca, Ellis dug into a pocket of his shorts and withdrew a small plastic dinosaur, which she guessed was a USB. 'Can you put it on this?'

As he headed to the man's desk, Rebecca wondered whether she should slip out, now she had the folder. But it seemed rude to go without thanking him properly, and she already felt a little guilty that Ellis was sharing his research when she hadn't told him what she'd learned by the pond at Huxley, nor about *Seven Tales*.

Rebecca had read the fourth story last night, stretched out on the futon in Amy and Tim's box room, and had liked it better than the rest. She wasn't sure why. Perhaps she was getting used to the tales or had appreciated it was the only one so far that had ended happily. What *The Enchanted Lute* had meant, though, Rebecca wasn't sure. If it was autobiographical, as she was now certain was the case with *The Collector and the Nixie*, could the princess be Rosalyn? Or was this too literal an interpretation? And if it wasn't, what had been Leo's thinking behind making her deaf?

'Sorry about that,' said Ellis, pocketing the little dinosaur. 'I'll walk you out, I was just about to go on my lunch.'

They wandered into a stark stairwell, where purple signs with arrows read, *Raspberry Ripple, Mint Choc Chip, Cookie Dough*.

'What's all that about?' asked Rebecca, gripping the steel banister.

Ellis followed her gaze. 'Oh, they're our meeting rooms.'

She shook her head. 'This place is ridiculous.'

'I knew you'd like it.'

Outside, as they blinked in the sunshine, Rebecca tried to remember where she was. To their right was Oxford Street, but which way was the tube?

'What are you up to now?' asked Ellis.

'I'm not sure . . .'

Their meeting with the agent on Thursday morning felt like a long way away – other than this research, how was she going to fill the time between now and then?

'You know, the British Museum is only about ten minutes that way?' Ellis suggested, with a nod.

'Is it?' Rebecca was unable to keep the eagerness from her voice.

'Fifteen minutes, tops,' said Ellis, laughing at her sudden enthusiasm. 'Come on, I'll show you.'

'Oh, I'll find it . . .'

'I don't mind,' he said, shrugging. 'I was only going to read my book.'

They started down a series of back roads virtually gridlocked with traffic, although the pavements were emptier here than in the shopping streets nearby. Rebecca tried to concentrate on Ellis's questions about Amy and Greenwich but was distracted by the smartly dressed office workers hurrying past with sandwiches and takeaway coffee cups. What was happening at Sudworth and Rowe right now? How were they faring without her? She'd phoned Gerry first thing, cringing as she cited *personal reasons* for taking time off, because it sounded like someone had died or she was suffering from an exclusively female ailment. Gerry had sounded panicked – 'Up to and *including* Thursday?' – but hadn't pressed her for details, presumably too afraid he might learn what the *personal reasons* were.

All thoughts of work were expelled from her mind when the pillared portico of the British Museum came into view. Weaving their way through the tourists and touts thronging by the railings, Rebecca and Ellis headed across the paved forecourt and up the museum's front steps, where she waited impatiently for the exiting crowd to subside.

She had been here twice before, once with Rosalyn when she'd been very young, and again as a teenager, with Lillian. That second visit had coincided with the height of Rebecca's obsession with ancient history, and she could still picture the empty tea cups and discarded sections of newspaper strewn across her grandmother's table when they'd caught up in the café at closing time.

Lingering on the threshold of the museum now, peering up at the daylight spilling in through the Great Court's glass roof, Rebecca remembered the thrill of that day: she could feel it still, but fainter, more distant, like an echo. In the gift shop, she'd bought her Anubis statuette, the one still cluttering up her old room. For once, the thought of it – the thought of all her archaeology trinkets – didn't embarrass her or remind her of her failure to keep up at Oxford. Instead, they prompted a twinge of nostalgia.

'Hey, Becs?'

'Rebecca . . .' she corrected, absently.

'I'll see you on Thursday, yeah? I'll email you the details of this agent.'

She turned to see Ellis easing a Tupperware from his bag. 'Aren't you coming in?' she asked.

'I'd better eat my lunch,' he said, indicating the museum's steps, where dozens more visitors were enjoying the good weather.

She gazed back into the building: the hall of Egyptian sculptures was in there, the Enlightenment Gallery, the *Rosetta Stone* . . . But, unlike him, they weren't going anywhere.

'Do you want company?' she asked.

He smiled. 'Sure.'

They settled on the steps, where the concrete was as hot as tropical sand. Beyond the railings opposite, a living statue was lurching at unsuspecting passers-by. Again, Rebecca thought of *The Enchanted Lute,* and the dryad whose dark, lichen-flecked skin had been like weathered bronze. Something about that fourth tale had stayed with her – or perhaps it was just her newfound belief that the stories might be more important than she'd first thought.

Beside her, Ellis was peeling the lid off his lunch. 'What've you got?' she asked.

'Couscous, chickpeas, tomato, an avocado that might be on the turn . . . It's a little recipe I like to call *Stuff I Found in my Fridge this Morning.*'

'Looks like you could use some chicken,' she observed.

'Looks like you won't be offered any.'

She laughed, and after he'd eaten a few mouthfuls, asked, 'So what've you been up to this morning?'

'Just working on a couple of ideas for future articles, stuff to pitch to my editor . . .' He shot her a sideways glance. 'I had a bit of a thought, actually.'

'Just the one?'

Ellis mimed poking her with his fork, then ventured, 'If we do manage to find your dad, it'd make a great story?'

'No,' she said immediately.

'I'm so glad you're giving this a chance . . .'

'I mean it.' She was only tolerating Leo's inclusion in the 90s' TV piece because she needed Ellis's help. 'A whole article would be way too much.'

'Why?' asked Ellis, genuinely curious. 'Don't you think people will want to read more than a paragraph about why and how the Stowaway disappeared?'

'I don't care if they do, it's none of their business,' said Rebecca, feeling the same protective instinct towards her father she'd experienced at Huxley and with Richard Lowrie.

'All right, all right,' said Ellis, placatingly. 'It was just a thought.'

His fork clattered against the inside of his Tupperware as he scraped out more couscous.

To change the subject, Rebecca asked, 'What were your other ideas?'

He gave her a sceptical look. 'Are you really interested?'

'Why wouldn't I be?'

'I seem to remember you calling SideScoop *pretty highbrow journalism* back in Exeter, and – correct me if I'm wrong here – I had the impression you were being sarcastic?'

Rebecca examined the toes of her shoes, which were dusty from the walk, and considered apologising. But when she glanced back at Ellis, he was bent over his lunch again, smirking. She wanted to give him a shove and, at the same time, touch the tip of her finger to that little dent in his cheek.

'Okay,' she said, 'what kind of articles would you most like to write? Not just for SideScoop, for anyone?'

'You mean, aside from *Pick a Colour and We'll Tell You Where to Go on Holiday*?' he asked, sounding more than a little sarcastic himself. Then, growing serious, he said, 'Profiles, I guess. That's how I started, when I was travelling – I just wrote about interesting people I'd met and sometimes it got published. I wouldn't mind doing a podcast one day, and I quite like reviewing . . . But yeah, profiles.'

They spent several minutes deliberating over their dream interviewees, their respective lists soon expanding to include historical figures and fictional characters. When Ellis finished his lunch, they then drifted towards the ice cream van outside the museum gates. Rebecca had to stop Ellis from paying – she owed him at least an overpriced 99 Flake for the research – so nudged him away from the counter. It was a careless gesture, but as her upper arm pressed against his chest, she was acutely aware of his warmth and height and substance; of the slight resistance of his body to hers.

'You've caught the sun,' he said, pointing at her face with his ice cream as they moved to stand in the shade of a tree.

She smiled, relieved this was how he'd interpreted the rush of colour to her cheeks. She felt nervy again, and her ice cream tasted of nothing.

'Well, I'd better get back to work . . .' Ellis continued, without enthusiasm. 'Say hi to those Egyptian mummies for me. They were my favourite when I was a kid. Me and my sisters used to pretend they'd cursed us.'

Rebecca wanted to delay him with questions. What kind of curse? When had he last visited? How many sisters did he have? As an only child herself, this last point felt especially pressing, but Ellis was already ducking out of the shade.

'I'll see you Thursday?' he said.

'See you then.'

He walked a few paces along Great Russell Street, then paused, turned back, and said, 'My flatmate's opening a bar on Wednesday night.'

'Oh?' Rebecca was now too used to him to be fazed by this apparently random conversation topic. 'Why Wednesday?'

'It's a soft opening.'

'A what?'

'He's just getting some practice in before the official launch on Saturday. *Anyway* . . .' Now it was Ellis's turn to study his shoes. 'You could come along if you wanted.'

Rebecca, blushing again, noticed he wasn't inviting her directly, merely presenting the information for her to take or leave.

'Only if you're free,' he said, before she could respond. 'I'll text you the details – have fun with all that.'

As he retreated, he nodded at her arm, the one not holding the ice cream, and when Rebecca glanced down she was surprised to find a transparent folder lodged in the crook of her elbow. For a moment, she couldn't think what it was.

9

Where Are They Now?

In Exeter tomorrow – meet you for lunch? xxxx

Rebecca considered the text from her mother, a little disappointed. She enjoyed their weekday lunches. It was restorative to escape the tedium of Sudworth and Rowe for an hour; to be treated to good food, maybe a small glass of wine, while Rosalyn regaled her with village gossip. Now, installed in Amy and Tim's cheerful living room, Rebecca was uncertain how to reply: what excuse could she give for being in London in the middle of the week? Unlike Gerry Rowe, Rosalyn was hardly going to swallow *personal reasons*.

She'd hoped the message might be from Ellis. The previous evening, encouraged by Amy and more wine, she'd agreed to go to his friend's opening, and had been obsessing over why he'd invited her ever since. Was he just being nice? Was his friend desperate for customers? Or had Ellis asked her because he was feeling at least a little of what she'd been feeling since Huxley? Whatever the reason, as he'd already texted her the bar's name, Pit-Stop, along with an address in Hackney and *see you there,* he had no reason to be in contact again.

With a sigh, Rebecca reminded herself that she needed to stop fixating on what had likely been a throwaway suggestion and focus instead on why she'd come to London in the first place. She forced her gaze back to the coffee table, deliberating between the folder of Ellis's research and *Seven Tales,* before reaching for the TV remote. Though it would tell her virtually nothing about the real Leo, what she wanted to do above anything else was watch *The Stowaway.* She wanted to watch *him.*

The programme was already onscreen, as she and Amy had watched episodes two and three – *Dick Whittington and his Cat* and *Beauty and the Beast* – on YouTube the previous night. While Rebecca settled back on the sofa, she hummed along to a few notes of the theme tune before realising what she was doing. Episode four opened in a tavern, into which the Stowaway sprung through a trapdoor like a jack-in-the-box. After crawling around behind the bar and helping himself to a number of people's drinks, he encountered a scruffily dressed Richard Lowrie, who was drunkenly boasting his daughter could spin straw into gold.

Once *Rumpelstiltskin* had ended, *Jack and the Beanstalk* loaded automatically, and when its eponymous hero had defeated his giant, Rebecca saw no harm in finishing series one with episode six, *Sleeping Beauty.* But she hesitated before continuing, suddenly troubled that there were only two series featuring Leo as *The Stowaway.* Perhaps she should ration the remaining episodes; if her search proved fruitless, this programme might be all she had left of him.

In comparison to the vibrant settings of *The Stowaway,* even Amy's sunny living room looked drab, and perhaps this was why Rebecca next reached for *Seven Tales.* She balanced the slim green volume on the tips of her fingers, like a white-gloved assistant at an auction house. The book's contents made it feel older than its seventeen years – or maybe she was handling it so lightly because this was the only copy. *Was* it the only copy? It hadn't occurred to her before but perhaps there were dozens of *Seven Tales* out there, each dedicated to someone else. Only, these were children's stories and, as far as she knew, the only child in Leo's life around 1999 had been her.

By then, her father had been gone for at least a couple of years, so, if this book was intended for her alone, it couldn't be just a bunch of stories he'd dashed off for her entertainment. The tales had to mean something, had to contain more than magic and make-believe. But if they really were autobiographical, could she decipher them?

Following the visit to Huxley, Rebecca could see how *The Collector and the Nixie* fitted Leo's early childhood, but what about the rest? Possibly, *The Golden Door* depicted his teenage years – hadn't Patricia mentioned he'd been bullied at school? – and she suspected *The Voyage to the Edge of the World* might cover the period of Leo's life after he'd stolen his father's credit card and bolted overseas, though she couldn't begin to imagine what all those pirates and sea monsters were meant to represent. And if the stories were in chronological order – which remained to be proven – she supposed *The Enchanted Lute* might concern the beginning of Leo's acting career. Perhaps the lure of the magical instrument was meant to symbolise the influence of whatever illicit substances he was first exposed to around that time.

But this was all guesswork – she knew nothing for certain. Besides, if by some miracle her speculations were accurate, who was to say Leo was an honest narrator? His whole career had revolved around his ability to pretend. Could a man who'd been immersed in the imaginary for most of his life be relied upon to write anything truthful?

But it feels truthful, Rebecca thought, turning to the next unread tale. She didn't know how, exactly, but this had to be the reason she was still carrying around this volume, and why she intended to read the remaining stories. In spite of her misgivings, she trusted him.

The Fifth Tale: The Woodcutter's Cottage

Once there was a man who was lost in a forest. It was cold, dark and frightening, and no matter which way he turned, he couldn't find his way out.

He wandered for many days, foraging for berries and nuts and drinking water from dirty puddles. The more time passed, the more afraid he grew. He saw eyes blinking at him between branches, and heard whispers in the rustling of leaves, though when he looked and listened more closely there was nothing there. The forest felt like a living beast that had swallowed him whole, and soon the man had spent so much time in its shadowy belly, he began to forget who he was, where he was from and why he had entered the place.

Then one day, the man stumbled across a cottage. At first, he thought his mind was playing tricks on him again, yet as he moved closer to the little house, he saw an orange glow of firelight through the windows, smelled wood smoke puffing out of the chimney and heard voices coming from behind the door. Reasoning not all his senses could be mistaken, he summoned the last of his strength and courage, and knocked at the door.

Moments later, a big, broad man appeared in the doorway. He had a dark bushy beard and an axe was slung over his shoulder, which, along with the logs piled up outside, suggested he was a woodcutter.

'Please, will you help me?' said the lost man. 'I have been wandering the forest for such a long time.'

The woodcutter invited him inside, where it was warm and cosy. The woodcutter's wife and two children helped him to an armchair by the fire and brought him a hot drink. Greatly relieved, the man thanked them, and admired the many beautiful wooden carvings inside the cottage, of squirrels, hedgehogs, foxes and even people. It seemed one of his hosts had a great talent for whittling.

'We are happy to feed and shelter you while you recover from your time in the forest, but we would like something in return,' the woodcutter told the man. 'Food here is scarce and there is little to thicken and flavour our stew, so in payment for your board we request you give us a finger from each of your hands. I will then carve you two new and better fingers out of wood.'

The man was so weakened from his time in the forest, he immediately agreed to this exchange. So, the woodcutter took up his axe, lopped off two of his guest's fingers and threw them into a pot on the stove. Then he set to work, whittling a lump of wood until he had made two splendid fingers, which he attached to the man's hands. After that, the family and their guest dined on the rich and delicious stew, and the man felt warm and content.

The woodcutter's guest stayed in the cottage overnight, recovering from his wanderings and the loss of his two fingers. The next day, the woodcutter's wife approached him and said, 'We are happy to feed and shelter you while you recover from your time in the forest, but we would like something in return. Food is scarce here and there is little to thicken and flavour our stew, so in payment for your board, we request you give us a toe from each of your feet. My husband will then carve you two new and better toes out of wood.'

The man looked out of the window at the dark and frightening forest, then agreed to this exchange too. So, the woodcutter took up his axe, lopped off two of his guest's toes, and threw them into a pot on the stove. Then he set to work, whittling a lump of wood until he had made two wonderful toes, which he attached to the man's feet. After that, the family and their guest dined on the stew, which was satisfying, but the man felt a little less warm and a little less content than he had the previous evening.

On the third day, while the man recovered from his wanderings and the loss of his two fingers and toes, it was the children who approached him. They repeated the words of their parents, this time requesting he give them one of his ears and the end of his nose. Once more, the man looked out of the window to the dark and frightening forest, and after some thought agreed to this exchange. Yet when he later sat down to dine with the family, his new wooden ear and nose attached to his head, the stew tasted bitter and he began to feel troubled and chilled.

On and on it continued. The man stayed in the cottage, recovering from the loss of his fingers, his toes, his ear and his nose, and every day the woodcutter or his wife or his children would approach their guest and request a hand, an ankle or an elbow in order to thicken and flavour their stew. Before long, the man grew alarmed about what might become of him if he stayed, but by the time he had decided to escape the woodcutter's cottage, it was too late: the family had taken both of his legs.

Eventually, there was no flesh, blood or bone left of the man and he became just like the wooden squirrels, hedgehogs, foxes and people inside the little house, who had also once been guests of the woodcutter. But the family liked the man above all these other creatures, for he had thickened and flavoured their stew very well, so the woodcutter's wife bored holes in the wooden man's hands, feet and head, and the woodcutter's children threaded those holes with string. Then they could move him about as they wanted, and they made him walk and wave and dance for their amusement.

When they grew tired of these games, the family left their puppet by the window, and sometimes the wooden head lolled sideways until it faced the forest. In the hollow of his timber body, what remained of the man recognised the place where he had been lost long ago, only it did not seem remotely cold or dark or frightening anymore.

Rebecca let *Seven Tales* lie open on her lap, its pages fanning into an arc that quivered from side to side, as though the book were breathing. She felt slightly sickened, as though she too had been subjected to that grisly stew and, for the first time, she was glad Lillian had withheld these stories for so long. She couldn't imagine her younger self reading *The Woodcutter's Cottage* and not being disturbed by its darkness. It disturbed her now.

Why had Leo written this vicious little story? What did it mean? And did she really want to know? Because if Rebecca was right in thinking *Seven Tales* was serialising Leo's life sequentially, this latest story likely covered his time in Lower Morvale . . .

The thought made her want to snap the volume shut and stuff it back in her bag. But most of its pages had now fluttered to the right, so she was staring at *For Birdie* again. Momentarily, it seemed the book had anticipated what she wanted to see, before she reasoned she'd turned to the dedication so often over the past week it was natural the pages should rest open at that point. Daring herself to read on, she slid her palms under the cover, but the movement sent the first page sweeping towards the others, revealing *Fletcher & Sons, 1999* on the inside cover.

Rebecca frowned: she'd been so focused on that date, she hadn't even registered the name. Reclaiming her phone from the coffee table, she typed *Fletcher & Sons* into Google and spent several frustrating minutes scrolling through joiners, estate agents and funeral directors. She had more luck on Companies House, where she was briefly excited to find an exact match in the form of an Edinburgh-based bookbinder – but the business had been dissolved three years ago and the listed address now appeared to belong to a wine bar.

Still, though: *Edinburgh*. Was that where he'd been in 1999? Eagerly, Rebecca began to type variations of *leo sampson edinburgh* into her phone and experienced another fleeting thrill at the emergence of several promising results. On closer inspection, however, they were only reviews of shows he'd appeared in during the Edinburgh Fringe of 1985 and 1986, before she'd been born.

Hadn't Ellis said that Leo had also toured with a Scottish children's theatre company? Was it possible, then, that after the breakdown of his marriage and being fired from *The Stowaway*, Leo had retreated to somewhere familiar, somewhere theatrical? Considering Rebecca now suspected *Seven Tales* had been printed in Edinburgh, it seemed more than possible, but she still didn't understand why neither she nor Ellis could find any trace of her father now, today.

Unwilling to dwell on the most obvious explanation for this, Rebecca clicked on Images, and found herself idly scanning the roofs and spires of a cityscape – of Edinburgh, she assumed, though she'd never been.

Or had she?

This thought – this doubt – seemed to come from nowhere, yet Rebecca couldn't dismiss it. Staring at the patch of cloud-mottled sky visible over Amy's balcony, she began to sift through her memory, panning for a bright nugget in the dark, until there it was: the street performers, the jostling crowd, the dark passageway she'd known she mustn't approach; that unexpected, troubling scene she'd recalled while running, but been unable to place.

Rebecca had no other memories of the city – the streets and buildings displayed on her phone screen might've been anywhere – but as reluctant as she was to rely on one hazy vision, her mind was now teeming with questions. What had been in that tunnel, where the ground had seemed to fall away? And when had she even visited? A long time ago, because she'd been small, and it must've been with Leo, because he'd been there – and at the same time not.

That doesn't make sense, Rebecca scolded herself. She gripped the top of her head, as though by compressing her skull she could squeeze out all the unimportant clutter it contained – old song lyrics and jingles, those formulas she'd learned for GCSE Chemistry – but no matter how much she strained her memory, she could conjure nothing else of Edinburgh.

Hoping it might jog her memory, she decided to inspect Ellis's research, but found no mention of Edinburgh beyond what she'd just seen online. Nevertheless, she spent a while looking through all the newspaper clippings, internet printouts and photographs the journalist had compiled. Much of the information relating to *The Stowaway* she'd already read, but there were a few articles she'd never seen: the announcement of the VHS release date; a local news piece about a school group who'd won a trip to the set; an interview with the costume designer. Better yet, Ellis had managed to find articles that offered an insight into the beginning of Leo's career, his pre-Lower Morvale days as a stage actor in London.

It appeared Leo's biggest role back then had been in a 1989 production of *Peter Pan.* The reviews Ellis had unearthed were unanimously positive and many singled out Leo, praising the energy he'd brought to the stage. Rebecca smiled at a black-and-white photograph of him in a ridiculous wig and frock coat, baring his teeth at the audience: he made a convincing, if not especially frightening, Captain Hook. She was briefly confused by a still from the same production, featuring Leo wearing a dinner jacket and a stern expression – neither of which suited him – before realising he must have played Mr Darling as well.

Peter Pan looked to be the last piece of theatre he'd done, which was odd, because aside from *The Stowaway*, the Captain Hook/Mr Darling roles seemed the most significant of his career. Did Leo make a habit of ducking out – or being forced out –

when he was on a high? But perhaps it wasn't so odd after all: 1989 was the year before she'd been born, the year Leo had married Rosalyn. Had he given it all up for her, for them?

It occurred to Rebecca she didn't even know how her parents had met. She'd never got further than the question of her father's whereabouts with Rosalyn, and if either of them had told her before Leo had disappeared, she'd been too young to remember. In the few recollections she had of that time, she'd either been with one or the other of them; puffing into straws to create bubble paintings with Rosalyn or tracing shadows in coloured chalk with Leo.

If she really put her mind to it, she thought she'd once heard their raised voices, partly smothered by the thick walls of Primrose Cottage . . . And on that day at the beach, when she'd been digging Leo and his shells out of the sand with her little red spade, her mother had been there, because Rebecca could remember Rosalyn calling her, summoning her back to the picnic blanket . . . This thought prompted a nip of annoyance: Rosalyn had been trying to separate them, even then.

Overall, though, her parents must've been leading fairly separate lives during her early childhood – which didn't surprise Rebecca, because they'd obviously been completely unsuited. The few male 'friends' Rosalyn had had since her marriage had been clean-cut, reliable and extremely boring, but her favourite fictional men – both in her classic novels and the risqué romances Rebecca wasn't supposed to know about – spent a lot of time striding across moors or rescuing women from kidnappers. Wrinkling her nose to be even contemplating any of this, Rebecca had to concede there was a wildness to Leo that Rosalyn might once have found attractive . . . But when she thought back on *The Enchanted Lute* and her idea that Rosalyn was the deaf princess, it suggested she had been *his* rescuer, not the other way around.

By the time Amy returned from work, Rebecca had sorted the photocopies into chronological order in the hope she could later cross-reference them with *Seven Tales*. Amy made no comment about all the paper scattered across her coffee table, and instead threw her handbag and keys towards the armchair, unzipped the top of her pencil skirt, and said, 'I see your boyfriend's been busy.'

'Who?' said Rebecca, emerging from a grainy copy of a theatre programme from 1988.

'Ellis,' said Amy. 'He's published that article, didn't you see?'

'What article? And—' Rebecca let out a huff of annoyance '— and don't call him that.'

'What, *Ellis*? It's his name, isn't it?'

'You know that's not what I meant.'

Amy plonked herself on the arm of the sofa and passed Rebecca her spangly phone, which was displaying the headline *Children's TV Stars of the 90s: Where Are They Now?*

Rebecca noticed what followed appeared longer than most SideScoop articles, which were usually mostly pictures. As she scanned the text, she caught glimpses of the names of programmes he'd mentioned during their first meeting – *The After School Club, Can You Capture the Castle?* – but skipped straight to the section on *The Stowaway*.

Back in '95, the undisputed star of BBC One's The Stowaway *was Leo Sampson, whose spirited lead performance as the wanderer lost in famous fairy tales quickly endeared him – and, by extension, the show – to a whole generation of children. But today it's difficult to ignore the presence of Richard Lowrie among* The Stowaway*'s cast. Now considered one of Britain's most esteemed veterans of stage and screen, Lowrie was usually relegated to the role of stern king* *or hapless father during his time on the programme (although he's particularly memorable as Zeus in the series two episode, Perseus and Medusa).*

The article went on to detail Lowrie's post-*Stowaway* career, then covered a couple of points from the interview the previous week, including that the actor's young grandchildren had influenced his decision to accept the role. Leo wasn't mentioned again.

'You look worried,' said Amy, as Rebecca handed back her phone. 'I thought you'd be pleased there's hardly anything about your dad.'

Rebecca was quiet for a moment. She was impressed by how adeptly Ellis had shifted the focus from Leo to Lowrie, and it was true she'd wanted her father to feature in this piece as little as possible. At the same time, though, the article's publication told her Ellis truly had given up on finding Leo, despite all the research he'd done. Did that mean he thought Leo lost for good?

'Ellis didn't say anything about this yesterday,' she said, mentally revisiting their conversation on the museum steps.

'Maybe he forgot?' suggested Amy, with a shrug. 'Weren't you busy feeding each other ice cream or something?'

Rebecca ignored this comment, especially as she'd just realised something else: 'And we're supposed to be meeting this agent on Thursday . . .'

'So?'

'So, why's he bothering with that if he's finished his article? Why's he still helping me?'

With a sigh, Amy reached out and gave Rebecca's topknot an admonishing flick. 'Oh, Becca,' she said, her expression somewhere between amused and pitying, 'why do you think?'

'Hello, Petal – you've found your phone, then?'

'What?'

'I thought you must've lost it, because you didn't reply to my text.'

'What text?'

'About tomorrow,' said Rosalyn, with a touch of impatience. 'I was thinking we could try that new place off Cathedral Close. You know, the little bistro . . .'

Rebecca pressed her fingers to her left temple. How could she have forgotten Rosalyn's message about lunch? She still didn't know how to get out of it, so regretted picking up this call – only, the day had generated so many questions, speaking to Rosalyn hadn't seemed a bad idea.

'I can't do tomorrow, Mum, I'm in London at the moment.'

'*London?*' Rosalyn sounded as though she'd just revealed she was on the moon. 'What are you doing there?'

Rebecca settled on a half-truth: 'Seeing Amy.'

'In the middle of the week? Is she all right?'

'She's fine, it was a last-minute thing. Can we have lunch next week?'

'Oh, I'm *so* disappointed, Petal, I haven't seen you since our holiday – I have pictures! When are you coming back?'

'Thursday.'

'You'll have to come to the village at the weekend, then.'

'All right,' said Rebecca, reflecting that a visit to Lower Morvale would also give her the opportunity to talk to Lillian – properly, this time.

While Rosalyn began to suggest various London-based activities, Rebecca urged herself to bring up Leo. She couldn't let this opportunity slip away. But despite everything she'd done over the past week or so, somehow it was much more intimidating to simply ask her mother, *How did you meet him?* Or, *Do you know if he's still alive?* Or even, *Why did you tell Nana I wanted nothing to do with him?* Whatever her question, she had to choose it carefully, because Rosalyn would likely try to shut down the conversation as quickly as possible.

'Mum,' she said, interrupting an anecdote about the British Library, 'have I ever been to Edinburgh?'

Though she enjoyed Ellis's method of lobbing questions at people, it would've been useful to see Rosalyn's face as she'd spoken. As it was, Rebecca only had silence to interpret.

'Mum?'

'*Edinburgh*?'

'Yes.'

'What are you asking that for?'

'Amy and I were thinking of going sometime – you know, for a minibreak.'

'A minibreak . . .' Rosalyn repeated, absently. 'Well, I think the festival's on at the moment, so it'll be very busy, very expensive.'

'Yeah, not *now*,' said Rebecca, growing impatient herself. 'Next year or something. We were talking about it last night. Amy's never been, but I couldn't remember whether I had . . .'

'No, of course you haven't,' said Rosalyn, suddenly firm. 'You haven't been to any of Scotland – you've barely been north of London.'

'That's what I thought,' said Rebecca, beginning to suspect she didn't need to see her mother's face to know she wasn't telling the truth.

After the call, she sank back against the lumpy futon that had become her temporary bed. Next door, Amy and Tim were absorbed in a courtroom drama, but Rebecca had retreated to her box room, intending to use the early night as an opportunity to mull everything over.

The trouble was, she couldn't control the direction of her

thoughts and, as much as she tried to wring her memory for something else of Edinburgh, Ellis kept popping into her head. Was there any truth to Amy's theory about why he was still helping her? The idea made Rebecca pleasantly jittery. She supposed his feelings might be clearer when she went to this bar tomorrow night, this Pit-Stop – if she went, that was, because now it felt daunting, and she kept weighing up excuses to get out of it.

Stop thinking about all that, she scolded herself, casting around for a distraction. Her gaze landed upon *Seven Tales,* which was sitting on the pile of research she'd tidied from the coffee table. Rebecca hadn't read any further since *The Woodcutter's Cottage,* the violence of which had shocked her. With its lonely woodland setting and that greedy, sinister family, she still couldn't shake the suspicion that the tale likely covered Leo's time in the village, with the Chases – though she felt hugely disloyal for even considering this, and far less sympathetic towards her father than she'd been of late. Nevertheless, now she was eager to be preoccupied by something other than Ellis, and with Rosalyn's lie about Edinburgh fresh in her mind, Rebecca reached for the little green volume and turned to the penultimate story.

The Sixth Tale: The Witch and the Sphinx

Long ago in a desert, a man discovered a golden egg buried in the sand. Delighted with this unusual treasure, he put it into his pack and told nobody what he had found.

Soon afterwards, a huge sandstorm separated him from the rest of his clan, leaving him lost with only a few rations. In the company of only his shadow, he wandered for many days, quickly running out of food and water. Then, just as he was close to death, he saw an oasis in the distance with a sparkling pool, lush green trees and a small hut. The man hurried towards this welcome sight, drank deeply from the clear water and begged for a little food at the hut, whose occupier was an ugly old crone.

'If I let you eat at my table, what will you give me in return?' she asked, leaning on a knobbly stick.

The man had but one possession now, and though he did not want to part with it, he offered the crone the golden egg. She accepted it at once and, while the man ate, placed the egg in her stove and lit a fire. As the flames licked the shimmering shell, it began to crack, until a beautiful red bird had hatched from within.

When the man saw this magnificent creature, he was overwhelmed with affection and begged the old crone to let him keep it. But she refused, reminding him he had given up the egg for a meal, and with a wave of her gnarled stick she created for the bird a golden cage.

'If you let me have this beautiful bird, I will give you anything you want in return,' said the man.

'There is something I desire,' replied the witch. 'Many years ago, a sphinx passed this oasis and stole three bottles from me. One contained Beauty, another Joy and a third Youth. These days, that same sphinx resides in a cave in the north of this land. She will recognise me, but if you go in my place and retrieve those bottles, I will give you the bird.'

The man agreed to this at once, but asked, 'How am I to travel to the north of this land when I have no possessions to my name?'

From a battered trunk, the witch pulled out an old leather mask, the kind that might protect a person's face from desert winds.

'This mask contains a spell,' she said. 'Those who look upon the wearer will see whoever they want to see and treat him kindly. But be warned, its magic is strong and you must only wear it when necessary.'

So, the man set off on his journey. As the witch had said, when he wore the mask, people treated him with great kindness. He was given a camel and supplies, and was invited to dine and travel with every group of merchants he passed. It felt good after the loss of his clan, but he heeded the witch's warning and used the mask sparingly.

Eventually, he reached the cave of the sphinx. She was a dazzling creature, part-woman, part-lion and part-eagle. When he saw her, the man bowed low and, knowing he must tell the truth, asked, 'Oh sphinx, may I be permitted to take a treasure from your lair?'

She looked down at him, her long tail swishing from side to side. 'You may,' she said, 'but only if you answer my riddle correctly. If you answer wrongly, I will kill you. Do you wish to hear the riddle?'

The man thought of the bright red bird, and replied, 'I do.'

So the sphinx said:

I'm always out of reach,
but I burn you just the same,
I bring both life and death,
do you think you know my name?

The man, who had never been known for his mind, considered this for a long time. He thought and thought, repeating the riddle to himself, until the hot sun overhead began to burn his nose – and then he realised.

'Sun!' he said. 'The answer is the sun.'

'You may enter,' said the sphinx, with a nod. 'Take only one item from my lair.'

The man hurried past her and into the cave, which was filled with many treasures. After much searching, he discovered an elegant crystal bottle labelled Beauty, which he pocketed. Knowing he must take no more, he began the long journey back to the oasis.

When he returned to the hut, the witch snatched the bottle from his hands and drank its contents in one gulp. Before his eyes, she began to transform: her back unbent, her teeth straightened, her warts disappeared, until she was very beautiful. But the man only had eyes for the bird, which had now grown bigger, more magnificent and acquired a lovely song.

'Now will you give this creature to me?' he asked.

'I am still wretched and I am still old,' said the witch, studying her reflection in a looking glass. 'You may have the bird once you have brought me my other bottles.'

So, he set off once more, only this time he was wearier and wore the mask more often. This made the journey easier, but he was given gifts he did not need and tarried too long with the silk and spice merchants, distracted from the course of his quest.

When he reached the sphinx for a second time, she did not seem surprised to see him. He repeated his request, and she repeated her response: if he answered her riddle, he would be able to take one object from her lair.

I fit inside your palm,
yet for many miles I'm sprawled,
I'm made of rocks and time,
can you guess what I am called?

It seemed to the man this riddle was even more difficult than the first, and he thought about it for so long he ended up sitting on the ground and running his fingers through the sand – and then he realised.

'Sand!' he said. 'The answer is sand.'

'You may enter,' said the sphinx, with another nod. 'Take only one item from my lair.'

This time, when the man crept into the cave, he was tempted to look for both potions. However, he was afraid of the sphinx's wrath, so when he found a round yellow bottle marked Joy, he departed.

Upon his return to the oasis, the witch seized the second bottle from his hands and drank its contents in one glug. She was then overcome with glee, but when the man requested she give him the red bird, which was now more splendid than ever, she refused unless he returned the last bottle.

So, the man set off for a third time, and he was so exhausted from his travels he did not take off the magic mask. As a result, he took a detour, and lingered with merchants for many months. When he finally remembered his mission, he tried to peel the leather from his face, but it was stuck to his skin and would not shift. Frightened, but determined to win his beloved bird, the man journeyed on.

When at last he reached the sphinx, he repeated his request and she repeated her terms.

'But think on this,' she added. 'I know you are taking those bottles

back to the desert witch, who first gained them by dark magic. So, tell me, do you really want to hear my riddle?'

The man realised this was a warning, yet he could only think of the red bird, so he replied, 'I do.'

The sphinx said:

You're daring and you're tough,
yet I see right through your mask,
and if you want your prize,
your name is all I ask.

The man's heart quickened. What was his name? It was the simplest riddle so far, but he had been wearing the mask so long he could not remember. How had they used to catch his attention in his clan? What name had his mother whispered? He had forgotten.

Knowing he was in grave danger, the man pretended to think, pacing with wide strides until the sphinx grew distant. When she realised what he was doing, she roared, rose up on her hind quarters and tried to strike at him with her lion's claws, but he was now beyond her reach and able to sprint over the hot sand until her lair was out of sight.

He returned to the witch angry and empty-handed.

'Where is my Youth?' she demanded.

'I do not have it,' he replied, 'but I want my bird.'

Before she could reach for her staff, the man seized the cage. But he was still wearing his mask, and the bird, not recognising him, gave a cry of fear. Screaming curses, the witch clawed at the other side of the bars and they each pulled until the cage door fell open and the bird tumbled out. It flapped its great red wings, flew out of the hut and soared high into the air, where it burst into flames.

'No!' cried the man, dashing out into the desert as the ashes of the phoenix began to drift down. 'Come back!'

'It is no use,' the witch told him. 'Eventually, some of those ashes may make another egg, but it will take many lifetimes to find it.'

The man did not hear her. He had sunk to his knees to try and gather up what remained of the bird, but all he was left grasping was sunlight and sand.

Rebecca pressed her fingertips to the centre of her chest, trying to allay that same ache she'd experienced on last week's run, when she'd finally allowed herself to remember him. It now seemed impossible she'd been so unaffected by the first few tales, and even her consternation following *The Woodcutter's Cottage* paled in comparison to being in the grip of this feeling, which had left her slightly breathless.

Were the stories changing, or was she? One thing was for certain: *Seven Tales* was becoming easier to interpret. Rebecca might not have known what the sphinx or all those bottles were supposed to mean, but otherwise she was fairly sure this story charted the breakdown and messy aftermath of her parents' marriage, while the mask the protagonist was obliged to wear was surely symbolic of Leo's time in *The Stowaway*. Though, again, Rebecca felt deeply uncomfortable – even angry – that, within a few stories, Rosalyn had transformed from a gentle princess into a conniving old witch.

Yet it wasn't just this cruel depiction of her mother that had left Rebecca gasping for breath, winded by words written so many years ago. It wasn't even her mixed up feelings towards the story as a whole, nor the relentless melancholy that infused this and all the other tales. It was that longed-for bird in its golden cage; it was that, for the first time in what was beginning to feel like a continuous narrative, she herself had appeared.

10

Pit-Stop

From the look of its exterior, Pit-Stop had started life as a repair garage. It was a prefab structure with four large windows that might once have contained roll-up doors and a concrete terrace, where the white lines of old parking spaces were still visible. Inside, though, the scene was softened by string lights – the bar's theming remained true to its motoring origins. As Rebecca entered with Amy and Tim, her gaze was drawn towards the corrugated iron roof, where a stripped car body was suspended like a skeleton in a natural history museum. It even smelled industrial, although she suspected the pong of paint and sawdust was due to the bar's newness rather than an attempt at authenticity.

'I thought tonight wasn't the official opening?' Amy called above the sudden blare of noise.

'It isn't,' replied Rebecca, who could understand her friend's confusion. Considering it was midweek, Pit-Stop was packed – although this was probably due to the half-price cocktails promised by the flyers littering the tables.

Fiddling with the ends of her hair, which she rarely wore loose, Rebecca studied the crowd. Most people were in their 20s and 30s, and the women, with their perfect flicks of eyeliner and deliberately clashing prints, seemed to have made much more effort with their appearance than she and her Exeter friends would've for a weeknight at The Crown.

'See, we're not too dressed-up,' Amy said, as though reading her mind.

Rebecca's hand moved from her hair to the hemline of the short, bottle-green dress her friend had lent her for the evening. Having only packed for a weekend at Huxley, she was borrowing everything from Amy, who had a much curvier figure. Conscious of this, Rebecca began to pluck at the low neckline of the dress, which lay very flat on her own chest, until Amy noticed and slapped her fingers away.

'Stop it, you look hot. Now where's this Ellis?' she demanded, like an older relative determined to be embarrassing.

'*Amy . . .*'

'All right!' Amy held up a hand, and several gold bangles clinked down her arm. 'But you remember our deal: no talk about work or Devon, and definitely no talk about your dad. Just relax, will you?'

Tim, who was tall, curly-haired and affable, remarked, '*Relaxing*, Becca, is this thing people do when they—'

'Oh, don't you start,' she huffed.

It wasn't that Rebecca thought having a night off was a bad idea – for the past few days, her mind had felt like a pot threatening to bubble over – she just wished Amy had let her spend it in the flat or at a quieter bar closer to Greenwich. Given how busy Pit-Stop was, Rebecca doubted Ellis would have noticed if she hadn't turned up.

'Drink?' suggested Tim, flyer in hand.

Amy peered around his arm to read it. 'What's in *Engine Oil*, d'you reckon?'

Rebecca, who hadn't been able to eat much of her dinner, had no intention of trying any dubiously named cocktails and was about to tell them so when she spotted Ellis, weaving around the tables towards them. Once again, something in her core jumped at the sight of him, as though she'd tripped and only just recovered her balance. His glasses made it difficult to tell for certain, but she thought she saw his gaze dart up and down her dress. To distract herself from the surge of heat this inspired, she tried to identify something annoying about his appearance and landed upon the dark red braces he was wearing over an off-white shirt, which made him look like he was going to a retro fancy dress party.

When he reached their group, she announced, unnecessarily, 'I brought my friends', then introduced Amy and Tim. Ellis shook Tim by the hand and then Amy, who he also kissed on the cheek. Amy didn't seem fazed by this – in fact, she appeared to have expected it – but Rebecca thought it a bit much, a bit *London.* Until, that was, Ellis leaned down to kiss her cheek too, murmuring, 'It's good to see you', in her ear.

His aftershave – which she'd not registered before – was slightly spicy. She would've been content to stand there and breathe it in a little longer, and perhaps this was why, when he drew back, she couldn't think of anything to say. Instead, she simply returned his smile: he really did look pleased to see her, which made her pleased to see him, in spite of the braces.

Amy glanced between them, then gave Tim a shove. 'Come on, you – *bar.*'

'First round's on the house,' said Ellis, shaking his head when Amy showed him the flyer. 'Derek'll give you a freebie. I'll introduce you . . .'

As they began to cut through the crowd, Rebecca glanced over her shoulder to check her friends were following, discovered Amy giving her the thumbs up and scowled.

Derek, it emerged, was the bar's owner, and Ellis's flatmate. He was big and stocky, with a dark beard, a Canadian accent and an air of having recently wandered in from the wilderness.

He seemed entirely underwhelmed by the evening, and when Rebecca, Amy and Tim congratulated him, he merely lifted his large shoulders, as though everything from the silver bar top to the illuminated shelves of craft beers and spirits had arrived there by chance.

He did, however, present them with four free Engine Oil cocktails in a tray shaped like a toolbox. The orangey concoction had the gloopy sweetness of children's medicine and, among its other ingredients, Rebecca thought she could taste Cointreau and maple syrup. By the time she remembered she hadn't intended to drink any cocktails, her tumbler was half-empty.

They planted themselves at the bar, where they saw plenty of friends and relatives come to congratulate Derek and his team. Initially, Rebecca stuck close to Amy, who had the enviable ability to chatter away to anyone. But the more Derek refilled her glass from what she hoped was a replica oil can, the more independent Rebecca's conversations became, until she was swapping theories about her favourite police procedural with one of Derek's cousins, and being talked through a running app by a girl who also worked for SideScoop.

Ellis remained close, making introductions and drifting in and out of her discussions. He seemed to know everyone, which at first Rebecca found irritating; she wanted to talk to him on his own, to recapture the intimacy of their conversations on the museum steps and in Huxley's kitchen. Soon, though, she decided there was something quite appealing about the way he kept returning to her barstool and, as Pit-Stop grew busier and louder, how they repeatedly caught one another's eye, their exchanges now more secretive.

The evening had a languid, resinous quality and, as it slipped by, Rebecca found herself nudged around the venue as though borne by some invisible current. At the games tables under the stairs, she beat Tim at air hockey, though if there were rules, she didn't know them. On a section of floor by the speakers, where people had started to sway, Amy tried to drag her into one of the dance routines they'd devised as teenagers for the village show. In the bathroom, while she reapplied lip balm, her hair was stroked by a girl she'd never met, who moaned to her friend, 'See, *this* is the colour I want . . .'

By the time she was back at the bar, waiting for a glass of water, her phone was buzzing in her bag. Automatically, she looked for her friends, but they were nearby, at the air hockey table again. Amy's arm was around Tim's waist, her thumb hooked into one of his belt loops and, as Rebecca watched, he leaned down to brush something from her cheek; a smudge of make-up, perhaps, or an eyelash. The sight made Rebecca feel slightly envious, though she herself found Tim about as alluring as a lamppost. She wondered when they'd get engaged; it was definitely a question of when, rather than if.

'Your friends are cool.'

She turned on her barstool: Ellis had found her again.

'Yours too,' she said, making a sweeping motion that included the entire venue.

He looked rumpled and sleepy and handsome. Her phone was ringing once more, but she ignored it. She wanted to tell him about Amy, about growing up in Lower Morvale, about *everything* – but at the same time she had a strong urge to snap one of his braces.

'What's so funny?' he asked.

Rebecca, who wasn't aware she'd been laughing, gave a contented shrug. Then, realising this was the first time that evening they'd spoken one-on-one, she asked, 'Are we still meeting this agent tomorrow?'

'Yeah, of course.' Ellis seemed surprised by the question. 'Why wouldn't we be?'

Rebecca considered telling him she'd seen his article, but, once again, she liked knowing more than he did, so gave another shrug.

Ellis edged closer to her stool, his elbow almost missing the bar as he leaned against it. 'How are you getting on with that folder?'

'Yes, fine. Although . . .'

She nodded in the direction of the air hockey table, 'I promised them I wouldn't talk about any of that tonight.'

She thought Ellis might ask what she was allowed to talk about – or perhaps point out she was the one who'd broached the subject. Instead, he reached out to twist at a bead of her borrowed bracelet, his fingertips tickling the thin skin of her wrist.

'Hey, Becs?' His voice so quiet she almost couldn't hear him. 'I don't suppose—?'

'*Bailey*!'

Yet another lot of Ellis's friends – how many did he have? – were calling him from across the bar. He hesitated, still playing with the bracelet, before glancing around at the group now beckoning him over.

'One sec,' he muttered. 'They're my sister's mates, I'd better— I'll be right back.'

Rebecca wanted to grab his hand, make him finish the question he'd started to ask. Instead, she watched him go and, as he was bundled into the group's embrace, her stare locked on a busty girl in bright red lipstick whose dark hair had been twisted into victory rolls – *was* there a fancy dress party she didn't know about? As this overdressed intruder began to shout in Ellis's ear, Rebecca felt suddenly sulky: *he* might be coming right back, but *she* would not be here – people wanted to talk to her too. Slipping from the barstool, she fumbled for her phone and squinted at the missed call alerts: *Chris Fenton.* Perfect.

It wasn't cold outside, but the night air was like a splash of water to her face. She was woozier than she'd realised. All the picnic tables in the car park-turned-terrace were occupied, but after passing through the apple-scented mist of a group vaping by the road, Rebecca carefully lowered herself onto a flat-topped concrete bollard, mindful she wasn't wholly in control of her own limbs. When she was certain of her balance, she smoothed the skirt of her silky green dress towards her knees, admiring the way it complemented her gold nails. She was glad she'd worn it.

Unlike Lower Morvale, there were no stars here, and because of the time of year – or maybe the smog – it wasn't even dark; the silhouettes of tall industrial chimneys were stark against the mallow-coloured sky. The street in front of Pit-Stop was empty save for a few parked cars, but Rebecca could hear the drone of nearby traffic and a siren keening above the pulsing bar at her back.

I'm out in London, she thought, stretching out and almost toppling off her bollard. After checking the vapers hadn't noticed this near-tumble, she crossed one bare ankle over the other, and decided, *If I wanted, I could live here – I could live anywhere.*

While she considered this unexpected idea, a fox trotted out of the shadows on the other side of the road and began to nose at a discarded burger box. Rebecca sat forward, but when a high-pitched laugh behind her startled the animal into stillness, her interest gave way to unease: the fox's now-motionless form reminded her of the carved creatures in *The Woodcutter's Cottage*. She shuddered, trying to dispel the association. She hated that tale.

Nevertheless, she reached for the book, before remembering she was wearing a tiny, pale gold handbag of Amy's, and *Seven Tales* – along with talk of work and Devon and her father – had been banned from this evening. It felt strange, even lonely, to be away from it. Since Lillian had passed it on, and certainly since Huxley, Rebecca had grown used to having the book nearby or catching sight of its title glittering at the bottom of her own bag.

Her mobile rang for a third time.

'*Chaser – oi oi!*'

Rebecca leaned away from her phone, waiting for Chris to stop shouting. Why had she answered again? A thoroughly unwelcome memory of their brief intoxicated tussle entered her mind and she grimaced.

When it seemed safe to return her mobile to her ear, Chris was saying, '—ruled for nine days?'

'What?'

In the background, she could hear their friend Steph repeating the question, and remembered it was Wednesday: pub quiz night at The Crown.

'Isn't this cheating?' she asked Chris.

'We finished ages ago. Don't you know?'

'It's Lady Jane Grey.'

'Aw balls, we could've won if you'd been here – top three at least. Where are you, Chaser?'

'London.'

'*Where*?'

'London.'

'*London*?'

Rebecca sighed, and while Chris tried to remember some of the other questions, she pictured him and the other members of We Mean Quizzness huddled in their usual corner booth, probably picking at a few bowls of chips. The scene felt cosy safe, and very far away. A part of her wanted to be there with them – and a lot of her now wanted chips.

'When are you coming back to work?' asked Chris.

'I don't know, Friday?'

'Yeah?'

She said nothing, unwilling to commit herself further. After a few seconds, Chris sniggered.

'Gerry says it's lucky you haven't signed that contract yet.'

'What do you mean?'

'He said he could just change the name and give it to the next person – you know, if you don't come back.'

'*What?*'

Rebecca's exclamation was far louder than she'd intended and caused the fox, which was still lurking on the other side of the road, to dart behind one of the parked cars.

'He was only joking,' said Chris, quickly. 'It was just a bit of banter.'

'Well you can tell *Gerry* . . .' began Rebecca, drawing herself up on her bollard, indignant but unsure where her sentence was heading. 'You can tell *Gerry* . . . I quit.'

'Aw, come on, don't be like—'

She jabbed at the screen of her phone until she managed to end the call, then made a *pfft* noise, which she hoped sounded scathing. Mostly, though, she felt hurt: she'd been working as a temp at Sudworth and Rowe for almost three years, but apparently it had taken three days for them all to start joking about her absence and making plans to hand her permanent contract to someone else.

If it means that much to you, why haven't you signed it?

She gave a dismissive flick of her head. It wasn't as though she'd had the contract very long. Deciding to check the date on the digital copy, she started to search through her emails, which were blurry – how many of those stupid cocktails had she had? – but as her thumb slid up and up, she was forced to concede it had been a while.

Her phone buzzed, signalling her inbox had updated itself,

and Rebecca blinked in surprise when she saw who'd sent the newest message: *Lillian Chase*. She'd never received an email from her grandmother before.

Dearest Becca,

I've been thinking a lot about our last conversation and what a mistake it was not giving you your dad's book until now. I hear you're coming to the village this weekend – perhaps, if you've had a chance to read the stories, the two of us could have a proper talk then?

Lots of love,
Nana xoxo

It took Rebecca almost a minute to read this email – her phone screen seemed to have duplicated itself and she had to resort to closing one eye to stop the words oozing out of focus – but she knew it would've taken her grandmother far longer to tap out the message on her tablet. Why had she sent it? To ease her conscience? And what did it matter, whether or not Rebecca had read *Seven Tales*?

The message should've come as a relief – Lillian was offering her answers – but instead Rebecca felt heavy; all her guilt and confusion had returned and were pulling her down, like weights on a diver's belt. She should've been more patient. She should've waited for this, rather than haring across the country, going behind her mother's back and risking her job for a man who hadn't cared about her in years – for a man who was probably dead. She didn't belong in London, in bars where they poured cocktails out of oil cans. She wasn't even wearing her own clothes. She wanted to go home. She wanted chips, and to go home.

When she stood up, the horizon tipped, and the ground turned to sponge beneath her shoes. Inside, the music was pounding and the hardware smell was now stifled by the odours of beer and perfume and people. Rebecca bumped through the crowd towards the chair where she'd left her jacket, which she prised from the blazers and cardigans piled on top. Reluctant to face her friends – Amy would laugh at her for being drunk – she decided to leave them at the air hockey table and head back to the flat alone; she could probably remember which tubes to take.

She was almost at the door again when she saw Ellis. He was halfway across the bar and seemed to catch sight of her in the same moment, because they both stopped. Rebecca's stomach gave a feeble flip, like a cautious pancake toss, but she wished she'd managed to slip out unnoticed. She couldn't cope with being teased and challenged right now; she was too tired to talk, too tired to think.

Ellis looked from the door to the jacket slung over her right arm and moved towards her. His walk was slightly teetering, his expression unusually serious – was he annoyed? Rebecca tried to cast her mind back to their previous conversation, which was foggy, while wondering how to explain why she was leaving without saying goodbye. She inhaled to speak, but by now he was right in front of her, much too close to her, and before she could make sense of what was happening, he'd reached out to cup her jaw and was guiding her face to his own.

Rebecca let out a chirp of surprise and froze, as stunned by his conviction as she was by the kiss. Her first thought was that he tasted of that cocktail; her second was that she must too. She closed her eyes, dizzy again. There was a swooping sensation in her torso and the rest of her felt untethered, like she was on a fairground ride.

Too soon, he let her go. She stared up at him, barely able

to believe what he'd just done. She thought he might laugh, try and pass it off as a joke, but he was still wearing that resolute expression, which was now almost expectant, as though he'd asked her one of his questions.

Rebecca knew her answer, but because his anticipation was intriguing – *exciting* – she took her time dropping her jacket towards the nearest chair, not noticing or caring whether it landed there or on the floor, and looping her index fingers around his braces. When she gave them an experimental tweak, Ellis stepped forward, so she repeated the action, backing unsteadily away from the door and taking him with her. His attention was on her hands, his slightly raised eyebrows suggesting polite interest in what was going on, yet he couldn't pretend indifference anymore: she could feel the rapid rise and fall of his chest against her knuckles, the heat of his skin through his shirt.

Once she'd steered them into a dimmer, less public corner, Rebecca slid her palms towards his shoulders and raised her face, knowing he'd kiss her again – which he did, immediately. They arranged themselves into an eager, clumsy embrace, their knees knocking together until her fingers fastened behind his neck and his hands moved to her waist, to her hair. He was warm and sweet and as she pulled him closer, she sighed against his lips, her body full of giddy desire, her mind completely clear.

11

The Agent

'Do you want to go ahead on your own?'

Blearily, Rebecca looked up from the cereal bar she was mashing between her fingers. The pretty blonde receptionist of G&B Talent was peering over at her, having just replaced the handset of her phone.

'Sorry, what?'

'Your colleague, he's a little late,' said the receptionist, nodding up at the grey numberless clock above her desk, which might've read quarter past ten. 'And Ms George is ready now, if you want to go through?'

Rebecca did not want to go through. She wanted to shrink to the size of a paperclip, slide between the cushions of this squashy chair and curl up in its dark, quiet innards until her head stopped throbbing. But she stuffed her uneaten cereal bar back into her bag – knowing it would make a mess – and said, 'Okay, thanks.'

The receptionist pointed down a short corridor. 'It's the first room on the right. I'll send your colleague through when he arrives.'

'Thanks,' said Rebecca again, suppressing a groan as she pulled herself to her feet, 'but it might just be me this morning . . .'

It wasn't exactly a surprise Ellis hadn't turned up, especially now his article was done. Perhaps it was even a relief. Shuffling down the agency corridor, Rebecca cringed as more details from the previous evening returned to her – had she been sitting on his *lap* at some point? What was the matter with her? What was the matter with both of them, pawing at each other in that corner like a couple of teenagers?

Thank God Amy had come looking for her: where and how might she have spent the rest of the night otherwise? Although beneath all her queasiness and mortification, there lingered a craving Rebecca suspected might've been satisfied had she and Ellis been left to their own devices – and at least, if she'd woken up next to him, she could've made him attend this interview.

Realising she'd been staring at a brass sign reading *Priya George, Talent Agent* for some time, Rebecca knocked at the door in front of her with a sense of mounting dread. How was she going to do this by herself, let alone with a pounding headache?

'*Come in!*'

The office beyond was small and monochrome: the desk, filing cabinet and leather chairs were black and the floor, walls and piles of scripts bright white. It might've resembled a cramped bachelor pad had it not been for the excess of headshots arranged about the walls like a macabre family tree. Rebecca, unable to resist gazing around at the sombre-faced actors, recognised only the few in the biggest frames.

Behind the desk sat an attractive woman who must've been in her late fifties, though her skin was smooth, particularly around her heavily made-up eyes, leading Rebecca to conclude she possessed either good genes or a good surgeon. With her dark shapeless clothes, artfully tousled hair, and an excess of gold jewellery around her neck and wrists, she exuded glamour, along with a haze of musky perfume.

'Hello, hello,' she said in a throaty voice, beckoning Rebecca towards her with a regal motion. 'Priya George.'

'Rebecca Chase, thanks for meeting me.'

'Of course, darling, of course.'

From her seat, Priya offered her hand and, after brushing Rebecca's fingers with her own, nodded at the two unoccupied chairs in front of her desk. Gratefully, Rebecca lowered herself into the seat on the left: the short walk had made her feel nauseous again.

'I was expecting two of you,' said the agent. 'Where's the man who was emailing me?'

'Um,' began Rebecca, without knowing what she was going to say, 'I think he's—'

There was a knock at the door.

'*Come in*!'

'—here,' finished Rebecca, amazed as Ellis then slouched into the room swinging his cycle helmet by its chin strap.

'Sorry, couldn't find anywhere to leave my bike,' he mumbled to Priya. 'Ellis Bailey, SideScoop.'

'Priya George – and not to worry, darling, we just started.'

The agent seemed to find Ellis more interesting than she did Rebecca, for she rose a few inches from her chair to shake his hand, then watched intently as he sank into the unoccupied seat and began to rummage through his bag. Rebecca, too, peeked sideways while he withdrew his notebook and phone, noting his movements were slow and that he hadn't shaved. When he stretched his legs beneath Priya's desk, Rebecca winced: she'd definitely sat on his lap.

'This is quite a collection you have,' he told Priya in a gravelly voice, indicating the headshots on the wall with a lazy wave of his pen. 'Who's your favourite?'

'Ooh, I don't have favourites!'

'Go on, I won't tell . . .'

She giggled, and began to point out her current clients, peppering each introduction with an anecdote. While she talked,

Ellis prodded at Rebecca's arm with his pen and, still wondering why he was here, she forced herself to meet his eye. He shot her an expression that was more of a grimace than a grin – which certainly wasn't the way he'd looked at her when they'd peeled themselves apart several hours ago – and, dissatisfied, she turned away. Maybe it would've been better to do this interview alone, after all.

Though unaware of the tension between her two visitors, Priya nevertheless seemed to realise their minds were elsewhere. She tapped her manicured fingernails against the desk and said, in the manner of someone about to embark upon an extravagant meal, 'So: *Leo Sampson*.'

Rebecca was almost surprised to hear her father's name. If nothing else, the events at Pit-Stop had driven him from her thoughts for the first time in almost a fortnight, and she'd been so focused on seeing Ellis, she'd barely considered the real reason she'd dragged herself to G&B Talent this morning. They hadn't discussed an approach for this interview. Should she pretend to be a SideScoop intern again and let him take the lead? It'd been an effective tactic with Richard Lowrie, but she wondered whether she was too fragile for games this morning.

Priya, who seemed unperturbed by their silence, mused, 'I haven't thought about him in years. I don't remember the last time he even crossed my mind before your email came in. Are you both journalists, by the way?'

'Actually, I'm Leo's daughter.'

Priya's eyebrows shot up. 'Are you really? How *extraordinary*!'

The agent appeared delighted by her own astonishment. Telling the truth had been the right decision, Rebecca decided: this was a woman who liked gossip.

'*Chase*, did you say?' continued Priya.

'It's my mum's name. I know I don't look like him, but—'

'No, no, I can see it,' said the agent, scrutinising Rebecca across the desk. 'You know, he had a very commanding stare – *captivating*, almost – and you're the same.' She jabbed her long nails towards Rebecca's face and then addressed Ellis. 'Don't you agree?'

'Erm—' the journalist, who'd been mid-yawn, looked startled '—Yes?'

'Leo's daughter, how extraordinary!' repeated Priya, with another deep chuckle. 'Hold on . . .'

She swung around in her swivel chair, stood up and opened the middle drawer of a filing cabinet.

'I don't keep them all,' she said, as she searched through its contents, 'but some people you hold onto. Ah, here he is!'

From a faded folder she extracted an A4-sized photograph, which she offered across the desk. Taking it carefully between the tips of her fingers, Rebecca noted this image of Leo was different from the many others she'd seen over the past few weeks: it was a black-and-white headshot and he was looking directly at the camera. Against the pallor of his face and the darkness of his tamed hair, his clear eyes were striking and a little sad. All of a sudden, Rebecca could see what Priya meant: there was something of herself there.

'Handsome, wasn't he?' said the agent, plucking the photograph from her hands. 'Not *classically* good-looking, of course: his nose was on the large side, and rather wonky now I look at it . . . But you didn't notice all that in person.'

She remained on her feet, holding the picture at arm's length and tilting her head from side to side, as though at a gallery and unsure whether or not she liked the artwork she was surveying.

Ellis leaned forward. 'Ms George—?'

'*Priya*, please!'

'Could we ask you a few questions about Leo? I'm trying to

piece together an overview of his career for the article I told you about in my email, and—'

'Why don't you just ask *him*?'

Ellis glanced at Rebecca, wordlessly seeking her permission to continue with the truth. Slightly distracted by the mention of the now-published article, she shrugged her assent.

'Because we don't know where he is. Nobody seems to have seen him for several years, not even Rebecca.'

'Really?' The thick black lines around Priya's eyes widened as she tore her attention from the picture at last. '*Curiouser and curiouser*!' Her dark, loose-fitting clothes rippled around her as she slid back into her chair. 'I think this calls for a coffee, don't you?'

Sounding relieved, Ellis requested his black, while Rebecca, frustrated by the interruption, asked only for water; her hands were still shaking from all the coffee a snickering Amy had pressed upon her earlier that morning.

As Priya phoned through their order – along with some very specific instructions about biscuits – Rebecca tried to curb her impatience by staring up at the wall of headshots, wondering whether she recognised any of the agent's clients. She was just contemplating a hard-faced actress who might've been in Amy and Tim's courtroom drama when a portrait out of the corner of her eye caused her a clunk of shock: it was the foundling from *The Golden Door*.

But no, of course it wasn't. After blinking a few times, she looked at the photograph properly, which depicted a jug-eared young man with dark, wide set eyes – the sort of person who must be a character actor, rather than a leading man. Rebecca frowned: she had to stop letting the fairy tales invade her mind like this. How could she have thought the foundling was here, in this office – in this *reality*? Maybe she was still a little drunk.

'Well, then,' said Priya, replacing the phone and twisting its cord around her index finger, 'what do you want to know?'

Ellis appeared to consider this; perhaps he'd not anticipated the agent would be so forthcoming. 'How did you meet Leo?' he asked, eventually.

'Oh, at some party – though don't ask me whose or where, I couldn't tell you.'

'Can I ask you *when*?'

''86? It was around then, because Marie and I – that's Marie Bowman, she's the *B* in G&B – we'd only just started the agency, so I was on the lookout for clients. Once Leo discovered that, he was determined to charm me – and he could be *very* charming, your father, when he chose to be,' Priya told Rebecca, who wasn't surprised to hear this.

'Do you know what Leo had been doing before he met you?' asked Ellis, who seemed to have taken it upon himself to lead the interview for now.

'Not really, I don't know if we ever talked about it.'

Rebecca, thinking of *The Voyage to the Edge of the World,* asked, 'Did he ever mention travelling?'

Ellis looked puzzled by the question, more so than Priya, who pursed her lips as she considered it. 'Possibly. I seem to remember something about touring in Scotland? But Leo never gave much away about his past, he was more focused on the future, on the next role. I admired that about him, at least in the beginning. Most actors are very lazy.'

Ellis, evidently trying to keep the conversation on track, said, 'Tell us more about this party, about Leo charming you.'

'Ah, yes,' said Priya, smiling. 'He was quite determined I should see him *in action*, as it were, so he invited me to his latest play – a little am-dram thing, you know. Wouldn't let me out of his sight until I'd promised to attend! I suppose *that* was what he was doing before he met me,' she added, in a more thoughtful tone, 'trying to get noticed.'

'How was the play?' asked Ellis.

'Oh, *dreadful*,' replied the agent, cheerfully. 'Those things always are. But Leo was good – very good, in fact. He had that spark you can't teach in drama school and whatnot. So I agreed to take him on. I knew it was a bit of a risk but, as I said, it was early days for G&B, so we couldn't afford to be too picky.'

'How was he a risk?' wondered Ellis, who was now taking notes.

'Let's just say I could see from the off he was rather rough around the edges. I knew not everyone would take to him – I just didn't expect *I* would find him such a handful.'

'How do you mean?'

Priya swivelled from side to side in her chair a few times. 'It's like there were two Leos . . .' she said, slowly. 'One was talented and charismatic and able to get work fairly easily, seeing as he charmed the pants off everyone he met – often literally, by the way,' she said, her raised eyebrows making Rebecca feel queasy again. 'He was the Leo I liked working with. But then there was this other Leo, who was difficult, unreliable; he'd turn up late, or not at all, and sometimes just wandered off mid-job – goodness knows why. And the trouble was, you could never predict which you were going to get. I'd pick up the phone without knowing if I'd be accepting praise for him or trying to smooth over one of his cock-ups. He was practically a full-time job.'

'Why do you think he was like that?' asked Ellis, which Rebecca thought a strange question; if Patricia's testimony was anything to go by, Leo had always had a disorderly streak.

'No idea!' Priya dismissed his query with a wave of her hand. 'But that kind of personality doesn't suit the actor's lifestyle – oh, you'd think it would,' she added, seeing their expressions. 'But acting's a funny sort of business: you're either in the middle of a production or a shoot, where you're constantly busy and surrounded by people, or you're sat at home, idle and alone, as you wait for the next job. It wasn't good for someone like Leo.'

'The downtime, you mean?' Rebecca asked.

'Yes, he couldn't stand doing nothing, so he was always pestering me for the next part, but he wasn't at his best when he was in the middle of a run either. He had a tendency to become consumed by the job, especially by whatever character he was playing.' She tapped the corner of Leo's photograph, which was still lying on the desk between them. 'He knew it was all pretend, of course, but I used to joke he thought it was real.'

Rebecca wanted Priya to expand on this, reminded of Richard Lowrie's claim that Leo had grown obsessed with the Stowaway's story, but Ellis asked, 'Did you ever talk to him about his attitude?'

'Oh, there wouldn't have been any point, darling!' laughed Priya. 'He didn't behave that way on purpose, it was just the way he was – actually, it was part of his appeal. And, like I said, he was very charming, so you couldn't stay cross with him for long . . . In retrospect, perhaps I should've got him a regular gig, like a soap, to keep him busy,' the agent mused, before shaking her head. 'But he would never have gelled with a big cast. Leo was the star and everyone knew it – him most of all.'

'Did he always work in theatre, then?' asked Ellis. 'Because, from what I've read, he didn't do much TV in the 80s.'

'Yes, that was the other issue,' said Priya, 'he was so *stubborn* about the stage. Usually it's the opposite, and actors are desperate to get themselves onscreen, but I think I managed to convince Leo to do a couple of adverts and that was it. He loved an audience, you see. He thrived on the thrill of live performance; the atmosphere, the instant feedback. So, I'd be lying if I said I wasn't a *little* put out when he later cropped up on *The Stowaway* . . .'

The agent looked as though she wanted to linger on this subject, but at that moment her receptionist backed into the office carrying a tray. *The Stowaway* now forgotten, Priya made a grab for the plate of expensive-looking biscuits, while Ellis began to gulp down his steaming coffee. More cautiously, Rebecca nibbled at one of the biscuits herself, but promptly stopped when it turned out to be lemon and lavender shortbread; its fragrance was making her stomach bubble with nausea.

Once the receptionist had departed, Ellis hugged his coffee cup to his chest and looked back through his notes. 'You said before that Leo was a *handful* – was he like that the entire time you knew him?'

'Mostly, yes.'

Struck by an idea, Rebecca asked, 'Do you think he ever took drugs?'

'Oh yes, of course.' Priya paused in the act of dunking her second piece of shortbread into her coffee to laugh at Rebecca's startled expression. 'Not in a *bad* way – it was the 80s, darling, we were all on something! Many of us still are . . .' She looked like she wanted to name names. 'He just dabbled, that's all. Everyone did.'

Stumped by this, Rebecca looked to Ellis, who was watching the agent intently. 'When was the last time you saw Leo?' he asked.

'Whenever he did that production of *Peter Pan* . . .'

''89,' said Rebecca, who'd read this two days previously.

'Sounds about right,' Priya said, taking a sip of coffee. 'I remember it was around this time of year, because the Circle were trying to attract the summer holiday crowd – such a silly idea, everyone knows *Peter Pan*'s a Christmas play.'

'He played Captain Hook and Mr Darling, didn't he?' said Rebecca, eager to show Ellis she was a lot more knowledgeable now than she'd been the previous week.

'As is tradition,' said the agent. 'Actually, it was one of the reasons I thought he'd thrive in that production: two characters for the price of one! And I was right, onstage he was extremely good. Of course, someone like Leo was always going to enjoy stomping around as a pirate, but it was for Mr Darling – an unrewarding sort of role – he received the most praise. He played up the father's repressive, cowardly nature until he was just as villainous as Hook, it was rather clever.'

Considering the picture of Leo's own father that had emerged from both their Huxley visit and *The Collector and the Nixie*, this interested Rebecca. But, again, Ellis seemed impatient to move on. 'So what happened *off*stage?' he pressed.

'Oh, the usual: he was late, he was emotional, he missed his cues, forgot his lines – sometimes he'd just make up his words on the spot, and you can't get away with that on something like *Peter Pan*, it's too famous. Obviously, none of this was new, but on that production, he was particularly difficult – the worst he'd ever been. Afterwards, I wondered whether he felt he was playing the wrong part . . .'

Having recently watched so much of *The Stowaway*, Rebecca found herself nodding in agreement.

'So he was fired?' said Ellis.

'Fired?' Priya seemed confused. 'No, darling, what makes you think that?'

'I thought you said you parted ways around that time? I assumed, because he was *the worst he'd ever been* . . .'

'We parted ways because of *her*,' broke in the agent, with sudden venom. 'After he met that bloody woman, he wasn't interested in the play or the theatre – in any of it.'

'What woman?' asked Ellis.

'Oh, I don't remember her name, I never actually met her. It was something fussy – Jocelyn?'

'Rosalyn,' said Rebecca, quietly.

She'd already guessed her mother might've had something to do with Leo's departure from the stage, but it was still a surprise to hear her mentioned: Rosalyn didn't seem to belong in the world of this story.

'Yes, that was it, *Roz . . .*' drawled the agent, with disdain. '*Roz* this, *Roz* that – oh!' A giggle escaped her as she suddenly seemed to realise how Rebecca knew the name.

Ellis came swiftly to her rescue: 'How did they meet?'

'At the play.' Priya gave another flippant wave, not noticing that Rebecca had sat up a little straighter at the question. 'She'd taken her nieces or nephews along, and they'd wanted to wait at the stage door for an autograph. She and Leo fell in love the moment they met, or so he kept telling me later – though he was always prone to exaggeration,' she sniffed.

At the word *nephews*, Rebecca had thought of the twins, but Rosalyn must've been babysitting Bea and Oliver, Morton's children from his now dissolved marriage. It was difficult to picture her po-faced older cousins waiting for an autograph from Captain Hook, even as children – but then, it was almost impossible to imagine Rosalyn falling in love at a production of *Peter Pan*.

'I still don't quite understand how Leo meeting Rosalyn meant the end of your professional relationship,' said Ellis.

'Because he wanted to run off with her, didn't he?' said Priya, as though this was obvious. 'He wanted to drop out of the play – a production at *the Circle*, no less – so he could disappear to Dorset or wherever it was! Well, I'm afraid that was the last straw for me. I'd run myself ragged looking after him, then I secure him the biggest role of his career and he wants to throw it all away for some—' she checked herself in front of Rebecca '—some *woman* he'd only just met!'

'So *you* let him go?' said Ellis.

'I didn't have much of a choice, did I?' Priya's tone was oddly defensive. 'After dropping out of a production like that, nobody in the industry was going to take him seriously – at least, I didn't think they would. How he got that part in *The Stowaway*, I'll never understand. He must've known someone.'

Rebecca, now growing frustrated with Priya's diversions, asked, 'How did he react, when you let him go?'

'Well . . .' The agent's fingers began to creep towards the last of the shortbread. 'I'm afraid we had a bit of a tiff – quite a big tiff, actually. I won't go into all the gory details, but I made it clear that I thought he was being rash and selfish, and told him it was the silliest idea he'd ever had, giving up everything he'd worked towards – *we'd* worked towards.'

'That can't have gone down well,' said Ellis lightly, and Rebecca had the impression he was pretending to side with the agent, just as he had with Patricia.

'No, it didn't,' said Priya. 'But by then, he'd worked himself up into the most ridiculous state – apparently, I didn't *understand* him, I never *listened* to him, I hadn't noticed he was *struggling* . . .' She rolled her eyes, as though they were discussing a melodramatic teenager. 'He kept saying she was going to save him – like he had it bad! Honestly, the way these actors talk sometimes, you'd think they were being forced to work down a mine!'

'So that was it?' said Ellis.

'Yes, off he went!' Priya waved the remains of her biscuit through the air, scattering crumbs over her desk. 'I heard through a friend he and *Roz* married a few months later, if you can believe it – I certainly couldn't, he was far too young for all that.' Then, addressing Rebecca with an unconvincing attempt at nonchalance, she asked, 'I don't suppose it worked out between them, did it?'

'Not really, no.'

'There you go,' said Priya, looking pleased, 'I knew it wouldn't.'

It took all of Rebecca's restraint not to roll her eyes.

'I assume you didn't stay in touch?' said Ellis.

'No . . .' Priya's expression turned wistful. 'Sometimes I regretted it, having to let him go. I assumed that was it for his acting career, so imagine my surprise when he popped up in *The Stowaway* – and when it was such a hit! I must admit that stung a little, especially as I'd always tried to get him into TV . . . I imagine it was the money that finally knocked him from his high horse. It usually is with actors.' She smirked. 'Perhaps he needed to pay his child support!'

Rebecca might've been offended by this but, reflecting on the masked hero of 'The Witch and the Sphinx', and how he'd been repeatedly sent across the desert for those magic bottles, she suspected there was some truth to Priya's theory.

'So you never had any contact with him again?' persisted Ellis. 'No Christmas cards, no emails . . . ?'

Priya shook her head. 'That's gratitude for you, isn't it? After everything I did for him! If you think about it, there wouldn't have been any *Stowaway* without me – at least, not for him.' Another flicker of malice crossed her features. 'You know, there are rumours he was fired from that show, and I'd bet you anything they were true. The papers said he left of his own accord, but he never appeared in anything afterwards, did he?'

Earlier, Rebecca might've pandered to her and revealed what Richard Lowrie had told them the previous week, but her dislike of the agent had been steadily mounting – especially since her vitriol towards Rosalyn.

Ellis started to ask another question, but was interrupted by the ringing of the office phone. After a short exchange with her receptionist, Priya announced, 'I'm afraid we're out of time, I have a client waiting . . . Oh, what a *bore*!' Her bottom lip curved into a childlike pout; apparently, she was having a good time.

Slightly more quickly than was polite, Ellis shut his notebook and pushed his chair away from the desk. But Rebecca remained seated.

'I realise you haven't spoken to Leo for a long time,' she began, 'but I don't suppose you know where he is now, do you?'

'I'm afraid not, darling,' said the agent, who did, for a moment, look genuinely pitying.

'And you don't know anyone who might've been in contact with him recently? You mentioned a mutual friend . . . ?'

But Priya was shaking her head. 'I'm sorry, I wish I knew more – no really, I mean that,' she added, in response to their obvious surprise. 'It might be rather fun to see him again, and it would certainly liven things up around here.'

She gazed at the portraits floating behind her head like square thought bubbles, regarding her other clients with less enthusiasm than before. Both Rebecca and Ellis chose this moment to thank her and start edging towards the door, but Priya beckoned them back.

'Tell you what,' she purred, opening a desk drawer and retrieving a couple of business cards. 'If you two find him, you tell him to give me a call, for old time's sake – no hard feelings and all that.'

She waggled the cards across the desk, like an indulgent doctor offering her patients a pair of lollipops. Rebecca had little choice but to take them, though made sure to crumple the cardboard in her fist.

When she turned, Ellis was holding open the door for her, his gaze fixed on the corridor ahead. Rebecca's insides wobbled – a feeling she could only partly attribute to her hangover – and suddenly she wanted to stay, let him go on by himself. She glanced back at Priya, hoping she might want a word in private, but it seemed the agent had forgotten them already: she was leaning back in her chair with Leo's black and white portrait, dusting his face free of biscuit crumbs.

12

The Video

Rebecca thought she'd feel better after leaving Priya's stuffy office but being outside was worse. The air was stagnant and, emerging from the agent's Soho townhouse, she was momentarily dazzled by the sunlight glaring off the tall windows opposite.

Staying in London had been a mistake. Amy might've been happy to provide her with a bed and clothes, but had that meeting really justified lying to her family and jeopardising her job? Rebecca knew no more about Leo now than she had on Sunday, when she'd left Huxley. Her time here had changed nothing.

Or, almost nothing, she thought, as Ellis followed her into the street. During their conversation with the agent, she'd briefly managed to bury what had happened at Pit-Stop, but now they were alone again, awkwardness swelled between them like a rapidly inflating balloon.

Ellis made the first attempt to puncture the silence. 'So, what did you think of her?' He jerked his head back towards G&B Talent.

Rebecca, grateful he'd said *something*, replied with the first thing that came to mind: 'I think she was in love with him.'

'Really?'

Ellis appeared to consider this. Rebecca had thought it obvious but, unwilling to linger on the subject of romance, continued, 'Apart from that, I'm not sure how useful it was.'

'No?'

'Well, she doesn't know where he is, does she? And it's not like she told us anything new.'

Ellis said nothing but clipped and unclipped the fastening of his bike helmet a few times, frowning. He seemed deep in contemplation – or perhaps he was just avoiding eye contact.

'Don't you think?' Rebecca prompted.

He finally let the chin strap hang loose. 'I think,' he began slowly, 'we should find some breakfast.'

Surprised, Rebecca's heart stirred feebly, and she told herself she couldn't drive back to Devon until she'd eaten something substantial – plus they could hardly discuss the finer points of their meeting with Priya on the street outside her office.

'All right,' she said, in what she hoped was an indifferent tone.

'There's a café round the corner that does brunch and stuff,' continued Ellis, with a nod.

Sluggishly, they made their way past an assortment of vibrant façades – pubs, boutiques, an independent bookshop – while Ellis made half-hearted attempts at conversation and Rebecca gave half-hearted responses. Every step she took cost her a great deal of effort, and the muggy weather was making her surroundings feel blurred; she might've been struggling against a ruthless current, like the captain in *The Voyage to the Edge of the World.*

Why had Ellis come to the meeting with Priya? Why was he still here? Perhaps he was simply curious and seeing the story to its conclusion or maybe he was planning to amend his article. Then a voice at the back of Rebecca's addled, sleep-deprived mind – a voice that sounded suspiciously like Amy's – suggested, *What if he's just here for you?*

The café turned out to be small and cheerful, although its yolk-coloured walls seemed muted after the sun-blanched street. Ordinarily, Rebecca might've disapproved of the mismatching tiles underfoot, and the crooked pinboards overflowing with posters for Zumba classes and West End musicals, but today she was more interested in the blend of aromas twisting around them: coffee, toast, *bacon*.

They found an empty table by the wall, and after settling herself into an uncomfortable metal chair that would've been better suited to a patio, Rebecca tried to wedge a folded napkin under one of its legs to stop it wobbling, until her head seared in protest. To her dismay, the café's laminated menus displayed the calorie count of each dish. Once she'd seen the number next to the full English – and reflected ruefully on all those syrupy cocktails she'd consumed the previous night – she resigned herself to porridge, and strove to ignore the wafts of sizzling meat emanating from the kitchen.

After a waiter had departed with their order, she glanced at Ellis, who was staring out of the window. At some point – possibly when she'd been fiddling with the chair – he'd got out his notebook. Perhaps, then, he didn't intend to talk about last night after all, or maybe he was waiting for her to bring it up: he was the one who'd invited her here, and to Pit-Stop; he was the one who'd kissed her. Maybe it was her turn to instigate something – but what, and how?

Immediately losing her nerve, she asked, 'So why do you think talking to Priya was useful?'

'I think it's useful talking to anyone who knew Leo,' said Ellis, his voice as distant as his gaze.

'But we didn't learn anything new about him.'

'Didn't we?'

'No.' She waited for him to contradict her, then realised he was rarely combative, so continued, 'Go on, then – tell me what Priya said that was so enlightening.'

'It was more what she *didn't* say . . .' He turned his focus to the glass salt shaker. It contained a few grains of dried rice, which looked grubby against the rest of its contents, like old toenail clippings. 'What I can't figure out is whether she was lying to us or whether she's been lying to herself for twenty odd years. I mean, she seemed honest enough – and really, why *wouldn't* she just tell us – but then what did she think he was playing at?'

'What are you talking about?' snapped Rebecca.

Finally, Ellis met her eye. 'Why do you think he ran out on that *Peter Pan* production and married your mum?'

The question took her by surprise, so she answered it automatically: 'Because they'd fallen in love.'

'Do you think that's true?'

'Yes!' She felt affronted, as though by doubting her parents' affection for one another, he was casting aspersions on her. 'Actually,' she reconsidered, 'I don't know. I can't remember them together – literally, I mean, I can't picture them in the same room. It was always just me and him, until it was just me and her . . .'

She trailed off, suspecting this was the first time she'd alluded to her memories of Leo – or lack of – in front of Ellis. But if he noticed, he chose not to comment and instead began to flip through his notebook.

'Do you remember when Priya talked about the last time they'd seen one another and they had that row?'

Rebecca nodded.

'Obviously, she didn't really go into what he'd said to her, but it was something like—' Ellis checked his notes '—she didn't understand him, she'd never listened or noticed he was struggling, and he thought—'

'—He thought my mum was going to save him,' Rebecca finished.

Ellis tapped at a point on his page. 'Save him from what?'

'Priya, probably.' Then, off his sceptical look, she tried again:

'Or the industry in general? If it's full of people like her and Richard Lowrie . . .'

She paused as a waiter brought over Ellis's coffee, her thoughts drifting from the agent to the veteran actor and then to Patricia, while her stomach scrunched with aversion.

'I think a lot of people turned their backs on him when he needed them,' she mused, when they were alone again.

'How do you mean?'

'Well, there was his dad, and Patricia, who didn't bother about him after Adeline died. Then Priya fired him when he was struggling, and I'm pretty sure *The Stowaway* people should've helped him if his drug issues had been that bad, not just got rid of him. And then—'

She caught herself: she'd been about to say, *And then my mum, and the rest of my family*.

'You're still feeling sorry for him, then?' Ellis noted.

Rebecca wouldn't have phrased it like this, because it implied Leo was weak or wretched – words she'd never associated with him before. In her memories, he was full of vitality: loud and mirthful, bright-eyed and pink-cheeked, frequently outside and always active; scrambling up slabs of granite, squelching through bogs, swinging on gates and low-hanging branches . . . Unless, of course, she was mixing him up with the Stowaway again.

'I just think he's been hard done by, that's all.'

Ellis stirred a dribble of milk into his coffee, watching as it formed a mini whirlpool, and said, 'So, rewinding a bit, why do you think he ran out on that play?'

'Oh, I don't know!' cried Rebecca, irritated by his tenacity – and irritated they were talking about this and not about what had happened last night, even though she hadn't the courage to bring it up. 'Does it matter? Maybe *Peter Pan* was boring. Maybe he fell out with the director, as well as Priya. Maybe he was ill.'

Something about the last of these flippant suggestions snagged at her attention and, more thoughtfully, she continued, 'You always hear about celebrities dropping out of things due to exhaustion, don't you? I always assumed that was code for drugs.'

Rebecca hoped Ellis could confirm or deny this, but he merely shrugged. She had the impression he was frustrated with her. Trying not to care, she ran a finger along the wall beside her, tracing a series of spots where the yellow paint had chipped away, while attempting to follow her own thoughts through the fog of her headache.

She supposed it was possible ill health had forced Leo to suspend his acting career to recuperate in Devon with Rosalyn. The unfamiliar notion of a fading Leo then led her reflect on something she hadn't considered – nor wanted to consider – since Amy had brought it up on Sunday afternoon: what if she was looking for someone who was no longer alive?

Until now, Rebecca had been reassured by the thought that, because he'd been the Stowaway, Leo's potential passing would've been big news, especially on websites like SideScoop. But now, in the malaise of her hangover, she had to acknowledge there was a chance Leo had died in anonymity. He might've fallen through the cracks, become wretched and emaciated, with matted hair, bloodshot eyes and a body marked by bruises and sores . . . The image made Rebecca feel sicker than ever – who, then, would know the magnificent man he'd once been?

At the same time, though, she couldn't really believe he was gone. Not with *Seven Tales* back in her bag, tucked between a half-eaten cereal bar and the packet of painkillers Amy had given her that morning. Somehow, the existence of the book told Rebecca that Leo was still out there, somewhere. Of course, this was completely illogical – a week ago she would've scoffed at herself – but she'd come to think of *Seven Tales* as an innate part of her father, so now it seemed impossible that one could endure without the other.

Scratching at the wall with a fingernail, Rebecca asked herself again why she now cared so much about Leo's fate. He'd still left her. He might've been misunderstood, even mistreated, but that didn't justify his long absence. And if he had been ill and had never recovered, it didn't explain the behaviour of her family, who acted as though they were afraid he might reappear at any moment. It didn't make sense; none of it ever made sense.

'Erm, Becs?'

She glanced around to discover the waiter was attempting to place a bowl of sloppy oats onto her paper placemat. Lifting her elbows – and hoping he didn't notice where she'd picked at the wall – Rebecca muttered her thanks, but was filled with self-contempt: why had she ordered *porridge*?

'Do you want some of this?' asked Ellis, who was spreading butter onto slabs of wholemeal toast. 'I've got loads . . .'

'No, thank you,' Rebecca said, with dignity.

She dipped the end of her spoon into her gluey porridge. It looked like vomit and didn't taste much better. There were blueberries and toasted walnuts scattered over the surface, but they, too, made her stomach shudder.

Ellis placed a slice of buttered toast onto a napkin and wordlessly ferried it over the table towards her. Rebecca acted as though she hadn't seen, but the familiarity of the gesture pushed Leo temporarily from her brain.

She laid down her spoon, took a breath, and asked, 'Are we going to talk about last night?'

Ellis chewed for what felt like five minutes, until Rebecca was expecting a reply bordering on the profound. When he finally swallowed, however, all he said was, 'If you like.'

'Don't do that,' she told him.

'What?'

She did an exaggerated shrug and dropped her voice half an octave: '*If you like.*'

He looked taken aback by the impersonation, but then gave her a sheepish grin. 'Sorry.'

'If you wanted to pretend nothing happened, you shouldn't have suggested this,' she continued, gesturing at the café.

Ellis's smile faltered. 'I don't want to pretend that.'

Now, it was Rebecca who was taken aback. They held one another's gaze and she was seized by a more pleasant shudder as she recalled the feel of his hand on the small of her back, his lips tracing a line down the side of her neck. To disguise her deepening blush, she picked up the piece of toast he'd slid across the table and took a bite: it was much more palatable than porridge.

Ellis then seemed to deem it safe to return to his food and, as she watched him tear into a fried egg and some hash browns, Rebecca realised it was her turn to nudge this forward.

'I don't have to go back to Devon today,' she said.

He paused. 'No?'

'It's not really worth rushing back for one day of work, is it?' she said, suddenly remembering she'd spoken to Chris Fenton last night – although about what, she had no idea.

'So . . . you might be around at the weekend, then?' said Ellis, addressing the question to the baked beans he was now prodding around his plate.

'Yes, probably. And if I am, maybe—' Rebecca cringed: why was this so difficult? '—Maybe we could do something?'

Ellis looked up, and for a moment his expression was completely open; she could read all his hope and desire and it made those same emotions swell in her. Perhaps this wouldn't be difficult after all.

But then his brow creased, and he set aside his knife and fork with a heavy sigh. 'Look, Becs, I think there's something you should know – something you should see.'

Was he trying to dodge her question? She watched him push aside his half-eaten breakfast to make room for his laptop, her bewilderment turning to dread.

'It's a video, I'll email it to you.'

'What kind of video?' she asked at once.

'It's from *The Stowaway* days, but—'

'Oh, I've watched that now,' she said, relieved. 'Half of it, anyway . . .'

'Have you?' He seemed briefly distracted by this, then shook his head as he inserted a familiar dinosaur-shaped USB into the side of his laptop. 'Well, you won't have seen this. Hardly anyone has.'

Now intrigued, Rebecca moved her chair to the other side of the table, hopeful that this video – whatever it was – would be more illuminating than their discussion with Priya. Ellis seemed startled to suddenly find her next to him, and she wondered whether he'd managed to shower this morning – and whether she minded if he hadn't.

'What is this?' she asked, peering at the screen, where a fuzzy video was paused.

'Behind the scenes footage from *The Stowaway* set. It was sent to me the other day.'

Rebecca tilted the laptop so she had a better view. 'Let's see it, then.'

'What, now?'

'It's only a few minutes,' she noted. 'Pass me those, will you?'

She pointed at the yellow headphones she'd seen him wearing in the SideScoop office, which were currently poking out of his bag. Hesitantly, Ellis handed them over.

'Becs,' he began, seriously, 'I'm really not sure this is the best—'

But the rest of his sentence was muffled as she slipped the headphones over her ears. Signalling she could no longer hear him, Rebecca plugged in the lead and pressed play.

At the base of the screen is a date: *10 APR 1997*. Its pixelated font is reminiscent of a calculator's, and along with the other numbers and letters dotted nearby it looks like part of an equation or a code. Everything else is gold.

The picture sharpens and the blurred discs of light rearrange themselves into the surface of a filigree lantern. Its glow illuminates oriental carpets, snake-charmer baskets, and treasure: coins, rings, precious stones, strings of pearls. But the scene is shrinking; seeping into its dark edges are lighting rigs and a floor marked with tape, until there is so much empty space, the treasure trove has been reduced to the size of a dolls' house.

The screen blinks, and a line of children file into view. They are around eight or nine years old, their grey jumpers stamped with a school logo, their maroon ties knotted with varying degrees of expertise. Two female teachers are trying to shepherd them into rows facing the set, but this is proving difficult; the youngsters are fidgety and distracted, wanting to gaze not just at the glittering props, but around the vast dark room and directly at the camera behind them.

For about a minute, little happens: the children shuffle where they stand, whispering to one another; a short middle-aged man wearing a lanyard attempts conversation with a few of the boys and girls at the front; a woman with a headset wanders behind the backdrop of the treasure store, which has been painted to look lumpy and shiny, like the walls of a cave. Then someone off-camera starts to clap. The children join in automatically, twisting around to see what they are applauding, before pointing and gasping as a figure clad in bright green and yellow comes bounding into view.

'*Hello*!' he cries, in a booming voice. 'Hello, hello, hello, hello—'

He begins to shake each child by the hand and they clamour towards him, pushing at one another to greet him first. After hailing every one of them – and ignoring both teachers entirely – the Stowaway swoops into the crowd, his arms outstretched like wings. Squealing with delight, the boys and girls scatter, their neat rows gone in an instant.

In distant times, so long ago,
a wondrous man did roam,
through magic lands he did not know,
to find his way back home.

The Stowaway's singing is tuneless, but so full of enthusiasm the children start shouting the words too. They skip around him, some trying to pluck at his hands or costume and in their grey uniforms they might been little moons orbiting a colourful planet.

The Stow-away, the Stow-away,
oh, listen to him well,
the Stow-away, the Stow-away,
the stories he will tell!

Following a few more renderings of the theme tune, the man in the lanyard edges through the dancing throng and says something to the figure at its centre.

'Puh, that's boring!' shouts the Stowaway. 'Hey, everyone, look what I can do!' He kicks up into a handstand. 'Look! Look what I'm doing!'

On shaking arms, he staggers across the tape-marked floor, his feet dangling above his head. A few of the children try to copy him but are quickly dissuaded by their teachers. When one of his trembling elbows gives way, the Stowaway collapses sideways into an untidy heap. The man in the lanyard dashes forward in alarm, but the brightly coloured figure is already bouncing up as though the ground is as springy as a trampoline.

The screen blinks again.

Now, the same children are sitting on the floor and this time their attention is entirely focused on the treasure-strewn set before them.

'Action!' someone calls off-screen.

All is still, except for a little girl in the back row, who kneels up for a better view.

'*Action*!'

The lid of the largest woven basket rises, revealing the Stowaway's head beneath. The children giggle as he moves up and down, pulling a new face at them each time he bobs into sight. When he rocks backwards and forwards, the basket topples over and he is spat out onto a coin-speckled carpet.

'Oh, hello there!' he cries, his body as floppy as a ragdoll's. 'I'm the Stowaway!'

The children cheer, and he leaps up to deliver his usual opening monologue, but so fast his words run together: '*Now I'm afraid I have an unfortunate habit of finding myself in other people's stories but I'm always searching for my way home so maybe this time*?' He gasps for breath but doesn't look around. '*Nope don't think I'm home*! But look at all this treasure . . .'

His speech slows as he reaches newer lines. 'Have you ever seen so much gold? So many jewels? Wherever can I be? It looks like I'm inside a giant treasure chest, but—but—'

He rolls his wrist until the woman with the headset hurries on with a script, which he regards with disdain.

'I don't need this,' he tells her, lobbing it away. 'I don't want it.'

The children laugh.

Encouraged, the Stowaway declares, 'Ali Baba's stupid anyway, we don't need *him*! Let's go on a different adventure – a better adventure! What do you say?'

'Leo . . .'

'A better adventure,' repeats the Stowaway, now pacing. 'Bigger and better – a quest! But what shall we look for, what shall we—?'

'*Leo!*'

The Stowaway glances at someone off-screen, then lets out an exaggerated sigh as he stomps back towards his script and retrieves it from the floor, prompting more mirth from the children.

'Wherever can I be?' he asks in a bored monotone, after finding his place in the scene. 'It looks like I'm inside a giant treasure chest, but all this damp rock must mean I've emerged into a cave! Ah . . .'

The Stowaway seems to realise he's in the wrong place and skips through all the gold and jewels to the back of the set. 'I can hear voices!' He presses his ear to the wall of the cave. 'Five, maybe ten?' No . . .' His eyes widen. 'More like 40 voices – and all of them sound like they're up to no good! Quick! I'd better hide!'

His sulkiness is forgotten as he clowns around trying to find somewhere to conceal himself, attempting to crawl under a carpet and squeeze into a tiny oil lamp, until, with much pointing and shouting, his young audience direct him back towards his woven basket.

The screen blinks once more.

The children are still sat on the floor, but this time most have their hands in the air. In front of them, the Stowaway dances from side to side, before pointing at a chubby boy in the second row, who excitedly asks, 'What's your favourite animal?'

'Brilliant question!' exclaims the Stowaway. 'My favourite

animal, my favourite animal . . . Hey, why don't you guess? Watch this!'

He clamps his arms to his sides and adopts a waddling gait. A few of the children call out the answer, but the Stowaway pretends he can't hear them.

'Anyone?' he cries, continuing to shuffle about in circles. 'Anyone at all? Come on, what am I?' Then, when the entire crowd screams *A penguin!* he jumps back with feigned shock. 'Woah, no need to shout!'

While the children fall about with laughter, the Stowaway calls for another question. This time, he chooses a girl on the other side of the group, who fiddles with the pink pom-poms securing the end of her plait for a few seconds, before admitting, 'I forgot.'

'You forgot!' beams the Stowaway. 'Well, never mind – I forget things all the time! Sometimes I worry my brain is made of jelly, and one day it will wobble right out of my ears . . .' He mimes how this might go, which elicits noises of both glee and disgust from the young crowd. 'Now, any more questions?'

Hands shoot back into the air. Many of the children are visibly straining to reach higher than their peers, and a few are whining *me, me, me!* But the Stowaway's attention is caught by a small boy with a mop of white-blond hair who is half-hidden in the back row.

'Avast!' he yelps. 'A pirate! Ahoy, matey – and what do you want to ask?'

The child's question is inaudible on the tape, but evidently the Stowaway hears it, because his face slackens with a surprise.

'Come here,' he says, urgently beckoning to the boy. 'Come on up to the front.' Then, in the awkward hush that follows, he manages to laugh. 'That is, if you can bear to stand beside this landlubber!'

After an uncertain glance at his teachers, the child does as he's told, and the Stowaway positions him opposite his classmates. He's wearing a pair of clunky plastic glasses, under which his right eye is covered by a white medical patch.

'Now, me hearty,' says the Stowaway, pointing at the other children, 'in your biggest, boldest pirate voice, can you repeat that question?'

The boy tugs down the sleeves of his grey school jumper until his hands disappear, before taking a breath and shouting, '*What's your name*?'

The crowd titters at his unexpected loudness, but the Stowaway remains unsmiling. 'What's my name?' he asks, beginning to pace again. '*What's my name*? It's a very good—That's it!' he cries, so abruptly the boy with the eye patch gives a start. 'I've just had the best—That'll be our quest, that's what we'll look for: my name! We'll find my name!'

He looks elated again, until the man in the lanyard reappears beside the treasure store, trying to object.

'No, Larry, this is perfect, they can help! They'll be—Look, children are more – more – open-minded, open-hearted, *open sesame*!'

'Leo, slow down, you need to—'

'What's my name?' the Stowaway demands of the boys and girls. 'Go on, try and guess. It's like in the story, you have to – *Rumpelstiltskin!* – you have to guess. Three guess, seven guesses, a thousand and one guesses! Because everyone has a—So why is the Stowaway just the Stowaway? Doesn't matter, not his story, but I have an unfortunate habit of finding *absolutely nothing*! On and on, and on and on, until all the tales are told . . .'

He sounds like a song that keeps skipping; the melody is discernible, the music all muddled. Tentatively, one of the teachers creeps towards the seated youngsters and crouches behind the last row, her arms half-raised, poised to sweep them all up.

'So we'll decide, we'll guess—' The Stowaway pushes a clump of dark hair from his eyes. 'This is going to work. We should go somewhere, can't think in here. Let's walk and talk, talk and walk. *In distant times, so long ago, a wondrous man did roam . . .*'

Now, his delivery of the theme song is not only out of tune, it's twice as fast as before. He can't seem to stop moving, even the pads of his thumbs keep skimming his fingertips, as though he's motioning for money, or trying to make a clicking sound, though his hands are a silent blur.

'Leo, we'll talk about the name later, I think you should calm—'

'*For fuck's sake, Larry*!' The Stowaway clutches at his head. 'Can't you see—Can't you see what I'm trying to—Wait, what are they doing?'

Both teachers are now motioning for the children to stand and pointing at somewhere off-screen.

'You're not going?' calls the Stowaway, horrified. 'You have to stay, we have to— Hey, come back!'

The children stare between him and their teachers, unsure who to obey. A few are still smiling, but most look unsure as they are prodded and pulled away. One girl has put her hands over her ears.

'*Come back*!'

The Stowaway looks wildly around, his gaze fixing upon the little boy with the eye patch, who hasn't strayed from the spot into which he was manoeuvred a few minutes ago.

'You'll stay!' cries the Stowaway, making a grab for the child's long sleeves. 'You'll stay, young pirate, and we'll find a vessel – we'll find the *truth* – and we'll—Don't need them, don't need anyone! Only the bravest, only the strongest, only the most—'

While he gabbles and shakes at the child's jumper, the boy blinks up at him with his one exposed eye, his expression more interested than afraid. Then a click-clacking of heels alerts the Stowaway that one of the teachers is marching towards him and he releases the boy at once, cowering from the woman's fury as she seizes her last charge and pushes him towards the other departing youngsters.

'Bring them back,' moans the Stowaway, gripping at Larry's arm as they are left alone in front of the treasure store. 'Please, bring them back!'

His colleague murmurs something, but the Stowaway shakes his head.

'I'm fine, I'm just—I don't see why—They were going to *help*!' He raises his hands to his temples again, his fingers curling into claws. 'Just let me – *stop talking* – let me think. Didn't I tell you I was tired?'

Larry lays a steadying hand on his shoulder, because the Stowaway is now bending forward, folding up on himself.

Elsewhere, there comes the sound of raised voices, and the ringing of a phone. The woman in the headset hovers uncertainly at the edge of the scene, before dashing forward to replace the upended basket.

'Is that still on?' Suddenly, Larry is staring straight at the camera. He readjusts his grip on the green and yellow figure, who is continuing to curl up like a caterpillar, and shouts, 'For Christ's sake, don't just stand there, *turn it off*! Can't you see he's not well? Turn it—'

Rebecca tugged the headphones from her ears, so focused on the now-blank screen she hardly heard the resurgence of her surroundings: the tinkling of cutlery on crockery; a faint but recognisable song playing from an overhead speaker; the hiss of the coffee machine.

She wished it had been pretend, part of a play or workshop,

and at the end there had been applause, and Leo had taken a bow. Only, she knew it'd been real, and not because there was no more footage, but because, a long time ago, she'd seen versions of this behaviour herself.

How was she meant to feel? Her impulse was to laugh, but that wasn't right – it wasn't funny. She didn't know what to do or say or think, and at first this was what concerned her above everything else: her own lack of response.

Ellis touched her lightly on the arm. 'Are you all right?'

Rebecca nodded, even though she wasn't.

After a pause, the journalist said, 'The following month, it was announced he'd left the show and the role was recast for the whole of series three. So Richard Lowrie was right – about some of it, at least.'

Still, Rebecca remained silent. How did she know she'd seen versions of this behaviour before? She continued to stare at the screen, almost willing it to start playing her paltry collection of memories – his tending her bee sting in the garden, or calling that clump of old sheep's fleece the beard of a gnome – so she could view him via an objective lens, rather than her own mind, which had smoothed all of his edges.

'Do you want to talk about it?' ventured Ellis.

Rebecca finally wrenched her gaze from the laptop. 'Talk about what?'

'About your dad being . . .' Ellis lowered his voice, looking worried. 'Well, about him being ill, really ill. I mean, it seems like he had some kind of mental health condition, probably—'

'No,' cut in Rebecca, attempting to stop rather than contradict him, because she wasn't yet ready to hear words like *mental health condition*. 'I don't want to talk about that.' Then, because it looked like Ellis might continue regardless, she nodded back at the screen. 'How did you get this, anyway?'

'A mate of a mate managed to find it in the BBC archives – obviously it never aired. I've been chasing it for a while.'

'If it never aired, how did you know about it?'

Her own question amazed her: apparently, at least part of her brain was still working. Ellis hesitated, almost flinching as he reached towards the laptop and, with a grim expression, dragged the cursor along the bar beneath the video.

Rebecca leaned back in her chair. 'Don't!'

Without playing it, Ellis scrolled back through the footage, so frame after frame of what she'd just watched flashed by: Leo cowering, Leo clutching his head, Leo pacing; Leo, Leo, *Leo* . . . Rebecca didn't understand what Ellis was doing, and wanted to shove his hand from the touchpad, but found herself staring at the screen instead, unable to bear it, unable to look away.

Eventually, Ellis seemed to find what he was looking for, and left the video paused at the moment Leo had brought the little boy with the eye patch up to the front. Circling the cursor around the child, Ellis asked, 'Recognise him?'

Rebecca squinted at the fuzzy image. 'Should I?'

Ellis said nothing but continued to outline the space around the boy's white-blond head, as though drawing him a halo.

'You were there . . .'

For a second time, Rebecca wanted to laugh: it seemed impossible Ellis Bailey had been such a shy, awkward child. But again, none of this was funny.

Ellis withdrew his hand from the laptop. 'Our class won a competition,' he said. 'Well, Jessica Dove did. She drew a picture, and we all got to visit the set and meet the Stowaway. I remembered there were cameras, because Mrs Brooke made us comb our hair before getting off the bus, but I couldn't think why we were being filmed . . . Apparently, it was for a documentary about fairy tales, but, as I said, they never used that footage.'

Now he seemed mesmerised by the screen, which was still frozen on the image of his younger self, but Rebecca had turned to stare at the older Ellis, who suddenly seemed like a stranger.

'You've known all this time . . .'

'No,' he said quickly, 'I haven't. I knew there was something odd about that day, about *him*. And I had the weirdest feeling it was my fault, like I'd said or done something wrong . . . But nobody explained anything. We just got back on the bus and it was never mentioned again.'

'I don't believe you,' said Rebecca.

She thrust the headphones towards him and dragged her chair back to the other side of the table. The sudden motion made her insides ripple – she felt shakier now than she had all morning – but she couldn't sit next to him anymore. This second shock seemed marginally easier to cope with than the first; she would react to this before trying to unpick what she'd just learned about her father.

Ellis closed his laptop so they had a clear view of one another. 'I'll admit, I've often wondered about him,' he said. 'I've always wanted to know what really happened on that visit. Sometimes I thought I must've imagined the whole thing, the way no one talked about it afterwards . . . But in a way that made it *more* memorable.'

This didn't sound dissimilar to Rebecca's own experience, but she was too agitated to care about that at the moment, so asked, 'Why are you here?'

'What?' Ellis glanced around the café, then at her, looking concerned again; perhaps he thought she too might be losing her mind.

'Why are you still helping me?'

'The article . . .' he said, slowly. 'I need to finish the *Where Are They Now?* piece.'

'But it's already finished, it's published,' said Rebecca, 'and you hardly even mentioned my dad.'

Ellis stared: evidently, he hadn't expected her to have seen it. Still, she willed him to say what she wanted to hear – *I'm here for you, I'm still helping because I like you* – even though this was looking increasingly unlikely.

'You're here because of that other article, the one you mentioned on Monday,' said Rebecca, the realisation slamming into her like a train as she recalled their conversation on the museum steps and the new pitch he'd allegedly only dreamed up that morning. 'You didn't talk to all those people or track down that footage for a few paragraphs in some stupid nostalgia piece – you've had something else in mind all along, something just about him.'

Ellis's uneasy expression confirmed it, but when he spoke his voice was firm: 'I talked to all those people and tracked down that footage because I wanted to know if what I thought I remembered actually happened.'

'And that's why you agreed not to write what Richard Lowrie said,' continued Rebecca, hardly listening to him. 'You knew all that stuff about drugs was a load of shit, and you knew there was a bigger, better story around the corner. You've been trying to get it out of everyone—' she was now staggered by her own naivety '— including *me*.'

She recalled what he'd advised at Huxley, about persuading Patricia to talk: *You need to let her share stuff in her own time, as though it's her own idea* . . . Was this the method he'd been using on her too? The first time they'd met, back in the new office, he'd thought she was withholding something. With mounting dismay, Rebecca realised *that* was why he was still here: he was biding his time, waiting for her to slip up.

'Is that what you take me for?' Ellis demanded, looking annoyed. 'Some sleazy tabloids hack?'

'So I'm wrong? You don't intend to write about him?'

Ellis sighed. 'It's not like this article would be a—'

'You do,' she cut in. 'You called and emailed all those people, you came to Exeter, to Huxley—'

'Huxley was your idea!'

'—you've got that whole folder of research.' Now, she did laugh. 'I can't understand how I missed it before!'

'And I can't understand why you're so against this,' countered Ellis. 'It's like I told you on Monday: it's a great story.'

'It's not a story!' Rebecca snapped. 'This is his life we're talking about, his *real life*!'

'All right,' said Ellis, raising his hands in a pacifying gesture. 'But just hear me out, will you? No, listen,' he pleaded, when she tried to interrupt him again. 'It's not as though I'm going to write some sensationalist crap with a clickbait headline: *You'll NEVER Guess What Happened to The Stowaway* . . . This would be a proper profile, a sensitive investigation into why a man at the height of his fame suddenly disappeared. You said it yourself, he was abandoned when he was struggling – he was fired, for God's sake! Don't you think people ought to know about that? And not just for Leo's sake: pieces like this, they're important, they can make a difference. Plus, imagine if we actually *find* him . . .'

Ellis let this last point hang, like a dangling cat toy she might make a lunge for, but Rebecca sat back, the metal edges of her chair digging into her spine and shoulder blades. Until this moment, she hadn't really believed – or perhaps hadn't wanted to believe – the extent of his deceit. But here it was, and not only was he unapologetic, he seemed almost proud of what he'd been plotting.

'You have this all worked out, don't you?' she said in her iciest voice.

'No!' cried Ellis, and even through her own agitation Rebecca was struck by how unusual it was to see him rattled. 'I really don't! You're acting like I've had this devious plan, when I was just following the story, seeing where it led. I wasn't expecting any of *this*.'

He traced a wide arc through the air, and Rebecca hated herself for wondering whether she was included in the gesture.

'I thought you were on my side,' she said. 'I thought you were helping me because you—' She stopped herself in time, her skin smarting with the shame of it. 'I thought we were friends!'

'We are!'

'Then why didn't you *tell* me?'

Her voice sounded high and plaintive, which made them both pause, although she was just as angry as before. Angrier, in fact, because the rest of it made a horrible kind of sense: of course he'd had his own agenda, of course he hadn't wanted to be her friend – or anything more. What she didn't understand, though, was why he hadn't said anything. Her stomach twisted, as though being wrung out like a sodden dishcloth: had he been laughing at her all this time, getting a kick out of her stupidity?

'Until I watched that video, I didn't know anything for certain,' said Ellis, cautiously. 'All I had were vague memories, just like you.'

'You don't know anything about my memories.'

'No, I don't.' He seemed to seize upon this point. 'I didn't even realise you cared about him this much: you never talk about him, about your time with him—'

'That's because it's none of your business!'

'—So how am I supposed to work out what you do and don't know? And how is it my place to tell you something *I* don't even know?'

Rebecca shook her head: these were just excuses, weak excuses.

'I thought maybe Richard Lowrie or Patricia or Priya might've been able to confirm it,' continued Ellis. 'I hoped because they'd known him, because they'd seen what he was like first-hand . . . But they were all useless, weren't they? Too bitter, too *brainless* to recognise what'd been happening right under their—'

'*You* should've told me,' Rebecca insisted. 'I trusted you, I went behind my mum's back to talk to you . . .' She trailed off, realising Rosalyn, too, had known all along, before returning to the betrayal at hand: 'You should've had the guts to say *something*.'

'Like I said,' Ellis began, his jaw clenched, 'it wasn't my place to—'

'Or maybe you didn't say anything because you knew I'd figure you out earlier, and you wanted to protect your precious *story*.'

Now Ellis was shaking his head. 'If that's what you think of me, fine,' he snapped. 'But I didn't make you do any of this. I would've given up after Richard Lowrie if it hadn't been for you. You're the one who's been pushing for answers, it's not my fault they're difficult, or that this is how you've had to find out.'

'Well, thanks very much for your compassion . . .'

'Really? *You're* calling me cold?'

'Fuck you.'

Hurt, Rebecca had imbued her response with venom, but Ellis merely rubbed at his forehead and sighed. 'Look, I'm sorry, I didn't mean—What are you doing?'

Rebecca was standing up, the backs of her knees knocking against her chair, which scraped over the mismatching floor tiles. The noise caused the customers at the neighbouring tables to stare – or perhaps they'd been staring already. Suddenly, the café was too hot, too loud; too much.

Ellis got to his feet. 'Come on, Becs, let's just—'

'Stop calling me that!' she snarled. 'Seriously, who the fuck do you think you are?'

She tugged at the strap of her bag, attempting to release it from the metal chair, and caught a glimpse of her uneaten porridge. The sight of the greyish sludge prompted a tremor below her sternum, as though her insides had coiled up and were ready to spring. She had to go. *Now.*

Ellis was still saying something, but she couldn't hear him anymore. Everything was smudging. 'No,' she said, leaning away from his outstretched hand, 'leave me alone . . .'

With a yank, she finally managed to free her bag, which bumped against the table and sent the spoon of her breakfast flying. She ignored the clang as it hit the floor, and pushed past Ellis, stumbling towards the door with her hand clamped over her fizzing mouth.

Outside, the sun was blaring. Rebecca collided with a group of tourists – who twittered apologies as she lurched between their shopping bags – and staggered down the street until she reached an alleyway. Whimpering, she bent double and was forced to cling to the nearest wall as the meagre contents of her stomach splashed onto the concrete.

13

Rosalyn

The humiliation stung the most. During the drive back to Devon, it pelted at Rebecca like a hailstorm. Everyone had known – Ellis, Rosalyn, Lillian. Her whole family had kept this from her for years, and she, feigning indifference towards her own father, had made their deception *easy*.

Why hadn't she asked about him sooner? Why hadn't she guessed? *He's not well*, the man in the video had said, but when Rebecca examined her cobbled-together memories of Leo – his loud renditions of Christmas carols, his trail of biscuit crumbs through the woods – she still struggled to equate his behaviour with illness. He'd just been bigger and brighter than everyone else – better, she'd thought. It hadn't occurred to her his blaze might be symptomatic of . . . What was it even called?

But she'd known *something*, hadn't she? She'd been sceptical of Richard Lowrie, Patricia and Priya. Had she doubted them because she could remember a different man from the one they'd all merrily slandered? Or had she simply been grasping for a reason other than drugs, grief and loneliness, or *it was just the way he was*, to explain his nature and why he was no longer in her life?

All these years without him, assuming he hadn't cared and resolving not to care in return, when the reality was . . . What, exactly? He'd been forced out of her life? He was holed up in a hospital, somewhere? He was dead? Rebecca wanted to shake the steering wheel and scream. Even now, she was still no closer to answering that question Ellis had posed to her almost a fortnight ago: *Where is Leo Sampson?*

Ellis. The thought of him caused Rebecca's now empty stomach to tighten with rage and shame. How could she have been so stupid? She'd known all along he was after some kind of story. She should've distanced herself from him as soon as she'd started her own search, not invited him to Huxley or confided in him or wrapped herself around him in that bar – *thank God* she hadn't slept with him, at least. Now, it was Ellis she resolved not to care about, Ellis she wanted to wipe from her memory. As well as erasing the events of last night and her idiotic belief that he'd actually liked her, she wanted to pretend it'd been her own idea to look for Leo and that his illness or condition – whatever you were supposed to call it – was something she'd come to understand by herself, not via that horrible video.

She missed the first exit to Exeter, then all the others that would've taken her from the M5 into the city. She'd thought she was heading home, back to her drab little flat, but it wasn't a shock to find herself speeding towards Dartmoor instead. Perhaps, at the back of her mind, Lower Morvale had been her destination all along.

The sight of Primrose Cottage made Rebecca's muscles clench with fury. As she slammed the car door shut behind her, she noted it was unusual Rosalyn hadn't yet pounced, almost as though her mother *knew* . . . But after marching across the driveway, Rebecca discovered the house was just as quiet as the last time she'd visited – although when she paused to listen for footsteps upstairs, she heard female laughter somewhere outside.

Rebecca strode down the hallway, past the kitchen and Rosalyn's study, but stopped short as she threw open the door to the back garden, her anger yielding to surprise. Framed by the cascading lilac flowers of a sweet-smelling buddleia, Rosalyn, Lillian and Daphne were reclined in deckchairs in the late afternoon sun, sharing what looked to be a large jug of Pimm's. Slouched nearby, his own seat entirely cast in shade, Morton was grasping at a bottle of beer.

A collective murmur of pleasure greeted Rebecca's sudden appearance, and Daphne waggled the glass in her hand so its ice gave a melodious clink. 'Yoo-hoo!' she cried. 'You're just in time for drinkies!'

'I thought you were coming back from London today?' called a beaming Rosalyn.

'I did. I drove straight here.' Rebecca tried to keep her tone flat, which was difficult when they all looked so pleased to see her.

'Well, come and tell us all about it, dear,' said Lillian, beckoning her over.

'Yes, for God's sake change the subject,' muttered Morton from his gloomy enclave, 'they've been talking about *cushion covers* . . . I assume you'll be drinking something sensible?' He reached towards the cool box beside his deckchair and produced another bottle of beer, which he offered to Rebecca.

'No, have some of this!' exclaimed Daphne, giving the fruit-filled concoction in the jug a stir. 'The strawberries are from our garden . . .'

'Why don't you go and get a chair?' suggested Rosalyn.

Rebecca was tempted. It would be so easy to collapse in the sun with a cold drink – a non-alcoholic drink – and pretend everything was fine. They seemed so settled, so content, and she felt an unwelcome surge of fondness as she glanced from one to the other, taking in Morton's ancient sandals, which showed off his hairy toes; Daphne's gigantic straw hat, which looked like a lampshade; Lillian's scratched white-rimmed sunglasses, which she'd found in a bog near Haytor.

But they're liars, Rebecca reminded herself, and the sun-soaked garden seemed to darken as, deliberately this time, she recalled *The Woodcutter's Cottage.* There were still details of the story she couldn't translate, but she understood that Leo had felt lost here, confined and chipped away at until almost nothing of him remained.

Rebecca fixed her gaze upon her mother. 'Actually, I was wondering if I could talk to you for a minute?' she said. 'Inside?'

'Sounds ominous, Becca-Bell!' laughed Rosalyn, but she peeled herself from her deckchair and pointed at the jug. 'Now don't you two finish that without me!'

While Lillian and Daphne giggled, Morton rolled his eyes at Rebecca, who almost laughed despite herself.

Rosalyn was wearing white cropped trousers and a sleeveless floral shirt, which emphasised her skinny limbs. As she kicked off her garden clogs at the door and pulled Rebecca into a hug, she said, 'Well, it's lovely to see you, Petal, although you might've given me a *teensy* bit of notice – goodness knows what I'm going to feed you!'

'I'm not staying long.'

But Rosalyn wasn't listening: 'I'm sure we'll find something. Now come in, come in . . .'

Mutely, Rebecca followed her back inside, and as she breathed in the rich, sylvan scent of Primrose Cottage, wanted nothing more than to crawl up to her old room, flop down on her childhood bed and sleep. But she forced herself to trudge past the stairs: she'd not come here for comfort.

In the kitchen, Rosalyn was already opening and closing cupboards, drawers, the fridge. 'Did you want Pimm's, or would you rather have tea? They do say it cools you down . . . How was the weather in London?'

'Hot. Tea would be good, thanks.'

As she slid onto one of the stools of the breakfast bar, Rebecca watched her mother fill the kettle, sniff at the milk jug, top up Brontë's water bowl. Why was she always flitting about? Rebecca wanted to throw a net over her, maybe trap her behind glass, like one of Victor's butterflies.

'Mum?' she ventured.

'How was Amy?'

'Um – yeah, good.'

'What's her flat like?'

'It's nice.'

Inwardly, Rebecca winced: she'd been so eager to get out of London, she hadn't waited for Amy to return from work. She hadn't even left a note or sent a text. The idea of explaining what had happened with Ellis was too mortifying – though Rebecca couldn't help feeling that, without Amy's meddling, she wouldn't have made such a fool of herself.

'She's in Greenwich, isn't she?' continued Rosalyn. 'Debbie'll be pleased you went – she does worry about Amy, all alone in that big city.'

'She's not alone, she's with Tim.'

'Yes, but you know what I mean, Becca-Bell – she's not nearby, like you. Are you staying the night?'

'No.'

Rebecca couldn't let this carry on. Yet she was mesmerised by the sight of her mother buzzing about the kitchen: it seemed remarkable Rosalyn was still exactly the same, when Leo – or rather, the Leo in Rebecca's mind – had completely transformed.

'Well, I hope you'll come back at the weekend,' said Rosalyn, 'and I'm sure you can stay long enough to look at a few holiday photos now. I'll go and get them.'

'No, don't—'

But her mother was already heading into the hallway.

Rebecca rubbed at her forehead, listening to the rush of the kettle and a snuffling snore from Brontë. She should've said something as soon as she'd arrived, regardless of the others being there. Because the longer she let Rosalyn believe everything was fine, the less inclined she was to say the things she wanted to say, the things she *had* to say.

'Here we are,' said Rosalyn, re-entering the kitchen with an envelope. 'I had them printed out, otherwise they just get lost on the computer, don't they?'

'*Mum*?'

'Yes, Petal?'

'I want to know where my dad is.'

Rosalyn paused, but after a spasm of surprise crossed her features she managed to smile. 'Rebecca, we already had this conversation, remember?'

'No, we didn't.'

'We *did*,' Rosalyn insisted in a sing-song voice. 'Just a couple of weeks ago. You'd been contacted by that journalist, and—'

'This isn't about that. *I* want to know where he is.'

Rosalyn blinked a few times. 'I don't understand where this is coming from. Are you trying to upset me?'

'Of course not.'

'Then why are you asking about this?'

Rebecca sighed. This was like talking to Ellis: question following question following question. 'He's my dad, I have a right to know.'

'And what about me?' asked Rosalyn. 'Don't I get a say in this?'

'In what? I just want to know where he is!'

Rosalyn shook her head. 'I don't believe this, I assumed you came here this afternoon for *me*! Never mind that we haven't seen one another for weeks, never mind that you missed our lunch yesterday . . .'

'I was in London!' snapped Rebecca. 'And do you want to know why?'

Rosalyn's expression implied she didn't, but Rebecca finally felt she was making headway and said, 'I've been looking for him.'

Before her mother could interrupt, she began a brief summary of the past few weeks' events, marvelling that this was really happening; she was forcing this conversation after all these years. She related her meetings with the figures from Leo's past she'd gone to for the explanation Rosalyn had never provided and, in particular, her weekend with Patricia, the great-aunt she'd never heard of.

By the time she'd finished, blotches of colour had appeared along Rosalyn's high cheekbones, and her gaze was darting between Rebecca's face and the address book on the breakfast bar. Until, without a word, she turned and flicked down the switch of the kettle. The water reboiled in seconds, but it seemed to take her an unusually long time to make two cups of tea.

'Mum?' Rebecca called over the sound of the tap, because Rosalyn was now rinsing a spoon. 'Mum, can we talk about this?'

'Talk about what?'

'Mum, I *know*.'

Rosalyn turned off the water, but stayed at the sink, staring at the snoozing Brontë, or the windowsill or the view into Primrose Lane. 'What is it you think you know, Rebecca?'

'Everything,' she replied, with an incredulous little laugh. 'I know he was ill, and for a long time – for most of his life, I think. I know he tried to run away from it and channel it into his acting, but when you met him he was struggling. And I know that after you split up and he became the Stowaway, it all began again.'

Rebecca had surprised herself: she'd barely had a chance to connect what she knew of Leo's life to what she'd learned from that video, yet the story had tripped off her tongue like a well-worn tale from childhood. When Rosalyn finally turned from the sink, however, she looked far from impressed.

'You don't know anything at all,' she said.

Her voice was quiet, calm – and so scathing Rebecca recoiled.

'Are you saying it's not true?'

'Oh, it's true,' said Rosalyn, 'but just because you've done all this *sleuthing*, doesn't mean you understand any of it.'

She returned to the breakfast bar, setting down Rebecca's tea with a clunk. Rebecca wanted to swipe it from the counter, just like Brontë knocked ornaments from surfaces with a swish of her paw; she wanted to see the orange *Pride and Prejudice* mug – Rosalyn's favourite – go splashing and smashing against the stone floor.

Instead, she forced herself to emulate her mother's chilly composure: 'Why don't you explain it, then?'

The look Rosalyn gave her was probing, as though sizing her up. 'All right,' she said, softly.

She remained on her feet, and for a moment she too looked like an actor, one trying to remember her lines.

'Imagine waking up and finding your whole house covered in flour,' she began, her eyes wide, as though she could still see it, 'because that's what happened when he decided he wanted a white Christmas. Imagine . . .' she trailed off, staring out of the window again for a prompt. 'Imagine the vicar calling you at three in the morning to say your husband was dancing around on top of the bell tower and could you please come and fetch him? Imagine discovering most of your savings were gone—' her words were coming out faster now '—because your joint account has been emptied to buy a luxury campervan, one he wanted to drive to *Greece*!' She glared at Rebecca. 'You can't,' she said. 'You have no idea what it was like to constantly be afraid of what he would do or say, where he would go – and whether he would even come back, because whatever was going on in his head was far more exciting than the dull little life you'd trapped him in!'

She broke off, breathing hard through her nose. But now she'd finally permitted herself to speak on this subject, it appeared she couldn't stop.

'And those were the *highs*!' she cried, her voice shrill. 'Those were the good days – for him, at least. Because there were plenty of bad ones; days when he wouldn't get out of bed, when he wouldn't move or speak, days when I feared . . .' She shook her head. 'It wasn't all fun and games.'

'I never thought—'

'Yes you did,' said Rosalyn. 'And it wasn't your fault, you were a child, but for *Leo and Birdie* everything was one big game: let's hitchhike into Exeter, let's dye all of our clothes green, let's go camping in the rain – and don't tell Mummy, because she'll just say no. He turned me into someone you avoided and lied to and resented. I was the villain in all of his stories.'

Rebecca lowered her gaze, but instead of seeing her untouched mug of tea her mind conjured a desert-dwelling witch. Then she recalled how Patricia had described Adeline and Leo as she had nodded towards the garden: *The two of them were always out there . . . playing their secret games, telling their secret stories.* When she looked up again, Rosalyn was perching on the stool opposite, apparently so drained by memories she could no longer stand. They regarded one another over the spotless surface and Rebecca found she did resent her mother – not for being the responsible one, but because now she didn't seem like a villain at all.

'I was very young when I met him,' Rosalyn continued,

quieter now. 'We both were. I didn't know anything about . . . *mental health problems.*' The last three words seemed to catch in her throat. 'I sensed he was a bit broken, but I thought he could be fixed – I thought *I* could fix him.' She clutched at one of her knuckles, as though afraid she too might start to fall apart. 'I tried to make it work, I did. At the beginning, I would've done anything for him. He completely dazzled me; I'd never known anyone like him before, not in real life, not outside of books . . .' She glanced down, and promptly let go of what Rebecca now realised was the bare fourth finger of her left hand. 'But then he began tearing us apart, Becca-Bell – you and me. And look!' A high, breathless laugh escaped her. 'He's still doing it now!'

'He's not doing anything,' Rebecca snapped, her anger reigniting. 'It's you who's caused this; it's your fault we're having this conversation now, instead of years ago.'

'You were too—'

'I wasn't too young! You should've said something, rather than pretend that he didn't exist, that he didn't *care.*'

'What on earth would I have said?' cried Rosalyn.

'The truth, maybe? He was ill!' Then, because she now wanted to know everything, Rebecca asked, 'What was it he had? What's it called?'

But Rosalyn was shaking her head, and it was this – her denial, or defeat, or whatever it was – that annoyed Rebecca more than anything her mother had said or done so far.

'He was ill,' she said again, and it felt right to say it, because she'd never heard it spoken aloud in this house before. 'He was ill!'

'*So what?*'

It took Rebecca a few seconds to register what her mother had scoffed and, even then, she struggled to believe it. But

Rosalyn's expression was entirely devoid of pity, so much so that Rebecca turned away in disgust.

'Where are you going?' her mother asked, as she slipped from her stool.

Rebecca didn't know. They weren't finished – far from it – but this was even harder than she'd imagined. She shouldn't have come here this afternoon. This conversation should have waited until she'd had a chance to reflect on everything, until she'd had some proper sleep.

'Rebecca?'

'Just give me a minute, will you?'

'Rebecca . . .'

She continued towards the door.

'Don't you dare leave!'

Rebecca froze. She was used to coaxing and guilt-trips and jokes that weren't really jokes; she was well-acquainted with long periods of silent treatment, and even the odd bit of bribery. But never, in twenty-five years, had her mother raised her voice like this.

She turned back to find Rosalyn on her feet, her face and throat flushed once more. 'If you come here asking about him, you don't get to walk out halfway through!' she snarled. 'If you want the truth, Rebecca, you need to listen to *all* of it!'

'Good – you should have told me all of it years ago!'

'Should I have told you he liked it?'

'What?'

'Being ill, he *liked* it.' Rosalyn looked triumphant now. 'He thought it made him different. *Special.*'

Rebecca frowned. 'Wasn't that part of it, though? The illness?'

'That doesn't mean he wasn't aware of it. He was addicted to his own condition and he didn't care. What did it matter if he caused chaos, as long as *he* felt good?'

Rebecca hesitated, wishing she had the knowledge and language to defend Leo – and wondering, for the first time that afternoon, whether he deserved defending. 'Are you saying he didn't try and get help?'

'Of course he didn't. He'd convinced himself he was supposed to be that way, and most of the time he didn't see anything wrong with it. Sometimes he even convinced *me*, but then all those ideas and schemes he had when he was in the grip of the thing, they were all just . . .' Rosalyn laughed. 'They were all just *mad*.'

Rebecca, unwilling to betray her ignorance, proceeded carefully: 'But if he'd seen a doctor . . .'

'He refused. He was too scared and too selfish, mostly the latter.'

'But—'

'No, he was. You don't remember what it was like, when we were consumed by it – because it consumed all of us, not just him. I begged him to get help – for my sake, for your sake – but, as I said, he liked it.'

He was ill, Rebecca thought, though this time she didn't say it. 'You still should've told me,' she insisted. 'As soon as I was old enough.'

'Old enough for what? To understand? I'm telling you now, and you still don't get it: you're determined to be on his side no matter what. You always were.'

'That's not fair.'

'No, it's not, is it?' Then, in the same curt voice, Rosalyn asked, 'Are you going to drink that?'

She was staring at the mug of tea still on the breakfast bar, and Rebecca, automatically compliant, returned to her stool. Rosalyn fetched her own mug from beside the sink and once more took the seat opposite, her detached expression intimating they were nothing more than strangers sitting down to a formal meeting. To give herself thinking time, Rebecca sipped at her tea. It was lukewarm, but it felt good to fill her hollow stomach with something, and Rosalyn had remembered she liked it strong.

'Was Edinburgh the last time I saw him?' she asked, eventually.

'Yes.'

Rosalyn didn't look surprised by the question, nor that she'd been caught out in her lie of earlier that week.

'When was I there?'

'August '97. How much do you remember?'

'Just bits and pieces.'

'Do you know why you were there?'

It was so irregular for Rosalyn of all people to be encouraging her to dwell on her past with Leo that, at first, Rebecca drew a blank. All she could think of were the stock images of the city she'd seen online earlier in the week: a castle, a craggy hill, a pillared monument. She tried to focus on the festival, the only part of the trip she could remember, and from the mists of her mind plucked the dancing girls, the juggler, the couple in the masks – or had it only been a man? And with that last thought, the performers vanished and instead she saw sun and sand and two figures grappling over a golden cage, while a red bird soared high into the air . . .

'He took me,' she breathed, her heart giving an unpleasant lurch. 'We were in Edinburgh because he'd taken me.'

Rosalyn closed her eyes, her brow furrowed, as though anticipating one of her headaches.

'Why?' asked Rebecca. 'What happened?'

Her mother took a long time to answer – she seemed to be bracing herself for something – but when she spoke her voice was level: 'After he left the village, we agreed he could see you once or twice a month,' she began. 'He lived in Bristol at the time, because that's where that programme was filmed, so I would drive you there and drop you at his flat – which was the crummiest hole you could imagine – and take myself off to the shops or the hairdresser for the rest of the day. Occasionally, you'd stay over.'

Rebecca strained to evoke something of these visits, but all she could picture was the purple sweet in front of the purple door, which she supposed must have belonged to the crummy flat. Once again, she recalled what Richard Lowrie had said about Leo's mood around this time: *He was upset about his daughter . . . His ex-wife was making it difficult for him to see her.*

'For a year or two it was fine,' continued Rosalyn, '*he* was fine. He had that show, I suppose. Then one day, the 23rd of August, he was bouncing around when we arrived at his flat and I knew he was having one of his episodes, I could always tell. I wanted to call it off, but we'd driven all the way there and you both would've made such a fuss, so I convinced myself it would be all right. Perhaps I thought his fatherly instincts would override his condition, I don't know . . . It was the stupidest thing I've ever done, leaving you there against all of *my* instincts.'

Rebecca stared: just as Rosalyn had never raised her voice before this afternoon, neither had she admitted to any kind of failure.

'You've no idea what it was like, going back to that flat and finding you gone – because I knew straight away he'd taken you. At first, the police kept saying he might've lost track of time, that you'd stayed too late at the park, but I knew. I *knew*.'

Tentatively, for she was afraid her mother would stop this story at any moment, Rebecca asked, 'How long was I gone?'

'Just under two days. I dropped you off at around 11am on the Saturday and you were found in Edinburgh the next evening. That might not seem very long,' she said, suddenly sharp, 'but bear in mind I had no idea – *no idea* – where you were. You can't imagine . . . And I knew he wouldn't hurt you, not deliberately, but I kept thinking he might drag you into a busy road or take you on one of his climbs, or . . .' She inhaled, her breath unsteady. 'You were six years old, Becca-Bell, and I thought I'd never see you again.'

Rosalyn leaned forward on her pointy elbows and clutched at her skull, as though the resurgence of these memories really had brought on a headache. Rebecca knew she should say something, do something; slide a hand across the space between them. But her bones had turned to lead.

In the silence that followed, she scoured her memory for something of this trip – of this *kidnapping*, she supposed. How had they got there? Where had they stayed? What had they done for almost two whole days? *Think,* she urged herself, *think.* But all she could summon was that same series of images from the cobbled, rain-lashed street and the feeling of bumping through a crowd: *Daddy! Daddy! Daddy!*

'I lost him,' she said. 'While we were there, I lost him.'

Rosalyn looked up. 'He lost you, more like,' she snapped. 'It's his fault you were wandering that city all by yourself, it's his fault you—' She stopped herself.

'What?' Rebecca pressed. 'His fault I what?'

Rosalyn's dark eyes were wide, like a startled deer. Then, with a small sigh, she said, 'There was an accident. You fell down some steps and broke your arm.'

Rebecca frowned, gripping at her right elbow. 'No . . .' she said, feeling for the smooth scar with her thumb. 'This was from my bike. You told me I'd fallen off my bike here, by the ford.'

But even as she said it, she could see, in that previously unplaceable memory, the dark passage where the ground had seemed to drop away . . . And she'd never been able to recall toppling off that little blue bike with its stickers and ribbons.

'It was in Edinburgh,' said Rosalyn, now with grim determination. 'You were on your own in a big crowd and got pushed towards some kind of steep alleyway, where you slipped on the wet paving. You were taken to hospital, of course, where, thank God, you were able to say who you were. Obviously, the police down here were already looking for you, so it all moved fairly quickly after that, though it felt like weeks and weeks until I got you back. And it could've been so much worse.'

Her quavering voice finally broke, and then it was she who reached out to knot her fingers through Rebecca's. Her grip was tight, painful, but Rebecca hardly felt it. Again, she was staggered by the gaps in her own memory; of the hospital, the reunion with Rosalyn, even of the accident itself, there was nothing.

Should she ask about Leo? He had got her hurt. Maybe not on purpose, but he was the reason she'd been there, on her own; he was the reason she had that ugly scar . . . Still, it was difficult to feel too aggrieved about something she barely remembered, and instead it was Rosalyn's haunted expression, Rosalyn's distress, that gave her pause. How much more of this could her mother endure? She'd never spoken of Leo so openly before. But wasn't that precisely why they had to continue? This might never happen again.

'He wasn't with me, then? After the accident? In the hospital?'

'No.' Rosalyn's expression hardened. 'I don't think he even knew about it.'

'What happened to him?'

'I heard he was picked up the police as well, but I don't know the details. He was on one of his highs, so who knows what he was doing . . .' She let go of Rebecca's hand to make a sweeping gesture, brushing the matter aside.

'And you didn't let him see me again,' Rebecca said, unable to keep a note of accusation from her voice.

'It wasn't like that, I wasn't unreasonable,' insisted Rosalyn. 'I hired a solicitor, of course – technically, we were still married at that point – and it was agreed he could see you when he'd sorted himself out: got a proper diagnosis, started taking medication, found a sensible job – all the things I'd been trying to get him to do for years. Until then, he wasn't fit to care for you.'

'But he didn't sort himself out?'

'If he did, I never heard about it. Do you know, I thought *you* of all people would be the one to convince him . . .' Rosalyn shrugged.

Rebecca tensed, interpreting this as a slight – although from which of her parents she wasn't sure. At the same time, though, it didn't quite ring true: ill or not, Leo wouldn't have just given up on her. Hadn't he left her *Seven Tales* two years later?

'I don't believe that,' she said.

Her mother looked steely again. 'Which part?'

'He must've tried to see me after the accident,' said Rebecca, her temper flaring again. 'You must've stopped him, kept him away somehow, and now—'

'I didn't!'

'—And now you're lying, just like when you told me I'd fallen off my bike, just like when you told me I'd never been to Edinburgh!'

'I did that to protect you!' Rosalyn cried, her face colouring again as she jabbed a finger across the breakfast bar. 'Everything I've done has been to shield you from this, Rebecca, *everything*!'

Once more, Rebecca balked at this uncharacteristic outburst of anger. It wasn't an admission of guilt, exactly, but perhaps it was all she was going to get. Maybe Rosalyn even believed what she was saying, but it couldn't be true: here was the only explanation for Leo's absence – at least, the only explanation that made any sense.

They lapsed into another silence, one that lasted so long it became almost comfortable. It appeared they'd arrived at a kind of stalemate – or perhaps they were both tired of arguing.

'I spent years dreading the day he would come back,' Rosalyn said eventually, staring towards the hallway. 'I used to picture him bursting through that door at dinnertime or making a scene at the school gate. Until, just like that, I realised: he was gone. And we haven't done badly without him, have we?'

'No,' said Rebecca, although she was reluctant to give Rosalyn the validation she seemed to crave. 'But where is he *now*?'

This was how it'd all started – *Where is Leo Sampson?* – yet the question always got forgotten, because asking it spawned so many others.

'I don't know,' said Rosalyn.

'You must – you can't just divorce someone and never speak to them again.'

'Don't be naïve, of course you can. Do you think he sent birthday cards or got in touch at Christmas? Do you think he helped out with your tuition fees? We hardly saw a penny of what he made from that ridiculous programme . . .'

'What's in your desk drawer, then?'

Rosalyn's reaction was one of confusion, rather than guilt. 'What?'

'The middle drawer, the one that's locked. There's nothing about him in there?'

'Oh for goodness' sake!' Rosalyn threw up her hands. 'There's just a bit of chocolate in there, that's all. A few sweets.' Suddenly she did look abashed, though Rebecca suspected this was connected to the uncovering of her secret stash of snacks rather than anything to do with Leo. 'I only lock it because Brontë once got in. Do you want me to show you?'

Defiantly, she pointed towards the hallway, but Rebecca didn't move.

'So you've no idea where he is?' she said, determined not to get distracted. 'None at all?'

Rosalyn sighed. 'The last I knew he was still in Edinburgh, but that was years ago, when all that legal business was being sorted. I doubt he's there now, considering what he was like, how restless he was. He could be anywhere.' She gave Rebecca a sharp look. 'And you're going to keep looking for him, aren't you?'

'I'm not sure.'

'You are,' Rosalyn said. 'After everything I've told you.'

'Mum, I think I should hear his side of the story . . .'

'Because you don't believe mine?'

'It's not that, it's just—'

'It's still not enough.' Rosalyn arranged her features into a smile. 'Well, *silly me* for expecting a bit of loyalty for once!'

'*Mum* . . .'

'No, it's fine, Rebecca, I'm used to it by now.' She rose from her stool and grasped at their mugs. 'I just thought, after all this time, you might finally be on *my* side.'

'I just want to talk to him!'

'Of course,' said Rosalyn, still affecting breeziness. 'And I assume you've prepared yourself for the possibility he might no longer be alive? That maybe that's why he hasn't tried to see you?'

'Yes.'

Perhaps Rosalyn had considered this the ace up her sleeve, because when it had so little effect, her whole body seemed to droop, as though the mugs in her hands were as heavy as dumbbells. She looked tired, wrung out, and so sad all of Rebecca's anger and frustration was smothered by something softer. Without thinking about it, she crossed the kitchen, transferred the mugs from Rosalyn's fingers to the sink and pulled her mother into a hug.

They were about the same height, but Rosalyn was so thin she felt brittle, and Rebecca was afraid to hold her too tightly. She was shaking, possibly from cold as much as anything else; her bare arms were rough with goosepimples. She smelled of flowery perfume, salon shampoo and home; she smelled of Mum.

Initially, Rosalyn didn't move, apparently stunned into stillness by Rebecca's rare demonstration of affection. Until, slowly, she turned her head so her mouth was next to Rebecca's ear. 'Just don't forget what he did to this family,' she whispered.

He is my family, Rebecca thought.

'Ah, this is nice!'

They broke apart to find a beaming Lillian standing in the doorway. The jug in her hands was empty, save for some mushy-looking fruit at the bottom, and she'd draped a lacy shawl around her shoulders, one side of which had slipped down her back and was trailing to the floor. At the sight of her twinkling grandmother, Rebecca almost smiled.

'I'm afraid Daffy and I might need a top-up,' Lillian said, with a guilty giggle.

'A top-up?' Rosalyn repeated.

Lillian's smile faded. 'Of Pimm's?'

'Oh . . .' Rosalyn squeezed shut her eyes again. 'Yes, help yourself . . . I think I might go and lie down, I'm not feeling too well.'

Dismissing Lillian's murmur of sympathy with a wave, Rosalyn headed for the door, before doubling back to the sink where she scooped Brontë from the windowsill. As she departed, clutching the enormous animal to her chest, Rebecca thought she looked like a child dragging around an oversized teddy she'd won at the fair, although nothing would've compelled her to laugh.

'Is everything all right?'

Reluctantly, Rebecca glanced back at her grandmother, who was placing the jug on the breakfast bar. The papery skin of her face was tanned from her holiday, and a bright pink flower had been tucked into one of her hairclips, probably by Daphne. Otherwise, she looked much the same as ever – and also entirely unfamiliar.

'Everything's fine,' said Rebecca. 'I'm going home.'

She started for the hallway, determined to ignore the concern and confusion in Lillian's expression.

'Becca, what's happened? Talk to me a moment—'

But Rebecca kept going. She'd done enough talking and didn't have a moment, not for Lillian; all her moments were now reserved for Leo.

'Is this about the book?'

In the porch, midway through sliding on her shoes, Rebecca paused. Lillian caught up with her, the long end of her shawl flapping towards the floor again, her cheeks darkening in the same way Rosalyn's had before. Taking in the sight of her, Rebecca was seized by another surge of rage.

'You should've given me that book years ago,' she said.

'I know, I'm sorry. But when Rozzy told me you wanted nothing to do with him—'

'She was lying. You should've known she was lying.'

Lillian nodded, accepting this, before continuing, 'It's just, after everything she went through . . .'

'What about everything *he* went through?'

'I know, dear, but—'

'And what about me? I thought he didn't *care*!'

'Oh, Becca.' Lillian shook her head with such vehemence the flower dropped from her hair clip. 'There was nobody in the world Leo cared about more than you. That was half the problem.'

Rebecca had wanted to hear this ever since discovering the

dedication in *Seven Tales*; a part of her had wanted to hear it all her life. But it wasn't enough anymore.

'How did you get it?' she asked. Then, off her grandmother's puzzled expression, she said, 'The book! Did he give it to you? Did he send it?'

'It just—It just *appeared*,' said Lillian, sounding tearful now. 'On the doorstep, at the house . . .'

'Was there a note?' Rebecca pressed, unable to believe she was still having to interrogate her family like this. 'A postmark? A return address?'

'No – there wasn't an envelope. It was in wrapping paper, bright yellow wrapping paper. I think it was for your birthday.'

'Which birthday?'

'Your ninth.'

'But there was no card?'

'I'm sorry, dear . . .'

She's lying, Rebecca thought. *They're all still lying.*

'So you don't know where he is?' she said, bluntly.

'The last Rozzy knew, he was—'

'In Edinburgh, yeah.'

Nudging her bare foot into its ballet pump, Rebecca reflected there was no Leo Sampson in Edinburgh – at least, there was no evidence of him there online. If he was still alive, it was likely he'd moved on, just as Rosalyn had said.

'You should go and talk to Mum, she's upset.'

Rebecca nodded towards the hallway, to what was visible of the stairs, but Lillian remained where she stood. 'Becca, if you are going to look for him—'

'I am.'

'—Have you considered the kind of person you might find? Have you read those stories?'

Rebecca almost laughed. 'Nana, I *know*,' she said, casting

around for a way to describe the worst of it, and alighting on Leo's own words: 'I know about the music that won't stop playing, about the shadows at the edge of the world. I get it now.'

Her grandmother didn't appear thrown by these references. At some point, she must've read *Seven Tales* herself. Fresh grief jolted through Rebecca as she turned away from Lillian and wrenched open the front door: that was *her* book. She should've been the first person, the only person, to read those stories – yet this, too, had been denied her.

14

The Man Without a Shadow

Rebecca's flat was just as she'd left it: the same crime novel was propped open on the sofa, the same clothes were dangling from the drying rack, the same shopping list was scrawled across the magnetic pad on the fridge. At first glance, the only indication she'd been away for almost a week was the junk mail scattered across the doormat and a few apples shrivelling in the bowl on the table. Somehow, she'd expected more of a change.

Unpacking only took a few minutes, because she'd expected to be away for just the one night at Huxley, but returning everything to its proper place – her keys to the hook in the kitchen, her phone charger to the socket by her bed – wasn't quite as satisfying as she'd hoped. Being back here should've felt reassuring; she'd missed her own belongings, her own space, especially today. But now, in spite of her exhaustion, Rebecca felt restless and unanchored, like she no longer belonged here herself.

When everything else was accounted for, she slipped a hand into the inside pocket of her bag and withdrew a small book with a faded olive-green cover: *Seven Tales*. She hadn't looked at it properly in almost two days, yet the stories themselves had been at the forefront of her mind, as though they now existed beyond the pages of this little volume. She felt she'd known about the collector and the nixie, the witch and the sphinx, and everything in between for much longer than she'd been in possession of this book. It now seemed impossible she'd only read these tales recently, and just the once. Because when she compared them to her memories of Leo, the latter were full of echoes: the feathers in her hair and clothes, knocking against bark for tree spirits, those little cardboard puppets of krakens and woodcutters and witches . . . Understanding seemed to shake Rebecca by the shoulders: had Leo been telling her versions of these stories all her life?

There was one tale left now. There hadn't been any time to read it today, nor last night, but maybe – as with the second series of *The Stowaway* – Rebecca had been putting it off, rationing her father's words in case they were all she had left of him. She thought of Rosalyn, and her words from just a few hours ago: *you don't get to walk out halfway through.* In response, Rebecca had insisted she wanted to know everything, but, as she began to leaf through *Seven Tales* in search of the final story, she wasn't so sure anymore; very few of the answers she'd found over the past few weeks had brought her much clarity or contentment.

The Seventh Tale: The Man Without a Shadow

Once upon a time, there lived a man who could shake off his shadow. He'd had this strange ability since boyhood, and all he needed to do was wiggle each foot and his shadow would slip from his body like an unlaced boot.

When he was younger, he detached his shadow for the sole aim of gaining a playmate, and they would chase one another through the woods or go exploring with sling shots and fishing nets. But as time passed, they remained separated for longer, because the man felt much lighter without his shadow's chilly weight dragging behind him. He didn't know why, but his dark counterpart unnerved him.

In turn, the man unnerved others. Though at first people would be drawn to his brightness, they soon grew distrustful and kept their distance, fearful he would burn them if they came too close. Except for the local shaman, who was intrigued by the man's unusual ability, and offered to sew his shadow back onto his body.

'But then we will be stuck to one another, my shadow and I,' said the man.

'Everyone is stuck to their shadow,' the shaman pointed out.

'Everyone but me!' laughed the man. 'Without my shadow, I am light! Why would I want to change?'

'Because one day you may see the value of being like others, and having a little darkness at your back,' said the shaman. 'Just be sure it is not too late.'

But the man was not interested in this warning, so he refused the shaman's offer and went on his way. Yet he continued to be unsettled by his gloomy double who, like him, was now fully grown. So, he kicked the shadow from his body and, pretending it was one of their games, cajoled the dark figure into a large tank. The trusting shadow went willingly, but as soon as it was inside the man slammed down the glass lid and fastened it shut with many bolts and padlocks. Without that cold weight at his back, he laughed and sang and danced, until he almost forgot he had ever had a shadow at all.

But the shadow did not forget him. Abandoned in the tank, it was forced to feed on loneliness, hopelessness, even emptiness, and with this dark nourishment it grew bigger and stronger, until it was so powerful it was able to break through the glass.

Following its escape, the shadow sought out its captor, and the man was alarmed at how large and fearsome his dark counterpart had become. He turned away and, when the shadow followed, broke into a run. The shadow gave chase, just as it had chased him as a boy, only now it wasn't a game.

Eventually, the man began to tire. He had reached a desolate coast when he was forced to stop, and it was there his dark double pounced. They struggled with one another, and now the shadow's touch made him feel sick and cold and afraid. The world grew dim, and though the man continued to fight, his shadow was too strong. In a desperate attempt to save himself, he hauled them both towards the edge of a cliff and, as they plunged into the turbulent sea, he and his shadow were separated.

While the man recovered from this ordeal, the shaman found him and, once again, offered to sew his shadow back onto his body.

'After what I just suffered?' cried the man, horrified. 'It will destroy me!'

'Not if you are one again,' replied the shaman. 'If you allow me to stitch you together, your shadow will be forced to walk behind you,

as part of you. If you do not, you will always be running from it, and that is a lonely life.'

'So be it,' said the man, stubbornly. 'I would rather be light and alone than have that creature dragging at my back.'

The shaman was right, and the shadow continued its pursuit, so the man kept moving, terrified of what would happen if the dark figure caught him again. He hitched lifts on the backs of carts and stowed away in the hulls of ships. He travelled to villages, towns and cities. He journeyed across moors and through vales. He hid, too, using masks and costumes, though his shadow knew him by shape.

Along the way, the man met many people; some kind, some cruel, most a bit of both. Captivated by his brightness, they would try to trap him, enticing him to linger a little longer by the fire or stay for another serving of stew, trying to carve out a place for him in their lives. Occasionally, he tried to explain the danger he was in, but they never understood. Their shadows were fixed and compliant, and they were used to the darkness at their backs.

So, it was a solitary life, just as the shaman had predicted, and for many years the man told himself this was the way it must be: the lightness was worth the loneliness. But as he grew older, he wondered what it would be like to have a companion, someone he could play games with, as he had once played games with his shadow.

Then one day, he heard a beautiful song. It was so enchanting it made the man's heart ache, and filled him with a joy he had never felt before. He followed the sound and, in the branch of a nearby tree, discovered a little bird. He had never seen a lovelier creature: she was small and delicate, with bright red feathers and a long golden tail.

When she noticed him, the little bird fell silent, but the man implored her to continue. 'Please, keep singing,' he begged, hopping from foot to foot. 'In a moment I must be on my way, but it would give me strength to hear your song again before I leave.'

'If you are in such a hurry, I will come with you,' she said, taking flight, 'then I can sing as we go.'

From then on, the little bird remained at his side, for, unlike everyone else, she could just about keep up with him, and did so willingly. Together, they would sing and laugh and play and, wherever he went, she would follow, no matter how far it was or how long it took to get there. She was lightness itself, lighter than even he without his shadow, and he loved her more than anything or anyone he had ever known.

When his dark double caught up with him again, the man had arrived at a magnificent city. As he glimpsed his shadow over his shoulder, he saw it had grown even bigger and stronger, until it hardly seemed his double at all. Terrified, he quickened his pace, desperate to elude his pursuer, but in his haste he forgot the little bird.

'Wait!' she cried, flapping her wings in vain. 'Slow down!'

But the man had sped too far ahead and could not hear her. He ran and ran, and only when he finally felt safe enough to collapse to the ground, did he realise he had lost more than his shadow.

Immediately, he began to look for the little bird, even daring to retrace his steps. He had never done this before and, as he went back, he noticed something strange: the ground over which he had run was blackened, as though it had been burned.

He continued to search while his dark counterpart continued to hunt him, yet somehow the bird's absence now felt worse than the man's fear of his shadow. Days turned to weeks, and weeks turned to months, and the weight of the man's loneliness and hopelessness and emptiness dragged at his heart, just as the weight of his shadow had once dragged at his back.

When he could bear it no longer, he sought out an old friend.

'Help me!' he cried, stumbling into the shaman's hut and bolting the door behind him.

He explained he could run no longer, and neither could he live without the little bird, while outside the shadow began to rattle at the door.

'It is as I told you from the start,' said the shaman. 'If peace and companionship is what you crave, you must allow me to sew your shadow back onto your body.'

'Can it really be done?' asked the man.

'You have been apart for a long time, so there will be pain, and the stitching will leave scars,' warned the shaman. 'But yes, it can be done.'

The man dared to peek out of the window of the hut, but instead of his shadow he saw the route he had taken to the door.

'Was that earth scorched by me or did my shadow cause that darkness?' he wondered.

'Does it matter, when you are one and the same?' asked the shaman.

The man had no answer to this, but he thought he now understood why people grew to fear him.

'If I stop running, I will still be alone,' he said. 'No one will accept me, not after the damage I have done.'

'They will not know you, not with your shadow at your back,' said the shaman. 'In starting anew, you can choose how they view you, what they call you. Being ordinary is the easiest disguise.'

As he spoke, the shadow continued to batter at the bolted door, until the whole hut trembled.

'Besides, you will not be alone, if you find your little bird,' continued the shaman. 'Or if she finds you.'

The man pictured his lost companion: her bright red feathers, her long golden tail, her sweet song.

'That is what I want, above everything,' he said.

The shaman nodded, and from a drawer withdrew a ball of silver thread and a long sharp needle.

'Then open that door, and let in your shadow.'

Rebecca looked up, almost expecting to find her father standing before her, as though by finishing these stories she'd liberated him from some spell. But all she could see was her own hazy outline; her reflection in the dark screen of the dormant TV. She flipped to the next page, and the next, but they were blank. Was that it? Where was The End? Where was *he*?

Inside the book's back cover, she rediscovered the small illustration of the crooked trees with keyholes branded into their bark. The artwork was comprised of stark black lines, which made it look old-fashioned, like a print from a wood engraving. It was exactly the sort of image that suited a book like *Seven Tales* – only, what was it supposed to represent?

The first time she'd seen it, when she'd only read *The Collector and the Nixie*, Rebecca had assumed the illustration belonged to a later tale. Now, *The Woodcutter's Cottage* seemed the best match, for hadn't its protagonist been trapped in a dark and frightening forest? Or perhaps the image was meant to depict *The Golden Door*, and how the foundling had escaped back to his own realm? Rebecca supposed it could even be a reference to *The Enchanted Lute*, and the magical tree that had once been inhabited by the dryad, but that seemed like a stretch. In fact, all these ideas felt more than a little tenuous – and why would only one story warrant an illustration?

He's trying to tell me something, Rebecca thought, pondering – for the hundredth time – why Leo had written her this book. What was its purpose? She'd accepted that the tales were fictionalised versions of his life, of his illness, but was there more within these pages? She thumbed back to the end of the last tale, rereading from the passage where the man without a shadow was separated from his beloved red bird – from her. *You will not be alone if you find your little bird*, the shaman had said. *Or if she finds you.* Had Leo intended *Seven Tales* to reunite them? Was the book meant to lead her back to him?

It wasn't fair: to be so near yet so far; to finally understand her father yet be unable to tell him. Why wasn't there *more*? It was so frustrating she almost wished she'd never laid eyes on the book; perhaps it would've been better to carry on believing he hadn't cared, to have never started any of this . . . And with that thought, the empty page following the last word of the final tale suddenly filled her with fury – its blankness seemed to mock her – and she flung *Seven Tales* towards the floor, where it made a thwacking noise, skidded under the table and fell still.

Immediately, Rebecca went to retrieve it: she hadn't meant to lob it so hard. Now it was now coated with dust, a few crumbs, a strand of her hair, while her throw had broken its spine; the pages were unpeeling, straining to escape. Dropping to her knees, Rebecca picked the cover clean of dirt and examined the damage inside. What was wrong with her? This was her last link to Leo.

She sat there for a long time, hugging the book to her chest, until she remembered Lillian's words: *It was in wrapping paper, bright yellow wrapping paper. I think it was for your birthday.* If it hadn't come in an envelope, how had *Seven Tales* just appeared on her grandmother's doorstep? Had Leo been in the village? Had he, or someone on his behalf, left it there? Rebecca wished she hadn't stormed out of Primrose Cottage without raising this – and she wished she hadn't been so short with Lillian. Never before had she caused her grandmother to look so hurt and, regardless of how much she was or wasn't being told, Lillian would have her best interests at heart.

When the light outside began to fade, Rebecca showered, changed into her pyjamas, and removed her gold nail polish, which had started to chip. After a whole pot of tea, she felt stronger, and considered laying out her work clothes for the morning, until, with a groan, she remembered the phone call with Chris, and wondered whether she had a job to go to. What had he said? What had *she* said? Rebecca clutched at her head, trying to elicit the details of that conversation outside Pit-Stop, but when she reflected on the bar, and last night, all she could think of was Ellis.

He'd been trying to phone her all afternoon, and she'd discovered two more missed calls after emerging from the shower. But he would give up soon. Something or someone would distract him and, within a week or so, he'd have forgotten all about her. The thought was almost reassuring: it would be as though they'd never met. Reassuring, and a little painful, because she'd allowed herself to hope. After years on her own – or, worse, suffering idiots and bores like Chris and her ex, Adam, she'd thought it might finally be her turn. At the very least, it'd been refreshing to find someone charming, and challenging, and *fun*; someone she'd actually liked, and who'd seemed to like her . . . *But he didn't*, Rebecca reminded herself, bitterly. *He didn't.*

During her unpacking, she had also recovered the folder of research Ellis had given her at the beginning of the week. She was tempted to throw it away now she understood why he'd carefully collated all that material, but instead found herself tipping out the folder's contents onto her living room table, where she began to organise it into piles, like this was just another filing task at Sudworth and Rowe.

Initially, she sorted it by type: photographs on one pile, newspaper clippings on another, fan site printouts on a third. Then she arranged the photocopies chronologically again, although all this really demonstrated was how much material related to *The Stowaway,* because soon she had a stack of reviews, interviews, press releases and promotional pictures, and relatively little else. Yet she persevered: perhaps, if she put everything into the right order, a pattern might emerge, and she'd be able to work out what had happened to him after Edinburgh. Plus, it was something to do.

When she'd been occupied with this for almost half an hour, Rebecca recalled the photograph from Huxley, the family portrait of Leo and his parents in the garden. Wanting something to add to the beginning of Leo's chronology, she searched through her phone for the image and had just spotted Adeline's yellow dress when a text pinged in from Ellis:

Pick up – I'm in Exeter.

Rebecca wished she hadn't seen it: there was no ignoring this.

'You're where?' she asked, after calling him back.

'Exeter St Davids Station,' said Ellis, sounding like he was reading from a sign or ticket.

'You're not serious . . .'

'I am. Can we go somewhere and talk?'

'*Now*?'

'No, next week – of course now!'

She was tempted to hang up on him, but warmth was spiralling down her spine: he was in *Exeter*.

'Hello?' said Ellis, after a moment.

'I don't want to talk to you,' she said, which was only half true.

'I know, but come on, Bec – *Rebecca*. I'm here, aren't I? I'm trying to sort this. Come and meet me.'

'You come here,' she snapped, and gave him her address.

He arrived around 15 minutes later, still unshaven, still in the same clothes as earlier. His eyes were bloodshot and the zip of his rucksack was gaping open. *What a mess*, thought Rebecca, trying to ignore the jump of her heart.

'You can't stay,' she told him, having thought about this in the interim. 'You'll have to find a hostel or something.'

'All right,' he agreed, stifling a yawn with his hand.

She stepped aside to let him in, watching as he took in the sight of his new surroundings: the running shoes by the mat, the potted fern in the hallway, the tangle of tote bags hanging from the cupboard door. A few days ago – a few hours ago – she might've been nervous about inviting him here, into her space; tonight, she'd answered the door in her pyjamas, her hair still wet from the shower.

In the living room, she gestured towards the sofa, but Ellis stayed standing, an expanse of laminate floor between them.

'I should've told you everything I knew from the start,' he said, without preamble, 'and I should've told you what I was planning. Here—'

Carefully, he threw something small and bright green towards her. Rebecca caught it without thinking, then opened her palm to reveal his dinosaur-shaped USB stick.

'What's this for?'

'That's all the work I've done on your dad,' Ellis explained. 'You can keep it, or throw it away, whatever you want. I've wiped it from my hard drive – you can check.'

Rebecca ran her thumb along the plates lining the creature's plastic back while summoning a name from the fathoms of her memory: *stegosaurus.*

'I think I got carried away,' Ellis continued, 'because I definitely didn't mean to upset you, or to muck up—' he paused, then motioned between them a few times, unusually tongue-tied '—*This*. I'm sorry.'

In the silence that followed, Rebecca could hear her own unsteady breathing. Did he want a response here, now? She told herself it wasn't necessary; she could just send him away, ask him to wait.

Instead, she said, 'All right.'

Ellis blinked at her. 'All right?'

She nodded, realising he'd expected her to make this harder for him – she'd expected the same. But for some reason she didn't feel angry with him anymore. Maybe his deception paled in comparison to that of her family or perhaps it was because, without him, she never would've learned the truth. Above all, he was here – he'd come all this way for her, for *this* – and that meant something, although Rebecca wasn't sure what.

Ellis risked a cautious smile. 'So . . . we're okay?'

'We're okay. But . . .' she held up the USB, 'what sort of person – what sort of *professional* – keeps his work on something like this?'

Ellis's smile widened. 'Come on, everyone loves dinosaurs.' He glanced down at his watch. 'Hey, that was under two minutes – I thought I'd be grovelling for at least twenty.'

'That can still be arranged.'

They met one another's gaze almost shyly and Rebecca wondered what to do next. Should she ask him to stay or tell him to leave? His presence was both comforting and confusing.

Ellis nodded towards the table, at the photocopies of his own research. 'Still at it, eh?'

'Yeah.' Seizing upon this topic, Rebecca drifted back towards the papers. 'I've been at my mum's – she pretty much confirmed everything – but she doesn't know where he is, or so she says. Which is why I was going through all of this again, in case we've missed something . . .'

She trailed off as Ellis inspected the well-organised piles of photocopies, realising how irrational and obsessive she must look. But she couldn't stop, not now. Having gone so long without Leo, she didn't want to waste another minute.

She had no idea how to explain this to Ellis, so braced herself for his reaction. But without teasing her or changing the subject, or even suggesting she get some sleep, he simply shrugged his rucksack from his shoulders and withdrew his laptop, saying, 'I'll have another look online.'

They worked side by side, she sifting through the paperwork, he scanning the internet for anything they might have overlooked, and Rebecca felt transported back to her student days: as she struggled to focus on yet another write-up of *The Stowaway*, she could've been cramming for an exam.

'You know, as his daughter, there are organisations you could try,' said Ellis, helping himself to more noodles; at some point, he'd ordered a Chinese takeaway and, when it had arrived – accompanied by wafts of ginger and soy sauce, its foil containers hot to the touch – Rebecca had been surprised by just how hungry she was.

'Such as?' she asked.

'Well, the police for starters, especially if they've dealt with him in the past. I don't know if he counts as a missing person, exactly, but there's plenty of stuff here about finding long-lost family members too . . .' With his chopsticks, he indicated the screen of his laptop.

Thinking back to Rosalyn's account of the aftermath of Edinburgh, Rebecca added, 'And my mum had a solicitor for the divorce, maybe they know where he is, or can find out somehow.' Although, even if these options were feasible, they would take time, especially the lawyer: Rosalyn was unlikely to give up that kind of information without a fuss.

Later, Ellis took their empty plates and the unopened bag of prawn crackers to the kitchen and, over the sound of the kettle boiling, called, 'I wouldn't have thought this was your kind of thing?'

He was holding *Seven Tales*. Suppressing the urge to leap from her chair and snatch it back, she said, 'It's a book of fairy tales.'

'I see that.'

'Written by him.'

'I—*Really*?'

She nodded, feeling oddly relieved to have finally told him. 'My grandmother gave it to me a few weeks ago. I'm pretty sure the stories are autobiographical.'

Ellis returned to the table but made no attempt to read or even open *Seven Tales*, in spite of his obvious curiosity. Rebecca appreciated this, and that he didn't question why he was only just learning of its existence.

'Are they any good?' he asked instead.

'I suppose so,' said Rebecca, who hadn't considered this before: as far as she was concerned, the book was a piece of evidence, not art.

'What are they like?'

'What do you mean?'

'Well, are they funny, or silly, or—?'

'No,' broke in Rebecca, although she understood why Ellis, whose perception of Leo was bound up with *The Stowaway*, might've assumed this. 'No, they're more . . . *sad*. Magical, but sad.'

They both stared at the book, until Ellis shook his head. 'I had no idea he wrote, he didn't publish anything – at least, not under his own name. I would've found it.'

'He wrote them for me,' said Rebecca, taking the book from Ellis's hands and showing him the dedication. 'That's what he called me, Birdie. I think he was trying to explain . . . well, *himself*.'

She removed her fingers from the page and let *Seven Tales* fall closed again. She thought she could see it now, the importance of this book: if everything she'd learned and remembered over the past few weeks was a jumbled jigsaw, *Seven Tales* was the picture on the box. Equally, though, it was more than just a collection of analogies. *He wrote them for me,* she'd said, and while that was true, she'd lost sight of the fact that Leo had created these stories a decade-and-a-half ago, when Rebecca – when *Birdie* – had been just nine years old.

Wordlessly, she pushed away paperwork, so her neat piles of research slid into disarray and balanced the fractured spine of *Seven Tales* against the edge of the tabletop, turning past its dedication to *The Collector and the Nixie*. It had been almost a fortnight since she'd first encountered this tale, back in her old bedroom at Primrose Cottage. Tonight, instead of treating it with cynicism, she would read it simply as a story, because that's what Birdie would've done; Birdie would've understood.

Once the nixie had returned to the water, Rebecca began *The Golden Door*, and although she was aware of Ellis moving away from the table, she didn't look up. The less she focused on what was outside of the fairy tale book, and the less she obsessed over what it was all supposed to mean, the more she appreciated an aspect of the tales it was impossible to categorise – their magic, perhaps – and for the first time she could feel it: his elation, his desolation, his everything in between.

By the time she'd finished *The Woodcutter's Cottage* the evening had turned dark and quiet. She didn't know how long she'd spent reading the first five tales; it could've been a few minutes, it could've been hours. Slumped on the sofa, Ellis had fallen asleep, his laptop still open on his stomach.

With a yawn, Rebecca got up to refill her glass with water – the takeaway had made her thirsty – and when she returned from the kitchen saw Ellis hadn't stirred. His laptop looked in danger of toppling to the floor, so she crouched down next to the sofa and, after a moment's hesitation, eased it from his hands. Closing the lid on his last search (*leo sampson role part acting 2016*) she placed the laptop on the coffee table and, reassured by Ellis's slow, regular breathing, chanced a proper glance at his face.

In sleep, he was unsmiling, and, with a shiver, Rebecca recalled how serious he'd looked the previous night, seconds before he'd kissed her. There was a chicken pox scar between his eyebrows she'd never noticed before, and perhaps only had now because his glasses had been pushed askew by a cushion. It looked awkward, and Rebecca longed to slide the frames from his nose and fold them neatly on top of his laptop – what was his face like without them? She longed to nestle into the gap between his arm and his body, lay her head on his chest and close her eyes . . . But even touching his glasses felt too intrusive, too intimate. Better to leave him to sleep, she decided, returning to the table and *Seven Tales*: he couldn't help her with this anymore.

As Rebecca started *The Witch and the Sphinx,* it was impossible not to think of Rosalyn, especially as she'd so recently provided her own version of these events. Yet in spite of all she'd learned during that conversation, it was still far from easy to read her mother depicted as a grasping old witch. *I was the villain in all of his stories,* Rosalyn had said, but Rebecca was beginning to think it more likely there was no villain in this real-life tale.

Wearily, she turned from the phoenix's flight to *The Man Without a Shadow.* It stood out, this final tale. Now Rebecca was calmer, now she could compare it to the others, she appreciated it was more of a summary than a standalone story. Had Leo been trying to ensure she understood it all? If so, one or both of them had failed, because she still felt she was missing something important. *You will not be alone if you find your little bird . . . Or if she finds you.* But how, Rebecca thought. *How*?

She flicked back through the book, its words blurring. She wanted to clamber between its covers and change every ending: fish the nixie from the pond again; convince the woodcutter's family to be kind; prevent the phoenix from taking flight. And she needed to finish that final tale.

He felt so close now, but her eyes were stinging, her head was heavy, and without meaning to she'd begun to imitate Ellis's deep, steady breathing. She was falling forward, slipping right through the pages . . .

... Except there aren't any pages, it's the screen of her laptop and the only information she can find is related to *The Stowaway: In episode four, the Stowaway (Leo Sampson) encounters a miller's daughter, whose father has boasted she can spin straw into gold.*

'It's like in the story,' says the Stowaway, who's standing on his hands in Huxley's kitchen, 'you have to – Rumpelstiltskin! – you have to guess.'

Go away, thinks Rebecca, as he begins to turn cartwheels around the table. *I'm trying to find my dad.*

She glances back at her laptop, which has transformed into an answer sheet, and hears the familiar voice of The Crown's quizmaster: 'Who played the title role in the BBC children's TV series, *The Stowaway*?'

I know this, thinks Rebecca, but when she looks up from the answer sheet her teammates, the quizmaster, and The Crown are all gone, and instead she's staring up at a sphinx who's flexing her lion's paws:

> *You're daring and you're tough,*
> *Yet I see right through your mask,*
> *And if you want your prize,*
> *His name is all I ask.*

Rebecca's eyes snapped open. Her head was resting on the closed cover of *Seven Tales,* its embossed gold lettering glinting at the edge of her vision. As she pushed herself up, she almost laughed: it had been right there – or not there – the whole time, and she'd never thought to question it.

'*Ellis*!'

'Huh?' He sprang into a sitting position, staring around in confusion until he seemed to remember where he was.

'I think I know why we can't find him.' Rebecca held up *Seven Tales*. 'Does anything about this cover strike you as odd?'

'Erm . . .' Squinting, Ellis adjusted his glasses.

'There's no author,' said Rebecca, too impatient to wait for his answer. 'Not here, and not inside either.'

'So . . . he *didn't* write it?'

'No, he did, it all fits: the stories, the dedication . . . But he could get fixated on names, remember? He was desperate to know the Stowaway's name – you saw it yourself – and according to Richard Lowrie that wasn't the first time. So why didn't he put his own name on this book?'

'Maybe he wanted to get it past your mum?'

'Maybe,' Rebecca allowed, and though she couldn't blame him she was frustrated he wasn't keeping up. 'But listen to what he wrote here, in the last tale . . .' With trembling hands, she flipped to the passage: '*n starting anew, you can choose how they view you, what they call you* . . . I think that's why we haven't been able to find him. It's right here, in the last story: he's changed his name.'

Ellis's expression was turning from befuddlement to concern. 'But if that's true, that makes everything harder, doesn't it? He could be anyone.'

'I don't think he changed all of it,' said Rebecca. She jabbed at the book's cover again. 'That squiggle, that's the zodiac symbol for Leo, and remember what Patricia said? His mother named him. So he would've kept *Leo*; he would've changed *Sampson*, his father's name.'

'Yeah, but still . . .' said Ellis, clearly contemplating how many Leos there were in the world.

Rebecca, however, was now thinking of Adeline, the wispy

figure in the yellow dress, the nixie. 'Everyone's been telling me I'm the only one he ever cared about, but what about *her*? She meant everything to him, and—' Rebecca broke off, realising something else '—and he gave her name to *me*!'

'Are you talking about his mum?'

'What if he took the other part? What if, when he got rid of his father's name, he took hers instead, her maiden name?' Rebecca's insides jolted as she finally caught up with her own hurtling thoughts. 'Oh shit, what was it?'

She began to pull at the papers on the table but knew she didn't have it: they hadn't recorded that dinner with Patricia. After all the notes she'd made, after all the research they'd done, the only piece of information she needed was the one thing she hadn't written down.

'I could have a look online?' said Ellis, reclaiming his laptop from the coffee table. 'It'll be on his birth record, surely? Or maybe we can find a record of Adeline's marriage to Victor . . .'

But Rebecca was hardly listening. She'd picked up *Seven Tales* again and opened it from the back cover. The answer had to be in here – Leo had to have left her some kind of hint, most likely in the final tale. But before she reached the end of 'The Man Without a Shadow', she found herself staring at the book's only illustration; that obscure image of the trees with keyholes in their barks.

'Lockwood,' she said, quietly.

Ellis stared at her.

'It's *Lockwood*,' she repeated.

'Are – are you sure?'

'Positive,' she said, now recalling Patricia's scornful voice: *Adeline should be locked up, we used to say at school* . . . Unwilling to dwell on the callous perceptivity of Adeline's classmates, Rebecca gestured towards Ellis's laptop. 'Search for it, search for *Leo Lockwood*.'

He did as she asked: 'There's a couple . . .'

'Search for *Leo Lockwood Edinburgh*.'

'Edinburgh?' He frowned. 'Where are you getting all of this from?'

She said nothing, too excited to explain that she was now following patterns, feelings, going by instinct – and instinct told her Edinburgh was a good place to start.

'There's a Leo Lockwood in Edinburgh,' said Ellis, his eyes fixed on the screen. 'It looks as though he works for a youth theatre company.'

'That's him,' said Rebecca at once.

'I don't know, this picture could be anyone . . .'

She crossed to the sofa and Ellis angled the laptop so she had a better view. He'd found the *About Us* page of a company called Acting Up, where each staff portrait was presented in moody monochrome, not unlike Priya George's wall of headshots. Leo Lockwood's photograph had been taken from a distance and he was almost entirely cast in shadow, like an old-fashioned detective. Rebecca squinted at this dark profile for several moments, trying to pick out his unruly hair or crooked nose, before her gaze slid to the text beside the picture.

Associate Artist: Leo Lockwood

Leo has been with Acting Up for over ten years, working as a mentor, workshop facilitator and director. An experienced stage and screen actor, he now prefers to stay behind the scenes, encouraging young people to develop their skills and confidence through theatre. Once more, Leo will be supporting the talented young team of this year's summer school production, The Emerald City.

'That's him,' Rebecca said again.

She jumped from the sofa, unable to sit still a second longer. She was fizzing from what she'd just read: all those precious new nuggets of information, all those insights into his existence *now*, not decades ago. She could hardly take it in, and perhaps she didn't need to – there was no point collating these clues anymore.

Ellis, however, remained staring at his laptop, his eyes unfocused behind his glasses. 'Even if it is him—'

'It has to be!'

'All right, let's say it is – what are you going to do?'

Rebecca stopped mid-pace. She hadn't thought this far ahead; perhaps she'd never expected to get this far. What *was* she going to do? Leave him a message via this theatre company? Again, this seemed too time-consuming – and it gave him the opportunity to avoid her, to stay hidden.

Where had that thought come from? A chill dropped through Rebecca's chest, like an icy drink swallowed too fast. *Leo has been with Acting Up for over ten years* . . . Had he really been in Edinburgh all that time? How could he have stayed in the same place, only a train ride or short flight away and not somehow let her know? *Because of Mum,* Rebecca reminded herself, with another jab of resentment. Rosalyn had said or done something to keep him away. It was impossible Leo had given up on his little bird; the man without a shadow was simply waiting for her, for now.

'I'm going to go there,' said Rebecca, deciding to ignore any further doubts, hoping they were only remnants of her last, disastrous trip to that city. 'I'm going to find him.'

Ellis's expression was unreadable. To Rebecca's frustration, he'd slipped back into his journalist persona. She wished she didn't care about his opinion, but it was no use; his support had become important to her.

'You could come with me if you wanted . . .'

She paused, pressing her lips together. This wasn't a walk to a museum or the opening of a bar. After everything that had happened between them in the past 24 hours, the time for affecting nonchalance had passed.

'I mean, if you could, I'd like you to come with me. I think I might need—' *you,* she thought '—a friend,' she said.

Ellis closed his laptop and as his dimples returned, he looked like himself again.

'When do we leave?' he asked.

PART THREE

15

Edinburgh

The significance of returning to Edinburgh in August wasn't lost on Rebecca: it was now 19 years to the month since she'd been there; more than a whole childhood since she'd last seen her father.

Ellis, however, was more concerned with logistics. After discovering the city's festival had increased the price of both accommodation and public transport to far more than either of them could afford, he suggested they make the journey by car and, by the time Rebecca had repacked her bag, he'd managed to convince an Edinburgh-based university friend to put them up for a few days.

Having driven back from London by herself the previous day, Rebecca was grateful for Ellis's presence during the lengthy road trip. Overnight, their relationship seemed to have reset itself to the beginning of the week and, between searching for obscure radio stations and pilfering more sweets, he initiated elaborate car games to distract them from the monotony of the M5. Unfortunately for him, Rebecca had always been good at variants of *I Spy* and *Twenty Questions*, but Ellis conceded defeat happily enough, so she pretended to believe the rules he invented to confuse her.

At some point after Bristol, they discovered a new way of keeping boredom at bay. Ellis, who she'd finally allowed behind the wheel – and who turned out to be a surprisingly good driver

– started asking about *Seven Tales.* His questions were tentative, as though he was afraid of overstepping, but Rebecca saw no point in withholding the fairy tales from him anymore. He was part of this now – he had been for some time – and, like Amy, deserved to be let in on her and Leo's secret.

So Rebecca tried to describe *The Collector and the Nixie,* and after realising she'd forgotten several key plot points, resorted to simply reading to him from the book, which she'd slipped back into her bag like a lucky charm. At first, she felt self-conscious to be sitting in the passenger seat of her own car, reading children's stories to someone she had more than friendly feelings for, but Ellis was an attentive audience. Save for the odd small noise of surprise or appreciation, he listened in silence and, when she'd finished reading each tale, he'd make comments and ask questions. Like her, he was eager to extract the fact from the fiction, but as he was more practiced at this, many of the details he picked up on were ones she hadn't considered before.

'Do you think the other specimens are supposed to represent Victor's other patients?' he wondered, after the first tale.

'*The Voyage to the Edge of the World* is one of the most mysterious, isn't it?' he mused, a little later. 'Because we hardly know anything about the time he spent abroad . . .' Then, after she'd read him *The Enchanted Lute,* he asked, 'So did that tree spirit know what was going to happen with the lute – is she supposed to be a baddie – or was she genuinely trying to help him?' He was also struck by the singularity of *The Man Without a Shadow,* and even asked Rebecca to reread the final page, which detailed the last conversation between the tormented protagonist and the shaman. Ellis was just as taken aback as she'd been by the open ending of the tale – and the book as a whole – yet seemed to find it more troubling than frustrating.

'Presumably Leo leaves it up in the air like that because, at the time, he was still living it,' said Ellis, frowning into the rear-view mirror as he prepared to change lanes.

'What do you mean?'

'Well, he doesn't reveal whether or not the man accepts the shaman's help and opens the door to his shadow – I guess because, in real life, Leo was still grappling with the idea of undergoing some form of treatment?'

Last night, Rebecca had been too preoccupied, especially by her own role in the story, to analyse this too closely, but it made sense. Especially because it tallied with what Rosalyn had told her earlier in the day, about Leo's refusal to see a doctor: *He was too scared and too selfish, mostly the latter.*

'But that was years ago now,' continued Ellis, 'and we still don't know what's happened since. We still don't know where he's been.'

'Yes we do,' said Rebecca, motioning at the road ahead.

'All right, assuming we have the right Leo Lockwood, maybe,' Ellis conceded. 'What I mean is, the reason the man without a shadow finally goes to the shaman for help is because he wants to be reunited with the little bird – with you. So where is he? Why are you the one looking for him and not the other way around?'

This was an echo of the doubt that had gripped Rebecca after seeing Leo's profile on the theatre company website, yet as they slid into the fastest lane of traffic, she told herself not to worry about it, nor any of Ellis's other musings. *Seven Tales* had served its purpose: the book had provided Leo's side of the story, and even pointed them towards Edinburgh. Picking over these details wasn't going to achieve anything, not when Leo himself would soon be able to answer any questions in person.

'We should've gone another way,' said Ellis, who was driving again – or rather, sitting at the wheel, because they were caught in another traffic jam. 'I don't think your satnav knows it's festival time.'

Rebecca didn't mind their crawling pace. After almost a whole day of motorway scenery, there was suddenly so much to see: a pillared neoclassical edifice, like the British Museum in miniature; a glass-fronted theatre whose façade was slightly concave; an austere but grimy university building, the arched entranceway of which was cluttered with bicycles. Which was to say nothing of all the posters and flyers: advertising everything from comedy to circus, they clung to brick walls and café windows, fluttered on railings and the poles of traffic lights, clogged bins and gutters or skittered loose along the pavements.

Rebecca wasn't the only one looking, either. Easily identifiable by their cumbersome cameras and souvenir shop bags, tourists dawdled along taking pictures and checking guidebooks, while their younger counterparts – the teenagers whose identical florescent backpacks suggested they were the temporary responsibility of a summer school – idled outside cafés and fast food restaurants, most of which boasted all-night opening hours for the month of August.

Competing with the sights and shops for the attention of these visitors were performers clad in matching hoodies or the costumes of their shows. They cheeped and preened in front of signs and scenery like birds of paradise, frequently swooping upon passers-by with flyers. As Rebecca and Ellis braked next to a shop window stuffed with whiskey bottles, Nessie toys, and Tam o' Shanter hats, a girl whose face was glittering with piercings dashed out into the road and shoved a leaflet through the car's partially open window.

'Electric violin recital?' said Rebecca, studying the picture of the s-shaped instrument.

'I'm all right, thanks,' replied Ellis, who was drumming on the steering wheel, unusually impatient. 'We're getting to the Royal Mile, by the way. It goes right up to the castle.'

Ellis, she'd learned earlier, had visited the city once before, with friends. Rebecca looked up the pedestrianised street he'd indicated, which contained a crush of people assembled under an immense blue banner reading *fringe*. Small shows and displays seemed to be taking place throughout the crowd, and though a few people rose above the throng – presumably supported by bollards, shoulders or stilts – it was too packed to discern exactly what was going on.

Had it been this busy before, when she'd got lost? Had she and Leo accidentally let go of one another's hands in the confusion? Once again, Rebecca strained to summon something else of that day – of this place – while, absently, she ran a finger along the raised line of skin below her elbow.

When they emerged onto a wide bridge, the buildings on either side of the road fell away, whipped out of sight like the black cloth at the end of a magic trick, and Edinburgh appeared. Ahead, a magnificent clock tower. To the left, a jumble of turrets, spires and domes. To the right, a rugged slice of wild land. Below, a series of railway lines criss-crossing into a station.

Rebecca wound her window all the way down. It was colder here, even for early evening, and gustier too, as evidenced by the Scottish Saltires straining against their flagpoles. It smelled of traffic and food, but there was also a hint of something fresher, which might've been the sea. The clouds were passing fast overheard, their downy bellies aglow with evening light.

I'm back, thought Rebecca, and her chest swelled as she tried to breathe it all in at once. *I'm here.* And somewhere, so was he.

Eventually, they arrived in a quieter neighbourhood, where

they were buzzed into an elegant Georgian tenement. Its spiralling stairwell grew brighter as they approached the skylight at its apex, and, a little breathless, stopped outside a door on the third floor bearing an elephant-shaped knocker. Its smart brass nameplate read *Ramsay*.

Upon throwing open the door, their host was revealed to be tall and skinny, with thick eyebrows and what would've been very dark hair had he not shaved it close, perhaps to disguise a receding hairline. He was wearing a lilac V-neck jumper, tight beige chinos and moccasin slippers.

'Did they get you?' he asked.

'Get us?' said Ellis.

'With flyers.'

'Actually, yeah – through the car window.'

'*Bastards.*' He gave Ellis a forceful kiss on the cheek. 'Hello, Bailey – and what the fuck do you look like, eh? Where are you shopping these days, the recycling centre?' He paused in the act of plucking at Ellis's faded T-shirt to look Rebecca up and down. 'And who's this?'

'This is Rebecca,' said Ellis, putting a hand on her back to guide her forward.

Trying to remain composed in response to both their host's glare and the gentle pressure of Ellis's fingers between her shoulder blades, Rebecca stuck out her own hand. 'Hi.'

The man's grip was surprisingly firm. 'Campbell,' he said, without specifying which part of his name this was. 'But you can call me Cam if you like,' he added, magnanimously. He had a melodious Scottish accent that was slightly at odds with his brusque demeanour.

'So, this is the place,' he continued, stepping aside to reveal a long hallway dotted with paintings of the African savannah and a wooden sculpture of a giraffe that was doubling as a coat stand.

'Ignore all the safari shite, I'm housesitting for my godmother, who spends most of her time terrorising the wildlife of Tanzania. Do you want the tour?'

Before they could answer, he was leading them down the corridor, waving towards the doorways he passed.

'My bedroom – don't look in there, it's a state; kitchen – help yourself to food, if you can find any; bathroom – there's no lock, you'll have to sing. And . . . guestroom.' After tweaking the corner of the double bed's red and blue check blanket, which looked more Maasai than Scottish, he waggled a long finger at Rebecca and Ellis. 'The sound carries to the living room next door, so no banging until after I've gone to bed, all right?'

Rebecca experienced a flush of heat so intense she might've stepped into a sauna. Ellis shifted his weight to the other foot, causing a floorboard to creak under the carpet.

'And, erm, is there a sofa?' he ventured.

Cam stared at him. 'Does this look like a bedsit, Bailey? Of course, there's a fucking sofa – didn't I just say there's a whole living room next door?'

'Cool,' said Ellis, and the floorboard squeaked again. 'You take the bed then, Becs.'

'Mm-hmm,' she said, noting the return of her nickname as she stared determinedly at the bright blanket. 'Thanks.'

'*Oh*,' said Cam, smirking. 'I assumed you were—'

'Keen to see this living room?' interrupted Ellis. 'Mate, you're totally right . . .'

He pushed their host towards the guestroom door, the pair of them arguing wordlessly on the way out. Left alone, Rebecca dropped her rucksack onto the bed and raised her palms to the hollows of her cheeks, waiting for her face to return to a normal temperature. This would be Ellis's second night sleeping on a sofa, she realised, with a flutter of guilt – or was it disappointment?

When her blush had subsided, she went through to the much-discussed living room, where the African décor continued: in addition to paintings of grasslands, the ornate fireplace was flanked by tall vases of dried bulrushes, and the mantelpiece was topped with bowls of what might've been giant seed pods.

'—If you'd been coming for the festivals, it would've been another matter,' Cam was saying.

'Cam hates the festival,' explained Ellis, as Rebecca perched on the arm of a chair.

'It's *festivals*, plural,' snapped their host. 'There's thousands of them: the Fringe, the International, the Book . . . I don't know, there's probably a fucking tiddlywinks festival by now.'

'Still, I'm surprised you haven't rented out that room,' said Ellis. 'You could make a fortune.'

'And have this flat overrun with *drama students*?' Cam gave him a withering look, and then twisted around to find Rebecca. 'Ah, there you are, let's have a drink. I've got wine – or I could make cocktails?'

'Wine's good,' said Rebecca, who'd only just recovered from the effects of Engine Oil.

'Yep,' agreed Ellis, just as fast.

In the kitchen, Cam sat them at a table with a bottle of Merlot while he began to make dinner. With a practiced air, he chopped vegetables with expensive-looking knives and tossed them into a sputtering pan, all the while complaining cheerfully about the number of people who descended on the city in August.

Before long, Rebecca had tuned out his lilting voice like background music and was once more reflecting on the fact she was in *Edinburgh*. Only, what if they'd come all this way for nothing? What if she had the wrong person, and the Leo Lockwood they'd found online wasn't her father at all? What if—?

Her next worry was interrupted by a nudge to her knee under the table. *Relax,* Ellis mouthed, with a reassuring smile. Rebecca smiled back, before – afraid she'd start blushing again – she glanced over at Cam, who now appeared midway through a rant about the price of shows.

' . . . Used to cost a couple of quid to see something decent, and now you pay £20 for the privilege of watching a grown man ride around on a kiddie's tricycle . . .'

Still, Cam's sourness didn't permeate his cooking, as the pasta dish he subsequently served up was rich and fiery – although a low bar had been set for food that day, because all Rebecca and Ellis had eaten were sweets and service station sandwiches. By the time they returned to the living room, Rebecca was finishing her second glass of wine and, as she settled between the sofa's animal print cushions next to Ellis, she felt pleasantly full and sleepy. Cam, on the other hand, seemed wide awake, and after topping up their glasses from a newly opened bottle, lowered himself into the armchair opposite and regarded them both through narrowed eyes.

'*So*,' he said, his expression so shrewd Rebecca feared he was about to bring up the sleeping arrangements again, 'why've you come up to Edinburgh now, and at such late notice, if not for the festivals?'

Automatically, Rebecca turned to Ellis, but he was motioning towards her, indicating this was her trip. She hesitated: she wasn't used to talking about Leo, especially with people she'd only just met.

'I think my dad's here,' she said.

'You *think*?'

'I'm pretty sure he is. I've been trying to find him.'

Their host continued to watch her expectantly and, feeling she owed him at least something, Rebecca began an abridged version of the last few weeks' events, one in which she neglected to mention *Seven Tales,* Leo's illness and his most famous role. Cam, she guessed, was only a few years older than her – presumably, he was the same age as Ellis – and in Rebecca's experience there were few people of their generation who hadn't watched *The Stowaway*. Even if she'd wanted to trust this near stranger with the truth, she was increasingly aware that it wasn't her truth to tell.

When she'd finished speaking, Cam's gaze flicked towards Ellis, and Rebecca supposed the journalist's involvement seemed puzzling, especially because she'd omitted Leo's fame from her explanation. Fortunately, though, Cam decided against pursuing the point and instead asked, 'What's the plan, then?'

'I'm not sure,' she admitted. 'I know he's working for a youth theatre company, and according to their website they're currently rehearsing at a venue called—' she reached for her phone to double-check '—St Jude's?'

Cam waved his empty wine glass towards the window. 'That's about fifteen minutes' walk from here.'

'I guess I'll go there, then,' said Rebecca. 'I presume he'll be there, because the first show's tomorrow night.'

She was struck by how simple this seemed – and by how calm she sounded. The wine and food had relaxed her a little, but her stomach was still bouncing with nerves, like a bag of popcorn in the microwave.

'You're just going to turn up?' asked Ellis, speaking for the first time in several minutes.

'Yes.'

From the silence that followed, she guessed neither he nor Cam thought this a good idea.

'Do you want me to come with you?' Ellis continued, after a moment.

Yes, she thought. 'Thanks, but I think I have to do this by myself.'

He nodded, and this time she had the impression he approved. Once again, Rebecca resented she cared what he thought of her.

'If you ask me, rehearsing a play sounds suspiciously festival-related,' remarked Cam, holding their bottle of wine next to a lamp to see how much was left. 'I feel deceived, Rebecca. I'm not sure I like you anymore.'

Rebecca, who was pleased he'd liked her at all, said, 'It's only youth theatre.'

'Ach, that's even worse.'

Later, when Ellis and Cam began reminiscing about university, and updating one another on the current antics of various mutual friends, Rebecca crept away to the spare bedroom. But she couldn't sleep. It was lighter here than in Devon and London – she hadn't appreciated how much further north she was until now – but this wasn't bothering her, and after one night at Huxley and several on Amy and Tim's futon she was getting used to being away from her own bed. She hardly even noticed the murmur of male voices and the occasional shout of laughter from the neighbouring room; Cam was right, the sound did carry.

Instead, it was thoughts of tomorrow that were keeping her awake. She couldn't help but dwell on Ellis's silence after she'd revealed her plan, which was exactly how he'd reacted last night when she'd told him she intended to travel to Edinburgh. But what other choice did she have? Rebecca had been loath to admit it, but she was afraid there was a chance Leo wouldn't want to see her.

Why are you the one looking for him and not the other way around? Earlier, she'd managed to brush aside Ellis's question, but it preyed upon her now, and no matter how long she considered it – and how much she wanted to blame Rosalyn – she could think of only two possible answers. The first, and most painful, was that Leo didn't care, just as she'd always been led to believe. Yet Rebecca *knew* he cared; the past few weeks had shown her that, over and over.

The more likely scenario she was forced to acknowledge, was that he'd had to stay away because he hadn't been able to open that door back in the shaman's hut; because he was still ill. With this in mind, she tried to summon her confidence from yesterday afternoon, when Lillian had voiced the same concern, but it wasn't so easy tonight.

Rebecca had never encountered anyone as ill as Leo had been in that video – as ill as he'd depicted himself in the fairy tales. She knew people with mental health issues, of course: Amy's Tim had been seeing a counsellor at some point, while her Exeter friend Steph sometimes made glib remarks about her *happy pills*. Somehow, though, conversations about therapy or medication always slid swiftly towards sunnier, funnier topics. Why didn't Tim and Steph share more? Why had she never *asked*?

Assuming Rebecca's instincts were correct, she and Leo were finally in the same place, their reunion mere hours away. So it was too late to back out now, regardless of how uninformed she felt. All she could do was worry about what sort of man she'd discover tomorrow – and whether it was even possible to prepare for someone whose shadow was still at large.

16

The Rehearsal

St Jude's was a small church whose derelict outer walls were dotted with newer, smoother bricks, as conspicuous as sticking plasters. Rebecca, who'd been expecting more of a playhouse, almost walked right past it, but her attention was caught by a familiar blue sign, versions of which she'd seen all over Edinburgh: *Fringe Venue 317*.

A poster for Acting Up's *The Emerald City* was tacked up inside the glass of an old noticeboard by the church's entrance. Through eyes itchy from lack of sleep, Rebecca studied its artwork, which featured slashes of green against a mottled monochrome background, and it took her a few seconds to realise this was a close-up of grass sprouting from cracks in concrete – although how this related to *The Wizard of Oz* she didn't know.

The church door had been propped open by a pot of black paint that seemed to have dried out, a paintbrush protruding from its centre. Beyond, Rebecca could hear voices and faint, tinny music that might've been playing through a phone or cheap speakers. The church porch had been lined with flipchart paper, presumably to protect its tiles from the debris that had accumulated just over the threshold: rucksacks and plastic bags, a half-eaten baguette, several scripts and a sprinkling of metallic green, which, on closer inspection, turned out to be loose sequins.

'Are you here to do the photos?'

A short, dark-haired woman of about her own age was peering

around an open door on the other side of the porch. She was squinting against the sunlight spilling in behind Rebecca, which – along with the black Acting Up t-shirt stretched tight over her plump torso – gave her the look of a mole emerging from its burrow.

'Sorry?' said Rebecca, with a jump of nerves: she hadn't meant to start speaking to anyone without formulating some kind of plan.

Uncertainty entered the other woman's expression. 'We're expecting a photographer?'

'Oh – no. I'm here to see Leo Sam— Leo Lockwood.'

The woman seemed to know the name, which was promising, but continued to blink until Rebecca realised more of an explanation was expected. Only, what else could she say? *I'm his daughter?* She wasn't about to announce her identity to this stranger before Leo himself.

'I'm the journalist,' she said, struck by a sudden inspiration. 'You know, from SideScoop?'

She hoped her tone would discourage further questions. If only she still had that lanyard from the interview with Richard Lowrie. Apparently, though, she didn't need it, because the woman's untidy eyebrows had shot up.

'*SideScoop*?' she gasped. 'Of course! Come in, and please ignore the chaos . . . Big day!' She raised her arms and imitated jazz hands, before motioning to the door at the other end of the porch.

St Jude's, it emerged, was a building with insides that had been hollowed out. There was no altar, pulpit, or pews, and the only furniture was a few rows of foldable black chairs – the kind Rebecca remembered from school dinners. The windows had been covered with dark cloth, as though Edinburgh was still enduring the Blitz, and the floor, walls and ceiling were all black save for a fire extinguisher, some peeling lines of masking tape and a couple of handwritten signs: *Don't leave your belongings in the theatre overnight! Remember to wash your paintbrushes!*

These directives were obviously aimed at the twenty or so teenagers dotted about the space. They were all wearing the same Acting Up T-shirt as Rebecca's companion, although most had customised it in some way, such as the girl who'd cut off the entire lower half to reveal her midriff. Around a dozen of them were at work – painting scenery, folding programmes bent over a sewing machine – while the rest were slouched over the metal chairs with scripts, although some appeared more interested in inspecting one another's phones, food and hair than in running through their lines.

The woman from the porch stopped and turned to Rebecca, who noticed a sticker on her chest that read *Heather!* and was covered with hand-drawn swirls and stars. 'If you just wait here a sec,' she called above the noise, 'I'll let Leo know you've arrived.'

Rebecca thanked her, the steadiness of her voice conveying a calm she didn't feel. As she watched the woman shuffle away, she noted there were only two other adults in the hall: in the opposite corner, an old man was bent over a stage light, apparently testing out different coloured filters, while halfway up a stepladder a woman in overalls with short platinum blonde hair was gesturing at two girls to hand her a swathe of shimmering green material, which she proceeded to staple along the top of the wall.

Where was Leo? Rebecca had assumed she'd spot him straight away and, when she didn't, she scanned the hall for some trapdoor or skylight – some portal from which, Stowaway-like, he'd erupt. She supposed he might be in another part of the church or out running an errand, but it felt so unlikely he'd be anywhere but here, right in the middle of the action; Leo didn't inhabit the periphery, he'd never lingered around the edges.

Had she made a mistake? Once more, Rebecca considered the possibility that the Leo Lockwood of Acting Up, of Edinburgh, wasn't her father after all. She'd been so sure back in Exeter, but now – having barged in on this rehearsal or whatever it was – she felt far less confident in the instincts that had drawn her here.

While she wondered what to do, she watched the progress of the iridescent green fabric, which, once stapled under the ceiling, rippled down the wall like sunlight in a sea grotto. The sight drew noises of appreciation from a few of the teenagers, and the woman from the porch – *Heather!* – paused to admire the now-glimmering backdrop, before she seemed to remember her mission and headed towards the older man with the stage light.

Rebecca repressed a huff of frustration: this was pointless, he wasn't here. If he was, she would know – they would all know. She wanted to call out, *Don't bother, I got it wrong!* But Heather was drawing level with her colleague, who was wearing paint-splattered jeans and a navy-coloured shirt rolled up at the sleeves and whose thinning hair was grey. As Rebecca studied this hunched figure, thinking him a little past the age where it was acceptable to be involved in youth theatre, he seemed to become aware of Heather, because he glanced up from his stage light, and in doing so revealed a familiar crooked-nosed profile.

Rebecca stepped back, a thousand volts juddering through her body.

It hadn't occurred to her he'd be so much older. Which was ridiculous, she now realised – of course he'd have aged. Yet somehow, like a figure in a fairy tale, she'd expected him to be almost exactly the same as the man in her memories, as though wherever he'd been, whatever magical realm he'd inhabited, no time had passed at all.

She wanted to run. She wasn't ready. But it was too late:

Heather had gestured across the church, and the man – *Leo* – had tilted in his seat to see past her hand. Before Rebecca could move, he was looking right at her.

His initial reaction was difficult to interpret, given the distance between them, but as his impassive expression dissolved, Rebecca thought she saw – just for a moment – his features flicker with fear. But maybe she'd imagined it, because a second later he looked exactly as she'd thought and even hoped he would look: stunned, comprehending, pained.

Heather was still talking, but Leo wasn't listening anymore. He eased himself from his chair and absently handed his colleague the stage light, failing to notice her body sag from its unexpected weight. Rebecca tensed as he began to walk towards her, his gaze never leaving her face. She couldn't make sense of what she was seeing: why was he so slow, so quiet? Why was he taking up so little space? He might've been trying to move through a forest without snapping so much as a single twig underfoot, and his guarded expression suggested he was approaching a wild animal; one that, if startled, might flee – or pounce.

He stopped a few metres away, apparently afraid to come any closer.

'Birdie?'

She couldn't speak. She couldn't breathe. Something sharp was swelling in her throat. His voice was soft, almost a whisper – it was nothing like she remembered. He was only half a head taller than her now and, close by, looked old: deep lines were etched into his forehead and the corners of his eyes and mouth, where laughter had once lived.

'It is you, isn't it?' he asked, his blue eyes – which were so like her own – very wide.

'Yes.'

It was only one word, but it seemed to overwhelm him, for

he raised a grimy hand to his face, pressing the nook of his thumb and index finger against his mouth. He didn't seem to realise he was still holding a red light filter.

'How—?' he began, before breaking off, the furrows of his forehead deepening. He tried again. 'How can you be here?'

Rebecca wasn't sure how to answer. She wasn't even certain the question was meant for her. His unrelenting stare was disconcerting, so she looked down, noting her fingers were clutching at the strap of her handbag like it was a lifeline.

At a loss as to what to say or do, she retrieved *Seven Tales* from the bag and wordlessly offered it to Leo. He stared at it for a long time until he finally seemed to understand what it was and dared to take it from her. Only then did he appear to register he was still holding a light filter and, for a few awkward seconds, he passed it and the little green book from hand to hand like an indecisive traffic light, before he bent down to lay the square of red film on the nearest chair.

It should have been a moment of triumph, reuniting *Seven Tales* with its author. But, as with Lillian before, Rebecca felt fiercely possessive as she watched this elderly version of Leo examine the clothbound cover of the book – *her* book – and touch the tips of his fingers to its gold lettering.

'I forgot about this,' he said.

Again, it sounded like he was talking to someone other than her. His hands, she noticed, were trembling as he opened the cover, and the pages blurred between his fingers like the wings of insects.

'I only just found out about it,' she said, feeling she should try and explain.

But Leo's attention was on the open book, his frown deepening as he flicked back through the pages. '*The Enchanted Lute*,' he read, before attempting a chuckle that in no way resembled his old bark of joy. '*The Voyage to the End of the World*, *The Golden Door* . . .' He shook his head. 'What on earth was I on about?'

Heat flooded Rebecca's face, though she was more angry than embarrassed. How could he speak so flippantly of the very object that had led her here, as steadfast as a compass? At the same time, though, she welcomed the rage beginning to sizzle under her skin: it was far better than her stupefied state of the past few minutes, far better than nothing.

'You wrote it so I'd understand,' she told him, stonily.

'Ah.' Leo looked up, clearly having realised he'd made some sort of mistake. 'Yes, I only meant—'

'I read it all, I understand everything.'

'Yes, it's just, it was a long time ago, and I wasn't—To be quite honest, I don't remember exactly what I wrote.'

She stepped forward and snatched back the book, clutching it to her chest. What was going on? Since school, she'd suffered recurring dreams of cramming for an exam only to turn up on the wrong day or in the wrong place, and it felt like that had happened now: she'd turned up to the wrong person.

Leo eyed the book now clamped under her arm, perhaps disappointed it had been taken away from him, and asked, 'How did you find me?'

'This,' she snapped, jabbing at *Seven Tales* with her other hand.

'Of course,' said Leo quickly, although she wasn't convinced he was keeping up. 'And does Roz—Does your mum know you're here?'

'She knows I'm . . .' Rebecca trailed off, because suddenly his expression from a few minutes ago made sense. 'You thought I was her, didn't you? When you first saw me?'

'Just for a moment, you look very like her.'

Rebecca winced: she was used to the comparison, but from

Leo – who'd made his feelings about Rosalyn abundantly clear in the latter half of *Seven Tales* – it stung.

'It's a compliment,' he insisted, 'you don't want to look like me! My God . . .' It seemed to hit him all over again as he studied her face. 'Birdie, you're all grown up!'

So are you, she wanted to reply.

Silence engulfed them. Rebecca knew she'd had weeks to prepare herself for this meeting, while he hadn't even had a minute, but she was impatient. She wanted him to catch up, to reach the point she had, so he could take some of the responsibility of deciding what came next.

'I'm sorry, I don't know what to say,' Leo admitted at last, running a hand through his grey hair, which was so flat and thin it made his head look small. 'Obviously I wasn't expecting you . . .'

This time Rebecca couldn't help herself: 'I wasn't expecting *you*.'

'No, I imagine I'm a little different to what you remember.'

This was such an understatement a bitter laugh escaped her. 'Just a little.'

'But you *do* remember me?'

Once more, she was hurt: did he think her inattentive or indifferent? Did he consider their scant years together forgettable? Granted, Rebecca had been trying to forget him for most of her life, but always in vain. Why did he keep saying the wrong thing? Not that she knew what the right thing would've been . . . Would she have been happier with stories and songs, with a figure more akin to the Stowaway? She doubted it, but at least it would've been in keeping with what she'd expected.

'Of course I remember you,' she muttered.

'Then I'm very surprised you're here.'

Leo stared down at a chalk X on the dark floor, just in front of his feet. This acknowledgement that he'd changed made

Rebecca want to bombard him with questions. Why was he different? What had happened to him? Was he better? She even considered bringing up *Seven Tales* again, so she could ask him in his own words, but what was the point? He seemed to have forgotten why he'd written those stories.

'*Lee-oh*?'

Heather was back, teetering on the edge of their conversation in such an exaggerated, irritating manner that Rebecca longed to relieve her feelings by giving the squat mole-like woman a slap. Instead, she forced herself to stare into the middle distance and was surprised when the interior of St Jude's materialised around her. Somehow, she'd blocked out the rattle of the sewing machine and the reedy phone music, the odour of paint mixed with the pong of cheese-flavoured crisps, the teenagers grooming and feeding one another like a troop of monkeys. For the past few minutes, nothing else had existed but her and Leo.

'Heather, I'm just in the middle of something here,' he was telling his colleague.

'O-kay,' she said, attempting to exchange a long-suffering expression with Rebecca, 'but you *did* say you'd run through Lewis's lines with him . . .'

Leo touched his fingertips to his left temple. 'Yes, and I'm sorry, but this is important. I'm sure Lewis can find someone else.'

There was something almost Rosalyn-esque about the way Heather then checked the watch squeezing at her chubby wrist. 'How long do you think this interview will last?' she asked Rebecca.

'Interview?' echoed Leo, bewildered, before shaking his head. 'Please, Heather, just—Just give us a minute, will you?'

Finally, his colleague gave up and, as Rebecca watched her bob away, she felt slightly less resentful of Leo, and not just because he'd called their conversation important. As Heather's pestering had continued, Rebecca had almost expected him to bolt. Some deeply ingrained memory or suspicion told her that was exactly how he'd have reacted before.

'I've come at a bad time,' she observed, more to start up their discussion again than to excuse her impromptu appearance.

'No,' said Leo at once, 'you haven't. It's just . . .' He gestured around the hall. 'This is the end of the summer school programme I've been leading for the past couple of weeks. We've a dress rehearsal this afternoon, then performances tonight, tomorrow afternoon and tomorrow night. So it's just a bit busy, that's all.'

This was the most he'd said in one go since she'd arrived. Rebecca was struck by how ordinary he sounded, like he was any old person discussing their job. He hadn't just aged, she realised; he'd changed in some deeper, more intrinsic way and, again, she wanted to know how and why, but couldn't think where to start.

'Is this part of one of the festivals, then?' she asked.

'Not exactly, although we're hoping some of the festival crowds might wander in. Usually it's just parents and friends who show up, but obviously people are more open-minded about new work at this time of year . . .' He seemed struck by an idea. 'I could reserve you a seat if you like?'

'No, thank you,' said Rebecca. 'I'm a bit old for children's stories now.'

She was trying to wound him, as he'd wounded her with his disregard for *Seven Tales,* but Leo said, 'Oh, it's not a children's story. Of course, it's devised around *The Wizard of Oz*, but the kids have gone quite dark with it, and it's about the impact of—'

'No thank you,' Rebecca said again.

This time, he couldn't miss her tone and looked away. His gaze landed upon Heather, who was talking to a lanky dark-haired boy holding a script – Lewis, presumably – and then white-hot jealousy erupted through Rebecca's whole body. Who was this boy? Who were all these teenagers, in comparison to her? Why should they have Leo when, at their age, she had not – and still did not, because even as she stood here now he was thinking and fretting and *caring* about them, these other people who were not her.

I was the rehearsal, she thought, her envy solidifying into crushing comprehension. With her, he'd only practiced fatherhood. This, though – the church, these teenagers, the play – this was all part of a dazzling final performance, one Rebecca had no part in.

'I should go,' she said.

'Go?' Immediately, his focus returned to her. 'Now? Are you coming back?'

'I don't know. I think this was a mistake.'

'It wasn't,' he told her, with more vehemence than he'd said or done anything so far. 'I'm sorry, it's just this play . . . You've caught me off-guard, that's all – and it's my fault, it's *all* my fault,' he added quickly, reading her expression. 'But it wasn't a mistake, please don't say that. I just—' he shook his head. 'I just can't believe you're here.'

There was something gratifying about seeing him gabble and grow agitated. It was reassuring to identify cracks in this new persona, to know he could be something other than quiet and slow. Yet as his mood veered back towards amazement, Rebecca softened: he was still absorbing this, she had to give him more time.

'What do you want to do?' he finished, helplessly.

'Maybe . . . Maybe we could go somewhere and talk?' she said, wondering why she was the one instigating this. He was the parent, and the one who had left; he should be taking the lead.

'Yes,' said Leo eagerly. 'Yes, we'll talk.'

She waited for him to suggest a place: perhaps the hall had some sort of break room, or he knew of a nearby café that wouldn't be overrun with tourists.

'How long are you here for?' he asked instead.

'What?'

'In Edinburgh – do you want to meet tomorrow?'

'Tomorrow?'

'Or today,' he corrected himself, nervous again. 'This afternoon, if you want, or—'

'I'm here *now.*'

He blinked, then looked around the church again. 'Yes – of course. If you give me a couple of minutes . . .'

Rebecca exhaled sharply. 'Forget it.'

'I just need to find cover. There's a photographer coming, and I can't leave the kids with only two other—'

'I said *forget it*!'

He flinched at her rage, but even this brought her no satisfaction.

'Good luck with the play,' she said, turning to go.

'Rebecca, please – wait.'

The teenagers, she now noticed, were staring, their scripts and phones and paintbrushes temporarily forgotten. Heather, too, seemed to have realised something was amiss, because she was peering over from the other side of the church, where she'd resumed her post by the porch. Their scrutiny made Rebecca falter – or maybe she stopped for him, because a part of her did want to wait, to start over.

But when she looked back, and even though Leo's face was a mask of anguish, she hardened again. He was fine – he was well. She'd spent all night agonising over facing a man who was falling apart, like in that video from *The Stowaway* set, yet somehow this was worse: he had a whole new life now, one that was more important than her – and evidently had been for some time.

Rebecca was still holding *Seven Tales*: her talisman, her map. She tried to stuff it back into her bag, but it no longer seemed to fit. In a burst of frustration and fury she tossed it towards the nearest chair, where it sent his red light filter tumbling to the floor. She didn't need it, not anymore. Perhaps she'd never needed it, because all that book had done was lead her to this stranger, this imposter— while Leo Sampson remained lost.

17

The Emerald City

'That was quick.'

Cam emerged from the kitchen as Rebecca let herself back into the flat, which smelled of coffee and laundry detergent. Today he was wearing a turquoise kimono patterned with flying cranes and carrying a wooden spoon.

'How did it go?' he asked.

'Yeah, fine . . .' She glanced down the narrow hallway, past the paintings of the savannah and the giraffe coat stand. 'Where's Ellis?'

'He just went out – I don't think he realised you'd be back so soon.' Cam looked slightly nervous. 'Do you want me to call him?'

'No,' said Rebecca at once, 'but thanks.'

She'd thought she'd wanted to talk to Ellis, but now found it was a relief she couldn't. She wasn't ready to tell him what had happened, not yet; she didn't want him to know all their efforts of the past few weeks had been for nothing.

'You'll never guess what he's doing,' said Cam, conspiratorially, '*seeing shows.* Apparently, he's decided to do some reviewing for that piece of shite website.'

'Oh,' was all Rebecca could think to say.

'What a traitor, eh?' continued Cam, jabbing in the direction of the front door with his wooden spoon. 'I've a good mind to throw him out, but he'd only land on his feet. Probably blag his way into the Balmoral . . . Coffee?' he asked, so abruptly Rebecca thought he was still talking about Ellis. 'Tea? Gin? No offence, but you look like you could use it.'

Nevertheless, Rebecca declined the offer, and was grateful when Cam then drifted back towards the kitchen without subjecting her to further questioning. She returned to the spare room, sinking onto the bed and throwing aside her handbag, which was very light without *Seven Tales*. She wished she hadn't discarded the book like that. Maybe it had served its purpose, but as an object it had become precious to her. It was the only part of Leo – the *real* Leo, not that stranger from this morning – she'd had left.

What now? Rebecca had walked back from St Jude's in a daze and returned to Cam's flat only because she had nowhere else to go. She supposed she should think about heading home, but even the idea of moving from this bed was exhausting. Besides, what was waiting for her back in Devon? Unemployment, most likely, not to mention some extremely difficult conversations with Rosalyn. Even imagining her own flat brought her no solace, because she'd left it strewn with all those papers – all those reminders of this utterly futile endeavour.

Now the memory of how she'd pored over those photocopies made her feel so stupid and sad that something twanged behind her lower ribs, sending aftershocks rippling through her skin. An ache at the base of her sternum began to rise, squeezing at her chest, her throat, until she was forced to exhale it, like a gasp in reverse.

There was a knock at the door, and both Cam and his wooden spoon reappeared. 'Forgot to say – I'm making scrambled eggs if you want some?'

'No thanks,' she said, her voice wavering.

Her vision had blurred, so she sensed rather than saw Cam move towards her.

'Are you all right?' he asked.

'Mm-hmm.'

'Rebecca?'

The bed sagged as he sat down next to her, and the white birds on his kimono writhed before her watery eyes. What was he doing? She could keep this at bay if he left her alone.

'What's happened?' asked Cam.

'Nothing,' she gulped, 'I'm fine . . .'

'No you're not,' he said, hooking his arm around her shoulders and pulling her against his chest.

Rebecca's instinct was to push him away: he didn't know her, he wasn't her friend. But she couldn't, because as soon as he'd reached out for her – as soon as he'd permitted her to do what she never, ever did – her whole body had begun to quake with anguish.

Cam said nothing as she cried, and instead it was the weight and warmth of his arms that offered the reassurance. They were both so bony it felt more like a clattering of elbows and shoulder blades than an embrace, but somehow that didn't matter, just as it didn't matter she'd known him less than a day – in fact, that only made it easier.

Eventually, Rebecca quietened. She felt woozy, and her head was throbbing, but after taking a few shuddering breaths against Cam's sharp collarbone she was finally able to curb her tears. Only then did his grip on her arm slacken, and he peered at the silky shoulder of his kimono.

'If there's snot on this, I'll be raging . . .' When she laughed, he released her, lowering his head so he could peer at her face. 'You look like shite. Let's have something to eat.'

He pulled her from the bed and chivvied her towards the kitchen with elaborate sweeps of his wooden spoon, as though it were a shepherd's crook. There, he tossed her a roll of kitchen paper and Rebecca, reasoning she had little dignity left, blew her nose loudly.

'Sexy,' declared Cam. 'Now here's what we'll do: I'm going to make us these eggs—'

'You really don't have to do that . . .'

'—I'm going to make us these eggs,' he repeated firmly, 'and you're going to sit and eat them, okay?'

'Okay.'

Obediently, she lowered herself onto one of the benches at the table while Cam set to work. For a few minutes, there was silence, save for the cracking of eggs, the sizzle of butter, the metallic scrape of the toaster. Feeling drained, Rebecca watched Cam dart around the kitchen for a while, before her gaze moved to the window and the strip of sky visible over the tops of the terraces across the road.

'Here we are,' said Cam a little while later, depositing cutlery and two steaming plates onto the table. '*Bon appétit*.'

As he slid onto the opposite bench, Rebecca found she couldn't meet his eye. There was a damp patch under the collar of his kimono, as though the cranes were beginning to melt.

'I'm sorry,' she said. 'I never cry.'

'I can tell.'

He patted his angular cheekbones, and when Rebecca mimicked the action, she felt the grainy remnants of dried tears and mascara beneath her fingertips.

'Shit . . .'

'Ach, leave it,' said Cam, as she wiped under her eyes with a scrunched-up and rather damp ball of kitchen paper. 'Who cares? Now, come on – eat.'

As Rebecca cut through the mound of creamy eggs and crusty toast her insides fluttered again, this time from hunger.

'This is really good,' she said, after taking a mouthful.

'I know,' replied Cam, 'it's the chives. Well, that and the fact I use a fuck ton of butter – it's best you don't know how much.'

They ate without speaking, which might've made for an uncomfortable meal had it not been preceded by the far more awkward few minutes she'd spent sobbing into his shoulder. When they were finished, Cam dumped both of their plates into the sink, flicked on the kettle, and asked, 'So what's up?'

Rebecca sniffed. 'I don't really want to talk about it . . .'

'Well, tough, because I just made you breakfast.'

She nodded: this seemed fair. Besides, she felt much better after the eggs, and the crescendo of the kettle on the other side of the kitchen made it easier to start talking. She began with what she'd kept from him the night before – her father being the Stowaway, Ellis's article, *Seven Tales,* Leo's illness – while Cam's jaw slackened, and the whites of his eyes became more and more pronounced. By the time she'd updated him on everything that had brought her to Edinburgh, however, Cam seemed surprisingly unfazed by the idea that she'd tracked down her long-lost father using a book of fairy tales – or perhaps he was simply feigning nonchalance – because he catapulted two teabags towards the kitchen bin, one after the other, and declared, 'I never liked *The Stowaway.*'

'Really?' Rebecca found this almost impressive. 'I don't think I've ever met anyone who's said that.'

'I just thought it was a bit sad, you know? The way he was always trying to get home but never could – never did.' He returned to the table with two mugs and a carton of milk. 'I don't know, kids' stories are always a bit fucking strange, aren't they, especially when you're an adult. They're never like you remember. Sugar?'

'No thanks.'

'Didn't think so. All right, come on – what happened this morning?'

'Oh God . . .'

As her visit to the old church returned to Rebecca in excruciating detail, she wanted to lean forward and collapse onto the tabletop – only Cam chose that moment to slide over her tea.

'I'm not sure what happened,' she admitted. 'It just didn't go how it was supposed to.'

'How was it supposed to go?'

'I don't know, not like that.'

Relating this was harder, so Rebecca addressed most of her account to her mug. It was too recent, too raw, and no matter how carefully she tried to convey the shock of discovering Leo so changed, she feared that – from Cam's perspective – her own response sounded just as disconcerting.

'It's not like I thought it would be easy,' she concluded. 'Of course it was going to be weird – I was prepared for that, I was prepared for practically anything. Just not . . . *him*.'

She lifted the mug of tea and finally took a sip, grateful for the excuse to partially conceal her face. Cam's dark eyebrows were drawn together – in thought rather than disapproval, Rebecca hoped, though when he offered no comment, she began to brace herself for a reproach.

'Go on, then,' she said, when she could stand it no longer. 'Be honest. Tell me I've messed everything up.'

'I'm not sure I can,' said Cam, still frowning. 'It doesn't sound as bad as you seem to think it is.'

She tried to contradict him, but he held up a hand.

'I realise he's not what you expected. But he's here and so are you, and at least you've *started* talking . . .'

'But he didn't want to talk to me!' cried Rebecca, her voice quavering again as she realised this wasn't just true of today, but every day for the past 19 years.

Cam, however, took her comment at face value: 'Of course he did. He was surprised, that's all. Did you really want him to just ditch all those kids and their play?'

'Yes,' said Rebecca, feeling there was little point in pretending otherwise.

'All right,' allowed Cam, 'but do you really think he *should* have?'

Rebecca exhaled hard through her nose but said nothing, because this was harder to answer. Deep down she knew those teenagers deserved Leo's presence – but so had she, and not just today. Plus, it wasn't as though he hadn't done it before: if Lowrie and Priya were to be believed, running out on jobs had practically been her father's party piece. The old Leo – the other Leo – would've left that church in a second, especially for her.

'It's like he's a completely different person,' she said.

'You know that after speaking to him for, what, five minutes?'

'Yes!' insisted Rebecca. 'That wasn't him, not the real him . . .'

'Hang on,' said Cam, 'if you were just a kid when he left, how do you know who the real Leo is? Maybe there were sides to him you didn't see – or maybe your memories of him are mixed up with *The Stowaway*?'

Rebecca sighed again, too weary to explain she'd never even seen *The Stowaway* until last week. She'd asked Cam to be honest, but that didn't make it easy to hear him challenge her, especially when she wasn't sure he'd fully grasped the extent to which Leo had changed.

'But he *was* the Stowaway,' she said. 'That character, that's what he was like in real life, I just know it. And I understand, he wasn't well; he made a lot of people unhappy, especially himself.

But I thought he was wonderful – he *was* wonderful, in spite of it all – and now he's just . . . normal.'

Aloud, it didn't sound particularly bad, so why did she feel so cheated? After everything she'd done, surely she deserved to find the person she'd been looking for, not some pale imitation.

'My dad's normal,' said Cam, after another pause. 'I mean, everyone's a bit weird in their own way, aren't they, but on the whole he's pretty ordinary. He likes football and having a beer in his local and that. He loves dirty jokes. I guess he's the sort of dad they make the Father's Day cards for. And we get on all right. We're nothing like each other, obviously, but he's nice, and he cares about me, and he's funny – well, he's not, but he thinks he is.

'My point is, there are worse things than normal. Normal is underrated. Honestly, if your dad's not a total tosser, you're already better off than most of my exes . . . And here's the other thing about dads – about anyone you're related to: you don't get to choose what they're like, however much you might want to. The only choice you really have is whether or not you want them in your life.'

While he'd been talking, Rebecca had set aside her mug in favour of playing with her piece of mascara-stained kitchen paper. She could appreciate what Cam was saying, yet the description of his own constant father only highlighted something Rebecca was even less willing to confront than the thought that the Leo of her early childhood was gone. *It was agreed he could see you when he'd sorted himself out,* Rosalyn had said, *got a proper diagnosis, started taking medication, found a sensible job* . . . Leo, it seemed, now resembled the man his ex-wife had envisioned, so where had he been? Assuming Rosalyn had remained true to her word, why hadn't he come back for his Birdie? Unlike Cam, she hadn't even had the consolation prize of a normal father.

'Are we done here?'

Rebecca looked up to find Cam pointing at her half-drunk tea. She handed him the mug, which he deposited in the sink with his own, on top of the dirty plates and frying pan. As he drizzled washing up liquid over the pile, its colour reminded her of that shimmering swathe of material in the old church. If only she could go back to that moment, right before she'd seen Leo, when she'd stood there watching that sheet of green fabric being stapled to the wall. If only she could start the scene again. But what would she do differently? Even if she could adjust to this new version of him, how could she accept her father had been here all this time, apparently fine? How could she accept he'd been fine without her?

'What if I don't know if I want him in my life?' she asked.

'Then you don't know,' Cam replied, picking up a pair of flowery washing up gloves. 'But then, why did you come all this way? Why did you subject yourself to me, and the festival, and ten hours in a car with *Bailey* – which must've been a fucking nightmare, by the way. Did you really do all of that because you were undecided?'

When she didn't respond, he turned on the tap, and as the sink began to fill, Rebecca sensed their discussion was over.

'What am I going to do?'

She was talking to herself, really; over the gushing of the water, she didn't even expect him to hear the question. But Cam, who'd been inspecting the foam rising behind him, remarked, 'The way I see it, right now you have two options . . .'

'Which are?' she asked, hopefully.

He held up the flowery washing up gloves. 'Either you make yourself useful with these, or you fuck off out of my kitchen.'

Acting Up Youth Theatre

presents

THE EMERALD CITY

Oz is dying. The trees are gone, the rivers are dry, the fields have turned to dust. With nothing left to lose, a resilient orphan named Dot decides to set out for the Emerald City, the last oasis of greenery in the land where, it is said, there lives a man with the power to cleanse the earth. But the journey is long and perilous, and East/West Ltd, the powerful corporation that profited from Oz's destruction, will stop at nothing to prevent outsiders from reaching the city and learning the truth.

Rebecca was glad she'd opened her programme and absorbed this synopsis before the play had begun, otherwise she wouldn't have had the faintest idea what was happening. Even having read it, much of what subsequently unfolded in front of the iridescent green backdrop – the strobe lighting, the synthwave music, the dancers wafting around aerial silks – made little sense, and it didn't help that the only dialogue was in some sort of dystopian dialect, presumably of the teenagers' own invention. Still, considering she'd anticipated jigging munchkins and earnest renditions of 'Somewhere Over the Rainbow', it wasn't too much of an ordeal, and she clapped politely as the young actors and crew took their bows, while the rest of the audience – most of whom were almost certainly parents – whooped and stamped their feet.

None of the youth theatre's staff had been visible during the play, not even at the curtain call, although by the time the audience had begun to amble towards the exit, Heather had rematerialised by the porch, while the platinum blonde woman in overalls was tidying the stage. Leo, however, was nowhere to be seen. Most of the youngsters had now disappeared through an arched oak door, which presumably had once led to a vestry, and Rebecca supposed he must be there too, congratulating his charges.

But what if he wasn't? She hadn't seen him since returning to St Jude's – what if he wasn't here at all? Guilt began to squeeze at her stomach. If Leo had appeared, unannounced, at Sudworth and Rowe, would she have been able to go back to filing and typing up reports afterwards, like nothing had happened?

She began to watch the vestry door as though she meant to memorise its every detail – the iron latch, the cracks and scuffs in the wood – and each time it opened she took a breath. But it was always only teenagers, laughing and jostling at one another, still euphoric from the performance.

Rebecca bit down on the inside of her cheeks. She should go in there. She should search that room and every corner of this church, and all the streets of Edinburgh if necessary, until she found him again. Because Cam was right: she hadn't come all this way for nothing.

'Rebecca?'

She spun around, but he had to call her two more times before she spotted him, standing on the other side of the stage, camouflaged among the parents. He'd donned a black Acting Up T-shirt for the occasion, but otherwise looked much the same as earlier, and was holding what she recognised to be the leafy cloak of the wizard.

'You came back,' he said.

'Yes.'

He braved another step towards her. 'I'm so sorry about earlier—'

'It's fine.'

'—I wasn't thinking, I didn't know what to—'

'Really, it doesn't matter.'

He began to fold the cloak in his arms but didn't take his eyes from her face. 'I was beginning to think I'd imagined you,' he said. 'With everything going on, with the play . . . I thought I might be losing it.' He allowed himself a small chuckle. 'Wouldn't be the first time!'

Rebecca stiffened: so he was able to joke about it? Unsure how to respond, but determined to be kinder than before, she said, 'I liked the play.'

'Did you?' Suddenly he was all eagerness again. 'It was great, wasn't it? Especially for the first performance. They did really well.'

The skin around his eyes creased as he smiled at the teenagers dotted around the church, none of whom were paying him any attention. Rebecca experienced another jab of envy, but forced herself to dismiss it, the conversation with Cam still fresh in her mind.

'I don't suppose you still want to go for that talk?' Leo asked, turning back to her.

She nodded, relieved he'd finally said something she wanted to hear. 'But it doesn't have to be now,' she told him, for she could see at least two parents waiting to swoop in on their conversation. 'I know you're busy, I wasn't expecting—'

'I can be ready in a few minutes,' he said. 'Unless you have other plans, of course?'

'No,' said Rebecca, wondering whether he thought she'd come to Edinburgh for the festival, and was simply looking him up while she was here. 'No, I can wait.'

'Are you sure? I won't be long, but—'

'It's fine, there's no rush.'

Even so, he kept his gaze on her as he backed away,

unwittingly cutting through the cluster of parents lingering behind him. After he'd disappeared through the vestry door, Rebecca returned to the metal chairs and studied the group of young performers huddled nearby. A few of them still bore traces of the play: one boy had a smear of green face paint along his jawline, while the girl who'd played Dot had kept on her clompy red boots.

As a woman stepped towards the green-jawed boy and started to wipe at his scowling face with a tissue, Rebecca's thoughts turned to her own mother. Rosalyn had cheered her on at every sports day, attended every concert during Rebecca's short-lived career as a violinist, waited late for every school trip to return. She'd been like these parents: proud, patient, present – too present, Rebecca had often felt, but wasn't that a hundred times better than not being there at all?

Their confrontation was still needling at her conscience; she couldn't shake the image of Rosalyn's flushed, tearful face, nor the sound of her voice raised in uncharacteristic anger. Rebecca reached for her phone and scrolled through her texts and call log, confirming Rosalyn hadn't been in contact – not so present after all, then. Was it surprising, though? Rebecca had practically called her mother a liar, when it was looking increasingly likely Leo had stayed away of his own accord.

The mother in St Jude's had now abandoned her tissue and was scrubbing at her son's green-tinged face with her thumb. Rebecca watched the boy squirm in protest, recalling how Rosalyn had always insisted on slathering her with sun cream in public; she could still feel the scrape of damp sand as lotion was rubbed under the straps of her swimming costume . . . And *that,* she realised, with another ache of regret, was why her mother had been calling her on the beach, that day Leo had buried himself in the sand; Rosalyn hadn't been trying to interrupt their archaeology game, but ensure that Rebecca, whose skin was as pale as her own, didn't burn.

When he reappeared, Leo was wearing a faded rucksack over a dark green raincoat, which, along with his paint-flecked jeans and scuffed trainers, gave him the appearance of someone practical – someone who might own a garden shed, perhaps. Together they proceeded through the old church, although slowly, for Leo kept being waylaid by questions and congratulations from teenagers and parents. When they finally reached the porch, which seemed much darker than before, Rebecca became aware of a chittering noise overhead, and saw the cobbles of the street outside were glossy with rain. She wavered on the front step, drawing her cardigan more tightly around her torso, and winced when a drip of cold water landed right in the parting of her hair.

'Here, take this,' said Leo, who'd been rummaging in his rucksack.

The umbrella he was offering her was a little worse for wear: a few of its spokes were bent, and its black underside was speckled with rust.

'What about you?' she asked, taking the handle.

'Oh, I have a hood here somewhere . . .'

He began to tug at the neck of his raincoat, attempting to unroll a flimsy scrap of material from its collar. As she watched him struggle, Rebecca considered suggesting they share the umbrella, but decided against it, content with the distance between them. On the edge of the porch, they might've been a pair of swimmers poised to dive, and when Leo glanced sideways his attention was caught by something just above her head.

'What?' she asked, feeling her parting, which was still wet from the raindrop.

'Nothing, it's just – you're a lot taller than I remember.'

'You're a lot older,' she countered, lightly.

He laughed, and for a second she saw him: the face was still lined, the hair still flat and grey, but mirth wiped away a little of his age and restored some of his spirit, some of his innate *Leo*-ness. In that instant, he was her dad again, and even when his smile disappeared as he contemplated the sodden street, Rebecca was comforted by the knowledge that, somewhere, this speck of him still remained.

Edinburgh, however, had changed almost beyond recognition. As they plunged into the rain – the umbrella squirming against wild surges of wind – Rebecca found it hard to believe this was the same bright city that had welcomed her the previous evening. Pitchy clouds coiled across the sky like ink through water and the downpour was beating a furious rhythm against the road and rooftops, as though chastening the cheer of the festival city.

The rain must have started suddenly, because all around them people were scurrying for cover, huddling in shop doorways and bus shelters or waving desperately to black cabs that were already occupied. In the dash to stay dry, soggy flyers were being trampled into kerbs, and abandoned hand-painted signs were dribbling into gibberish. As Rebecca and Leo pelted through a pedestrianised zone, they found performers striving to protect props, musical instruments, electrical equipment. A juggler's fire torches sputtered and smoked, the make-up of mime artists streamed, a troupe of dancers' feathery tails drooped and dragged through puddles. It seemed to Rebecca everything was smudging; Edinburgh was a chalk pavement picture, dissolving and draining away.

How easy it would be to get lost here, she thought.

Eventually, they shook off the crowds, but as they hurried down a series of residential streets, the lashing rain was still incessant and Rebecca was growing cold and annoyed: why hadn't they just stayed in the church? Then Leo indicated a small pub up ahead, whose hanging sign identified it as The Unicorn. This seemed a lofty name for an establishment with grimy windows and peeling black paintwork, but Rebecca wasn't about to spurn shelter.

The Unicorn's front room was dominated by a wood-panelled bar, a motley collection of elderly men, and the pervading aromas of beer and vinegar. The pub was bigger than it first appeared, for after nodding at the barman Leo led Rebecca through a labyrinth of small low-ceilinged spaces – some of which housed dartboards, fruit machines and even a cramped-looking pool table – until they reached an empty back room whose main feature was a stone chimney breast, its fireplace half-hidden behind a screen of mesh and wrought iron.

'I hope this is all right,' said Leo. 'It was the only place I could think of that wouldn't be packed.'

'It's fine.'

After they'd claimed a couple of chesterfield chairs upholstered in maroon leather, he volunteered to go back to the bar and, because Rebecca was cold, she asked for a red wine. Once Leo had departed, she sank into her wingback seat and slipped off her soggy shoes, placing her bare feet on the tartan carpet, which was threadbare but mercifully dry.

The nearest wall was cluttered with framed sketches and paintings, most of them depicting views of what she assumed was Edinburgh, and all of them yellowed with age – or perhaps cigarette smoke. As Rebecca tweaked the corner of the nearest picture, which wasn't quite straight, she began to regret her choice of drink: the wine wouldn't be good here.

Was this Leo's local? She knew nothing about his life, beyond his work with Acting Up. What did he do with the rest of his time? Did he have any friends? Perhaps they assembled here, as she and her friends congregated at The Crown.

'Here we are,' said Leo, as he set down a wine glass that was cloudy from the dishwasher.

He'd only ordered himself half a pint, and Rebecca wondered whether this meant he didn't intend to stay long.

'Well, cheers.'

He raised his glass rather than tapping it against hers. She mimicked the action and took a cautious sip. Unsurprisingly, the wine was sour.

They looked at one another.

'I'm glad you came back,' said Leo.

'You already said that.'

'Did I? Well, it's true.'

Rebecca dug her toes into the worn fibres of the carpet, reminding herself to be gentler, more patient. But now they were facing one another – now the distractions of the play and the rain and the rest of the pub were gone – she didn't know what to say or do; how to act, how to feel.

'Where are you staying?' he asked.

When she told him, he nodded, apparently familiar with the area, before commenting, 'It must've been difficult, getting accommodation during the festival.'

'Not really, we're staying with a friend.'

'We?'

'I'm here with another friend.'

She considered elaborating on the subject of Ellis Bailey but couldn't think what to say or feel about him either.

'And this Edinburgh friend,' persisted Leo, 'he – or she – isn't renting out the spare rooms?'

'No, he hates the festival.'

Leo nodded again – not, she suspected, because she was saying anything very interesting, but because she was saying something. A tasselled wall lamp was shining directly down on him, while a tatty red velvet curtain had been half-drawn across the doorway behind his chair, presumably to combat a draught. Perhaps Rebecca had theatre on the brain, because this put her in mind of a stage, and she was suddenly gripped with sadness that she'd never see him perform again. Not just because he'd stopped acting, and there were only two series of *The Stowaway*, but because there would be no more puppet theatres or shadow plays or spontaneous anecdotes about trolls and gnomes and trees that moved at Midsummer . . . It was yet another part of him that was lost.

'When did you arrive?' he asked.

'Yesterday.'

'And you came from . . . ?'

'Devon.'

'*Devon* . . .' he repeated, his tone wistful.

'Exeter,' she clarified, because as much as she disliked divulging anything, she didn't want him to assume she was still in the village.

'That's where you live, is it? Where you work? I don't even know what you do.' His restraint was beginning to slip. 'I don't know your job, your hobbies, whether you went to university . . .'

'I did.'

'Of course you did,' he said, smiling. 'Of course you've inherited your mum's brains – and thank God!'

Rebecca glared at him: she wished he'd stop comparing her to Rosalyn.

'Where did you study?' he asked, undaunted. '*What* did you study?'

She took another gulp of the cheap wine, before saying, 'I don't really want to answer these questions.'

She feared this might throw him, but he continued to nod, apparently unsurprised by her reticence. Perhaps he'd anticipated it; perhaps he hadn't expected any answers at all.

'Not now, anyway,' said Rebecca, encouraged by this reaction. 'Maybe later we can talk about that stuff, but I came here to find out about you.'

He opened his mouth to speak, then seemed to reconsider and gulped at his beer instead.

'What were you going to say?' she challenged.

He managed to hold her gaze. 'Just that earlier you seemed to know a lot about me already.'

'What?'

'From the book, the fairy tales?'

She cringed to recall how she'd shaken *Seven Tales* at him that morning, insisting she understood it all, before experiencing another wrench of regret that she'd tossed the book away. How could she have been so careless? She hoped he'd picked it up but was too ashamed to ask.

'You didn't finish it,' she told him instead. 'In the last tale, the shaman offers to sew the man's shadow back on, so he can—' she took a breath '—so he can find the little bird again. Because that's what he wants above everything. Then there's nothing else. It's unfinished.'

It appeared to take Leo a moment to recall the story, but when he did – and when he seemed to understand where she was heading – his whole body shrivelled like an empty drink can being crushed in a fist. If mirth restored some of his youth, misery aged him: his filmy eyes became sunken, half-hidden under a heavy brow, while the veiny hand he clasped to his mouth tugged at the lines criss-crossing his face.

'Oh, Birdie . . .'

Rebecca gripped at the buttoning on the arms of her chair, partly so she wouldn't recoil. 'I want to know the end,' she said.

'I'm sorry?'

'What happens next? Tell me the rest of the story.'

Leo began to shake his head. 'I'm not sure I can . . .'

'Why not?'

'Because—Because I don't really know how to do that anymore; how to invent tales about shamans and shadows. I think it's gone,' he said, both his voice and his hand trembling as he splayed his fingers, releasing something invisible into the air. 'I've run out of make-believe.'

This came as no surprise to Rebecca.

A part of her had known it from the moment she'd spotted him in the church, hunched in that chair, clutching at those light filters. And it hurt – it hurt so much it felt like a hammer to her heart – because that was the Leo she'd longed to find; the ceaseless storyteller, the endless entertainer. For all his faults, for all his troubles, he was the only dad she'd ever known.

Perhaps, though – being who he was now – the man before her might make this more straightforward.

'So tell me the truth,' she said.

18

The Eighth Tale: The Lost Storyteller

Not so long ago, not so far away, there lived a man who was always lost. Wherever he went, whether it be city or forest or desert, he could never get his bearings, even if

No, wait

That isn't right: it should start with you.

Once, in a little kingdom nestled in a great valley, a princess was born. To her father, who was sometimes gripped by a terrible sadness, it felt like the sun had come out after weeks of cloud and rain. So delighted was he by his new daughter, he was able to forget that the realm belonged to his wife, the Queen, while he hailed from a faraway land, one that

I know.

I can't do it anymore. It's not enough anymore. And you asked for the truth.

The trouble is, I'm not sure you'll believe me. There'll be no nixies or magical lutes, but you'll think I'm still making up stories when I tell you everything I've done since we last saw one another has been for you.

There: I said you wouldn't believe me. That's understandable, it doesn't make much sense. And perhaps I'm exaggerating. Perhaps, deep down, some of it, a lot of it, was for me too, but

This still isn't coming out right.

I suppose the true story starts when you and I were separated. That's where we left off, when I left you. That trip to Edinburgh, it was meant to be a new beginning. I'd been fired from *The Stowaway* a few months beforehand, and I was upset by how little I was seeing you – and paranoid Roz would try to cancel the few visits we had. So I got it into my head we should start again, just the two of us. Not in the village, or Bristol, but somewhere I felt at home – the first place I'd ever really felt like myself.

I was in a manic phase, of course. I spent most of my *Stowaway* earnings on a deposit for a flat up here, which I filled with the strangest, most impractical things: a candyfloss maker, a paddling pool, one of those giant piano keyboards . . . I was also convinced I was being watched – by Roz, by the media, by MI5 – so I arranged everything as Leo Lockwood. It was one of the reasons Roz's solicitor later called it a *calculated kidnapping*.

Only I messed it up. By the time I'd got you here, I was too excited, too agitated. It's mostly a blur now, but I remember dragging you all over the city, wanting to show you your new home, and it was so busy that when I let go of your hand, I—

Well, you know what happened next.

Afterwards, I was arrested. Not for taking my six-year-old daughter from her mum and then abandoning her, but for trying to climb Castle Rock – those crags in the middle of the city – without any kind of permission or equipment.

That's what they told me I'd been doing, anyway. I don't really remember, but it sounds plausible: I was always prone to climbing when I was on a high, I liked to be king of the castle. Maybe I was still trying to find you.

The first thing I remember from the hospital is being asked questions. Hundreds and hundreds of questions. And whatever I said, or did, it was enough to diagnose me – *re*-diagnose me, I should say. I already knew I had bipolar disorder. I've known since my first arrest, when my father marched me to a London hospital, and he and the other doctors terrified me with talk of drugs and electric currents and whatever else they were planning – I didn't hang around long enough to find out. I was 17 years old, and they called it manic depression back then.

At some point in Edinburgh, I must've told the doctors or police that my name was Leo Lockwood, because suddenly that's who I was. I must've given them my Edinburgh address as well, because I don't think returning to Bristol was ever discussed. It wasn't a great loss – I had no friends or family there – but later it occurred to me this must've protected me from the press. It never got out, you see, that the Stowaway ended up in a loony bin . . .

Sorry – I still don't really know how to talk about this.

Even then, it was you I wanted. It was you I asked for, again and again. They told me you were fine, you'd been found and were back with your mum, but I didn't trust them. I needed to see you for myself, but by that point they'd decided to keep me in, which isn't as common as you'd think. An *observation period*, it was called.

My doctor at this time was called Ravi. He was very softly spoken, with this little moustache that made him look like a 40s film star. During the four months I was in hospital, I only saw him once a week – mostly I was reviewed by junior doctors and nurses – but Ravi was the one who helped me understand what had happened to you. To us. You were the only thing we talked about in the beginning. I couldn't shake the suspicion it was all just a big conspiracy Roz had concocted to get me away from you: in my confusion, in my paranoia, that was easier to accept than the idea I'd abandoned my little girl.

My Birdie.

It was the first letter from Roz's solicitor that finally convinced me. Something about having it in my hands – that thick paper with its legal jargon and fancy little logo at the top – made everything feel clearer, more real, and I realised I wasn't the victim of some elaborate plot or prank. Still, I don't know how to explain it, what happened in my head after that. How can I explain it, what happened in my head after that?

When I was about eight, I found a grey cat at the bottom of the garden, which I called Smoky and decided to adopt. I was quite lonely as a child. It was only me and my father – and sometimes my aunt, but she wasn't much fun. Anyway, this cat, Smoky, tolerated me for a while, probably because I fed it all sorts of things I found in the kitchen, but then one day – and not for any reason I can remember – it scratched me. Quite badly. My father, who was a doctor, had to put a dressing on my arm. But it wasn't the scratch that upset me, it was the fact that this creature I'd cared for had just turned on me, and with such violence. I was so shocked, so hurt – and years later, when I read and reread that solicitor's letter, I felt exactly the same way about my condition.

I'd convinced myself I could tame it, you see, and that people like your mum, who told me I needed help, didn't understand I had it under control. Roz used to say I enjoyed being ill. Maybe that was fair, maybe it wasn't. The thing is, I didn't see it as an illness – I enjoyed being *me*. It's easy to look back now and see the damage I did – and I do look back, all the time – but it wasn't until I'd sabotaged my relationship with you that I finally recognised I was in the grip of something monstrous.

You're probably wondering about the hospital. For most of my life, I'd dreaded ending up in a place like that, and somehow it was both better and worse than I'd imagined. Obviously, it's not like the old days: there aren't any straitjackets or belts on the beds. Mostly, I remember the smell. It was sterile, like a normal hospital, but because it was an old building there was a mustiness to the air. I used to think it smelled of my father's study, which didn't help.

It was so bright. Every room had those strip lights you get in schools and offices, but they seemed more powerful there than anywhere else. Maybe it was to keep an eye on us. My mother would've said it was to keep away the shadows. I remember once, when one of those lights kept flickering, it sent another patient into a frenzy. He started throwing all his belongings at the ceiling – his shoes, his book, his toothbrush. After that, they changed the bulbs straight away.

The food was terrible, like school dinners, and it was impossible to sleep surrounded by so many people. I hated feeling confined and being told what to do, because everything there was decided for me: when I woke up, when I ate, when I saw the doctors, when I went to bed . . . In the first few weeks, the sheer monotony of it made me want to peel off my own skin, but I got used to it eventually. My agent once told me I was the sort of person who needed routine, and maybe she was right.

I didn't make many friends. I'm not sure anyone did – most of us just wanted to get out. There wasn't much trouble, though. People were polite. I suppose the real battles were raging inside everyone's heads. And secretly, I think every person there believed they were different from the rest – that they'd ended up in that place by accident, not because they were really ill, not like everyone else.

That's what I told myself, anyway.

Besides, I knew my way out. According to Roz's solicitor, some judge in Exeter had ruled I couldn't see you until my condition was under control, so it was clear what I had to do. It's strange: for so long I only cared about myself, but that never extended to my own health. You were different, though. For you, I'd get better. For you, I'd *be* better.

It's not even getting better, not really. It's *recognising triggers* and *developing coping strategies*. It's talking, so much talking.

It's mood stabilisers – placing that little tablet onto your tongue and finally swallowing. It's trying this pill, that pill, how about we move you onto these pills? It's not feeling like yourself, and being told that's good, that means it's working. It's giving up, running away and being brought back – or bringing yourself back, because they discharged you too early. It's starting again. And again. And again. It's spending every reserve of energy you have striving for something that – deep, deep down – you're not even sure you want. It's erasing those parts of yourself you thought were shiny and special, and taking it on faith that, when you're done, something more than nothing will remain. It's accepting that no matter how many triggers you recognise, strategies you develop, moods you stabilise, this will never, ever leave you, and – in the end – all you can do is learn to live with it.

It's exhausting.

There were activities we could do at the hospital – *alternative therapies,* they called them. Pilates, pottery, that sort of thing. Drama workshops were out, so I started with painting, although I've never had the patience for arts and crafts, not like your mum. Then this writer came in: Tess? Tessa? She was very smiley and freckly, and smelled of cinnamon.

During those sessions, she had us listing the sounds of our childhoods and writing poems, using signs we found around the hospital. Only, I wasn't interested in *Family Room 3* and *please wash your hands,* so I started writing the fairy tales instead. Perhaps it was inevitable: the sound of my childhood was my mother's voice, telling me stories.

Tasha – that's what the writer was called.

I wrote the first draft of that book in a kind of delirium. It only took about two days. I barely slept or ate, just frantically scribbled until it all came out.

The stories were always for you. I was afraid your mum and the rest of your family would be telling lies about me, so I wanted to defend myself, explain myself. I'd also got it into my head that the book would reunite us; that if I stuffed it with enough clues about who and where I was, I wouldn't need Roz's or anyone else's permission to come and find you, because you would find me. Never mind you were barely seven years old at this point.

So, when I'd finished, I gathered together all those crumpled pieces of paper – which were covered in nonsense, of course – and started pestering the staff for an envelope big enough. Fortunately, one of the nurses figured out what I was up to and Ravi convinced me to let him hold onto my so-called book for a while, until I left the hospital. Which was probably for the best: I wasn't actually allowed to contact you back then.

It was winter when I was discharged for the final time. I remember that not because it was cold, but because the streets and shops were full of Christmas, which meant everything was so luminous, so loud. I wasn't just pushed out, of course. I had a lot of support at the beginning: they signed me up with a GP and a counsellor, and this gruff man from social services, Doug, came round every week to eat all my biscuits – I used to buy these expensive ones before each visit and arrange them neatly on a plate, hoping it would make me look extra stable. Extra sane.

Fortunately, I still had my flat up here, and this time I tried to furnish it properly. I went shopping for pans, cotton sheets, lamps, a houseplant – which died, immediately. It was overwhelming: there were so many colours and types and prices. Roz had always dealt with that stuff or else I'd made do with whatever I'd found in the cupboards of wherever I was living.

I was getting it ready for you, of course. Nesting, in a way. During my counselling sessions, I'd learned I had to be *responsible, reliable, trustworthy*, but I didn't know how. Perhaps if I had all the right props, though – all the right sheets and pans and plants – I'd be able to pretend.

Roz wasn't fooled for a minute. Your mum always knew when I was pretending. So when I steeled myself to call her, to ask her, to tell her I was better – or better than before, at least – she didn't believe me. She said . . . Well, she said a lot of things, because it was the first time we'd spoken since I'd taken you. I only heard one thing, though:

No.

You can't really blame her, not after what I did.

But still . . .

What was I supposed to do then? Ignore her? Show up at Primrose Cottage? *Ta-da*! Or go back to how I was? Flush all those little pills down the toilet – or maybe swallow them all at once.

I wouldn't have done that. I swore, when you were born, never again. Not that it's a choice: when you're feeling that low, that helpless and hollow, when you aren't feeling anything at all – there's no alternative, no other release. But as wretched as I was after that call with Roz, there was still a little hope for me – there was still *you* – and I couldn't bear the idea of leaving you like that; not like my mother left me.

I didn't flush my pills away either. I'd come too far, and maybe I knew I wouldn't be able to do it again. I had to keep going, keep submitting to it all – the meetings, the medication, whatever I had to do – because that was the quickest, easiest path back to you. Relatively speaking, I mean. Obviously none of this was remotely quick or easy.

Besides, everyone kept telling me Roz would come around. I just had to prove myself, she just had to trust me again – nobody understood she'd barely trusted me in the first place. If I wanted to see you again, I had to wait.

So I waited.

And waited.

And waited.

And while I waited, I tried to get used to how it felt, not feeling like myself. It was as though I'd invited someone into my house, and he'd not only moved in, he'd started making the place his own: repainting the walls, throwing out my possessions, changing the locks . . . Only, it wasn't my house, it was my head, and I'd asked for this. I'd summoned him inside.

How were we to live together? How was I to live with myself? Because I hated him, this person I was becoming – how muted he was, how ordinary. For the first time in my life, I felt like a spectator. Passively, I drifted from task to task, appointment to appointment, from days to weeks to months to years, all the while asking myself: is this what normal feels like?

Is this it?

A few months after I left hospital, sometime in the spring of '98, I tried Roz again. Maybe she could sense a change in me, because I sensed a softening in her. Don't get me wrong, she was obviously still upset, still furious, but when she said she wasn't yet ready for me to see you, I realised she was no longer telling me *no*, but *later*.

To prove I was taking my recovery seriously, she gave me a long list of requirements I had to meet, many of which I was already doing, like taking medication and going to counselling. But she was adamant I should find a proper job, a sensible, well-paid 9-5 – only for someone like me, still very ill, this was easier said than done.

I started in a café, Beanie's, which was miserable. I kept spilling drinks and giving the wrong change, and I felt intimidated by the other staff, who were all students with better things to come, while I was in my late 30s and qualified for nothing. But it got me out of my flat, and gave me a little purpose, even if that purpose was just making terrible coffees – and often more than once, because the customers always complained.

Then someone in my therapy group told me about an admin job at a small theatre. Which I also struggled with, because I could barely use a computer, but my colleagues there were more understanding – I think they could tell I was a bit broken. And it helped to be back in a theatre, even if it was only behind the scenes.

It was through that job I later bumped into Colin, who I'd worked with on a Fringe show before you were born. While my career had soared and plummeted, Colin had been working steadily as a producer, and had recently set up a youth theatre company called Acting Up.

For a long time, I couldn't understand why he offered me a job. We'd never been close. He wasn't even interested in my fleeting fame, because by then I'd been Leo Lockwood for a while and completely disassociated myself from *The Stowaway*. On the few occasions someone would recognise me, it was easy enough to convince them they were mistaken.

I've since come to realise that Colin is just decent, kind. He recognised I needed a second chance – or whatever chance I was on by then – so he gave it to me. You know, in my worst bouts of illness, I used to think everyone was against me, but during my recovery it seemed like the opposite was true: most people want to help you when you're trying to help yourself.

Acting Up gave me another reason to stick to my care plan. Dozens of reasons, actually – the kids, the other staff, the shows – but when I first joined, my biggest concern was getting it right for Colin. Letting him down when he'd put such faith in me was unthinkable.

And this, I've found, is what it's all about: finding those reasons to keep going. They don't have to be big. I used to think only the highest of highs had any value; the rushes I got from my illness, of course, but also from drink, and drugs, and sex – sorry, but you asked for the truth – and from performing, which for me was the best high of all.

But I'm not sure I believe that anymore.

Around the time I joined Acting Up, I got a rescue dog, Chilli, an old mongrel from a local shelter, and he found joy in everything. The ping of the microwave, the view out the window, his blanket – which was actually one of my fleeces he'd stolen from the laundry basket. Most of all, he found joy in *me* – the me I was then, and am now, not the me I'd once been.

God, I miss that dog.

So, I try to be like Chilli. I try to find the good in small, ordinary things: a favourite song; my morning walk; whatever mess of a meal I've made in cooking class. And, over time, I've found it's enough.

It's more than enough.

I've become distracted, haven't I? I've told you everything apart from what you wanted to know.

I was waiting, let's go back to that. Waiting and waiting for your mum to trust me. And around that time – which must've been the end of '98, maybe the beginning of '99 – I rediscovered that early draft of *Seven Tales*.

It was at the bottom of a bag I'd never got round to unpacking after the hospital, and my first impulse was to throw it away. The sight of it made me feel sick with shame, because, of course, it was a mess. The parts that weren't completely illegible were full of rants about Roz, my illness and *The Stowaway*, or else random asides about what I'd seen on TV or in the hospital grounds. In some sections, I'd addressed you directly, like I was writing a letter. More than once, I mixed you up with my mother.

But among all that, there were stories: seven tales that described my life and my illness, up until just after the point we were parted. They made a strange kind of sense, if you ignored all the rubbish and bad spelling, and this made me think. One of Roz's excuses for keeping us apart was that you were still too young to understand everything, and I couldn't shake the feeling that no matter how ill I'd been when I first wrote them, the idea of using fairy tales to explain myself wasn't a bad one.

So I started to redraft my book, to shape it into something coherent. It was slow, painstaking work – the kind I'd never been good at – but I persevered for your sake, and for mine. As much as I struggled to focus, there was something comforting about returning to the world of make-believe each evening. I'd been picking over my past since I arrived at the hospital, and it hadn't got any easier over the years. But looking back through the fairy tales, through that veil of pretend, was simpler, safer, and in many ways more honest, because in spite of all those magic spells and impossible creatures, everything else – how I had *felt* – was true.

By the time I'd finished, it was late August – two years since I'd been hospitalised, two years since I'd last seen you. I hadn't yet joined Acting Up or adopted Chilli, but by then I was on a fairly even keel, probably for the first time in my life. I'd done everything Roz had asked of me, so when she continued to be evasive I realised the only way to prove how much I'd changed was to show her, to show both of you, by bringing the book to you in person – and the timing couldn't have been better, because of course late August meant it was almost your birthday.

So I went back. Around five years after I left, I returned to Lower Morvale, that place I'd felt so trapped and lonely – and at the same time so happy, because I'd been there with you. Naturally, it hadn't changed. The same cars were parked outside the same cottages, the window of the tearoom had the usual selection of cakes and that funny old neighbour of your mum's said hello to me outside the church, as though I'd been there the whole time.

Your birthday was on a Sunday that year, and it was the most beautiful day. I remember walking down Primrose Lane in the bright sunshine and smelling a barbeque on the other side of the hedge, and hearing music and the shrieks of lots of little girls running around the back garden . . . I was so close. But as I approached the bunch of balloons tied to the front gate, I had this horrible feeling I wouldn't get to you. I was expecting Roz to stop me, I think, or maybe Lillian, but as it turned out I didn't see either of them that day – and of course I didn't see you.

I saw Morton.

Your uncle and I had never got on. Even at the beginning, when things were good with Roz, I seemed to infuriate him. I think he found me ridiculous, and resented that I'd charmed his sisters and mother so easily. Maybe he'd grown used to being the man of the family since your grandfather died, I don't know, but his dislike of me had only increased over time.

Anyway, on this day – on your ninth birthday – Morton was loitering around the driveway of Primrose Cottage with a beer. I remember he was wearing a tiny purple party hat, which someone had obviously forced him into and which he must've forgotten about. It was quite hard not to laugh at that.

Nothing else about our conversation was funny. I'm not even sure you could call it a conversation, because Morton did most of the talking. Your uncle isn't exactly chatty, but he was always very good at finding the right words to knock me down. He told me I wasn't part of the family anymore. He told me Roz hated me and would never forgive me for what I'd put her through. He told me I was a coward, a freak, a psycho . . . And I was prepared to hear all of this, because none of it was any worse than what I'd told myself over the years.

What I wasn't prepared for, though, was hearing exactly what had happened to you in Edinburgh. I still remember precisely what he said: *You could've killed her. You understand that, don't you? Your own daughter almost died because of you.*

But I didn't understand. I didn't know. As far as I could remember, I'd abandoned you in the middle of the city, that was all – that was enough – and if I'd ever realised or been told anything else, it'd been lost in my confusion and sedation during those early days in the hospital. Even Roz had never mentioned an accident, never used it against me. Morton, though, was happy to fill me in on the details: how many places your arm had been broken in, how long you'd had to wear a cast for, that you still complained it hurt to hold a pen or throw a ball . . .

Your own daughter almost died because of you.

So I went back. For the second time in five years, I turned my back on Primrose Cottage and walked out of your life.

It wasn't because I didn't want to see you. I *needed* to see you. I've discovered, since we last saw one another, just how much I'm able to adjust to a whole new lifestyle, a whole new me – but it's never been possible to adjust to your absence. There's no medication for loss, no coping mechanism that can fill the gap left by your own child. And it is a gap. Without you, I've been incomplete, there's been a Birdie-shaped hole in my heart. But that encounter with Morton marked a turning point. It forced me to stop obsessing over what was best for me, and ask a question I'd never really considered before:

What was best for you?

I had everything to gain from a reconciliation, but what effect would my sudden reappearance have on you and your life? How could you possibly benefit from a reunion with your useless, volatile dad, who – back then, at least – might've relapsed at any moment? Even if I didn't put you in danger again, I had nothing to offer you anymore. Especially because, soon, you'd no longer be the little girl of my memories, but a teenager and then a bright, brilliant young woman who wouldn't need me. Who'd be able to see right through me. Who would, I was sure, be better off without me.

And this seemed fitting, somehow – not for you, perhaps, but for me. It made sense that I should be deprived of the only person, the only relationship, I truly cared about. It was my punishment. The loss of you was the price I paid for everything I'd done. I believed – I still believe, in fact – I've never deserved you. I'm not certain I deserve you now, but you're here. You're *here*.

I can't quite believe it was the book that did it. As I said, that had been my intention at the start, but on my way out of the village that day, when I found myself still clutching the present I'd wrapped so carefully back in Edinburgh, I decided to leave it on Lillian's doorstep more as an apology than anything else. Your grandmother had always been good to me, more patient than most, but I'm not sure I really believed she'd pass it on. She probably thought it was another one of my games. Maybe it was. I certainly didn't expect to see it again.

But I hoped you'd look for me, of course I did. I've imagined our reunion a million times. But it had to be you who chose this, not me. I couldn't just charge back into your life and mess everything up, not again. I had to keep waiting.

I know this sounds inadequate. I can't imagine how you're feeling right now. And I'm sorry – I'm so sorry – but you must believe it was all for you: for you I got better, and for you I stayed away.

It was all for you.

Birdie?

Birdie? Say something, won't you?

Rebecca?

19

The Trig Point

The wilderness at the edge of the city looked enchanted. Like a sleeping giant, perhaps, or a mound teeming with tunnels of treasure-seeking dwarfs. Or maybe it was the consequence of a clash between sorcerers, an epic duel during which ancient rock had been wrenched from the earth . . .

Rebecca frowned: she'd been reading too many fairy tales.

It was a bright, brisk morning, and the only evidence of last night's rain was the still-sodden grass, its dampness threatening to seep up the sides of her trainers. The wind was trying to nudge her forward, ruffling her ponytail and chilling the backs of her knees, but she stayed where she was, still contemplating the bumpy profile of Arthur's Seat.

Edinburgh's hills bore little resemblance to the tors of Dartmoor, yet Rebecca's thoughts drifted towards the landscape of her childhood as she probed her memories for Leo. They were different now. When she pictured them wading through a stream together, she could also see him staring mournfully into the ripples, searching for his own reflection; when she heard him calling her as he hopped over tree roots and clusters of bluebells, it was over the sound of her own ragged breath, as she struggled to keep up with him.

Whether these recollections were real or half-imagined Rebecca didn't know, but they plugged some of the gaps in her memory. It would take some getting used to, having this sadder, truer version of him in her head. Yet as she turned from the hills and spotted him hastening over the soggy grass towards her, right on time, it was stranger still to see him in real life. He was wearing the same jacket and rucksack as yesterday but had swapped his trainers and jeans for walking boots and waterproof trousers. Teased by the breeze, his thin grey hair stood on end, as though a faint imprint of the Stowaway was still smudged into his outline.

Maybe this was wishful thinking, but when it came to her father Rebecca's double vision was clearing, and since last night she could see how this Leo and the one of her childhood might be the same man. Mostly, though, his account in The Unicorn had suffused her with sorrow: for him, of course, but also for the blame she'd placed on Lillian and especially Rosalyn, whose stories had matched his after all – and for the fresh betrayal of learning the role Morton had played in driving Leo away. Was this the price she had to pay for having her father back, the unravelling of these other relationships?

'Morning!' Leo called.

Rebecca raised her hand in greeting, and he responded with a self-conscious wave of his own. He looked even older today: as he smiled, the daylight carved deeper lines into the corners of his eyes and mouth.

As he stopped in front of her, Rebecca braced herself for some kind of physical contact – a hug, a kiss on the cheek, a pat on the arm – but Leo seemed content to stay where he was. Perhaps he was also comparing her daytime version to yesterday, taking note of the faint freckles on her nose and cheeks or the overlarge raincoat she'd borrowed from Cam that morning. Or perhaps he was just pleased she was there. The previous evening – the play, the storm, the old-fashioned pub – had had a dreamlike quality, and maybe he, too, was struggling to believe it'd actually happened.

Rebecca nodded towards the highest peak, where it was just

possible to discern the tiny silhouettes of other walkers. 'Is that what we're climbing?'

'If you still want to?'

'Yes.'

This plan had come about last night, after his explanation, or confession – whatever it'd been – had made her need to retreat, to reflect. Starting again today with a walk had felt like a good idea. And though nothing seemed any simpler this morning, Rebecca was tired of going nowhere, of being mired in accusations, misunderstandings and guilt. She wanted to move.

They set off across the grass, cutting through a sedate stretch of park, although soon their surroundings turned more rugged, and they joined one of the trails coiling around the hillside, their chosen route skirting a wedge of rust-coloured rock as fibrous as whalebone. As they began to climb, Leo tried to engage her with questions. Had she slept well? How long had it taken her to walk to their meeting point in Holyrood Park? Rebecca responded as politely as she could but was unable to summon much enthusiasm for these pleasantries. She barely even noticed the impressive views of Edinburgh as she strode past slower walkers – albeit carefully, for while the path was wide the drop to their right was steep. Instead, her focus was on the ascent. She'd spent too much time indoors lately; too many hours in the car, or in cafés and pubs. Now, as her heartbeat quickened and her calf muscles twinged, a fierce joy soared inside her, as invigorating as the jostling wind. If she'd been alone, she would've broken into a run.

But she wasn't alone, and as the trail dipped, Rebecca stood aside to wait for Leo, who was stuck behind the young family she'd recently overtaken. He was a little out of breath, but otherwise unaffected by the climb and when he drew level with her only a few moments later, she realised his measured gait was swifter than she'd thought.

'It opens up in a minute,' he said, apparently sensing her frustration. 'It isn't usually this busy – although normally I walk between the hills, over there.' He gestured to his left as they fell back into step, then admitted, 'That way's a bit easier.'

'How often do you come here?'

'Almost every morning. It helps to start the day with a clear head.'

Rebecca nodded. 'I run.'

'You do?'

'Yeah, most mornings as well. Usually around the river, if you remember?'

'Yes, yes . . .'

'I live by the Quay, so it's convenient.' After a brief pause, she added, 'I did the Great West Run two years ago, the half marathon.'

'You did? That's wonderful!'

As he began to ask about the route, her time, her training, Rebecca smiled, realising she didn't need to feign modesty; his praise was genuine, his curiosity boundless. Briefly, though, she wondered whether the other Leo – the one she'd been searching for and was still mourning – would've reacted with quite the same enthusiasm.

Once they'd exhausted the topic of running, Leo returned to her comment about living by the Quay and, again, Rebecca had the impression he was carefully collecting up every crumb of information she dropped about herself. Yet she felt less inclined to respond to his enquiries about her flat, her job, Exeter. The more of her life she shared with him, the harder it would be to disentangle herself if this didn't work, if she never saw him again. But it wasn't fair: last night she'd insisted upon the truth, and he'd told her everything.

After looping around the wrinkled crest of rock they'd been

following, Arthur's Seat loomed back into full view, although much of its scrubby bulk was cast in its own shadow. The route to the summit divided in two around a squat half-buried boulder that protruded from the ground like a self-important tollbooth; the right fork of the path zigzagged steeply to the top, the left meandered around a contour of the lumpy slope and out of sight.

'I still can't believe you're here,' Leo said, turning left. 'I still don't understand how you found me. It can't have just been the fairy tales.'

Once more, Rebecca found herself comparing this version of her father to the one of her childhood. The other Leo would've understood that, ultimately, she'd been led here by patterns and feelings. Hadn't that been his original intention, the reason he'd first scribbled down those stories? But the man walking beside her couldn't remember the clues he'd scattered through those pages in the hospital, nor appreciate the chain of events – the game, almost – he'd later instigated, in leaving her that book.

'I did have a little help,' she admitted.

'From Roz?'

'God, no! I don't think she knows where you are,' said Rebecca, experiencing another pinch of remorse. 'No, from— Well, from a few people, really, but I suppose it all started with this journalist . . .'

As she began to speak of Ellis, recalling how brazenly he'd sauntered into her office just over a fortnight ago, Rebecca was struck by how used to his presence she'd become, to the point that she was now longing to see him. They'd exchanged several texts, but yesterday they'd been in and out of Cam's flat at different times and he'd been asleep when she'd left this morning. Of course, he was busy with the Fringe – and, unlike their host, Rebecca was impressed by how quickly Ellis had managed to turn this impromptu trip to his advantage – but she wondered whether he was also keeping his distance on purpose, to give her space.

The path tracing the hillside was quiet, temporarily sheltered from the rasping wind. This made it easier to relate the story of her search, as did the knowledge she wouldn't be overheard, because they'd lost the crowds to the larger trails. As they passed through a small thicket, the hush was so striking they might've been back in the woods around Lower Morvale, or in another realm entirely, for there was an eeriness to the scrawny thorns tangling around them.

Leo, too, was silent as Rebecca spoke, although he was unable to suppress splutters of surprise when she mentioned her meetings with Richard Lowrie and Priya George, and was so astonished by the revelation she'd visited Huxley that he almost tripped over another sunken rock.

'I'm not sure you could've found many people who resented me more,' he remarked, when she was finished. 'Outside of Lower Morvale, of course.'

'I don't know, Priya seemed pretty happy to talk about you . . . She even wanted me to pass on her card.'

'Did she?' Leo gave an exaggerated, almost Stowaway-like shudder, which made her smile. Then, his expression turning solemn, he let out a long puff of air and said, 'I can't believe you went to *Huxley*.'

Rebecca pictured the unhappy place he'd grown up: the gloomy house, the overgrown garden, the pond in which his mother had drowned. 'I didn't like it there,' she said.

'No, neither did I.'

When he was quiet for a few moments, she glanced sideways and found his face bore the same haunted look as last night, when he'd related the worst of his illness. His skin seemed stretched too tight over his skull, giving him a gaunt, sickly appearance. Rebecca tried to think of something consoling to say – she felt she should acknowledge Adeline in some way, the grandmother she'd never known – yet it was Leo who spoke first, his voice soft and low.

'It never occurred to me you'd go to people like Priya or Richard. But then, I didn't think too much about how you might find me. I didn't dare to hope. I suppose I assumed Morton might say something – I think I told him I was living in Edinburgh during our conversation that day – or that Roz's solicitor might be able to track me down. I'd forgotten about the fairy tales, of course.'

'Yeah, well, Uncle Morton never bothered to mention that conversation,' said Rebecca, bitterly, 'and getting the details of Mum's lawyers seemed like more hassle than it was worth.'

'More hassle than going all the way to Kent, interviewing actors and agents and trying to decipher a bunch of children's stories?'

'You've obviously forgotten what Mum's like.'

Finally, this made him laugh, although only a little. 'I'm very grateful,' he told her. 'I'm not sure I deserve your loyalty.'

Rebecca shrugged: she wasn't sure she deserved his gratitude.

A more comfortable silence followed, before Leo asked, 'And this journalist, Ellis, is he still going to write his article?'

'Oh—no,' said Rebecca, surprised. 'No, of course not.'

'Then why's he in Edinburgh?'

'He—' She faltered. 'Well, he's here for me, because he's—Because we're friends.'

'I see,' said Leo, a lightness entering his tone that suggested he saw more than Rebecca had intended.

'He's also reviewing shows at the Fringe,' Rebecca continued, wishing she'd thought to say this first.

'Ah.'

In spite of the wind, which was starting to pick up again, she felt her cheeks grow hot, but when she peeked sideways at Leo, he appeared more thoughtful than amused.

'Do you think he *would* write the article, if you asked him to?'

'I expect so, yes – in fact, I'm sure he would. But—' Again, Rebecca was thrown. 'Well, it doesn't matter now, does it? And if it did, I'm not sure it's my place to ask, not anymore.'

'I suppose not,' agreed Leo.

They'd begun to climb again, and after pulling themselves up a series of steps, they emerged onto a grassy ledge where the view was dominated by a swathe of water arcing around the horizon like a powder-blue ribbon. A couple of crows pitched overhead, their hoarse calls piercing the burble of multilingual chatter coming from the other walkers, who had rematerialised; the knotty trail Rebecca and Leo had been wandering had converged with a wider, rougher path, one populated by everyone from pensioners to neon-clad runners.

Soon, it became apparent the presence of all these people would mar the completion of the climb. Their scramble to the summit frequently stalled as they stood aside for those shuffling back down, and when they finally reached the top, Rebecca was dismayed to discover the hill's craggy crown so busy it might've been the platform of a delayed train. She grimaced as she picked her way across ridges of rock, loose strands of her hair lashing at the side of her face. At another time, this peak would've offered an unbroken panorama, but today the vista was stippled with too many figures in the foreground.

'Come on,' said Leo, who'd put up his hood against the gusty weather, a look Rebecca found almost embarrassing – he might've been a garden gnome. 'Touch the trig point, and then we'll get out of this wind.'

Touch the trig point, climb to the highest rock, race you to the granite cross . . . His words sparked in her mind, illuminating more memories. In addition to all the games and stories, one of his favourite activities had been moving between the markers and monuments of Dartmoor, no expedition complete until they'd slapped their palms to ancient stone. Perhaps they'd even revisit those routes, Rebecca mused, if at some point he came back to Devon to see her. Assuming she'd want him to. Assuming she wanted to return there herself.

This last thought was unexpected and a little unnerving, so she pushed it aside and considered the white triangulation pillar, which was poking from the highest chunk of rock like a stumpy lighthouse. She felt slightly foolish as she clambered towards this apex and raised her arm, but Leo was already pressing his own fingers against the graffiti-clad post. When she mimicked the movement, the proximity of their hands over the scribbled surface resembled a child's early artwork.

A few minutes into their descent, they found a secluded crag jutting from the slope, which provided shelter from the relentless wind. The ground was still wet from the previous night's rain, so Leo gave Rebecca his jacket to sit on, while he perched on a tuffet of grass, protected from the damp by his waterproof trousers. He seemed entirely accustomed to the changeable weather, which even out of the breeze was only a little muggy today, as though summer here was already nearing its end.

They were still relatively high up, so now Rebecca could appreciate an unencumbered view of Edinburgh, which might've been a miniature toy town. She had the sense she was at one end of a topographical timeline. Below, the architecture bordering the parkland was modern; functional-looking flats and offices neighboured quirkier contemporary structures. Further in, the city's core was older, pulled into peaks by spires and towers, and dominated by the crease of Castle Rock. On the other side, it was prehistoric; the hazy hills and estuary at the horizon creating an elemental sweep of land, water and sky. It prompted in Rebecca a surge of wonder, to chart this passage of time, to have all that history unfurled at her feet.

Leo, meanwhile, was unpacking various items of food from his rucksack: croissants, bananas, hardboiled eggs.

'What's this?' asked Rebecca, as he placed a couple of Clingfilm bundles onto the grass between them.

'Savoury muffins, it's a recipe from cooking class. Although I must admit my baking's never quite the same when I do it at home . . .'

'No, I mean all of it.'

'It's breakfast.' He seemed puzzled by her reaction. 'Is it okay?'

'Yeah – more than okay,' Rebecca said, and not just because all she'd eaten that day was the remains of a squashed cereal bar she'd found in her bag; for the first time in almost two decades, her father had made her breakfast. She pictured him earlier, in the kitchen of wherever he lived, carefully packing up this picnic for her, for them, and something about the image caused her heart to catch.

'Thanks,' she added, helping herself to one of the muffins.

'I probably went a bit overboard, but I didn't know what you'd like,' Leo continued, now producing a couple of miniature yoghurts, the kind she'd loved as a child – was that why he'd brought them? Before she could ask, he held up a Thermos flask. 'Tea? I'm afraid I'm not allowed to drink coffee anymore.'

'Tea's great – all of this is great.'

She took a bite of the muffin, which was light and herby. Then, because she was warm, and they were getting in the way, she pushed up the long sleeves of Cam's jacket. Leo flinched.

'What?' she said.

'Is that . . . ?' He was staring at her now-exposed forearm, at the shiny scar beneath her right elbow.

'Oh – yes.'

The Thermos cup trembled in his hand. 'Rebecca, I—'

'It doesn't matter,' she said, because she didn't need his apology or explanation, especially not now, during this breakfast. 'I barely remember it.' She tweaked the sleeve back down her arm. 'Honestly, it's fine.'

Leo relented under her firm gaze and peered into his rucksack again. Moments later, he extracted a small, olive-green book from its depths. 'I wasn't sure if you'd want this back, but . . .'

With a rush of relief, Rebecca reached eagerly for the tales. She juggled the book from hand to hand, reminding herself of its size and weight, of the fuzziness of its clothbound cover and only just resisting the urge to press her nose to its pages and inhale.

She could remember her ninth birthday, when she should've first received this book: not just the barbeque and the games in the garden, but that Rosalyn had made her a cake shaped like a desert island, and that a girl from her class had thrown both her shoes into a hedge. And, like Leo, Rebecca was now consumed by the knowledge of how close they'd been that day. If only she'd seen him. If only, for some reason, she'd snuck from her own party and intercepted him at the gate, or in Primrose Lane. Would it have changed anything?

'I read them – or reread them, I suppose – last night, after I got back from the pub,' said Leo. 'They're not bad.' He sounded surprised.

Rebecca, who was now brushing crumbs and pieces of lint from the book's cover, asked, 'Did you really not remember them?'

'I remembered . . . bits. And they *feel* familiar – but then they would, wouldn't they?'

Reflecting that this was how they'd felt to her too, Rebecca said, 'I think you must've told me versions of these tales when I was little. I didn't realise at first, but I'm sure I've heard some of them before.'

Leo nodded, his expression faraway, as though he, like she, was combing his memory for fragments of the fairy tales. 'I certainly borrowed quite a lot from my mother's stories,' he said. 'She always used to talk about her shadow . . .'

They were back at Adeline again; the waif-like figure in the yellow dress, the nixie whose name he'd shared between them. Reminded of something she'd been pondering, Rebecca turned to the Lockwood illustration at the back of *Seven Tales*. 'Did you draw this?' she asked, showing Leo.

'No, that was by another patient, Gordy. He was always doodling, so I asked him to sketch that particular clue, and when I revised the book later, I couldn't quite bear to take it out.'

Again, Rebecca reflected on how odd it was that she'd ended up following at least some of his clues, just as he'd initially intended; she'd almost understood him better when he'd been ill. She thought about saying as much to Leo, but he now seemed lost among the trees with the keyholes in their trunks.

Struck by an idea, she retrieved her phone from Cam's jacket. 'Here,' she said, swiping back through a few views of Edinburgh, some artefacts in the British Museum, plus several attempts at a selfie with Amy. 'I took this at Patricia's.'

There was something familiar about Leo's look of mournful disbelief as he took the phone and saw the photograph of himself and his parents in Huxley's garden. It was, Rebecca then realised, the same reaction he'd had upon seeing her.

When he spoke, his voice quaked. 'Do you think you could send me this?'

'Of course.'

In that moment, Rebecca would've gone back to Huxley and fetched him the real thing; she would've raided that miserable old house for every photograph of Adeline it contained.

'I remember this one,' Leo continued, more steadily. 'It was my father's favourite. I wanted to take it with me when I moved to London, but he wouldn't allow it – he wouldn't even let me get it copied. He was always like that, trying to keep her for himself. I suppose I was, too. And she was always drifting away from both of us.'

Just as before, when she'd stood in the clearing of that thicket, the unwelcome image of Adeline floating lifelessly in the murky water returned to Rebecca's mind.

'I found the pond,' she ventured, cautiously. 'Patricia said she drowned by accident, but . . .'

She let the sentence hang as Leo made a noise of disapproval. 'My aunt believed everything my father told her,' he said. 'And my father believed only what reflected well on him. He thought if he kept my mother dosed up and shut away, he could cure her – of her depression, but also of her indifference towards him. So when it didn't work, and she lay down in that water with rocks in her pockets, he had no choice but to convince himself she'd slipped.'

Leo didn't bother to conceal his bitterness, which surprised Rebecca, and she wondered whether she'd already grown used to his mild demeanour. Not that his response wasn't justified: *The boy,* Patricia had said. *He was the first to go looking for her, and almost drowned himself trying to pull her out.*

With fumbling fingers, Leo zoomed in on the photo, either to see Adeline close-up or to cut out Victor. 'She must be about your age here,' he said, his tone softening as he looked from the phone to Rebecca. 'I think you even look a little alike.'

Rebecca wasn't sure how he could tell – Adeline was mostly a blur now – but it wasn't worth contradicting him. 'I wish I could've known her,' she said.

'Me too.' He touched his fingertips to the screen again and gave a start as he accidentally flicked to a previous picture. 'Sorry, I didn't mean to—' He smiled. 'Is this your cat?'

Rebecca peered at the photo she'd sent from the kitchen of Primrose Cottage to reassure Rosalyn the previous week. 'Urgh, no, she's Mum's. That's *Brontë*.'

Leo chuckled. 'Brontë?'

'Don't be fooled, she's a horrible animal.'

'No, it's just . . . The name, it's very Roz.' He was still smiling. 'She always wanted a cat.'

His expression was fond, surprisingly so for someone who'd depicted his ex-wife as a witch. Feeling oddly reassured, Rebecca recalled her mother departing from the same kitchen, the same cat clutched in her arms, and felt a surge of affection herself.

Leo passed back the phone, helped himself to a banana, then leaned sideways to tap at the book still clutched in her other hand. 'I don't suppose there's a *Seven Tales* by Rebecca?'

'A what?'

'A book that would tell me all about you?'

'Oh – no. There wouldn't be enough for one tale.'

'I'm sure that's not true.'

She was gripping tightly at the corners of the cover. In the daylight, and next to the effortless green of the grass, it looked faded, and very small – far too narrow a volume to contain so much of someone. Once more, Rebecca felt it wasn't fair, to be holding the whole of his past in her hands while offering up so little in return.

'What do you want to know?' she asked, warily.

'Everything,' he said.

As she began, she was conscious her own story was very ordinary, yet Leo listened with such focus she might've been recounting a great epic. He wasn't a silent audience either, and was constantly cutting in with questions: *Is this the same Amy you stayed with in London? What made you choose History?* But Rebecca no longer resented his curiosity. Often, his input made her account richer, because it teased out interesting details that she, an impatient and inexperienced narrator, had glossed over.

Some of his queries, particularly those relating to her present, were difficult to answer. But she tried to be truthful, as he'd been with her, and it was surprisingly easy to admit to him her worries, her doubts, her mistakes. This Leo seemed to understand; he had long ago accepted his own fallibility.

'I'm sure I could go back,' she said, after revealing she'd skipped a whole week of work – and possibly quit her job on a drunken impulse. 'I'm sure they'd have me back.'

'But?' prompted Leo.

'I don't know,' said Rebecca, because it was hard to explain she couldn't see herself there anymore; she couldn't imagine carrying on exactly as before. 'What do you think I should do?'

'*Me*?'

'Yeah, you seem to have it all figured out.' With the spoon of the yoghurt she'd just eaten, she gestured at the view of Edinburgh, trying to indicate what little she knew of his life here.

'Do I?' He seemed astonished to learn this, then quickly looked uncomfortable. 'Regardless, I'm the last person who should be giving out advice . . .'

'I'm not saying I'll follow it.' Then, as he smiled, she urged, 'Go on, tell me. I want to know.'

'Honestly?'

'Honestly.'

'I think you can do better than this office, this . . . *Sudworth and Rowe*.'

'How do you know that?' she challenged.

'I just do.'

She had expected him to cite everything she'd just told him: her good grades, her love of history, her confession she'd expected more for herself. Instead, his response had been baseless, almost childish, yet he'd sounded so sure of himself – so sure of *her* – Rebecca found it difficult to disbelieve him.

What would she do instead? She knew, of course – she'd known since she'd been a young teenager – but certain moments during the past few weeks had brought her ambitions into sharper focus: the conversation with Ellis in Huxley's kitchen; their visit to the British Museum; even that feeling she'd had a few minutes ago, when contemplating the view. It was a relief, really, to finally acknowledge it – and to accept that, at some point, she'd taken a wrong turn.

They'd finished eating now, and as Leo began to drop discarded eggshells and banana peels into an old carrier bag, Rebecca said, 'I'm sorry.'

He paused, the plastic still crackling in his hands. 'What've you got to be sorry for?'

'I don't know, yesterday? I wasn't very nice when I came to the church. I should've warned you, or – I don't know,' she said again. Then, remembering Ellis's accusation over another breakfast, which still stung, she admitted, 'Sometimes I'm not the most compassionate person.'

Unexpectedly, Leo laughed.

'What?' she demanded. 'What's so funny?'

'Oh, Birdie,' he said, gently, 'how else could you be here?'

Rebecca inhaled, and something loosened in her chest, until her lungs felt much fuller than usual. Her eyes were itching, and she had to cover them with her fingers to suppress the tears threatening to follow. Why did she keep *crying?*

She hoped Leo would be too busy with his bag to have noticed her composure slip, but when she opened her eyes, she saw him drop his arm, as though he'd moved to comfort her before reconsidering. Now his hand was resting awkwardly between them. She thought of when she'd wavered in front of the trig point, and because she'd had enough of hesitating, she reached out and covered his fingers with hers.

For a long time, they didn't speak or look at one another, or even move, save for Leo twisting his wrist until their cold palms were pressed together. As a moment of contact, it was far less bold than all the times she'd grabbed for his hand as a child, but neither was it as formal as a handshake, an introduction of strangers. Instead, it was somewhere in between – and for now, Rebecca thought, it was enough.

20

The Interview

As Rebecca let herself back into Cam's flat, she almost knocked into Ellis. They both jumped, and so did her heart – not just from the surprise of nearly running into him, but because the sight of him was so familiar, so reassuring. While they laughed over their near collision, she watched him closely, as though to make sure he was all there: his crinkled clothes, his prominent dimples, his air of sleepy affability. It was all she could do not to throw her arms around his neck.

'How was the walk?' he asked, holding open the door for her.

'Not bad, actually. We talked.'

'How's your dad? No, wait – how are you? Is everything okay?'

'I think so, yes.' As she said it, she realised it was true. Then, noting he was wearing both his SideScoop lanyard and rucksack, she asked, 'Are you on your way out?'

'Got another show to see. A colleague should be picking me up any minute . . .' He slid his phone from his jeans pocket. 'We could probably get you a ticket? Or do you want me to stay?'

'Thanks,' said Rebecca, touched, 'but you go – I've quite a bit to do here.'

'Fair play.'

They performed a shuffling little dance over the threshold until they'd swapped places and he was standing in the stairwell, she on the giraffe print doormat.

'I'll see you later, then,' he said, shifting a strap of his bag into a more comfortable position on his shoulder. 'We're in charge of dinner, by the way.'

'Oh? What are we making?'

'Dunno yet, I'll pick up some stuff on the way back – then you can tell me all about your dad while we cook.'

'Which reminds me, I might have another idea for you to pitch to SideScoop,' she said. 'Or somewhere else, actually . . .'

'Really?'

'Yeah, it's—' But she shook her head. It would take too long to explain now, what Leo had suggested during the clamber down Arthur's Seat, especially as she still didn't know what to make of it herself. 'Never mind, I'll tell you later.'

'You sure?'

'Of course, enjoy the show.'

'Will do. On the poster, half the cast are dressed as dolphins – I can't wait to tell Cam.' As Rebecca laughed, Ellis's phone buzzed in his hand. 'Ah, that's my lift.'

He gave her a small salute and began to jog down the steps. The skylight was casting a pearly glow through the stairwell, brightening flecks of the faux marble floor and tufts of Ellis's untidy hair. Rebecca watched him until he was halfway to the floor below, feeling short-changed that they'd only had this minute or so together, which was perhaps why she then called, 'When are you coming back?'

'After this, four-ish?' He glanced up, his expression mischievous. 'Why, will you miss me?'

Rebecca's impulse was to assure him she wouldn't, but she stopped herself, daring to answer another way: 'What would you say if I said yes?'

Ellis paused, suddenly looking more thoughtful, then reascended two or three steps, so they had a better view of one another. 'I would say . . .' he began, slowly. 'I would say, when we're done in Edinburgh, we should go somewhere.'

'Where?'

'I don't know, the Highlands? The Hebrides? We could take your car.' With the toe of his shoe, he traced part of the floor's jagged pattern, which almost resembled lightning. 'Assuming you could get more time off work, that is.'

'Um, don't *you* have a job?' said Rebecca, who didn't think now was the moment to reveal she'd all but decided to quit Sudworth and Rowe.

'Yeah, but I'm in their good books at the moment, because of all this reviewing. Apparently, I've shown *great initiative,* coming up to Edinburgh.'

'You're unbelievable . . .'

'Thanks. And if they make a fuss, I can just pitch this trip as an extension of the festival stuff. You know, *Ten Places You Shouldn't Miss While You're in Scotland* . . . Go on, it'll be fun.'

As casual as he made it sound, Rebecca was momentarily daunted by the magnitude of this plan. Only, they were out of excuses to spend time with one another: their alliance had run its course; their friendship too, perhaps. But they had something else, and Ellis's bold suggestion offered a chance to figure out what it might be – what they might be.

'All right,' said Rebecca. 'Why not?'

'Cool.'

They looked at one another for a few seconds, during which Rebecca felt tingly and skittish, as though the air between them was charged. Then Ellis gave her a quick smile and continued down the stairs. She watched him walk away, still slightly dissatisfied by their encounter – though really, what more did she want?

'Ellis?'

He turned, and before she could think about it too much –

before she remembered they were sober and she might trip, or he might stop her, and there really wasn't enough time – she had dashed down the stairs, stopped two steps from where he was standing, and kissed him.

It was a hasty, clunky kind of kiss – Ellis had to catch hold of her elbows so they didn't overbalance – but it was also full of purpose, full of promise. Her body whirled with warmth as she felt his grin tweak at her lips; she was grinning too.

At a buzzing noise, they broke apart, and Ellis stared at his phone as though he'd forgotten what it was.

'You should go,' murmured Rebecca, tucking his lanyard under the collar of his shirt. 'I'll see you soon.'

'Yeah . . .' Ellis kept hold of her hand as he backed down the stairs, only letting go at the last possible moment. 'See you.'

'Bye.'

Rebecca wasn't really conscious of returning to the flat – she might've floated back to the front door – and neither was she sure why she then headed to the living room, except for its association with Ellis. The sofa was half-hidden under a tangle of blankets, cushions and clothes, while the coffee table was scattered with flyers and tickets, highlighter pens, an unopened chocolate bar and a guidebook to Scotland that looked second-hand.

Dreamily, Rebecca sank back into the nest Ellis had created for himself on the sofa. It smelled of him, a warm and slightly spicy scent immediately evocative of Pit-Stop. After a few minutes of mentally replaying what had just happened in the stairwell, she finally allowed herself to bask in memories from that evening in London – to recall their eager mouths, their roaming hands – before she began to imagine what might happen when they were away again, alone again . . .

Her eyes snapped open: she couldn't fall asleep here. What if Cam walked in and discovered her, Goldilocks-like, in someone else's – in *Ellis's* – temporary bed? Besides, she thought, pulling herself up into a sitting position and trying to remember all the plans she'd made on the way back from Arthur's Seat, there was too much to do.

She wanted to go to the shops, buy a bottle of wine for dinner, a present for Cam, a conciliatory postcard for Lillian – and Amy, too, who would surely cackle over one of those pictures of a Scotsman's kilt being lifted by a strong breeze. Then she'd email Gerry at Sudworth and Rowe. If she was going to leave, she should resign properly, and perhaps if she produced some detailed handover notes – ones that explained her filing system and how to work the coffee machine – she might end up with a decent reference. With a quiver of nervous excitement, Rebecca realised she could even start looking into volunteering on digs again, and temporary museum work; opportunities that would support a Masters application next year.

First, though, and before she did anything else, she needed to phone Rosalyn. Rebecca had no idea what she was going to say, only that she had to say something. Given the circumstances of her last visit to Edinburgh – and the lasting effect it must've had on Rosalyn – she should at least check in; be honest and firm about where she was and who she'd found. It would take time to forgive her mother – to believe her actions had been purely protective – just as it would take Rosalyn time to forgive her for defying the parent who had raised her for the one who had not.

Best, then, to face it all as soon as possible; best to start today.

St Jude's, or *Fringe Venue 317*, was empty. The signs had been tugged from its walls, the fabric from its windows, while all the chairs had been stacked into precarious-looking towers at its edges. With most of the dusty black floor now exposed, the interior of the old church appeared boxy, like the inside of a pinhole camera, and Rebecca found it difficult to believe all those teenagers, helpers and parents had squeezed into this space. Aside from a few curls of masking tape still clinging to the walls, the only evidence Acting Up had been here at all was the green fabric of the backdrop, which was currently collapsed in shimmering folds across the floor, as though a vast mythical beast had shed its skin.

Leo hadn't noticed her come in. He was sweeping at the other end of the church, around the section of floor that had served as a stage. Rebecca studied him for a few seconds, watching his slow, careful movements, listening to the swishing of the broom and the clinking of the keys half-hanging from his jeans pocket. He might have been a janitor.

When he doubled back on himself, she remarked, 'You've already done that bit.'

He glanced up, smiling. 'Maybe – but I keep finding these wretched sequins everywhere.'

Letting the broom handle clatter against the nearest wall, he bent to retrieve something from the floor. He held it up between finger and thumb to show her, but from Rebecca's vantage point the gesture looked like a question: *okay?* She responded in kind as she approached him, which made his smile widen, and then surprised herself by reaching out for a hug – although he barely had a chance to raise his arms in return before she'd pulled away again.

'You look tired,' she told him, partly because there were shadows under his eyes, but mostly because she was embarrassed about the hug.

'Well, it was quite an eventful weekend.' He gestured to the hall, to her, then seemed to realise there was still a green sequin stuck to the end of his index finger. As he tucked it into his pocket, his gaze moved to the door behind her. 'I thought you were bringing . . . ?'

But he paused at the sound of approaching footsteps, and with a jolt of apprehension Rebecca turned in time to see Ellis strolling into the church. He was examining a handful of flyers he'd presumably found in the porch, and when he looked up seemed momentarily startled to find them both staring at him.

'Oh – hi!' He hurried forward, his arm outstretched towards Leo. 'Ellis Bailey.'

'The journalist I was telling you about,' said Rebecca, her heart still thumping as they shook hands. 'And Ellis, this is—' She hesitated, undecided between *Leo* and *my dad.*

'—the Stowaway,' said Ellis, nudging his glasses further up the bridge of his nose, as though to see Leo better.

Rebecca looked to her father, wondering how he'd take this, but he seemed distracted by Ellis, whom he was studying with a slightly puzzled expression, as though the journalist wasn't what he'd expected. It wasn't until he spoke that he gave any indication he'd even heard the name of his former character.

'It's been a long time since anyone's called me that,' he remarked, mildly. 'I suppose I might have to get used to it again . . .'

Like before, it sounded as though he was talking to someone else – or perhaps just himself – a habit Rebecca was starting to find irritating. Ellis, however, was unfazed, and after giving her a quick grin, told Leo, 'It's great to meet you at last.'

'Yes, I hear you've been looking for me.'

'You could say that . . . Hey, is one of these your play?' Ellis fanned out the flyers in his hands, as though trying to tempt Leo into a card trick.

'Yes,' said Leo, picking out *The Emerald City's* black-and-white artwork from the rest. 'Although it was the kids' play, really.'

'What was it about?'

Leo seemed encouraged by Ellis's interest, and grew more animated as he began to describe how the teenagers of Acting Up had devised their production. The mention of his young charges provoked another twinge of envy in Rebecca, but she ignored it, more interested in the dynamics of this meeting.

It was difficult to gauge, given how little she knew Leo and how inscrutable Ellis could be, especially in work mode, but she sensed each was trying to impress the other. Ellis, in particular, seemed somehow brighter than usual, as though he'd turned up the charm to full blast. Rebecca reasoned this was natural, considering what they'd come here to do, but with another jump of nerves she supposed her own presence was also affecting what would otherwise be a purely professional meeting. It was strange: even now, none of them knew exactly what they were to one another.

By the time she'd tuned back into the conversation, Leo was outlining the story of *The Emerald City*, to which Ellis was responding with a lot more insight and curiosity than Rebecca herself had demonstrated, even after seeing the performance. How typical, she thought, that they'd already established a better rapport than she and Leo after half a weekend together.

'I should've reviewed this instead,' said Ellis, turning to include her in the discussion. 'It sounds a lot better than some of the stuff I've been writing about over the past few days.'

'Speaking of . . .' prompted Rebecca.

She was feeling increasingly uneasy; standing here talking about the play was only delaying the inevitable.

'Yes,' agreed Leo, 'let's sit down, shall we? If you two grab a few chairs, I'll find us some cups.'

He began to wander towards the vestry door, while Rebecca and Ellis headed to the nearest stack of metal seats.

'What?' she asked, because for some reason Ellis was smiling to himself.

'Nothing, it's just . . . It's really him, isn't it?'

She frowned. 'Didn't you believe me?'

'I did,' Ellis assured her, unfolding one of the chairs. 'It's just a big deal, I guess.'

Rebecca wasn't about to disagree, and it was only then she remembered this was the second time Ellis had met her father – although she trusted he wouldn't reveal the details of their first meeting until he thought Leo ready to hear them.

As they picked up two more chairs, she reflected this wasn't all she trusted Ellis with; Cam's indomitable presence in the flat meant they'd had little opportunity to continue what they'd started yesterday, in the stairwell, but Rebecca was now increasingly impatient for their forthcoming road trip, for reasons mostly unrelated to the appreciation of Scottish scenery.

'Also, I've changed my mind: you do look like your dad,' Ellis decided.

'Oh, be quiet,' she said, unsure whether this was a compliment, a joke or merely an observation.

Before she could find out, her phone pinged, and she was surprised to see the text was from Rosalyn.

Their call the previous day hadn't gone exactly as Rebecca had anticipated. Rosalyn hadn't changed the subject or started ranting or hung up. Nor had she demonstrated any outward curiosity about her ex-husband: how he was, what he'd said about her, whether he now met the requirements that she'd set, almost two decades ago. In fact, she'd hardly said anything at all; instead, as Rebecca provided a brief account of the weekend, her mother had *listened.*

This atypical quietness had been difficult to interpret. Maybe Lillian had had a word, advised her against blurting out something she'd later regret, or it was possible that, following their showdown at Primrose Cottage, Rosalyn had nothing more to say. Yet Rebecca had sensed resignation, so it didn't feel completely naïve to wonder whether her mother's feelings were shifting, settling; perhaps the purging of all that hurt and rage and guilt had even been a little liberating.

Still, it hadn't been an easy call, and afterwards Rebecca had assumed they'd both retreat for a while to recover. The fact that Rosalyn had texted so soon was as unexpected as her pensive silences.

Nana & I are thinking an afternoon tea in Exeter for your birthday this year – maybe with fizz?? xxxx ps I see there's an Impressionism exhibition at the National Gallery of Scotland??

Rebecca read this message several times, trying to identify some catch or hidden message, but it felt typically Rosalyn. Though she herself had very little interest in art, the indirect acknowledgement that she was in Edinburgh was encouraging, while the suggestion of the tea was the kind her mother always made around this time of year. The thought of Rosalyn and Lillian talking about her, making plans for her, flooded Rebecca with both affection and relief. Plus, it was her birthday soon: her ninth might've been on her mind lately, but she'd completely forgotten about her twenty-sixth.

Afternoon tea sounds great, thanks. Will try and catch the exhibition xx

By the time Rebecca looked up from her phone, Ellis had arranged the chairs into a triangle, while Leo had returned with three mismatching mugs and the same Thermos flask as yesterday. The metal seats creaked as they took their places, and Rebecca thought they must look absurd, sat in the centre of an empty hall as though about to start devising a drama themselves.

'I hope it's okay, meeting here,' said Leo, perhaps reading her expression. 'It's so difficult to find anywhere quiet during the festival and I have to come back later anyway to hand over the keys to the next lot.'

'Who are the next lot?' asked Ellis.

'A theatre company from down south somewhere. I believe they're putting on a kind of ghost story . . .'

Rebecca shot Ellis a look that forbade him from asking any more questions, so he began rooting through his bag, saying, 'The space is great. I might even include it in the piece, it adds . . .' he produced a pen and waved it at their bare surroundings, like a magic wand, ' . . . *atmosphere*.'

Leo was now painstakingly pouring out tea, so Rebecca, in an attempt to curb her impatience, searched her own bag, where she located *Seven Tales*. Neither Ellis nor Leo questioned why she then laid it on her lap, like a script; perhaps they were too used to seeing it in her possession – or maybe they, like she, felt it natural the book should be there.

'So how's this going to work, then?' asked Rebecca, once they were each clutching a mug of tea.

She was looking at Leo, but his attention was fixed on Ellis. 'I think we should leave that to the expert, don't you?'

Ellis scratched at his chin with the end of his pen. 'I wouldn't go that far – I'd be lying if I said I'd done a profile or long read quite like this before. Obviously, it'll be sensitive, and you'll get the final say about what's published – both of you,' he added, and Rebecca swallowed her objection. 'As for the angle we take, though, that's kind of up to you.'

This he directed to Leo, who went quiet for several moments, until Rebecca thought – or perhaps hoped – he might've given up on the whole idea. When he finally spoke, however, he sounded resolute.

'I want to be honest,' he said. 'I think I've been avoiding my past for a long time, and I didn't even realise until you showed up, Rebecca, asking for the truth. I suppose I'd forgotten that, in a way, I was still pretending. But now you're here, and just about putting up with me . . .' He smiled. 'All of a sudden, putting up with myself doesn't seem quite so bad.'

Rebecca met his gaze, and though his blue eyes were very clear, she felt like she was peering into a kaleidoscope of all the versions of himself he had been, and continued to be: not just the Leo of her childhood and the Stowaway, but the boy whose dearest companion had departed for the water, the explorer who'd strayed into a land of shadow and the player who'd been forced to keep performing; she could see the man who'd felt pursued and persecuted, exceptional and invincible, outcast and alone; and she could see the father who had lost his Birdie.

A painful lump began to swell in her throat, so she was grateful when Ellis then turned to her, saying, 'Actually, we might have to consider your involvement in all of this.'

'What do you mean?'

'Well . . .' He hesitated, perhaps anticipating she might shut him down straight away. 'Considering everything that's happened; how you've gone on this big search, and been guided by that book . . . And the fact that we're here, and you *found* him . . .' He gestured between Rebecca and Leo with his pen a few times, joining them with an invisible thread, so they wouldn't lose one another again, before returning his attention solely to her. 'It's your story too, isn't it?'

At these words, Rebecca felt a glow of some bright but largely unfamiliar emotion. Pride? Satisfaction? Relief? Whatever it was, it prevented her from dismissing Ellis's suggestion. She might not be totally convinced by what they were doing, but neither was she ashamed of anything Leo had to say, nor anything she herself had done to bring this about – and again, she trusted Ellis.

He, clearly encouraged by this reaction, adopted a louder, more buoyant tone: 'As for how we approach today, I thought Leo could talk, I could listen and we'll see what happens.'

'That's how he approaches everything, by the way,' Rebecca remarked to Leo. She still didn't know whether she was annoyed or amused Ellis had got his article after all. '*We'll see what happens*.'

'Becs, it's an approach that *works*,' said Ellis, indicating Leo with another flourish of his pen.

The corners of Leo's eyes crinkled as he looked between them a few times. 'It suits me,' he said.

Perhaps in response to this expression, Ellis busied himself with his phone. 'I'm also going to record you, if that's all right,' he continued, quickly. 'If I can get this thing working . . .'

Rebecca touched Leo on the arm, which felt unnervingly thin and fragile, like the hollow wing bone of a bird. 'Are you sure you want to do this?' she asked.

She'd been dogged by these doubts ever since he'd first suggested sharing his story. Having finally come to terms with his cloistered lifestyle, Rebecca found it difficult to understand why he'd want to do anything to jeopardise it. She hoped Leo didn't think it was expected of him, by her or by Ellis. There was no need for penance, no obligation to publicly confess.

In the end, though, it was Leo's choice – it was Leo's right – and Rebecca wondered whether his new occupation might also be informing his desire to speak freely; now, he was a role model, one who could provide hope and perspective to any of his young charges – and others – who might be grappling with similar experiences. With this in mind, Rebecca suspected her discomfort ran deeper than a desire to protect her father from the readers of SideScoop, or whoever else might publish this prospective profile. Maybe now she'd found him, she wanted to keep him to herself. But this was as a senseless as it was selfish; he'd always be hers.

Leo patted her hand. 'I'm sure,' he told her. 'I think it's time.'

Rebecca glanced at Ellis, who was absently running his pen across a corner of his notebook. He seemed to be waiting for something and, after a moment, she realised what, and gave him a small nod. Her fingertips were tracing the embossed gold lettering of *Seven Tales* on her lap, while, at the edge of her vision, she caught sight of another sequin on the floor, winking at her.

Ellis's phone made a chirruping noise as he pressed record.

Leo leaned forward.

'Are we ready?' he asked. 'Shall I begin?'

Acknowledgements

I've been telling stories for as long as I can remember, and though writing has a reputation for being a lonely sort of business, on the whole I've found the opposite to be true. My path to publication might've been somewhat meandering, but it's been populated by people who have made the journey a lot of fun, and without whom I doubt I'd be writing these words now.

First, though, a few places: I'm so grateful for the years I spent at St Margaret's School in Exeter, where I learned – among so much else – the drive and diligence it's taken to write this book; I'm also extremely appreciative of my time at Royal Holloway University of London, the University of Edinburgh, and Arcadian Lifestyle Publishing, where I was able to explore the mechanics and magic of fiction, and where my lifelong fascination with fairy tales was heartily encouraged.

I'm delighted that *The Lost Storyteller* found its home at Hodder Studio, and am so thankful for the enthusiasm, dedication and kindness of the whole team – especially as they were working against the less-than-ideal backdrop of a pandemic: Niamh Anderson, Sarah Clay, Matthew Everett, Bea Fitzgerald, Rebecca Folland, Myrto Kalavrezou, Grace McCrum, Callie Robertson, Will Speed and Ellie Wheeldon. In particular, I couldn't have asked for a better editor than Sara Nisha Adams, whose insightful suggestions added both sense and spark to the story, and whose passion and vision for this book so closely matched my own. I'm also hugely grateful to my magnificent agent, Jo Unwin, who championed this novel from practically the moment she received it, and who took such good care of it (and me!) during the rollercoaster that was 2020, and beyond.

I'm incredibly fortunate to have the most wonderful friends, who never fail to ask, 'How's the novel going?' I wish I could thank you all individually, and hope you know that your interest and encouragement made me feel a lot less foolish for aiming for something that, at times, seemed completely impossible.

Special thanks, however, must go to members of writing groups past and present, whose generous feedback and brilliant work has kept me striving to be better: Lizzie Bell, Cheryl Caira and Cat Schaupp; Elodie Olson-Coons, Kirsty Mackay and Helen Patuck; Candace Bagley, Daniel Shand and Alice Tarbuck. Also to Hannah Grego, Joe Murray and Lucy Scholes for all their writerly advice and wisdom, usually shared over a wine (or three). To Charlotte Christesen, for always offering both her London expertise and her spare room. To Andrew Jeffrey for his youth theatre intel, and Krisztián Kiss for the author photos. To Florence Vincent, first reader extraordinaire, for helping me tidy those last loose plot strands, and for persuading me the manuscript was in shape for submission. And to Joely Badger, the novel's fairy godmother, for being with this story ever since I first mentioned the idea, once upon a time during some dragon-spotting on Dartmoor.

Until fairly recently, my family hadn't even read this book, yet their support over the years has been immense and unwavering. So I'd like to say a huge thank you to my partner, Chaz, for not only celebrating my successes, but for mopping up my tears – so many tears! – and for unquestioningly doing all the tidying or taking the baby when I said I was writing (*mostly* I was…) Also to my parents and my brother, James, for absolutely everything, but especially for never suggesting I get a proper job; I am so lucky to have you. And, last but never least, to my daughter, Lia, whose arrival forced me to stop faffing and finally send her book sister out into the world; dream big, little one.